KYN KRONICLES BOOK 4

SHADOW'S CURSE

JAMI GRAY

Cover Art: Deranged Doctor Design, www.derangeddoctordesign.com

Publisher: Celtic Moon Press Revised edition, 2018
ISBN: 978-1-948884-22-8 (ebook) ISBN: 978-1-948884-23-5 (print)

First edition, January 2015, Black Opal Books ISBN: 978-1-626942-19-6 (ebook) ISBN: 978-1-626942-20-2 (print)

SIGN UP FOR FREE
READS FROM JAMI!

Join Jami's newsletter to be the first to hear about new releases, free books, special prices and other nifty events.

Sign up at: https://www.subscribepage.com/jami-gray-books

WHAT READERS SAY...

About Arcane Transporter:
"Taking a refreshing approach to fantasy magic, this fast-paced, economical thriller is told from a highly likable perspective." — Red Adept Editing

About PSY-IV Teams:
"This story is an emotional roller coaster, from betrayal, anger, fear, love..." — InD'tale Magazine

About the Kyn Kronicles:
"...a fantastic paranormal action novel is quite possibly the best book I've read this year. I could not put it down, and had to exercise serious self-control to keep from staying up all night to finish it." — The Romance Reviews

About Fate's Vultures:
"...if you like your characters with a bit more bite, with secrets, with hidden agendas, and all those sorts of things, and your worlds are a far more deadlier place, then this is for you." — Archaeolibrarian

Also by Jami Gray

ARCANE WONDERLAND

Last Call

Bitter Spirits

Rune & Tonic

ARCANE TRANSPORTER

Ignition Point (*Prequel Novella*)

Grave Cargo

Risky Goods

Lethal Contents

Collision Course

Blind Spot

Terminal Drift

THE KYN KRONICLES

Shadow's Edge

Shadow's Soul

Shadow's Moon

Shadow's Curse

Shadow's Dream

Shadow's Fall

Tangled in Shadows (*Short Story Collection*)

FATE'S VULTURES

Lying in Ruins

Beg for Mercy

Caught in the Aftermath

Fear the Reaper

PSY-IV TEAMS

Hunted by the Past

Touched by Fate

Marked by Obsession

Fractured by Deceit

Linked by Deception

BOX SETS

PSY-IV Teams Box Set I (Books 1-3)

The Collapse: Fate's Vultures (Books 1-4)

The Kyn Kronicles Box Set (Books 1-6)

Arcane Transporter Box Set I (Books 1-3)

Arcane Transporter Box Set II (Books 4-6)

"Out of suffering have emerged the strongest souls; the most massive characters are seared with scars."
~ Kahlil Gibran, Lebanese Poet

Acknowledgments

For all of those who've stumbled and lost, only to rise again, more determined and stronger than ever ~ this one is for you.

As always, to my favorite two misters of mayhem, my boys, and my ever patient Knight ~ love you all.

CHAPTER I
PRESENT DAY, DEEP IN THE
TAURUS MOUNTAINS IN TURKEY

DARKNESS SPREAD ITS OPAQUE CLOAK OVER THE COBBLED PATHS winding between the stone buildings while silence crouched and waited. In this small corner, goats walked streets too narrow for cars, and the human inhabitants were tucked inside their humble homes. Inside the inky confines of a rustic alley, a figure slipped from the shadows and through the unlocked wooden door of one of the homes.

"You're late, Darius." The sharp greeting came from the man lounging with casual elegance among the jewel-festooned pillows on one of the low-slung couches.

"And you're in a pisser of a mood, Zayn." Unfazed by the rude welcome, Darius snagged an olive from the table. Popping it into his mouth, he grabbed an empty cup and poured a drink.

Taking a handful of olives and his cup, he walked across the lush, overlapping rugs and sprawled on the other sofa. He studied Zayn as he chewed, taking in the overly long white shirt paired with sand-colored linen pants. Despite his sun-streaked blond hair and the small abode's rich haven of comfort, Zayn still managed to convey a Middle Eastern flare.

"Until we find out who is behind Mulcahy's death, I don't see that changing." Zayn lifted his own cup, his sleeve fluttering with the movement. "What did you find out?"

Darius chased the olives' lingering salty tartness away with a quick sip and wiped his fingers against the dark denim covering his thigh before answering. "We were right to question the account received from the Northwest Kyn. There is more to the story than they are sharing." And he intended to uncover just what that "more" entailed.

Zayn's lips twisted into a grimace. "No surprise there. No way would Natasha cough up the whole story."

No, the little demon queen was too intelligent to show her hand to the Council. It didn't stop the whispers, though. "There are rumors she could be behind his death." And if the rumors were true, Darius would ensure she'd be facing someone much more dangerous than the Kyn's Council.

"I thought they shared a history."

Darius gave his companion a dark frown and shrugged his shoulders. "Shared history doesn't mean shit when power is on the line. Mulcahy's death created some damn explosive opportunities. She's grabbing as many as she can. What does that tell you?"

"She's an intelligent woman?"

Zayn's quip drew a snort from Darius. "Of that, I have no doubt. She didn't get to her current position on looks alone."

"No, she's not one to let emotional attachments get in the way of her plans." His tone as dry as the winds of summer, Zayn advised, "Be careful that she doesn't return you and your ego in nice, bloody pieces."

Leaning back, Darius stretched his arms across the back of the couch, confident in his appeal to the fairer sex. He'd been described as a study of shadows. From his olive-toned skin to his dark, shoulder-length hair and closely trimmed goatee, the description was warranted. The only unsettling bit of color was his eyes—ice-cold blue, ringed in fiery red. A deep chuckle escaped. "Would you miss me?"

"You?" Zayn shrugged. "Not so much. But there might be few others with a different opinion." Humor bled away, a startling seriousness taking its place. "This change. It's been hundreds of years in the making. Unfortunately, Mulcahy's death has accelerated things. If they aren't handled correctly, the outcome could be extremely detrimental to our goals."

"I haven't forgotten." Hard to forget when the line they walked was razor thin.

A small nod. "We won't be welcome."

Darius's smile was anything but friendly. "Their welcome is not my worry. Nor should it be yours."

"Don't underestimate them. Ryan Mulcahy was not the only reason the Northwest Kyn have become who they are."

"Yet, he's the one who held them together." A fact that someone out there knew all too well, or Mulcahy wouldn't be dead. Darius's hand tightened into a fist, his knuckles showing white through his skin as he fought back the grim wave of fury and grief.

"Perhaps. But he hasn't done it alone." Zayn paused. "Do they know about you?"

They could apply to so many—the Council, the Northwest Kyn, those behind Mulcahy's death—but in this instance Darius knew which *they* was implied. The Northwest's Wraiths, a shadowy group of warriors who stood between the American public and the nightmares haunting the dark. "No. They know only what they need to." And until he discovered who was playing for whom, it would remain that way.

Zayn rubbed a hand over his clean-shaven chin. "The potential for a shitstorm is tremendous."

"There's no 'potential' about it." Too much was at stake to walk delicately now. "Mulcahy's death changed the game. Without him, there is no one left to bridge the emerging division of the Council. Sides will be chosen. We need to stack the odds in our favor." Odds that had shifted with one violent act.

Zayn raised his cup in silent agreement. For a few minutes, quiet reigned. He broke it with, "Did DiMarcco give you your orders?" When Darius remained mute, Zayn gave a small smile of acknowledgement. "Our esteemed leader won't admit to worry. Instead, he and the rest of the Council will couch it in false concern and empty platitudes. Yet they are watching and waiting. Will Mulcahy's Kyn rise or fall?" He slowly rolled the cup cradled in his hands. "Of course, it would not surprise me if some are trying to assist their desired outcome."

Council maneuverings were a given, especially as current events threatened to tear the last threads from the fragile veil hiding the Kyn from mortal view. Some on the Council weren't opposed to the impending revelation, so long as their agenda reigned supreme. "Dissension is an insidious ploy. It can turn on a whim. Many are unprepared for what they wrought." A lesson Darius had watched more than one learn the hard way. "I don't think the outcome will be what anyone expects."

"Still, tread carefully. The path isn't as clear as it once was, and I would not put it past the high-and-mighty Council to offer you as a scapegoat should it be needed."

"Or you," Darius drawled.

Zayn sighed but didn't dispute the claim. He swirled the content in his cup, grief clouding his features. "I'm going to miss the bastard. He was bloody brilliant." He looked to Darius. "His people should prove interesting."

A predatory grin broke across Darius's face as anticipation hummed under his voice. "If nothing else, they will make our visit all the more entertaining."

CHAPTER 2
OUTSIDE PORTLAND, OREGON

THE HAUNTING NOTES OF A MELODY DESIGNED TO CUT THROUGH heart and bone faded away, leaving echoes to intertwine with the cool breeze. Sunlight wove through clouds holding the promise of rain. Here, in this old, half-forgotten forest, safe from mortal eyes, a throng of inhumanly beautiful creatures gathered to pay their respects to one of their own, Ryan Mulcahy. The head of the Northwest Fey House would be sorely missed, his absence leaving behind slow healing wounds. But that was not all it had left behind.

Natasha Bertoi stood apart from the gathered mourners, remembering, watching, taking in the obligatory masks of somber grief. Some hid ugly truths and bitter needs, yet genuine sorrow still existed. The evidence was etched in the unnaturally still countenances of those who felt his loss most keenly.

All four Kyn houses—Fey, Magi, Lycos, and Amanusa—were represented, a testament to the man who looked beyond bloodlines and old prejudices. It was what made Ryan, perhaps not so much loved, as respected.

As with any leader, much more lay hidden from

common knowledge. Politics, machinations, old feuds, and new alliances—they all played a part in a leader's decision. And those decisions often served a bigger purpose.

But death disrupted even the best laid plans.

The aching hollowness in her chest burrowed into her bones. Long suppressed memories rose and blotted out the present. The sun-dappled forest faded, replaced by stone walls. Ghostly wails of agony drowned out the melodious murmurs of somber peace and solace. Around her, melancholy faces shifted to haunted masks of death. The ache morphed to an agony not lessened by time...

Natasha stood over what once was her closest confidant and friend, the only individual she trusted without question—her sister. She felt...empty, her emotions carved out with a brutal hand. Blood chilled against her skin. Faint screams and dull explosions provided background music— the hellish notes never more appropriate. Around her, the small stone room held the corpses of those she once considered hers to protect. Instead, their choices forced her to exact a fatal punishment.

"Natasha, we need to leave," a smooth, baritone warned.

She knelt, careful to keep clear of the spreading blood, and wiped the rust-colored stains from her thin, deadly blade against the gore stained material pooled at her feet. Only when the blade was clean did she rise. Her gaze was riveted on a face as familiar as her own, death's stillness leaving a deceptively peaceful mask behind. Each detail seared into her brain, a brutal reminder of how treacherous family could be. For hundreds of years, she and her sister had played among the Kyn and their secrets, using them to further their own agendas and protect their people. Yet, she had missed the biggest secret of all—Irina's never-ending thirst for more.

Damn you, Irina.

Natasha's attention switched to the male crumpled next to her sister, the one who egged her sibling's twisted need higher and deeper. Fury and betrayal curled around the numb edges of Natasha's heart and mind. Her arm and blade whipped down and out. There would be no miraculous return from death's cold embrace for this Kyn male.

His lying, conniving head flew from his body.

Sickening emptiness crawled through her.

Fingers, warm and strong, wrapped around her wrist. Their grip forced her to turn and meet deep, brown eyes, narrowed and cold. "They're coming."

Under her skin, the demonic nature, which made her one of the most feared of the Amanusa rode a wave of rage and destructive hunger, stirred. "Let them," she hissed.

Everything she worked for, schemed for, was for naught. Now, innocents would pay and there wasn't a damn thing she could to do stop it. All because she had trusted the wrong person.

"You don't get to play the martyr now, Bertoi," the man beside her snapped, his elegant face cold, unbending. "There's no time to wallow in your mess. If you want to fix it, we must leave. Now."

"There is no fixing this, Ryan." How far did her sister's lies and betrayals run? Had her insatiable need for chaos destroyed everything? "I can't out run the Council's dogs. She made sure of it."

Ryan Mulcahy, the deadly Fey warrior who captured

Natasha's curiosity since he first walked through her mother's halls, wrapped an arm around her waist and yanked her to his chest. Their blades met with a kiss of metal that covered her unexpected gasp. He held her gaze, his face etched in unfamiliar, merciless lines. "With her death, their hunt is finished. The Council will see only a lovers' fatal quarrel. Unless they find you here."

"We are—were—sisters. It is enough to condemn me in some Council eyes."

He gave her a small shake. "They have no proof. Witnesses will testify you set sail an hour ago on my ship. All Councilman DiMarcco will see is that the most obvious threat to his seat has been eliminated."

She shook her head, her mind whirling as bits and pieces twisted and turned, creating a more devious picture than even she had dared to imagine. "They will hunt me."

A flicker of dark knowledge in his gaze made her stomach clench as his arm around her waist tightened. "You are not their target."

The surety of his answer sent shock rocketing through her and turned her into a statue.

In that moment, her vague suspicions crystalized into brutal certainty, and one last illusion shattered. This time the emotional break barely caused a flinch.

She studied him, the hard angles of ruthlessness revealing his true nature, quashing whatever misguided hope lingered. *Fool, such a stupid, little fool.* With her world in pieces and nothing left but her pride, she lifted her chin and forced her lips into a mocking smile. "Darling, you've been keeping secrets. How...interesting."

Emotions too fast to read flashed across his arrogant face. His dark gaze, the one she once found so fascinating, turned into burnt umber. Lips she spent many a night exploring, curved into a cruel smile he had never aimed at her before. "Did you think I'd share everything with you, little one?"

He dipped his head down, his mouth ravaging hers. Although her body perked up, her shattered heart remained untouched. When he lifted his head, a swift, sorrowful shadow flitted then disappeared under a hard, determined light. "Whether you choose to believe me or not, you are safe. This—" He waved his sword over the carnage behind him without looking away from her, "—is on Irina. If you fail to move forward, she'll have won in truth. Is that what you want?"

"What I want no longer matters." Bitter and mocking, the words fell between them.

He frowned. "You would abandon those who are counting on you now?" He shook his head. "I didn't think you were that breakable, love."

His insinuation snapped her spine straight. "Because of her and the snake she allowed into her bed, suspicion will fall on me, regardless of the illusions you spread."

"Let them wonder," he said. "Let the speculation run rife. It can only help in the end. You will need the whispers to strengthen your position."

There was a remorseless sort of truth in his words. In a world populated with predators, it was better to be feared than loved. Mercy was a weakness. Starting now, it was a concept she must embrace to garner the future she wanted.

She flattened her empty palm against his heart, feeling the steady beat—one last time—taking comfort from his strength. Then she let it fall and stepped back, forcing him to release her.

Free from his hold, she straightened her shoulders, lifted her chin, and tucked the broken emotions inside her into a dark corner. "Betray me, Mulcahy, and what happened tonight will be a pretty dream."

Never again would someone catch her unawares. Time to fully embrace her nature and ensure her own future.

He sketched her a brief bow. "I would expect nothing less, Natasha." He held out his hand, torchlight glancing off his silver ring, the ring she should have realized would have warned her of who she really dealt with. "Shall we? We have a boat to catch."

In the air, light shimmered and bent, revealing their escape route, a nebulous door into the walkways between the mortal and Kyn worlds, the Shadowed Paths.

Ignoring his offered hand, she swept past him and fought the urge to look back. There was nothing left for her here, nothing but blood-soaked lies and heart-rending betrayals. A sweet song of death and chaos sang, the melody a welcome one to her demonic nature.

Ryan followed, closing the doorway between worlds just as the sounds of Irina's reinforcements broke through the wooden door.

Natasha slipped away and left more than her sister behind.

Quiet murmurs rose and fell from the gathered mourners, bringing Natasha back to the present, where she stood over Ryan's resting place. Unlike mortal funerals, there was no casket sitting beside a gaping, earthen maw, waiting to be filled. The heavy stench of roses didn't suffocate all who attended. No wailing or gnashing of teeth broke the quiet. Instead, his ashes were given back to the earth in a simple, ancient ceremony, one that survived longer than mortal memory—its simplicity reminding her of other times, other places.

She blinked away the press of tears, her gaze caught by an unmoving couple standing in the sea of attendees. Gavin Durand and Raine McCord.

Some of the crowd stopped to offer condolences to the eye-catching couple, but not many. Most kept a safe distance from the dark-haired woman standing silent and cold at Gavin's side. Wise of them. Ryan's niece, Raine, made no secret of her intention to find the one behind her uncle's death. Or her suspicions of Natasha's involvement.

Her wariness made Natasha secretly proud of the girl. Granted, Raine was looking in the wrong direction, but that would soon change.

A flash of color caught Natasha's eye as a tall, regal redhead stopped in front of the couple. Carys Iver, the newly named Head of Fey House and Ryan's predecessor.

Gavin's distantly polite expression relaxed as he took Carys's offered hand. Even Raine's remote expression regained some life. Too far away to hear their conversation, Natasha had no doubt her name was being bandied about. A fact confirmed when Raine lifted her head and caught Natasha's gaze.

Meeting that predatory speculation, Natasha dipped her head in acknowledgement, surprised when she got one in return. *What stories was Carys sharing?* When Natasha stepped in to fill one of the many holes left by Ryan's death in the Northwest Kyn power structure, pesky whispers began to circulate—whispers that the one behind his death existed closer to home. She hadn't stopped them. Why bother? They provided such a lovely distraction for her to work around. There were other, much more important things to focus on.

"Who's that?"

The question came from the young man standing at Natasha's side. Turning from Raine, Natasha looked to where her protégé, Jamie Ryder, indicated. Spying the man standing at the edge of the clearing, her lips curved with anticipatory glee. Deep inside, a low, dangerous purr rumbled to life as her demonic nature stirred. *Ah, seems she wasn't the only one interested in replacing Ryan.*

The stranger's appearance signaled the entry of a new player. Finally, it was time to play. She kept her malicious satisfaction out of her voice. "Seems the Council has decided to pay us a visit."

The man was garnering quite a bit of attention. He ignored it all, his lazy perusal touching on each attendee before moving to the next. Something in his regard brought to mind a lion choosing his next meal.

"You know him?" Jamie's question interrupted her contemplation.

"No," she murmured. Placing her hand on his linen covered arm, she decided to change that. "Let's introduce ourselves, shall we?"

The stranger watched them approach.

She did a little evaluating of her own. Dark-blond hair, liberally laced with gold, with a hint of curl. Composed of sharp angles with the shadow of a beard over burnished skin, his face spoke of a bloodline found in the far eastern deserts. The tall body, impeccably draped in silk and linen, whispered of subtle strength. And yet...

She drew closer and when only a few feet remained between her and this visitor, gave Jamie's arm a light squeeze. Heeding her signal, he stopped. She continued forward on her own and held out her hand. "Natasha Bertoi."

With an old world elegance, too natural to be feigned, he brought her hand to his mouth. A spark of male appreciation glinted in his unusual gold irises. The thin ring of red around them marked him as surely at it marked her and Jamie. He was Amanusa, a demon. His lips brushed against her skin. "Zayn Aimeric."

There was a faint accent to his name, one hinting at spices and shifting sands. Intriguing. "Were you friends with Ryan?"

Wry amusement flashed. "Some days, others it was questionable." He looked beyond her and, when his attention returned, his amusement had vanished, replaced by a more serious demeanor. "His loss is far reaching. The Council sends their condolences. They are concerned the repercussions may echo for a long while."

"They certainly will," she murmured. "Although we are honored—" she managed not to choke on the word, "—by the Council's attention, sending a personal emissary wasn't necessary."

His smile was full of mocking edges. "That remains to be seen." He sketched a small bow. "I'm here to help the Northwest Kyn."

"Help?" She raised an eyebrow. "Or evaluate?"

"Whichever proves necessary."

"Hmmm."

She considered her options. Kicking his interfering ass out of Portland would cause more problems than it would solve. However, maneuvering her own players would be challenging enough without adding in this rogue piece who'd been set into play by the Council. He could upset her entire game.

Holding his gaze, she wondered if he knew who was behind Ryan's death and what it might cost to retrieve it.

Dropping her lashes to break their connection, she set the question aside. There would be time to find out, and then, well...

Anticipation fired through her blood, curtailing her frustration at his possible interference. Perhaps his presence could prove useful. "How long do you plan on staying?"

"Until I'm no longer needed." An ambiguous answer. His attention drifted behind her.

She knew who stood there before she turned. Their approach had hardly been quiet. She stepped aside and turned to greet the advancing couple. "Gavin Durand, Raine McCord, may I introduce Zayn Aimeric." Deliberately, she placed her hand on Zayn's arm. *A deterrent or warning?* Even she was uncertain. "He's here to extend the Council's condolences."

Appearing unruffled by the deriding edge underlying her announcement of who he represented, Zayn held his hand out to Raine's companion. "Mr. Durand." The two men made quick work of the handshake. Zayn turned and offered the same to Raine. "Ms. McCord, my deepest sympathy on your loss."

The breeze played with long strands of ebony while icy silver eyes remained cool. It wasn't until Gavin subtly nudged her that Raine unfolded her arms and, with obvious reluctance, took Zayn's offered hand. "Mr. Aimeric." Her steely gaze slid to Natasha and narrowed. "I was unaware the Council was expected today."

"My apologies, I was asked to stop by on my way back from another meeting," Zayn said, reclaiming Raine's attention. "Your uncle had friends among the Council. His passing poses questions we would like answers to."

She stiffened noticeably at his words. "Yes, answers would be nice."

Inwardly, Natasha sighed. *Did the silly girl think her familial relationship to Ryan had been hidden from the Council?* Sometimes, she forgot how young these lethal children were. Gavin and Raine had no true concept of the power behind the eleven-member Council of the Kyn. The group held their authority in tight fists because they made sure to know everything.

Oblivious or uncaring of who she faced, Raine pushed, "Are you here to help uncover the one behind his death?"

A practiced frown creased Zayn's brow, but Natasha didn't miss the flash of cunning Raine's question triggered. "I was under the impression your Lycos leader disposed of the one who set the spell that killed Mr. Mulcahy."

Natasha let her lips curl. An apt cue if she ever heard one. Time to set things in motion. "Vidis is not one to take betrayal lightly. That particular traitor is no longer anyone's concern. However, we have discovered some interesting developments." Developments she was in no rush to share with this not-so-ignorant man.

"The Council is here to serve their people." His polite response contained intriguing layers of implications, ones she would love a chance to explore, but first, rules must be set.

"As much as we appreciate your offer, we'd be happy to discuss business at a more appropriate time." Falling back on her recently announced position as Chief Executive Officer of Taliesin Security, the public corporate front housing the Kyn, she offered, "Perhaps tomorrow afternoon around three at the office? I'm sure I'm not the only one with questions for you."

Taking her clear dismissal in stride, Zayn inclined his head in acknowledgement. "Until tomorrow."

He took his leave of Gavin and Raine. When he reached the edge of the clearing, another man stepped from the shadows. *Hmm, seemed their Councilman didn't feel entirely safe alone.*

Natasha and the couple beside her remained quiet, watching the two men walk away. Once they were out of sight, Gavin turned to her. "What the hell is going on, Natasha?"

Suspicion darkened his eyes to jade, while fury sketched thin white lines around his mouth. Next to him, Raine fairly vibrated with tension.

Unruffled by their hostile attitude, she motioned Jamie over. Raine and Gavin had good reason to doubt her motives. However, it was time to make sure they understood she wasn't the threat they should be worried about.

"The Council wants to play in our sandbox." Taking the arm Jamie offered her, she held Gavin's gaze with her own. Needing to impress the seriousness of what was happening, she let her demonic nature slip its leash of flesh and rise like a mirage around her. A stark visual reminder of what made her the Northwest Demon Queen. "It's our turn to remind them who they're playing with."

CHAPTER 3

Later that afternoon, back at their hotel, Darius settled into a chair across from Zayn. He stretched his legs and watched the gas firelight dance over his faded jeans and heavy sweater. On Zayn's lap was a paper file. "That from the Council?"

Zayn raised his glass, the warm colors of a good brandy swirling in its depth. "All the important information on the four Northwest Heads of House—Warrick Vidis, Cheveyo, Natasha Bertoi, and their latest addition, Carys Iver."

Darius considered the thin folder. "Seems a little light."

Zayn tipped his glass in acknowledgement before taking a sip. "Someone slacked on their homework."

"Or the Northwest is better at keeping secrets than our Council."

"Don't underestimate Natasha Bertoi, my friend. There was a reason she and Ryan worked so well together." Zayn kept his focus on his glass, his thoughts hidden. Finally he asked, "Have you sent out the summons?"

"An hour ago." Darius's hands, scarred with a myriad of thin lines from old scrapes and cuts, folded over his stomach. Firelight glinted off the silver ring on his right hand.

"There will be challenges," Zayn murmured, swirling his drink.

"I expect nothing less." Challenges he could handle, but it had been interesting to watch Mulcahy's funeral. The undercurrents floating through the gathering had been hard to miss. "The little queen's decisions are causing quite a stir."

"I would expect nothing less of her." A pause. "Anything of interest?"

Darius shrugged, thinking through what he heard. "Perhaps, but I want to listen a bit longer."

Zayn set his glass aside and rubbed a hand over his face. "We're entering a dangerous game."

Darius smiled. "Ah, but those are the best kinds."

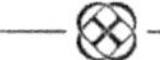

"They didn't waste any time." Warrick Vidis, the alpha wolf of the Northwest Lycos House, prowled the length of the seventh floor conference room. His unsettled presence lent a feral edge to the tense atmosphere, making the spacious room feel crowded.

Against the windows of the building housing Taliesin Security, the rain promised earlier washed the early evening light in a watery curtain.

Natasha heaved an internal sigh. Too bad the rain couldn't wash away the volatile tempers circling the room. Zayn Aimeric's presence stirred up an already simmering pot. Not for the first time, Ryan's absence cut deep. His ability to juggle the tempestuous natures of the other heads of house had been remarkable, and admirable. Now, everything and everyone was off kilter, including her.

"What did you expect?" she asked, genuinely curious of their answers.

In the chair across from her, Cheveyo, the most powerful witch in the Northwest and head of the Magi house, drummed his fingers against the table. His obsidian gaze switched between her and Vidis. "We're under scrutiny."

And this surprised them? Natasha fought not to roll her eyes. "I warned you both this would happen."

Vidis spun around, his wolf obvious in the bared teeth and amber lightning streaking his eyes. "We do not need your 'I-told-you-so's.'"

His snarled challenge roused the more savage aspect of her nature.

Must not kill the dog. Her mental reminder didn't do much to reign in her frustration, but the minute breathing room allowed her to reach for a calm she didn't feel. "Look beyond your anger, Vidis. Engaging with the Council requires a level of ruthless practicality beyond claws and teeth."

"Although those may come into play later," murmured Carys, drawing their attention. Their newest member didn't even blink under the combined stares.

"Perhaps." Natasha agreed. "But until then, we'll have to play this Zayn Aimeric carefully. He may not only be our key to uncovering the real power behind the spell that killed Ryan, but we can't afford to be seen as weak." She deliberately leaned back in her chair. "The last of Ryan's responsibilities must be filled."

Cheveyo studied her with wary calculation. "You've made your position quite clear, Natasha."

His intense regard didn't faze her. She knew what he saw—a cold, ruthless bitch wrapped in a small, blonde package. A perception she encouraged. It would do no good for him to see beyond that. For anyone to see beyond that.

She let her lips curl. "Neither you, nor Vidis, wanted the chains of running Taliesin Security," she reminded him. "Or did I miss something?"

Instead of answering her question, he posed one of his own. "How long do you plan on balancing your roles?" His question was valid. "We agreed that as a founding member of Taliesin, the CEO position should fall to you, but between that and your own House, you have your hands full. Too full to balance the marketing demands our company requires. Especially now. Without Mulcahy, our standing as the premier provider of corporate and private security services may suffer. We need to name a new Chief Marketing Officer before these small fires turn into a raging inferno."

The normally taciturn witch made a valid point. As the curtain between the humans and the magical race of beings, known as the Kyn, frayed, maintaining Taliesin's public image was more crucial than ever. Even though a small number of humans knew of the Kyn's existence, recent events and the prevalence of technology made it difficult to stay in the shadows.

Before Ryan's death, Natasha held Taliesin's Chief Marketing Officer position, a job she enjoyed immensely. She spent years cultivating connections and building the reputation of the security company. She hadn't wanted to take on the CEO role, something Cheveyo didn't understand, and she refused to explain. Unfortunately, no one else was strong enough to hold the company together, and she'd be damned before she let Taliesin falter.

"I have some candidates in mind." Individuals groomed as carefully as her connections, ones who could slip into her stiletto heels quite smoothly. "But that is not the position I'm talking about."

Vidis slammed his hand on the table, causing Cheveyo to jerk in surprise.

Natasha refused to react. If the big, bad wolf thought he could intimidate her, he could think again. What did he think existed in her house? Tame little devils? Of the four Kyn houses, her Amanusa held the most dangerous and treacherous creatures in the Kyn. And they were all hers.

"Do you think we would let you take over all of Mulcahy's duties, Bertoi?"

Why must he always growl? It was such a stereotype. Using the distracting thought to maintain her temper, she slowly stood and placed her hands directly across from his as she stared into his furious gaze. For a long moment, they engaged in a silent battle of wills, neither willing to back down.

Needing the alpha wolf to understand who and what he faced, she allowed the creature inside her to come out and play. "All? No. The important ones? Yes."

Her voice took on an unearthly depth and, on the table, her manicured nails thickened and grew, an edge of black coloring her impeccable crimson manicure. "If you disagree, find me a better replacement, Vidis. Taliesin Security must remain the powerhouse Ryan built. It is all that protects the Kyn from the humans. You and Cheveyo have both made it abundantly clear you did not want the responsibilities of CEO. I will not have the fate of the Northwest Kyn or Taliesin left in an unknown's hands. Nor will I leave any openings to be exploited by a Council tool. Not one."

"Including the Wraiths?" Cheveyo's voice cut between them, garnering both of their attention. A power in his own right, he didn't even flinch as he continued, "Will you try to control them as well?"

She blinked. *Was he serious? Control the Wraiths?* No one controlled the Wraiths, not really. The twelve-member, highly elite team of Kyn, gathered from every house, were the last bastion of justice between the humans and the nightmares lurking in the shadows. They spanned the width of the United States and Canada.

Until his death, they answered solely to their captain, Ryan. They remained fiercely loyal to him, out of love or fear—she didn't know which, nor did she care. What mattered was that they were a very lethal, useful instrument, one not publicly acknowledged, even though stories abounded of their possible existence. As far as she knew, the only ones outside of the Wraiths who were aware of their existence were sitting in this room.

And on the Council.

She straightened, dismissing Vidis. "I am not looking to control them, Cheveyo." Having such a group at your beck and call was...seductive. "Yet, if we don't replace their captain, the Council will. I am not willing to put such a decisive weapon in their hands, are you?"

Cheveyo inclined his head in acknowledgement. "Then don't stand in Gavin's way."

She arched a brow. "You would hand the reins to a child?"

Red rushed up to color Cheveyo's sharp cheekbones. "He's a grown-ass man," he snapped, his legendary control disappearing under her constant cuts.

Her laugh carried a mocking edge. "Compared to who? You? He's what? Thirty?"

"Age isn't everything, Natasha," Carys interrupted. "Ryan trusted Gavin at his side for years. I think that speaks for itself."

Exasperation wiped away Natasha's patience and she waved Carys's words away. "I'm not talking about age. I'm talking about knowledge." The stubborn expressions around her sent her temper slipping. "I have walked this earth for hundreds of years. Longer than any of you. Only Ryan had seen more than me. The Council has had eons of manipulating the Kyn. They know each house's weaknesses, their strengths, how to set each against another. All so they can achieve what they want. Their attention has turned to us, and we have no idea how long they've been watching."

With each word, her fury rose, dragging her demon closer to the surface. The temperature in the room dropped drastically. Carys stiffened in her chair, while Cheveyo's normally copper skin paled. Even the unflappable Vidis stilled.

"If we cannot present a solid front, you are asking the Council to annihilate us," she spat out. "You want to pit a man, who's just learning the extent of his abilities, and the unpredictable woman he stands with, against them?" Her hands curled into fists, then relaxed. "We must use this unsettled time to move ahead in this game or we will lose everything."

Cheveyo's throat worked as he swallowed, but his voice remained steady. "The Council is not invincible, Natasha. If we are to stand against them, the Wraiths must work with us, not against us. Let them choose their own captain."

"You said it yourself," Carys added. "The Northwest can't afford to be divided. Even on this."

Tucking her anger and frustration away, Natasha

regained her frigid control. "A choice can only be made if they are given options. If he can't stand against me, he deserves to lose." If he couldn't unify the Wraiths against her, he'd never hold them against the Council.

"Perhaps," Vidis answered. "But you'll gain nothing if you force yourself on them."

Finally, they were starting to get the picture. Keeping her pleasure hidden, she looked down and smoothed a non-existent line on her white pantsuit with a studied nonchalance. Only when she was certain that nothing showed on her face but her normally expected arrogance, did she look up. "If Gavin can win the vote, the Wraiths are his. If he fails—" she gave a delicate shrug, "—I will do whatever is necessary to keep them out of the Council's hands."

CHAPTER 4

BUSINESS IS A COMBINATION OF WAR AND SPORT.

Natasha ran a crimson nail over the etched edges of the small statuary bearing André Maurois's quote. In her opinion, the French novelist had certainly nailed it.

Ryan gave her this piece many years ago, shortly after she secured a vital government contract. A tongue-in-cheek reminder of the bloodless battle she waged, and won, for their fledgling company. At the time, women were not known for wheeling deals with men, especially military men.

Yet, Ryan was never one to follow conventions.

From the beginning of their business partnership, he allowed her to forge her own path as she walked next to him. His ability to see beyond the obvious countered her drive for control. Together they created something unique to the Kyn world—a successful enterprise that allowed them to hide in plain sight. A dangerous achievement. So dangerous, someone went to extreme lengths in an attempt to destroy it.

She sat back down at her desk, her gaze not focused on the expanse of her office, but turned inward to a more treacherous landscape. Unfortunately, after dealing with the anger and fury of the other heads of house, her emotional grip was slippery at best.

Chaotic grief escaped its leash and seeped around the formidable barriers she erected to deal with the loss of Ryan. Here, where she was safe from scrutiny, she could let herself grieve. Things had moved fast, requiring rapid-fire responses in order to stem the oncoming tide, and allowed her to ignore the press of emotions. Until it caught her unawares.

Her fingertip traced her signature authorizing the public reveal of Taliesin's reconstruction, a media event designed to reassure the human business world that Taliesin Security stood strong in the wake of their unexpected loss. Strange to see her name in place of Ryan's.

In a matter of weeks, there would be no sign of the physical damage wrought by the spell that killed him. The reconstruction melody of heavy thumps and high-pitched metal saw blades would disappear as the physical pieces were put back in place. No visible scars would be left behind as reminders of what they lost. Of what she lost.

Betrayals made for strange bedfellows. A fact she learned at Ryan's hand a very, very long time ago in a blood-soaked stone room in a desert land. He shattered her foolish heart, while ripping away her naive blinders, then offered her an alternative to certain death. Within a singular moment, he had secured her loyalty in a way no other had before or probably would ever again. Because of that, there was no way she would let his death go unavenged. Whoever was behind that spell—and Vidis's little bastard brother was not the true mastermind—would pay. Pay in very arduous ways. It was the least she could do for the only one she called friend. Damn, she missed him.

A quiet buzz jerked her out of her grim thoughts. Frowning at the phone on her desk, she depressed the speaker button. "Yes?"

"Ms. Bertoi, Sector Chief Victor Osborn is here to see you."

Well now, wasn't this interesting? Tucking her grief away, her insatiable curiosity took front and center. What news would call for an unexpected visit from the Preternatural Crimes Division? "Please send him in."

While she waited for the head of the government-sanctioned group who worked with the Kyn on decidedly other crimes to appear, she straightened the mess of papers, setting her desk in order even as she tucked her wilder emotions away.

When the door opened, she rose to her feet, her professional mask firmly in place and a polite smile on her lips. "Chief Osborn," she greeted, walking around her desk to take his hand. "To what do I owe the pleasure?"

He met her halfway, his hand outstretched. "Ms. Bertoi."

"Natasha, please," she corrected, shaking his hand. Once he released her, she waved him to one of the chairs in front of her desk. "Won't you have a seat?"

Instead of resuming her place behind her desk, she settled into the second chair.

"Natasha," he murmured, taking a seat. He wiped an ineffective hand over his wrinkled slacks, before giving up and sitting back. "I apologize for interrupting you during this difficult time. I heard Mulcahy's private funeral was today. My condolences."

She dipped her head in acknowledgement. "I don't

mind the interruption, if you're here to share information on the investigation."

A grimace came and went. "I wish I had better news for you." He met her gaze with an unusual shrewdness. "We've hit a dead end on the geneticist, Brant Sutler."

A shift in his guarded expression made her ask, "Literally or figuratively?"

His lips quirked, before he stilled them. "Figuratively."

A small spurt of surprise flashed. Not the answer she expected. "And the drug he created?"

Osborn shook his head. "No more public reports of wild wolf attacks, nor any sign of Kyn having control issues."

She gave him points on his polite phrasing. When psychotic werewolves decided to shift in front of humans, "control issues" was the nicest thing you could call it.

"Both Sutler and his drug seem to have disappeared into thin air." Frustration lent a sharpness to his words.

And if the bags under his eyes were anything to go by, he had chased every trail he could find. "Did Division have any luck tracing Sutler's financials?"

There was no way the human could have developed a drug powerful enough to force an unnatural shift on a wolf without some serious monetary backing. Jamie was tugging on a similar thread, but from an angle that Osborn had no knowledge of. Still, it didn't hurt to see if the humans had stumbled upon any additional tidbits.

"Not yet. His accounts are inactive. Not that there's much in there. A few hundred in savings, and his last paycheck in checking. No movement on any charge cards or his travel visa. We'll be expanding the search, but it's going to take time."

"Time is not our friend," she warned. "The longer your

people take to find answers, the more unsettled my people become."

His expression didn't noticeably change, but a wary anticipation sharpened the air. He drummed his fingers against the chair's arm as he studied her. "I warned you before, your people are not the only unsettled ones in this, Natasha."

"While I appreciate your warning, Mr. Osborn, you also indicated a definitive decision had not been made. Has that changed?"

His mouth thinned. "Mulcahy's death appears to have accelerated the conversations on revealing the Kyn to the general public."

Not surprising. A few key incidents in the past months left the thin curtain between the Kyn and the humans perilously frayed.

Hours before Ryan's death, Osborn told the Northwest Heads of House that the U.S. government was considering reneging on the 1946 Agreement and outing the Kyn.

"While we agree an eventual reveal is necessary," she said. "It would serve your leaders best if they remembered who and what they are dealing with."

Osborn's stiffened in his seat. "Threats don't go over well with my government."

She smiled, pleased when an uneasy frown marred his face. "Mr. Osborn, the Kyn don't issue threats."

Standing in the front receiving area, Natasha waited until the elevator doors closed behind Chief Osborn before turning to Rachel, Taliesin's trusted receptionist. Even at this late hour, she remained as crisp and professional as ever. "Rachel, is Mr. Ryder still in?"

Rachel dipped her head, her manicured nails sounding an efficient rhythm as she checked her system. "I'm showing him still available, Ms. Bertoi."

"Wonderful." Noting the woman's pale, drawn face, Natasha allowed a bit of warmth into her voice. "Why don't you head home? There's nothing that can't wait until tomorrow."

Quickly veiled surprise added much needed color to Rachel's complexion, but she only nodded in acknowledgement.

Natasha made her way to the door leading to the back offices. She reached out, only to have Rachel's gentle, "Don't stay too late, Ms. Bertoi," touch an unexpected soft spot.

Natasha's fingers tightened on the doorknob, but she simply nodded before pulling the door open and slipping into the hall. By the time she hit Jamie's office, her composure was firmly intact. She gave a perfunctory knock then stepped through the partially opened door.

Seated behind his desk, Jamie visibly started and came to his feet. "Natasha? Did I miss a meeting?" His black shirt was rolled halfway up his arms, and there was no tie in sight. He ran a hand through his already artistically messy brown hair and gave his desk a quick once over before coming around to meet her. He waved to the lone chair in front of his desk. "Have a seat."

"Relax. I just wanted to follow up on a few things with you." She moved into the office, closing the door behind her. "Where are we on Brant Sutler?"

As she settled into the chair, he leaned against the desk's edge and slipped his hands into the pockets of his gray slacks. "Nothing on Sutler, but we did find the human hired to assassinate Vidis."

"The one who shot Xander instead?"

Jamie nodded. "He's dead."

She crossed her legs. "No surprise. I'm sure whoever hired him was very unhappy with his performance."

Jamie's gaze acquired a dangerous light. "He may not have taken out the Northwest Alpha, but going after Vidis's mate did create a scene."

"Hmm, yes, it did," she agreed. "Quite the chaotic mess. I have to say it was beautifully done."

"Would've been better had he used silver bullets." He shrugged his shoulders. "But you get what you pay for."

Used to the lust for turmoil that every demon thrived on, she remained unfazed by his calculated observation. "Pay for?"

"We did manage to trace a recent payment in the shooter's account back to Vidis's brother, Dmitri. Unfortunately, it dead ends there. No sign of who provided the money."

Someone was very, very good at covering their tracks. "How much?"

"Half a million."

Interesting. "A partial payment then. The shooter's death? Was it one of ours?"

He raised his eyebrows, amusement lighting his eyes. "Are you asking as CEO or captain of the Wraiths?"

As much as she normally enjoyed sparring with the impertinent young man, today was not one of those days. She arched an eyebrow and infused her voice with ice. "Does it matter?"

Jamie's normally easygoing mask slipped and something older and darker peeked out, wiping away his youthful illusion. "You truly want to hold all the power, don't you?"

A subtle note in his voice made her wonder if something more was at play in the recent tensions in her house. Something beyond the simple machinations for her seat. "Not all," she corrected. "Just the important pieces." She tilted her head to the side and considered him. "Jealous?"

A flash of red, then he threw back his head and laughed, dispelling her momentary paranoia. "Nope, not a bit." His laughter faded and he waved a hand, as if erasing his momentary challenge. "Have at it, Natasha. I'm interested in seeing what comes of all of this." He straightened with a lithe movement and leaned closer. "Just remember who helped you along the way."

Reaching up, she patted the side of his face. "I never forget what others do for me."

He pulled back with chagrined amusement.

Folding her hands in her lap, she asked, "Are you going to answer my question?"

"I don't think it was one of ours. It actually appears as if whoever is behind this whole mess is tying up loose ends. The police found the shooter in Idaho. They listed it as an open murder. No clues, no evidence, nothing. Chances are good it will graduate to a cold case."

"Hmmm." She added this newest piece of information to her collection. "That doesn't bode well for the little geneticist on the run, does it?"

"You think whoever was behind Mulcahy's death will find Sutler before we do?"

She rose to her feet. "I think, if the human has run to ground, there are more hounds than us on his trail."

"Poor little tool," Jamie muttered. He turned and caught

sight of the clock on the back wall. "Damn, I have to go." He moved back around his desk, powered down his computer, then reached for the jacket draped over his chair. "I'm running late for a get-together."

And so was she. "Let's meet tomorrow morning. We have a few more items to go over before our meeting with the media relations coordinator from the Chamber of Commerce."

They aligned their schedules as they walked down the hall and through the now empty reception area. As the elevator doors closed behind Jamie, Natasha headed to her office to collect her things, her mind turning over all she had learned.

If the Kyn, or more specifically, the Wraiths, could get to the geneticist Brant Sutler first, their chances of uncovering a solid connection of who in the preternatural world had targeted the Northwest Kyn would rise dramatically. There was no solid proof tying Vidis's brother, Dmitri to another, but there was no way the lone wolf could acquire half a million dollars for a hit. Not to mention the expense of having Sutler create a drug targeting shifters. Granted, Tomás Chavez, the Southwest Alpha could have the means to fund such an endeavor. He made no secret of his hunger for Vidis's blood.

But there was that thrice-damned spell—cast from ancient magic that had been around longer than most of their suspects, human and Kyn combined. While she didn't think Chavez had the finesse to craft the magic behind Ryan's death, gods above and below knew revenge could make one very creative. Even as she gathered her things, she checked the time and decided to pursue that avenue later. Tonight, she had a meeting to make.

Her mind continued to riffle through hidden agendas

and convoluted schemes, an activity one of her blood thrived on. Although she held suspicions on where all this would lead, identifying the money source could be a game changer. In the end, she intended to be the one making the changes.

She brushed her fingers over Ryan's gift before turning off the light. "Time to begin our campaign, my old friend."

CHAPTER 5

Streetlights cast hazy pools across the glistening cement as Natasha stopped outside the darkened doorway of an abandoned pub. Tucked among the Pearl District's collection of art galleries and trendy restaurants, Zarana's had sat empty since the death of its owner six months earlier. Yet the skin-ruffling energy of warding magic still hummed at its entrance

A sudden bark of laughter down the sidewalk drew her attention. Even dreary weather couldn't dampen people's desire to socialize. Having even meager crowds out helped to disguise her presence and let her become just another gallery gawker. She was about to turn back to Zarana's when movement caught her eye.

Two men strolled down the far side of the street. They passed by a well lit restaurant and she caught sight of Jamie's familiar features.

She stepped back into the pool of shadows, not wanting to be seen. At least not yet. As they drew closer, she decided it was time to move indoors. She called on her maternal Fey bloodlines, kept secret from everyone, except Ryan, and stepped into the shadows.

Like most Amanusa, she preferred to remain very tight lipped about her bloodlines. While the Amanusa were the mixed offspring of the twelve original Fallen Angels and whatever Kyn female they managed to impregnate, all could lay claim to one of six bloodlines originating from the Fallen—War, Earth, Secrets, Enticement, Death, and Iniquity.

Unfortunately, blood didn't guarantee power. The more diluted the genetic line, the weaker the demon. And if you had the misfortune of a human mother, your chances of surviving puberty were slim. The fight between the profane and divine tended to break the strongest of human minds, reducing them to a level beyond psychotic.

So, while Natasha's mother carried enough Fey blood to allow her surviving daughter to Shadow Walk, Natasha's true power lay in the strength of her Amanusa ancestry. As one of the Blood of Secrets, her nature feasted on the beautiful, unexpected results of manipulation, lies, false promises, intrigue, and secrets.

Which was why she decided to Shadow Walk tonight. Not only would it allow her to bypass the wards and use the small backdoor left behind by the previous demon owner, but she would also be able to remain unseen by those gathered inside.

She moved along the paths twining between the mortal and magical realms as icy winds whipped around her without finding purchase. Locating her exit point wasn't difficult. What cost her time was the delicate reconfiguration of the warning system that penetrated even to this in-between place.

An admirable example of warding work, probably

Gavin's, but as she noted once before, experience generally trumped age. Not to mention that the devious nature of a demon held its own advantages. Finished with her maneuverings, she stepped into Zarana's main room. Her skills were such that her presence would go unnoticed until she decided otherwise.

Observation spot chosen, she surveyed the room. Gavin leaned against a dust-covered bar and next to him was Raine. A small, memorable blonde stood with them. Her lightning-quick hand movements ruffled the sleeves of her gauzy poet shirt, even as the short, sassy plaid skirt swung at mid-thigh. One knee-high leather boot tapped against the floor.

Xander Cade, Vidis's mate, and the only other female in the lethal Wraiths. Compared to Raine's sleek, no-nonsense red thermal shirt, jeans, and boots, the shifter resembled a Hell's-Angel-meets-Goth-Fairy mix. "Any others Shadow Walking?" Xander asked.

"A couple," Gavin answered. "The rest should use the front door."

Or the backdoor, Natasha corrected silently. Granted, Gavin had no idea she carried the necessary blood to use such paths. Not many of those with Fey blood had the magical strength to take advantage of traveling the strange, twisted roads without getting lost. It took a certain level of mental and magical strength. Like the type found in the Wraiths. But Ryan had shown her how.

"Incoming." Raine's murmured warning came before Natasha's magic twinge in recognition of the newest arrivals.

Gavin and Xander came to attention.

Two men stepped out of the shadows about ten feet apart. The first one stood a couple of inches above Gavin's six-foot-four height and sported neatly trimmed, dark hair, his eyes hidden behind superficial wire-framed glasses. He was immaculately dressed as if returning from some impressive lunch—one where crystal and cloth napkins were standard fare. His civilized illusion was flawless.

"Niall," Gavin greeted, receiving a short nod in return. He turned to Niall's companion. "Gideon."

"Durand." The depth of Gideon's voice vibrated bone. In faded jeans and a chambray shirt, he missed Gavin's height by a couple of inches but gave the impression of an unmovable boulder. Solid was the word that sprang to mind. Completely opposite in looks, the two latest arrivals shared identical impassive expressions and a lingering inhuman beauty inherent to those with Fey blood.

The door opened, outdoor sounds and rain-laced air sweeping through the darkened room as Jamie held the door wide for another. "Fahd, after you."

Ignoring Jamie's mocking arm flourish, Fahd swept in. Slender and dark, he didn't walk so much as flow across the floor. The sense of an impending lightning strike lingered in his wake. Jamie followed, pushing the door closed.

"Gentlemen," Gavin greeted.

"Durand." The melodic voice matched Fahd's exotic coloring. He sketched a smooth half-bow to Raine and Xander. "McCord, Cade."

His movements carried the same old world elegance of their Council visitor, Zayn Aimeric. Not unexpected. Fahd was an excellent courtier.

Jamie raised a hand and flashed a taunting smile to Raine and Xander, before taking a seat at one of the tables. Fahd joined him. On the other side, Niall and Gideon took up positions against the wall, leaving Gavin, Raine, and Xander squarely in the middle.

Natasha continued to watch, curious. So far, only seven of the twelve Wraiths were present.

"How many more are we waiting on?" Jamie leaned back in his chair until it was balanced on two legs.

"One," Gavin said.

"Still leaves us short."

"The others can't make it in."

Before anything more could be said, the final member entered. A chill breeze chased him in, even as he closed the door. Clothed in a dark overcoat and pressed slacks paired with a gray shirt, the man took in the room's occupants before dismissing them, focusing solely on Gavin. "Durand."

"Sullivan."

The twist of distaste in Gavin's greeting almost made Natasha smile. It seemed Kevin Sullivan had already ruffled some feathers. Since Ryan's death, she kept tabs on this one. Not only because of his position in the Wraiths, but because this was the same demon encouraging the discontent in her house. If her intel was correct, he would be the one who would cause the most issues tonight.

Sullivan deliberately sat apart from everyone else.

Gavin didn't waste time on unnecessary pleasantries. "The Council's representative arrived today." Based upon the lack of reaction from the room, word had already spread. When no one said anything, he continued, "We need a new captain before we're given one."

"What do you propose we do?" Sullivan's question bordered on insolence. "Vote?"

Unruffled, Gavin met the red-ringed gaze of the arrogant demon. "Yes."

Even from her hidden position Natasha could see the deepening of crimson in Sullivan's eyes at Gavin's unshakable composure. "We're still short," Sullivan snarled. "Don't you think we should all be present for this conversation?"

"Our other four are out on assignment. Once we come to a consensus, they'll be brought up to speed."

"Generous of you," Sullivan sneered.

Gavin folded his arms, his stance relaxed. "Do you have another suggestion?"

A dull flush rode under Sullivan's skin, but he held his tongue.

Natasha gave the first confrontation to Gavin.

Gavin turned back to the others. "With the Council rep in town, our options will dwindle fast. If we don't set a captain in place now, we may find ourselves becoming exactly what Mulcahy feared."

"Tools." A derisive bite colored Fahd's comment.

Gavin nodded. "Giving the most powerful and political Kyn in the world access to an elite squad of assassins and hunters is asking for trouble."

"There's no guarantee he is here for us," Niall said.

"Are you blind?" Feminine disgust brought every male head in the room toward Raine. She lifted her chin. "The Council rep isn't here for shits and giggles, boys. If you don't think he'll make a play for the captaincy, you're all fucking idiots."

Natasha swallowed her urge to laugh at the myriad of frowns Raine's scornful comment provoked. No matter how deadly Raine and Xander were, the other male Wraiths tended to forget that what lay underneath the curves could be more deadly than their chosen weapons.

"Do you not want it, McCord?" Gideon's deep voice echoed through the room. He didn't move from his position, simply stared at Raine.

"Nope, not even if you offered it dipped in chocolate." She bared her teeth. "However, I'd be happy to answer to Gavin."

The flash of humor on Gideon's face was so quick, Natasha would have bet good money that she was the only one who caught it. "What a surprise."

"Let's make this fair then, shall we?" Sullivan drawled with frigid disdain. "I'll officially throw my hat into the ring."

"Oh, shocker, that one," Jamie muttered.

Sullivan turned with reptilian slowness to pin the younger demon with a glare. Unfazed, Jamie simply smirked.

Niall's unruffled voice wound through the tension. "Besides you and Durand, who else is offering to stand for such a position?"

"Our friendly neighborhood Councilman, Zayn Aimeric," Raine offered.

"Natasha Bertoi," Jamie volunteered, never looking away from Sullivan while an anticipatory delight danced across his face.

"Seriously?" Xander asked. "Natasha already claimed the CEO position at Taliesin. Isn't that enough for her? She doesn't need the captaincy as well."

He just grinned in reply.

Fahd spoke up. "Natasha is not a choice I would be comfortable with. There is no guarantee she wouldn't use us to accommodate her own goals."

His comment made Natasha reevaluate the depth of dissent in her court. Of the three demons gathered, only Jamie seemed to be in favor of her bid. While Sullivan was always a self-serving bastard, for Fahd to question her ability to hold the Wraiths was more disturbing. Perhaps it was time to remind those gathered exactly what kind of leader they must choose.

She stepped out of her concealment, her voice cutting through the room with icy precision. "And you think Gavin or Zayn would be any different?"

Her sudden appearance caught everyone's attention and the room's tension skyrocketed.

"Natasha, nice of you to join us." Gavin's growl told another story, but she appreciated his efforts at civility.

Brushing an imaginary fleck of dirt off the sleeve of her jacket, she strolled across the floor, knowing the elegant lines of her white pantsuit fairly glowed against the dim interior. "I wouldn't have missed this for the world, Gavin." Coming up behind Jamie, she brushed her blood red nails over his shoulder as she passed. Her attention landed on Fahd. "I ask again, do you think Gavin or Zayn would hesitate to use any of you to further their own position?"

Fahd remained relaxed under her piercing regard, his voice steady. "The Wraiths stand as the last guard against those who would see the world washed in blood. Politics can have no place in justice."

His answer had her giving a low laugh meant to send uneasy chills chasing over skin. "Oh, Fahd, don't fool yourself. Not all of your assignments have served Lady Justice, regardless of what Ryan told you." When the room remained silent, she raised her eyebrows, turning in a slow circle. "What? No rushes of denial?" She clicked her tongue in admonishment. "That's something, at least." Looking beyond Fahd, she zeroed in on Sullivan.

He tried not to squirm but failed to stop his tiny, involuntary twitches.

"Do you really think you could hold this group together?"

"Better than you, Bertoi," he sneered, hollow bravado echoing behind his words. "Stick with the bloodless weapons. They're less likely to chip your nails."

She suppressed her urge to roll her eyes at the childish taunt. *Was that the best he could do?* She was amazed at the amount of trouble this one half-wit managed to generate. His obvious immaturity made her question how accurate her information was on the rumblings in her court. But it was one more reason that he couldn't be allowed anywhere near the captaincy. Idiots didn't have long lifespans.

Natasha drifted closer until she stood directly in front of Sullivan. Wanting to get her point across, she let her demon rise to the fore and hover around her, allowing her to loom over the fool. She leaned in until their faces were inches apart. If not for the furious energy singing between them, their position could have been mistaken for a kiss. "Do you know why both the captaincy and your petty aspirations to my seat will forever go unfulfilled? Mmmmm?"

Sullivan's lips tightened into thin lines as his gaze darted between her eyes and face without settling. This close, she couldn't miss the red bleeding over the brown of his irises. He struggled to contain the monster under his skin, knowing he now faced down the biggest threat in the room. His jaw was so tight, she was surprised it didn't crack his teeth.

When it became obvious he couldn't speak, she continued, "Because you don't have the balls to see shit through, little boy." Her voice barely rose above a whisper, yet the hiss echoed through the room. "Until that changes, stay the fuck out of my way."

He paled.

Satisfied she had delivered her message, she straightened without breaking eye contact. "Unless, of course, you'd like to make your challenge official?" A little bloodletting would do a demon queen good.

"Enough, Natasha." Gavin drew her focus like a magnet. "You can't bully this group into doing what you want."

She held his gaze and fought back the urge to push a little further, a little harder. When Gavin refused to look away, she let her lips curl into a condescending smile and drew back from Sullivan.

Gavin addressed the entire group. "The nominations will stand. Each member will chose who they feel would best serve as captain."

Xander, who at some point had hopped up on top of the bar, swung her legs, the silver chains on her black boots chiming. "Gavin has seniority. He can hold his temper better than any of us, which makes him invaluable in dealing with—" she gave a significant glance at Natasha, "—others. He was Mulcahy's second, so I'm nominating him."

As Natasha agreed with her observation, she simply smiled at the younger woman. Besides, upsetting Vidis by taunting his mate gained her nothing.

"Seconded," Raine added.

"Seniority? Level head?" Jamie snorted. "Did you forget how close the humans are to outing us? Or that the Council is targeting us as well? If the Northwest Kyn plan on coming through this, we need someone who can spin the public and parry the Council's advances. No offense, Durand, but I'd pit Natasha against odds like those any day."

"A sound argument," Gideon said. "I'll second Natasha's nomination."

How generous of him, and unexpected, but she'd take it.

"Anyone else?" Gavin asked.

"I'll second Sullivan's nomination," Fahd added, avoiding Natasha's gaze. When the rest of the group turned to him, he shrugged. "Options are always nice to have." Not a ringing endorsement, but when dealing with demons, one must always be prepared for the unexpected. They loved to stir shit up, and this was turning out to be no different.

Gavin turned to Niall. "Anyone you want to nominate?"

Niall shrugged. "I'm still considering the options."

"Fair enough," Gavin murmured.

"Anyone want to second Aimeric's nomination?" Raine drawled.

When no one answered, Gavin said, "Then I suggest everyone consider the nominations carefully." He met Natasha's gaze, the mocking glint warning her that he wasn't done yet. "Did you all receive the same invite?"

Everyone but Natasha nodded.

Intrigued and a little miffed, she asked, "Invite?"

"Our presence is being demanded tomorrow night at Mulcahy's home."

This was unexpected and disturbing. "By?"

"Zayn Aimeric." Raine shrugged. "Or so we think. The details are a little sketchy."

Natasha frowned, puzzled by their seeming lack of concern. "None of you are curious about this?"

"Whoever it is will be facing eight Wraiths," Gavin said. "I don't think it's us who should be worried."

Granted, Gavin had a right to his arrogance, but still she'd make sure to join tomorrow's gathering.

When she added nothing more, he continued, "I'll notify the other four. They can vote by proxy. We'll call the final vote tomorrow night."

One by one, the Wraiths left the way they came, until

only Gavin and Raine remained behind with Natasha. A watchful silence stretched between them. Gavin never fidgeted under Natasha's regard, a trait she admired. Even Raine kept still, waiting.

"Do you think you're ready to take this on?" Natasha asked.

Gavin studied her. "This or you?"

Refreshing not to be underestimated. She smiled, knowing how it would unsettle the two before her. "Are they not the same?"

"I'm not stepping aside." Grim determination laced every syllable.

No, Gavin couldn't, actually, not if he and Raine wanted to survive. But they didn't know she understood that. She gave a merry laugh. "Then good luck to you, Gavin." Taking a step back, she stood on the threshold of the Shadowed Paths and gave her final volley. "You're going to need it."

CHAPTER 6

A SHARP RAP ON THE DOOR DRAGGED NATASHA'S ATTENTION AWAY from her corrections on the latest press copy.

"Natasha, it's time." Jamie stood in the doorway, letting in the chaotic chorus of heavy thumps and high whines of metal saw blades. A muffled shout sounded, followed by a crash, causing him to wince. "They're in the conference room."

Setting aside her work, she rose from her desk and grabbed the tailored black-linen jacket from her chair. Passing the penholder, she snagged a lacquered Chinese hairpin. "Who's here?"

"Vidis and Cheveyo."

Untucking her hair from the jacket's collar, she made a few quick twists and set the hairpin in place. "Carys?"

"On her way." Jamie remained in the doorway. "Rachel indicated her meeting ran over."

With the exit blocked, she pulled up short, even as she secured her jacket's lone button over her crimson silk shell. Jamie's normally easygoing expression was shadowed by something darker. Smoothing the material down over her hips, she canted her head to the side. "What's wrong?"

"Why haven't you taken out Sullivan?"

She gave his unexpected question a slow blink. "Excuse me?"

"Why are you allowing that bastard to spread his poison through Amanusa House?" He pushed away from the doorframe, stepped inside her office, and closed the door behind him. Leaning against it, he studied her. "You and I both know the Council is here to exploit the cracks in our leadership. Sullivan will just rip the existing ones even wider, especially if he gains control of the Wraiths."

Jamie's caustic tone scoured over her, riling the demon living below her skin. Although she held grand plans for her protégé, not even he had the right to question her decisions as the Amanusa Head. That he felt he could, brought her demon roiling to the surface in a reflexive rush, shimmering the air between them. "So because he disagrees with my decisions, I should, what? Make an example out of him?"

Color drained from his face as her lethally edged questions cut through his disdain.

"Is that what you think makes for a strong leader, pet? Disposing of those who don't fall into line?" Her lips curved, revealing the sharpened points of her teeth, a physical change prompted by her straining nature. "If I relied on such simplistic tactics, there wouldn't be much of a house to rule, now would there?"

Little beads of perspiration appeared on his forehead, but he gamely held her gaze while he shook his head slowly.

Satisfied with his reaction, she straightened and took a step back, giving herself a chance to reclaim control over her instinctive need to see him bleed. Once sure she wouldn't leave Jamie with a lasting mark of her displeasure, she continued, "If Sullivan's petty aspirations for my seat don't worry me, neither should they worry you. If he wants to whisper that my hand crafted the spell, so be it. He's playing a child's game of rumors. One I don't have the time, or patience, to indulge in."

Jamie visibly swallowed but dared to press his concern. "Those rumors are turning the other houses against us. It makes yo—" He verbally stumbled and quickly changed his next word, "Us, the Northwest, look weak to the Council."

She raised an eyebrow. No way to miss his obvious pronoun change. She considered explaining why his observations were incorrect, but something held her back. Instinct, past experience, or her hunger for havoc, she wasn't sure which. And preparing to step into the political ring with the Council and the other Heads of House was not the time to delve into it.

However, a warning would not be remiss. "You aren't giving our house or the Kyn as a whole, enough credit. Those intelligent enough to understand what is truly at stake understand that Mulcahy's death gained me nothing and could cost us a great deal."

"You gained Taliesin," he muttered.

"You thought someone else would run the company?" Who had he expected to step up? Vidis? Cheveyo? Neither man had what it took to run a multi-million-dollar company. Nor could they straddle the fine line between aggression and compromise with various government agencies and rival businessmen. Vidis's temperament was too close to that of his wolf, and Cheveyo, well, he had enough problems to handle.

When she silently held his stare, Jamie clenched his fists, his own temper finally breaking free, despite his obvious nervousness at confronting her. "Look, fine, you're the best one to run Taliesin. I'm not questioning your appointment. I meant what I said last night. I'm thrilled you're in the running for captaincy, but it's no secret every house has a few rats who report back to the Council. Who's to say Sullivan isn't our rat? What if this is a ploy to bring down another one of our leaders?"

He was making some valid points, ones she considered herself. And because she had, she gave him the same answer she'd come to. "The Council tools are never so obvious. They prefer to work where they can't be seen. Sullivan is not subtle enough to be their pawn. It's a necessary trait for Council tools. Unlike the one behind Ryan's death, Sullivan doesn't hold enough power or influence to create the necessary fissures the Council relies on."

"You willing to bet your position on that, Natasha? Your life?" For moment, an unsettling anger ran behind his face, almost too fast to catch. "Because if the ones behind Mulcahy's death are examples of who, or what, we're facing, I'd be a bit more concerned, if I were you."

"But you're not me." More than concern haunted her, but a leader never revealed their doubts, not even to those who stood beside them. "I would never risk more than I'm willing to pay, Jamie. Sullivan is a distraction. The real threat is the one waiting for us in the conference room." She gave a pointed look at the closed door.

His shoulders slumped, but he stepped aside. "I hope to hell you know what you're doing."

"Better than most," she said, opening the door.

As Jamie dogged her heels, Natasha closed in on the conference room where voices from within floated into the hallway.

They stopped outside the room and Jamie asked, "Do you need me to stay?"

"No."

He turned to leave and made it a step before he stopped and turned back. "I'll pick you up around nine tonight?"

Ah, yes, the private meeting at Ryan's. "I'll be here." It was one appointment she didn't want to miss.

He dropped his head and left.

Professional smile firmly in place, she swept into the room and brought the conversation to a halt. Zayn looked up from his conversation with a frowning Vidis, while Carys and Cheveyo sat on either side of the empty chair at the head of the table.

Good, everyone was here.

She made her way to the seat between Cheveyo and Carys. "My apologies, my previous meeting ran over." Taking her seat, she laced her fingers together and rested her hands on the table's surface. "Welcome to Taliesin, Mr. Aimeric."

"Zayn, please," he murmured.

"Zayn, then." The other three heads remained silent, ceding control to her. Today there would be no delicate dance. They needed some answers. And perhaps those same answers would help her smooth Jamie's ruffled feathers. "We appreciate the Council's thoughtfulness in sending you for Ryan's service."

"As I mentioned before, his passing has left its mark."

"Yes, it has," she murmured. "However, me and mine would like to ensure we address the true reason behind your visit. You are here for more than condolences."

"You and yours?"

"Taliesin, and our Kyn community," Carys interjected.

If not for the fact that Natasha knew Carys held no love for the Council, even she'd have been fooled by the civility in the woman's tone. In fact, having Carys as the new head of Fey House pleased Natasha on multiple levels.

Not only did Taliesin's chief legal counsel possess a razor sharp mind, Carys's desire for answers on Ryan's death rivaled Natasha's. Enough so, should there come a time when lines must be crossed to get those answers, lines Cheveyo and Vidis may not be comfortable crossing, Natasha knew she would find a certain level of support from Carys.

Zayn inclined his head, his pleasant expression never wavering. "The Northwest Kyn have become a unique power here in the new world, one the Council has been happy to work with. While congratulations are in order for both you, Ms. Iver, and you, Ms. Bertoi, Mulcahy's death leaves behind some very... unique problems."

"Which problems would those be?" Vidis asked, something predatory crawling behind his eyes.

Zayn turned to the wolf, a considering light in his red-ringed yellow eyes. "In the last few months, the Northwest Kyn has been involved in some highly public situations. Situations that verge on the cusp of becoming problematic. The Council would like to offer our assistance in resolving any remaining complications."

"Such as?" Natasha was truly curious to hear his answer. "Both the CEO position and the Head of the Fey house are filled. Taliesin's professional standing at both the federal and local levels remains solidly intact. What could possibly be worrying the Council?"

"The Wraith's Captaincy."

And there it was, the real reason Zayn was sent to Oregon. "The Council holds no authority over the Wraiths."

Anticipation fired in those unusual eyes, even as Zayn deliberately relaxed into his chair. "The Council understands the vital role the Wraiths play in our co-existence with the humans. Therefore we would like to offer our input on who will assume this position."

Did he really think his "input" would go over uncontested with the Wraiths? What could prompt that kind of arrogance? He hadn't struck her as a fool. At least not yet.

"I just bet they do," muttered Cheveyo, his comment turning Zayn's smile into a tight-lipped grimace.

Before anyone else could stoke the fire, she said, "The Wraiths are here to keep both human and Kyn safe from all threats. There is no room for politics in justice." It didn't escape her that she raised the same concerns, voiced against her, to Zayn. *Thank you, Fahd.* "If we allow the Council to interfere, they will not be able to maintain that impartiality."

"Truly, you don't think the Council would stoop to such a level as to use such a group to enforce their political views?" His question dripped with polite disbelief.

The man deserved an award for his performance. If it weren't for the brightening of red around his pupils, a telltale clue of his waxing temper and a sure sign his Amanusan nature was clawing for attention, she might believe him. "Please, Zayn, don't play us for fools. Any time a political machine is given access to such a tool, they will always utilize it." A fact she witnessed the Council prove time and time again. She held his gaze. Dropping all pretenses, she let her demon prowl forward and let him see just how far she was willing to go to keep the Council out of Wraith affairs. "The Wraiths will not answer to the Council."

His amusement vanished. "They must answer to someone."

"They will," Vidis said, his voice low. "Their captain."

"And who will that be? Gavin Durand?" He tilted his head in her direction. "You?" He shook his head. "Don't be obtuse. Mulcahy's pets owe their existence to the Council. They are too dangerous to hand over to just anyone."

Three insults in three sentences? From someone who was such an experienced Council member, the blunder was quite clumsy. Unless, of course, he was trying to provoke them—a minor success, considering the brightening sheen of amber in Vidis's eyes and Carys's sudden, focused attention. Even Cheveyo's spine snapped straight while his hands disappeared below the table. Perhaps she should call a halt to this little charade before blood was spilt. The tension in the room climbed as the silence stretched and the monster under her skin hummed in joy.

With a silent sigh, she tucked away her predatory anticipation of imminent bloodshed and focused on business. "The Wraiths owe their existence to Ryan Mulcahy, a fact that they understand all too well. His death was not well received. In fact, I do believe they would love to ask you a few questions of their own." Ignoring the indignant look on his face, she continued, "As a matter of fact, there's one particular question bothering me. Perhaps you can answer it?" Time to push.

Zayn deliberately sat back in his chair and made a go ahead gesture.

How magnanimous of him. "What has the Northwest Kyn done to frighten our esteemed Council?"

A scowl settled over his aristocratic features. "The Council is not frightened, Ms. Bertoi. They are concerned. In the last few months, your people have been involved in some highly troubling situations." He turned to Cheveyo. "We are still dealing with the fallout from your visit to the Southwest." His gaze slid to Vidis. "And yours. Their alpha has laid serious accusations at your door. Not to mention the rogue who cut a bloody swath through the human nightclub a few weeks ago." He swiveled to Natasha and spread his hands wide. "Mulcahy's death was the last straw, and now there are whispers that perhaps your House is unsettled."

When she refused to react to his dig, he continued, "Whatever is at play here is dangerous. Not just to your people, but to the Kyn as a whole. Our agreement with the human authorities is being severely tested by such events. The Council agreed to the Wraiths' creation, so long as their first priority remained intact. Keep our race safe and hidden. Discretion is vital to that goal. If the Wraiths fail at that, then it becomes the Council's problem. Something the Northwest Kyn seem to have forgotten."

Mental wheels spun as she considered what Zayn didn't say. If the Council considered the Wraiths a problem, who did they think could stand against them? Old memories stirred, little things she tucked away for decades.

"Is the Council truly so blind as to not see that the time for secrecy is coming to an end?" Cheveyo's question cut through the room. A muscle ticked in his jaw. "Technology has shrunk the world, erasing boundaries, including the ones we have hidden behind for centuries."

"It is not time to step out of the shadows."

The witch's lips twisted into a grimace. "You better check your damn watch, because you're running behind."

Zayn arched an eyebrow. "You're questioning the Council's wisdom?"

"That's not wisdom," Carys snapped. "That's being unrealistic."

"I'll be sure to share your opinions with the Council, then." His mocking tone matched the glare he leveled at Carys.

"Please do." Natasha stepped in. "The Wraiths can only do so much, Councilman, without turning the humans against us." When his attention centered on her, she continued, "I'm sure certain Council members will find it reassuring that their people understand change is imminent and necessary."

His eyes narrowed. "Reassuring?"

She blinked in mock innocence. "Was this not the exact subject under discussion last month?" His spine straightened. *Yes, we have ears of our own.* "I do believe we are not the only Kyn who understand that if we don't arrange our reveal to the humans on our terms, we may be facing a new era of persecution." Deliberately she used Ryan's exact phrasing, one he shared with her after his last go around with the Council.

Zayn's lips thinned as her words found their mark.

"When," she stressed, "not if, the curtain is drawn back, the only ones able to keep the most violent of us from making brutal headlines in the mortal world will be the Wraiths. Ryan knew exactly who to choose to create a group capable of doing just that, especially since the humans are poorly equipped to handle our less than pleasant aspects. Their captain must be of their choosing. Otherwise, they will be of no use to the Kyn or anyone else."

"That choice is not yours to make," Zayn said.

"Nor yours," she shot back. Taking a steadying breath, she leaned back, and looked around the table before coming back to Zayn. "It strikes me that the Council is much too interested in, not only our actions, but those of our Wraiths."

He rose to his feet, straightening his tie. "I've already explained our concerns."

Refusing to let him off the hook, she shook her head. "No, there's more to it." Her fingers began to drum on the table as she studied him with narrowed eyes. "If you're so eager to meet with the Wraiths, perhaps you can help them with something."

"What would that be?"

"They have questions about the spell that killed Ryan. You see, Mr. Aimeric, it was very, very old." And the demon before her was no young fool, regardless of how he played things.

His hand froze and he lifted his head to meet her gaze. "How old?" An odd intensity edged his question, one that was lacking until now.

Cheveyo leaned forward. "Ancient."

Zayn slowly considered each of them. He stopped on Vidis. "It was my understanding that your brother was behind the spell."

Vidis's smile wasn't nice. "Dmitri held no affinity for spell crafting." His wolf evident in his amber gaze, he stared at Zayn. "He was, however, a very good tool."

Thoughts too fast to follow flashed across their visitor's face. As he processed their implications, he set his jaw. "Perhaps I can offer my assistance to the Wraiths."

"I'm sure they would appreciate any insights you could provide." Pursing her lips, she rested one crimson tipped fingernail against her chin. "However, may I suggest you refrain from referring to them as 'Mulcahy's pets' if you value your appendages?"

After a distinct pause, he inclined his head. "I'll take that under advisement, Ms. Bertoi."

"Good." Flashing him a smile guaranteed to loosen his bowels, she murmured, "Best of luck to you, Mr. Aimeric."

CHAPTER 7

WIND DANCED THROUGH THE QUIET STREETS AS THE FIRST questing fingers of night began to appear. Cool and scented from the evening's earlier rain, the accompanying breeze tripped and tumbled over leaves, sending them scurrying along to pile against the silent house. Clouds played peek-a-boo with the moon, bathing the private residence in an ever-changing pallet of whites, grays, and blacks.

Natasha stepped off the Shadowed Paths and onto the edge of Ryan's property. She held still, taking time to ensure she was alone.

After the tension filled meeting with Zayn, she spent another hour dealing with various situations requiring immediate attention from Taliesin's new CEO. Having business impede on her personal agenda was nothing new. However, the sheer volume of things to be addressed made her even more aware of the urgency in naming her marketing replacement. Which probably wouldn't happen for a while, since a few more pressing concerns vied for her attention, such as filling the captaincy and getting rid of

Zayn Aimeric. Oh, yes, and quashing Sullivan's juvenile attempts for her seat.

She expected today's meeting to raise more questions than it answered, but the type of questions Zayn's answers provoked made tonight's detour even more important. If, what she suspected was true, her plans were about to be upended. When the dust finally settled, she intended to be on top, not crushed underneath.

Crossing to the front door, she paused long enough to slip by the wards. Simple enough, as they hadn't changed since her last visit. As easy as it was, there was no doubt that stronger, more difficult ones waited inside. If she was lucky, she wouldn't have to mess with any of those.

Once inside, she didn't bother to turn on any lights. There was no reason. What she wanted didn't lay in the common rooms. Turning down the hall, she headed directly to the room she wanted. Ryan's office. The door was closed and heavily warded.

Standing before it, she took a deep breath. Time to see just how close a friend Ryan considered her. Raising her hands to shoulder height, she kept her palms facing the door. Magic pulsed under her hands, like a living curtain between her skin and the wood. Ryan's ward would recognize friend from foe. She whispered a phrase, felt the magic pause, then curl around her in an unbreakable grip. It nipped along her skin, testing her intentions. The pressure increased, like red-hot pins piercing nerve endings, until she gritted her teeth in an effort to quell her reaction.

Her demon didn't like the unsettling sensation. It prowled inside her, swiping at the invasion and straining her control. *Damn, it had been a long day.* Finally, about the time she reconsidered letting her more chaotic nature loose, the magic flared then disappeared.

Blowing out a breath, she dropped her hands, the muscles in her arms trembling. Grasping the knob, she turned it and pushed the door in. The air quivered then stilled. Nice to know Ryan liked her.

Stepping inside, she shut the door softly behind her. Thanks to the drawn shutters, not even moonlight penetrated the shrouded room. Not that darkness ever proved a challenge for demons. Too much of their time was spent in the inky world. Yet, she still flicked on the desk lamp, letting the soft light spill over the desk.

Traces of Ryan's life lay scattered over the surface. A neat pile of files lay clustered near the phone. Some report on Taliesin letterhead held center position. Red ink in his masculine handwriting marked up the pages. A handful of pens lay in disarray around it, and a half full glass still sat to the side. The flat computer screen was dark, and a book rested face down, jacket cover spread next to it.

She ran a finger along the bent spine, tracing the title and well-known name of the king of horror. She never understood why Ryan choose this particular genre. Reading should be an escape. And their world held more nightmares than even this particular human could convey.

Everything indicated a man who would be returning shortly to finish his business. The incongruous scene hurt because Ryan wouldn't be back.

Slowly moving around the desk, she sank into the leather chair. Faint traces of his familiar scent drifted to her, the smell tightening her throat. *Suck it up, my dear. Now is not when you want to lose focus.*

There wasn't much time before her next appointment

so she got work and began to go through each of the desk drawers. When nothing interesting appeared, she swiveled the chair, and studied the office.

Big windows, currently hidden behind the shutters, would overlook the wildness crouched in his backyard, offering glimpses of the lake just beyond. Two padded chairs and a couch faced off with the desk, the wall behind graced with a painting portraying a land Ryan hadn't seen in years. The last two walls held row after row of bookshelves. The man loved his books and souvenirs. Objects, some valuable on the art market, others valuable only to the one who collected them, lay scattered among the shelves.

She studied each shelf. *Would it be in plain sight?* Ryan once told her hiding things in the open was much better security than hiding them in lockboxes. Deviousness might be key to the Amanusa, but it didn't mean they were the only ones with a monopoly on it. It was one of the things which made Ryan so successful with Taliesin. He could out think most of the criminal element that comprised their company's bread and butter. Who better to catch a thief, than one of the best? Had he chosen to work toward different goals, the Council would have been wise to be concerned.

The house shifted, the subtle creaks yanking her head up and around. Her ears strained, trying to ensure it was just the house, and not an unexpected visitor. The wards would provide a warning, but she proved they could be breached. When silence resettled, she rose, turned her back to the door, and went back to scanning the shelves.

A photo box caught her eye. A delicate sketch surrounded by dried violets and a faded, frayed ribbon.

Hard to tell what color it had been in this light, but she recognized the face in the sketch. The sharp chin, the up-tilted eyes, dark hair a rippling curtain of warm mahogany, and a knowing smile. Catriona, Ryan's younger, and only, sister. Raine McCord's mother.

Picking up the decorative box, Natasha studied the feminine face captured by a loving hand. Probably Ryan's. On the boat trip from Europe to here, she caught him sketching a small boy scrambling like a monkey up one of the tall masts. After they settled in Oregon, she couldn't remember him ever sketching again. Yet, this was proof he had done it at least once. The paper was modern, not the heavy vellum of the past.

"He did that just before I was born." Raine's voice was bland, quiet. "Mom and I made that for him before..."

So, not the house settling. Natasha turned, careful to keep her face empty.

No matter how much the girl tried, Raine couldn't completely hide the depth of pain at losing her mother to a human's twisted experiments. It lurked under everything she did, every choice she made. Had Natasha been more inclined toward emotional reactions, she would have hurt for the younger woman standing before her. But pain created the warrior and the warrior was what would be needed to survive in their world.

Yet, right now, perhaps Natasha could offer some small comfort to Ryan's last, surviving family. "She was well loved."

Those silver eyes didn't blink but stay focused, very reminiscent of the hunting stare common to big cats. Natasha held that considering gaze, unimpressed. What lay under her skin was more than a match for what lay under

Raine's—regardless of whatever quirks science or genetics left the girl.

"Why are you here, Natasha?"

"Perhaps I should ask you the same thing," Natasha murmured. "Where's your shadow?"

Amusement actually cracked through the blank mask. "Gavin's out overturning some rocks." The brief amusement faded. "What are you looking for?"

"Answers."

Raine crossed her arms over her chest, her dark brows lowering. "And you think those are here? In Mulcahy's office?"

"Not think," Natasha said, her fingers sliding along the edges of the photo box. "They are. It's just a matter of finding them."

"Finding what?"

Natasha shook her head. How blind had Raine's anger toward her uncle kept her? Time to rip those pesky blinders off. Her fingertips skimmed over a rough spot. "Proof." Heading back to the desk, she ignored the younger woman's frowning gaze. "You never answered my question last night." Angling the box under the desk lamp, Natasha noticed the small, almost imperceptible break she felt.

"It's been a damn long day." Raine came closer and leaned her hands on the other side of the desk, watching Natasha's movements. "Which question?"

Fingers stilling, Natasha lifted her head and trapped Raine's attention. "If Gavin becomes captain, what keeps him from using you to further himself?"

Those silver eyes began to burn with an eerie incandescence. "Don't. You aren't going to drive a wedge between Gavin and me, Natasha. Worse than you have tried and failed. Miserably."

Ah well, not her best effort, granted, but it was worth a shot. Changing tactics Natasha asked, "Did you ever wonder how and why your uncle created the Wraiths?"

Raine frowned. "Is this a trick question?"

Dear hells, no wonder the girl infuriated Ryan so often. "No, McCord, this is not a trick question." Natasha went back to her study of the photo box.

"The Wraiths were created to keep the big, bad shit from tearing a bloody swath through the human world and making the presence of the Kyn known. So long as the humans can't prove how dangerous we are, they can't justify wiping us out."

Natasha slid the edge of her nail into the small break and pried. "If that's the case, then why don't you answer to the Council?"

"I thought that was who Mulcahy answered to."

Raine's answer actually made Natasha laugh and raise her head. "Did you meet your uncle, child? He never answered to anyone."

Thunderclouds drifted over Raine's face. "Don't call me a child." The demand held the edge of a growl.

"Then stop acting like one." Turing her attention back to the box, Natasha lifted a section of the frame, and exposed a hollow opening. The lamplight danced across something wedged inside. Satisfaction flared and she smiled, tilting the box and giving it a soft shake until the hidden object landed in her palm. Setting the box down, she traced a fingertip over the etched metal as memories crowding close. Gently pushing them back, she cupped the object and held her hand out to Raine. "Do you recognize this?"

Raine leaned closer, studying the ring. "No, should I?"

"Unless you remember your bedtime stories, no."

Natasha held the silver ring up, letting light dance across it. "Have you ever heard of the Sarielian Order?"

Raine shook her head.

"Think of them as the Wraiths' predecessors. Before the Kyn came to America, the European Houses needed a neutral group to police their own, to keep the worst of us out of sight of the humans. Too many times we failed to stop those who believed humans were dispensable. The burning of Alexandria's Library, the Inquisition, the Crusades, each time the humans rose in revolt, we lost more and more of ours. One very astute and clever leader decided if we were to survive these mortal purges, we needed a group to operate outside of politics and moral boundaries to ensure we didn't offer the humans ready-made excuses to wipe us out. The Council agreed and the Sarielian Order was established."

"So, what? Mulcahy created the Wraiths based on this Order?"

Quick little cat, but Raine still missed the bigger picture. "Yes, he did."

"Mulcahy was part of the Order?" Confusion made her voice sharp. Before Natasha could answer, she kept going. "No, no way."

Mulcahy had been more than part of the Order, but that wasn't something Natasha planned on sharing just yet. Curious as to what was flying around in Raine's head, Natasha leaned back in her chair and asked, "Why do you find that so hard to believe?"

Raine's head lifted, her chin jutting obstinately. "You just said he'd never answer to anyone. If something like this Order existed, it would answer to the Council."

Maybe, maybe not. Some of the things Ryan shared with Natasha made her wonder how accurate that assumption was. "You don't believe such a group could remain outside of the Council's influence?"

Raine snorted. "Please, if the Order is just a higher version of the Wraiths, there's no way they aren't being used by the Council. Unless they have someone like Mulcahy in charge."

"I'm not sure if your cynicism is a blessing or a curse." Natasha held the ring out to Raine. "Take it. It's yours."

Straightening, Raine studied Natasha with a strange intensity.

Natasha let her, in no way shaken by the intense regard. Scarier than Raine tried to shake Natasha's composure with no luck. Raine had many years to go before she'd be up to par.

"What game are you playing now?"

"I'm not playing any games." Not right now. This was too important. Natasha needed this young woman for her plans to succeed.

Raine snatched the ring from her. "Bullshit." With that exclamation, she threw herself into one of the chairs facing the desk. One hand tapped on the armrest, the other clenched around Ryan's ring. "Why are you suddenly so..." she searched for the right word, "...amenable? I'm nothing more than a pain in your ass."

Oh, how true, but Natasha had moves to make and promises to keep. "You will always be a pain in my ass, Raine. That doesn't mean I don't find you useful." She crossed her legs and smoothed out a non-existent wrinkle, a small moment to recollect herself. "How much of your uncle's history do you know?"

Those silver eyes narrowed and Raine's fingers stilled. "Obviously not as much as you."

Natasha dipped her head in acknowledgement. "True,

but what I can tell you is that the ring you hold changes our current situation."

Raine looked down and opened her hand. The heavy silver lay against her palm. "How?"

Time to throw the girl into the deep end. "The current Council is highly divided on the whether or not to reveal our presence to the humans."

Raine's head lifted. "That's not big news."

"No, but what you don't know is that the same faction that wants to keep us hidden, has another goal. This one, not publicly known, would turn their own people against them. Thanks to the intermingling of bloodlines among the Kyn, there are very few purebloods left. Most of the younger generations are mixed blood. Yet their blood is not the only thing that has changed, so has their magic. There is a small, but very dangerous group hidden among the Council who would rather see these mixed bloods wiped out, even if it means temporarily aligning with humans."

Something too fast to read flashed over Raine's face, but she schooled her features before Natasha could identify it. "They destroy the mixed bloods and there will be no more Kyn."

And no more you or Gavin. "I agree. Yet, this faction is firmly convinced the only way for the Kyn to maintain their status is to remain as pure as possible."

"No," Raine sneered. "That's not why they want to wipe us out. If you're going to tell me stories, Natasha, tell them right."

Hiding her smile at Raine's disgust and unintentional slip, Natasha leaned forward. "Fine. If you don't think it's for racial purity, why do you think they want to wipe out mixed bloods?" Let's see how deep of a grasp Raine really had on what was happening around her.

"They're scared." Cold, cutting, and utterly ruthless, Raine's answer hit the bull's-eye.

This time Natasha let her smile free. "You're damned right they're scared. Mixed blood means new abilities, ones they have no idea how to control or defend against." Time to go for blood. "Abilities like yours and Gavin's."

Raine's face paled and her mouth fell open.

Natasha held up her hand and cut Raine's denials off. "Stop." Did the girl really think she hadn't guessed what was going on between her and Gavin? Granted, Natasha might not have all the details, but those two shared something unique and powerful—an ability Natasha had only seen once before. Now she needed to make sure it stayed on her side of the upcoming fight. "I don't want details." Not yet. Best to let Raine think she and her lover still had some secrets. "We have bigger challenges coming our way. First, we need a name, one we can connect to this Council faction and Brent Sutler."

"We have someone on that."

"Then they need to move faster." Natasha ignored the streak of fury on Raine's face at her snapped command. "In the meantime, perhaps we can use Zayn to help garner that information from another direction."

"Why? Because he's with this Order?"

"Perhaps."

"He works for the Council, Natasha. If we do find a Council connection, no way in hell can we guarantee he'll hand over the bastard who killed Mulcahy. We have nothing to indicate he's even on our side of this damn mess."

Natasha rose from her chair and came around the desk until she stood in front of Raine. She plucked the ring out of Raine's hand and held in front of the girl's face. "This tells me he just might be. If he has a connection to the Order, this will mean something. Something above the Council's games. At one time Ryan was one of his. Ryan stepping down to run the Northwest Kyn doesn't change that fact."

Understanding brought color to Raine's face. "You're putting a hell of a lot of stock in a supposed friendship. That could be dangerous." First-hand knowledge swam behind her words.

"Alexi was a bitch, darling." Natasha put the ring back in Raine's hand. It belonged to her now.

Raine's head jerked up at the cavalier words.

"What? Did you think I blamed you for tearing out her throat?" Natasha laughed when she caught the confirmation in Raine's expression. Her laughter faded and her more primal nature prowled forward, wanting to ensure Raine understood something. "She betrayed me. She betrayed Ryan. She betrayed the Wraiths. What you did to her was much more merciful than what I would have done." Her words reverberated with the unvarnished truth. "I do not tolerate betrayal."

"If you're wrong about Zayn, you could be signing all our death warrants, because neither does the Council." Raine's warning was soft, but honed with a cutting edge.

"There are those on the Council who want to see us destroyed, have since we began."

"You think someone at their level is behind his death?"

Natasha nodded. "Ryan was a threat to their authority."

Raine tilted her head. "If that's so, then why did they allow Mulcahy to leave in the first place? Hell, why would they allow him to leave the Order? You can't tell me they couldn't have stopped him at any time. Yet, they just let him walk away?"

"Yes." The one word was all Natasha would give Raine.

Rehashing history wouldn't help now. Besides there were parts she didn't want to go into with Raine, or anyone for that matter. Natasha stepped back and leaned against the desk's edge. "Officially the Council doesn't control the Sarielian Order. However, that doesn't mean certain members aren't...tied to individual Council seats."

"You think Zayn's working with someone." Raine narrowed her eyes. "Who?"

The girl was quick. "I don't know. Yet. What I do know is the Council is scrutinizing us. They need a way inside the Northwest and Ryan's death created fractures they can use. The Wraiths are their best shot to gain influence. If the Council falls to those who would turn on their own, the Northwest is their strongest opposition. Destroying us now, leaves them uncontested." And everything she and Ryan had worked for would be gone, her promises nothing but dust in the graves of those she failed to protect. "We unveil which Council member is behind Ryan's murder, we'll gain our own foothold within their ranks."

"So which side does Zayn fall on?"

Natasha shook her head. "I don't know. He could be here to find out who's behind Ryan's death or he could be the one behind it. However, someone is trying to sidetrack us."

"By what? Sowing dissension in your house?"

The fact that even Raine had noted the issues within her people set Natasha's teeth on edge, but it didn't negate the point that the girl was spot on. "Among other things. Don't worry, that issue will be remedied soon."

"How exactly?"

Did she really expect an answer? Natasha set the wooden photo box back to rights then returned it to the shelves.

"Oh my gods." The stunned exclamation behind her made Natasha's spine stiffen. "You're setting yourself up as bait."

Turning around slowly, Natasha studied Raine. "Are you channeling your uncle?"

Ryan's ability to foresee the future had been very handy. *Did Raine possess that trait as well?*

Raine shook her head. "I wish. It would make things much easier." She considered Natasha. "You've made sure everyone knows you want what Mulcahy had, everything you can grab. But you don't, not all of it."

Instead of answering, Natasha held her tongue, curious to see how much Raine managed to piece together.

"You and Mulcahy, you two had a relationship." Not really a question.

"We had something even rarer, a friendship." One Natasha wished she could have again, but she was so far removed from the woman she had been, it would be impossible to replicate such a thing at this late date. Taking in the astonishment on Raine's face, Natasha asked, "Why do you find that so hard to believe?"

"Have you looked in a mirror lately?" Raine muttered, her gaze sliding away. "You're not exactly Susie Sunshine." For a singular moment, self-directed mockery and disgust bled through.

Understanding dawned. *Ah, yes.* "Monsters have friends too, dear."

Startled, Raine blinked at her.

How funny. Rendering Raine speechless was quite satisfying. "I need to go." Natasha was to meet Jamie at Taliesin, and she had no need to advertise her impromptu visit to Mulcahy's. "Do ask Gavin to have your person dig a little faster on Brant Sutler, would you? I'd really like to know who's pulling his strings." She crossed the room.

Raine's voice stopped her at the door. "Do you really want the captaincy, Natasha?"

Smiling to herself, Natasha didn't answer. Let the girl wonder. A little uncertainty never hurt anyone.

CHAPTER 8

Ryan Mulcahy had been a lucky bastard, Darius thought as he leaned against a thick tree trunk, waiting for his invitations to be answered. The small, private island nestled on Oswego Lake held a beautifully crafted home tucked among the forest. A rare oasis within the suburbs. Perhaps he should have visited his old friend here more often. The home was currently dark, a silent mourner in its owner's passing. Yet a sort of haunting quiet lingered, reminding Darius of the older forests in Europe. Strange to find such a thing here, among the Americans and their incessant need for...well, everything.

Privacy was a grand thing. Something ensured by the solid security gate standing guard between the island's single access road and the rest of Lake Oswego. It was one reason why Darius chose Mulcahy's home to call the Wraiths together. The other, well, that subtle statement would have made his old friend, the master of non-verbal power plays, grin. *"Positions of power can be captured with more than a sword."*

"Let's hope no one bleeds tonight, old man," Darius

muttered. These trained warriors would not be expecting him. No, they thought Zayn Aimeric would be meeting them. The unexpected never went over well with warriors.

Besides, these particular ones were more on edge than most. A fact that Zayn's retelling of his afternoon meeting confirmed. Understandable. On some level they must realize that without their leader, they were vulnerable. And hunted. Their combined skills were too dangerous to be left unmanaged.

A breeze kicked up, shushing through the newly re-cloaked branches. As it danced away, the soft flow of the lake kissing the shore crept in, a rhythmic sound, as if nature was indulging in meditative breathing. A strange whimsical thought. Observing Mulcahy's funeral yesterday must have affected Darius more than he realized. Though why, he wasn't sure. He and Death shared an intimate relationship, one forged by blood and time.

Watching the somber gathering from the hazy embrace of shadows allowed him to observe certain individuals and get a sense of the board before he officially entered the game. His ability to blend into the background had saved his ass on more than one occasion. This time, more than his ass was at stake. Mulcahy's death was proof of that. The reminder of the loss scraped over the thin chains restraining his rage, but years of experience kept them firmly in place. Now was the time to analyze, not strike.

He agreed to the Council's request, couched in polite terms, to come to the Northwest and uncover who or what was behind their string of troubles, not because they asked, but because he owed it to Mulcahy to uncover the truth. Though they would never admit it, but the Council was scared, and they might have good reason to be.

Darius folded his arms. Before coming to Portland, he

did a little digging on the Northwest players, going beyond Mulcahy's tidy reports to the Council. Mutterings and rumors abounded, but what he found raised more questions, not unusual since the former head of the Northwest Kyn tended to play things extremely close.

Mulcahy held his four houses together admirably, better than most Kyn. His ability to ride out the rise and fall of internal politics was a point of envy for some, respect for others. As CEO of Taliesin Security, he provided a plausible home for those Kyn who would normally stand out in the mortal world. The world class security company allowed the Kyn to utilize their unique talents in keeping people and objects safe. Admirable, if you were into that kind of altruistic thing.

However, times were changing. Science and politics made for more treacherous battlegrounds than blades and spells, even as they caused an ever-widening rift in the Council. As each year passed, scientific advances diminished the gap between the human and Kyn worlds.

Mulcahy's niece and her lover were proof of that, both subjected to a human scientist's greed for power. Those experiments wrought unknown changes for both Raine and Gavin. Some on the Council were extremely interested to see what the two could do, while others muttered dire warnings. So far, neither Raine nor Gavin portrayed any magical deviations, but speculation ran rampant.

Personally, he thought if anything had changed, those two were smart enough to keep it under wraps. They understood that some things should remain hidden, even as the existence of entire races of mythical creatures was poised to explode across the world's stage. A fact some Council members failed to grasp, as they continued to bury their heads in the sands of the past. Lines were being drawn—move forward with change or stand fast in the past.

Darius knew which choice would benefit the Kyn, but the Council, eleven of the most powerful nearly immortal creatures, were acting like petulant, spoiled children, because the new kids had cooler toys.

His lips curled in disgust. *Can't teach an old dog, new tricks.* The overly used expression certainly fit the obstinate group. Some things would be much simpler if he could just shoot the damn dogs. Unfortunately, the blowback wasn't worth it.

Which brought him back to tonight's meeting. Mulcahy's death heralded an unprecedented change for the Northwest Kyn. While nature abhorred a vacuum, a proved adage as two of Mulcahy's positions were quickly filled, the most crucial role remained open. More than one individual was eyeing the hole with anticipatory glee.

The most concerning was Natasha Bertoi, the alluring Head of the Amanusa House. Or, as Raine had been heard to call her, the Bitch Demon Queen. Darius found it an apt description. The quintessential female might appear fragile, with her pale, blonde hair, petite curves, and baby blues, but under that deceptive facade lurked a power to be reckoned with, one Darius had no intention of underestimating. Not satisfied with Taliesin's CEO position, she was now making a play for the captaincy of the Wraiths. He could not allow her to worm her way into that particular position. Not if his plans were to succeed.

The sound of an approaching vehicle broke through the night.

Darius lifted his head and listened. The muted thump of two car doors echoed. A third followed. If he was a betting man, he'd place money that Gavin, Raine, and Xander had arrived. The three most pivotal Wraiths shared close bonds. It would be interesting to watch how well those bonds fared over the coming challenges. That is, if they survived the next few days.

He kept his grin to himself and pulled the shadows closer, hiding his shape from the approaching trio. No sense in giving up his edge, not until he was damn good and ready.

They came around the corner of the house, Gavin in the lead, the two women following behind. The man stood a couple inches taller than Darius's six-foot-two, but the way he moved screamed lethal predator. It almost made Darius want to see how well they'd match up in a physical contest. Perhaps another time.

Gavin's gaze scanned the clearing. When he came to where Darius stood, halfway between the waking and mortal world, he paused. A small frown creased his forehead.

Next to him, Raine zeroed in on his discomfort. "What?"

Gavin continued to stare at the spot where Darius stood. "I don't know," he muttered.

Darius's pulse spiked then leveled. *Could Gavin sense him?* If so, he would be the first, in more years than Darius could count, to do so. Intrigued by the possibility, he waited to see what Gavin would do next.

Raine stepped closer, ignoring the hand Gavin shot out to stop her. Her head tilted, and she was close enough that Darius could see her eyes take on an unearthly glow, like miniature silver stars. "This is Mulcahy's home. He had more shit up his sleeve than anyone we know." She turned away to face Gavin and the silent Xander. "Chances are it's something he left behind."

Gavin studied the spot then seemed to come to some

internal decision. "Maybe." He looked over his shoulder at Xander. "Pick up anything?"

She closed her eyes and drew in a deep breath, testing the scents in the air. After a moment, she opened her eyes and shook her head. "Nothing I can pin down." She tucked her hands into the pockets of her black cargo pants, shrugging her shoulders. "It could be something left behind by a visitor."

Gavin didn't look happy, but he let it go. "Let's make sure we're alone. The others should be here soon."

The three split up, working their way through the woods.

Darius held his place. Nice to know his instincts were alive and kicking. There was definitely something more going on with Gavin and Raine than what Mulcahy had shared with the Council. Under Darius's skin anticipation thrummed.

The steady vibration of another vehicle approached. From opposite sides Gavin and Xander appeared where the yard met the forest, waiting for the newcomer. There were no telltale footsteps, no brush of cloth against cloth to give away the arrival. Instead, one moment empty darkness existed, the next a tall, unmistakable Fey appeared. A burly, giant stood at his shoulder. If Darius's notes were right, this would be Niall and Gideon.

"Don't you boys go anywhere alone?" Raine's question came from behind Darius.

"Can't Shadow Walk beyond Mulcahy's interior boundaries," Gideon's deep rumble answered.

The distinctive purr of a muscle car spilled through the night. More arrivals.

"Looks like frat boy from hell is here." Raine made her way past Darius to stand next to Gavin.

"You know how it is." Xander snickered as she perched on a fallen log. "Ryder has to compensate somewhere."

"I don't know. Natasha seems to like him just fine," Raine drawled.

Her comment caused an unexpected flash of anger that caught Darius by surprise.

Xander grinned. "The poor boy has such dangerous taste in women." She wiggled her eyebrows suggestively. "Natasha. You."

Raine's upper lip curled, flashing white teeth. "Bite me, wolf."

"Thanks for the offer, but I'll pass." The delicate tattoo didn't detract from the mischievousness of Xander's grin. "Besides, I've recently acquired a top-notch chew toy. He's much tastier than you."

Darius wondered how Vidis would feel about being labeled a "top-notch chew toy."

Before Raine could shoot back a rejoinder, Jamie Ryder came around the corner with a companion. Darius noted Raine's frat boy assessment was spot on. Pick him up and throw him on a college campus and you'd lose him in the crowd. Even knowing what lived under Ryder's skin for him to hold the position he did, Darius couldn't understand what about this punk would appeal to the very complex woman standing beside him.

"Natasha." Gavin's greeting sounded perilously close to a curse.

"Gavin." Her voiced slipped over Darius like cool silk. Much like the shimmering blue material falling like water over her generous curves. *Such a lush female for one so petite.* Tailored black slacks hugged her hips and made her legs seem longer. Or maybe that was the three-inch heels on her boots. Even her concession to the cool night, a hip length sweater, tempted a man to delve underneath and touch. The ice-queen's gaze took in those gathered. "If Fahd and Sullivan are running late, rendering a decision before Zayn shows will prove difficult."

"Oh don't worry, Natasha," Raine said with a barely disguised sneer. "I think we can accurately guess their votes."

Raine's challenge wasn't unexpected, so Darius was surprised to see a shimmer in the air around Natasha, as if some small heat wave surrounded her. A sign her demon was about to slip loose. What left her so on edge as to threaten her legendary control? Even from his hidden position, he picked up on the distinct ruby glitter in her gaze.

"So certain of your lover, little girl?" Her voice dropped in decibels.

Raine stepped away from Gavin and closed in on the smaller woman. No evident fear, just an anticipatory hunger. "At least he won't throw our lives away for his games. You'd destroy us if it served your purposes."

Both women were so focused on each other, they were blind to their audience. Gavin took a step toward them, only to have Xander's quick head shake stop him. Niall and Gideon remained impassive, yet not missing a thing. Ryder's shit-eating grin grew wider. The little fucker was getting a kick out of this.

Natasha's laugh held dark implications. "You have no concept of my so-called purposes. The Wraiths cannot be led by altruistic aspirants. Do you have any concept of what is coming toward us?"

A perfect cue if he ever heard one. Dropping his concealment, Darius stepped into the conversation. "Do you?"

CHAPTER 9

THE STUNNING MALE WHO APPEARED OUT OF THIN AIR BEHIND Raine left Natasha blinking in shock. It wasn't Zayn Aimeric, but a niggling sense of familiarity tugged at her. Thick, black hair created a startling contrast to the ice-cold blue eyes glowing with an unearthly light. The thin red ring surrounding his pupils made her inner beast purr in delighted recognition of one of her own. His strong jaw carried an inky vestige of a beard. His full lips were framed by the neatly trimmed goatee.

He leaned negligently against a thick tree, his arms folded across his solid chest. He was not as tall as some of the men gathered, but tall enough. Add in his wardrobe choice of all black and he reminded her of a panther—sleek, deadly, and savagely tempting.

Recovering faster than the others, Natasha ignored the dangerous curiosity he provoked and stepped around Raine to face this unexpected development. "Change," she said, answering his earlier question. "Pivotal change."

His teeth flashed white in a grin. "Is there any other

kind?" He straightened and the tension in the air sang to a new level. "This question of the Wraith's leadership is a moot point."

"We beg to differ," she countered. Yet as the surrounding shadows fell farther back, recognition hit, amping her curiosity. Zayn's bodyguard from the funeral. She fought back her demonic nature at the attractive lure of his arrogance. "And you are?"

He executed a mocking half bow with an elegance that bespoke of age. The flash of a silver ring caught the moonlight. "Darius Abazi."

"Darius Abazi," she repeated, mimicking the exotic lilt he gave his name. "Why did you call this meeting?" Memories spun, suspicions splintered and reformed, but she waited to see if they would bear fruit.

"A trained unit requires an experienced commander. The Council will not endorse an unproven captain." He spread his arms wide, palms up. "Consider me your evaluator."

"What the fuck?" Raine's muttered oath meant she just realized who they faced.

While Natasha silently agreed with Raine's profane assessment, the others remained ignorant of who this man represented. Perhaps not Gavin, she amended as he stepped to Raine's side, his jaw set tight.

A move Darius missed as the other Wraiths claimed his attention with various hostile reactions to his claim. He arched a dark eyebrow, sardonic amusement evident. "Did you think you were the only such group in our world? You're lethally dangerous and require a strong, disciplined hand. Anything less will lead to chaos." His gaze skimmed over each one, before touching on Natasha last. "I hate to burst your bubble, but you are not the top predators in our world."

Was he challenging her?

He continued to hold her gaze as reactions continued to erupt around them.

Maybe.

"And why should we believe you?" Gavin challenged.

"We don't know you from jack," Jamie added, coming closer.

Darius appeared unfazed, his unruffled confidence lending credibility to the whispered stories growing stronger in her head.

If he was who she believed him to be, this was going to be such fun. She smiled in anticipation. Let him think she was acknowledging his unspoken gauntlet.

"What's with the grin, Natasha?" The question came from Xander.

Natasha almost laughed aloud. "Would you like to inform our little group who you really represent, or may I?" she asked Darius.

He cocked his head. "You think you have me figured out?"

Unable to suppress it, she let her laughter ring free. "Boys and girls, we are being honored by one of the Sarielian Order."

For a moment no one spoke.

"The rumors are true then?" Niall's taciturn question sounded overly loud.

Natasha finally turned her attention away from Darius. "As true as the ones surrounding the Wraith's existence."

"What rumors?" Xander asked.

Raine and Gavin held silent and watched.

"A group similar to ours," Niall said. "Yet older, more powerful. They exist to give nightmares to the nightmares."

Xander got up off her log and stretched, her fingers flexing while gold brightened her hazel gaze. "Guess we shouldn't be shocked there would be a group to police the police."

"Yeah, but then who watches them?" Jamie's normally easygoing expression was now deeply grooved with a frown.

Natasha fought the urge to roll her eyes. "Did none of you consider where Ryan might have culled his idea for such a group in the first place?" Why did it feel as if she was forever asking the obvious?

Gideon was the only one who spoke up. "He worked with the Council to address a need."

"I'm not here to give a history lesson," Darius cut in. "Suffice it to say, I'm here to ensure you don't forget your purpose."

Raine stepped forward, Gavin's restraining grip not much of a deterrent. "You may answer to the Council, but we don't. Our job is to protect our people, regardless of where the threat comes from. And right now, our only concern is uncovering the one behind Mulcahy's death, not playing politics."

There were times Natasha yearned to teach the girl a lesson, but there were others, like now, where she would love to applaud Raine's ballsiness, no matter how unwise.

But Raine wasn't quite done. "Unless you're here to make sure we don't uncover a link between the Council and Mulcahy's death?"

Darius's amusement disappeared under the whip of accusation, a feral darkness prowling forward, providing a glimpse of his true nature. "The Order does not kowtow to politics or to the Council. The truth behind Mulcahy's death will be revealed, regardless of who it implicates." He held the young woman's gaze. "My word to you."

Oaths were not given lightly in the Kyn world, as they had a way of coming back to haunt you in some very not-so-nice ways. Raine's aggression didn't completely dissipate, but it noticeably lessened. Enough so for Gavin to release her.

Natasha wanted to shake her head at Raine's naive assumption. *Really, taking a demon's oath at face value?* Had the girl learned nothing from her past experiences? Still, Natasha held her tongue. For now.

"We choose our own captain tonight." Gavin's ability to hide his inner thoughts was not such a welcome skill at this particular point. It made him difficult to read. "With or without the Council's or Order's approval."

Darius inclined his head. "Then your new captain best be prepared to prove that his—" he slid a glance her way, "—or her, intentions don't compromise the Wraiths' effectiveness."

The sound of spitting gravel and a revving engine cut through the night. A heavy door slammed, the echoes barely fading before Gavin's name, laced with fury, was called.

Everyone turned toward the summons. Fahd burst around the corner of the house, a wave of rippling energy spreading before him, an indicator his inner demon was clawing at the reins. He came to a stop inches from Gavin, his normally swarthy face pale, the glow from the red Amanusa rings bleeding over his dark eyes.

Natasha's stomach clenched. Something was very, very wrong to upset the normally levelheaded demon to such an extent. "Fahd, what happened?"

He turned his attention to her, his other form apparent to her in the watery echo looming around him. "Sullivan is dead." His voice reached bass levels.

The unexpected words sliced through her. *Dead?* What the hell had Sullivan done? "What?"

Fahd's growl swelled and he went to move around Gavin, but two things happened simultaneously. Gavin blocked him and Darius slid in front of her. Shocked by Fahd's unexpected aggression, she stood there, trying to process the quickly changing situation.

"Is this how you plan on leading us, Natasha?" Fahd hissed. "Eliminating those who disagree with you?"

Raine added her strength to Gavin's in restraining Fahd. *What the hell was he talking about?* "Me?"

He struggled against Gavin and Raine, clearly intending to get to Natasha. "He was killed by a demon. Then left in such a way as to expose us to the humans."

Infuriated that he would think she would risk her people for such a fool as Sullivan, her beast surged forward unfettered. This was not the time for control. The air cooled considerably, the night taking on a hint of red and yellow.

"Let him go." The command came out in a hiss. She could feel her human form slipping. Gavin and Raine didn't move fast enough. "Now!" A sharp shove of magic accompanied her demand, pushing Gavin and Raine away from the other demon. "How!" She took a step forward. "Dare!" Another step. "You!" Until she was inches from Fahd.

Her human form might be small, but her beast dominated his. She was his queen, a fact he seemed to have forgotten. She released her hold a little more, the energy around her gearing up.

Fahd bared his teeth. Flashes of his other self peeked

through as his control frayed. "I dare because no other would have taken him out in such a blatant way. It speaks to an untouchable arrogance. It is your handiwork."

With clawed hands she dragged Fahd into the Side and out of the mortal realm. Startled shouts were abruptly cut off as the demon realm formed around her and her subject. The Side was a dimension only accessible to those of Amanusa blood, a place where their human skins fell away and their true forms took dominance. It was where she enforced order for her House. And order seriously needed to be enforced now.

Stretching to her full eight-and-a-half-foot height, she sank her lethal black claws into Fahd's scaled azure chest, the sharpened points slicing deep, drawing blood. "You dare accuse me of arrogance? You have no idea of what my so-called handiwork includes, *sisna*." The demon slur reverberated around them as she dragged the slightly smaller demon up until mere inches separated their faces, her ebony horns scraping thin layers off of his. "However, I'd be happy to demonstrate my work to you."

"Natasha, stop."

The ground-shaking roar yanked her head around. She ignored Fahd's sharp cry as one of her horns scored a deep groove along his forehead, leaving a smear of ruby red.

Another demon stood behind her. Massive and savage, he was half a head taller than she, his bone-white horns a marked contrast to his deep obsidian coloring. Masculine beauty existed in a savage harmony with the beast. Ice-cold blue eyes stared back.

Recognition hit. Darius.

"Release him," he growled.

Turning her back to him in an obvious dismissal, she gave Fahd a brutal shake. "Do not think to falsely accuse me again, or I will make sure it's the last mistake you make." She flexed her claws, driving them deeper. Fahd's grimace gave way to a soft gasp as she scraped past muscle and tendon, touching things never meant to be touched. Savage hunger rose, clamoring for more—more blood, more pain. Snarling, she threw him away.

A shimmer flickered, as Fahd called his wings into being. Flaring them for stability, he stumbled to his feet. Like most of the more powerful Amanusa, the savage blend of beast and man created a menacingly, beautiful creature, even as his lips peeled back from sharp, jagged teeth. His lean face retained enough of its human characteristics to reveal his grimace. Straightening slowly, he kept his complete attention on her.

"It's not a false accusation." The lesser demon flicked his gaze at Darius then back at her. "See for yourself." His wings settled then faded away, even as he crossed his muscles arms across his scaled chest, ignoring the dripping blood.

The conviction in his voice brought Natasha up short. Trying to work beyond the anger pulsing through her, urging her to rip him limb from limb, she considered him.

Her people fell into two categories, strong and weak. He was not one of the weak, but offering her access to his mind could be fatal—for him. Yet Fahd didn't falter, holding her gaze, his fury burning bright. Never before had he challenged her. As a matter of fact, he would be the last one she would have expected to rush to such a judgment.

Calling on the ability granted to her by her Amanusa bloodline, she tore through Fahd's inconsequential mental shields and delved deep. She wasn't gentle in her quest, the need to punish riding her hard. Ignoring his pained shout and Darius's snarl, she shifted through his mind until she found what she was looking for.

Secret desires, hidden dreams whispered to her, offering her such sustenance, but that wasn't what she wanted right now. As delicious as it would be to indulge, she searched for one thing, a hint at his true purpose. It couldn't hide from her. She was a scion of the Blood of Secrets. Yet, no matter how far she dug, she failed to find a driving need to take what was hers. So if he wasn't out for her position, or to sabotage her chance with the Wraiths, why accuse her? She drew back to herself, ignoring Fahd's pained oaths. Puzzlement edged out fury. Something wasn't making sense here. She began to pace.

"Natasha!" Bone white claws grasped her arm, wrenching her around to face Darius, his red-ringed, blue eyes just as startling in this form as his human one. "Did you kill Sullivan?"

"Excuse me?" she snapped, her patience beyond an end. *This...boot-licking, Council lackey dared to question her?* Her beast rose in a wave of turbulent fury, subsuming her human intellect. Yanking free of his hold, she let her magic ripple out from her.

While Fahd dropped to a knee, grimacing under the wave of magical pressure, Darius stood unmoving, staring her down with a hair tearing arrogance. "Did I stutter?"

Her world went red, her emotions transferring to the Side, rocking the ground under their feet. Calculated responses disappeared, even as she tried to re-establish her hold on her beast. She bared her teeth. Claws flashed and three deep gouges appeared like red ribbons along Darius's sharp cheekbone.

He barely flinched. Instead, he captured her wrist before she could strike again, twisting it painfully and drawing her against his hard, unmoving body. His apparent self-restraint, while her own frayed, sent heat, fury, and a disturbingly animalistic need slamming together in a violent haze. He leaned his head down until his entire visage consumed her sight. "Get your ass in control, woman."

"Fuck you," she spit, no longer the Amanusa Queen, just one seriously, pissed off demonic female—albeit one with lethally sharp points.

Her response triggered a low, sub-sonic growl to vibrate between them. His eyes flashed from red to crystal blue, his beast obviously testing his limits. "We need to return."

For a moment, they remained locked together in a savage battle, neither one willing to give ground. Putting her indomitable will to use, Natasha re-established her dominance, cramming her demon back into its incorporeal cage. Uncaring of the physical pain, she ripped free of his hold and spun away without a word.

Between one breath and the next, she donned her human form and stepped back into the mortal world. She paced, smoothing her hands over her hips, wishing her demon would settle as quickly as her clothes. Behind her, she felt the energy shift as Darius and Fahd returned as well.

"What the hell is going on?" Gavin strode toward her, his gaze flickering behind her then back to her.

"Fahd is convinced I killed Sullivan."

"Did you?" The question came from Gideon.

His accusation sent her beast into another feral frenzy, clawing under her skin. The urge to strike back was so strong her surroundings disappeared under a red haze. She fought back. There would be no more lapses in control. "No."

"Prove it," Fahd hissed.

She chose to ignore him, instead focusing on the silent, infuriating man beside him. She lifted her chin. "I need to see the body."

"We need to see the body," Raine corrected.

"This is not a field trip," Darius bit out. "I will accompany Fahd to the scene."

"We didn't put you in charge," Niall said.

"You need an impartial opinion, one who can't be accused of tainting the investigation. Therefore, I am in charge," Darius said.

"No." The word shot through the group. When Darius turned to face him, Gavin deliberately folded his arms across his chest and widened his stance. "You may be here at the Council's behest, but none of us are comfortable with you investigating Natasha on your own."

A small, cold smile broke over Darius's face. "You don't trust me."

Gavin didn't blink. "We don't trust the Council." The inescapable truth in his words rang through the night.

The two men held each other's stare, neither willing to back down.

Who knew how long the standoff would have lasted, had Xander not cut in with, "I'd prefer that Gavin represent the Wraiths on this. As captain. Anyone else?"

Strong and unflinching, Raine answered the shifter, never looking away from Darius. "Seconded."

Niall and Gideon stepped closer, coming up to stand beside Raine and Xander, directly behind Gavin.

Gideon spoke for both. "We agree."

"Agreed." Fahd realigned himself with the other Wraiths, leaving Jamie to stand off to the side. Alone.

The young man looked between the unmoving group,

then at Darius and Gavin. Finally, he turned to Natasha, indecision clear on his face. He raised an eyebrow in a silent question. She inclined her head just enough to indicate she noted his hesitancy. Blowing out a hard breath, he moved to join the Wraiths, leaving her the sole individual between the two men. "Agreed."

Darius's smile sharpened as he faced the six, silent Wraiths and their newly chosen captain. "Pick one person to accompany you, Captain." The last word held a mocking note.

"Two," Gavin shot back. "Raine and Natasha."

Darius's smile faded, allowing the predator to peek out. "You tread dangerous ground."

This time it was Gavin's turn to smile, his expression an eerie echo of Darius's earlier one. "I'm simply honoring my oath to protect my own."

With a growl, Darius spun on his heel, striding away. "Fahd," he barked. "You'll drive me."

Vindictive pleasure washed through Natasha when Fahd paled, but he hurried after the other man. She turned to Gavin, curious. "Why?"

His jade green eyes stayed hard. "Why what?"

"Why stand against him for me?" She considered him. "Some part of you believes I'm guilty. Why not just let him deal with me?"

"Whether you did it or not, you're ours," he said before walking away.

Natasha turned to Raine, only to be met with a smile filled with teeth. "If you are guilty, we get to kill you, not him."

The feral claim made Natasha laugh in delight. "You think my death would come easy?"

A strange combination of anticipation, and something

she couldn't quite grasp, scuttled behind the younger woman's expression. "Oh no, easy never cut it for me." Raine spun and followed Gavin.

Natasha trailed behind, ignoring the others as they began to leave. Her players were taking up their positions nicely. Deep inside, her demon was humming in satisfaction. Although Sullivan's death added a small kink, things were going so much better than planned.

CHAPTER 10

The ride over to Sullivan's house was heavy with tension. Although no one spoke, Natasha watched Raine's profile run through a myriad of expressions. The symphony of non-verbal cues drew Natasha closer to a certainty that what existed between Raine and Gavin was much more complex and dangerous than expected. While a telepathic link between two Kyn was not unheard of, it generally evolved between mated shifters, like Xander and Vidis.

So how would one exist between Gavin, a witch-Fey, and Raine, a predominantly Fey warrior?

It could be a by-product of their exposure to the humans' experiments, but Natasha wondered if there was more to it than that. Although Ryan was never able to solve what existed in Raine's paternal line, the girl's ability to shift into a leopard was not a common one among the Kyn.

When Gavin's gaze slid to the rearview mirror to zero in on her, Natasha decided to add the possible telepathic link to her treasure trove of knowledge about this intriguing couple. It went right next to Raine's ability to see magic, the very same ability that made her such a prime target for the

Council and truly one of her uncle's family. An unguarded memory pushed forward...

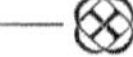

"She believes her ability to visualize is because of Talbot's experiments, not because of her blood." Ryan paced between Natasha and the fireplace, his hands clasped behind his back. His worry morphing to frustration.

"Why not tell her the truth?" She sipped her wine, unwilling to uncurl from her chair.

He stopped next to the mantle and stared into the flames. "Because I'm not sure what the truth is."

His unexpected answer curdled her stomach and soured the lingering taste of the wine. "Could the human's science experiment recreate your gift?"

He looked at her. "He had Raine and Catriona for months. There's no telling how much or how many of their abilities he managed to alter. If he discovered this specific skill, what would keep him from increasing it to an even more dangerous level?"

"Such as?"

"If you can see magic, you then gain insight into how it works and why. The next logical evolutionary step would be to alter those traits, adjusting things to your preferences."

"Is that a true seeing or a logical conclusion?"

He frowned. "Speculation."

Unsettled by Ryan's dire predictions, she set her wineglass aside, stood, and walked toward him. "Darling, you've managed to keep your own gift hidden from the most discerning eyes." Stopping in front of him, she tapped one nail against his chest. "She is your niece, Ryan. Time and time again she's proven how well she can hold her own against any who come against her. Why would this be any different?"

A bleak sort of grief whispered behind his eyes before his gaze shuttered. "Because the vultures are circling."

His dire tone triggered a well-hidden protective streak. "I've always wanted a feathered cap," she quipped.

As one of their last conversations crowded close, the echoes left chills dancing over Natasha's skin. Refusing to rub them away, she held Gavin's jade gaze. Part of her would love to eavesdrop on their telepathic exchange. When his attention jumped back to Raine for no apparent reason, Natasha smiled. Yes, the two definitely shared a link, which meant chances were very high that Gavin could "see" what Raine did when she traced magical signatures. That would be useful, especially tonight.

Gavin's features darkened and, this time, he actually turned in his seat to face her. "What's the smile for, Natasha?"

"Just thinking, pet."

"About?" His one word growl indicated his waning patience.

"Fahd's expression when you tell him the one behind Sullivan's death wasn't me." Let's see how far these two would go to keep their secrets.

He quirked an eyebrow. "And why would you think we'd tell him that?"

"Because magic doesn't lie."

Raine's hands tightened on the steering wheel. "Yes it does."

"Not to you two, it won't."

Gavin's face went still and predatory, while Raine stiffened in her seat.

Undaunted, Natasha continued, "When we get there, Raine will trace whatever magical signatures remain. Between the two of you, you'll be able to pinpoint, if not who, then what, killed Sullivan."

Although Gavin didn't look at Raine, that strange sense of an unspoken conversation returned. "One, you're in no position to give me orders. Two, you're not making sense."

Ah, denial, the tried and true first attempt. This time it was her turn to pin Gavin in place. "You may now be the captain of the Wraiths, but I am still the CEO of Taliesin and the leader of the Amanusa. You do not want to challenge me. Nor do you want to try and play me for a fool. If we weren't being hunted by the Council, I could afford you the luxury of believing your secrets were safe. However, I would be a piss-poor leader if I didn't understand who and what lived under my rule. It is how Ryan made sure the Northwest became the power it is today, and it is how I will continue to ensure we remain that way. So, as I told Raine earlier, I may not know all your secrets, but I do know enough to utilize what weapons I must to keep our enemies at bay."

Gavin opened his mouth to respond, but Raine cut him off. "If you were the one behind Sullivan's death, we won't protect you." She turned her attention from the road to the rearview mirror. "Even if losing you gives the Council another opening."

Impressed by the ruthlessness lurking in those gray eyes, Natasha gave a small dip of her head in acknowledgement. "I will never expect your protection." Because the only one who ever protected her was now dead, leaving her the sole protector of his legacy.

The two exchanging a puzzled look at her answer. Raine turned back to the road and Gavin asked, "What exactly do think we'll find tonight?"

Natasha leaned back and turned to watch the weak streetlights blur by. "More questions."

Natasha surveyed the quiet Hawthorne neighborhood. Craftsman style homes and mature trees lined the softly illuminated streets, lending a surreal, Thomas Kincaid atmosphere. Fahd's black sedan prowled into a narrow driveway, forcing Raine to leave her SUV against the curb on the street. A slow perusal confirmed Sullivan's neighbors were tucked safe behind their curtained windows. When the SUV stopped, she waited for Gavin to open her door.

Calm and composed, she gave no outward appearance of the worries tightening her stomach into an uncomfortable ache. She fell into step beside Gavin as they made their way up the steps to the porch with Raine trailing behind. A scowling Fahd opened the door, leading the way inside, while an ominously silent Darius followed.

Inside, Natasha went left to a large great room, only to come to a stop next to the stone fireplace. Darius stood in the middle of the room next to a tasteful sectional. No signs of violence marred the room. A discarded newspaper and a remote sat on the coffee table, while an empty glass perched under a decorative lamp on the small side table. A hall disappeared just beyond the stairs. By the main door, a pair of men's running shoes were casually tossed to the side and now rested under the coatrack holding the necessary accessories for a rain-filled life. The neutral colors screamed hired designer, but it still felt lived in.

Raine frowned as she looked around. "Where is he?"

"Master bedroom, end of the hall," Fahd answered, leaning against the stair's cherry newel post.

Raine and Gavin rounded the foot of the stairs and disappeared down the hall.

Darius's gaze went from them to Fahd. "What's upstairs?"

"Two smaller rooms. One's an office, the other a guest room, slash storage." Fahd kept his attention on Darius. "No broken windows, jimmied locks, or damaged doors. His car is in the garage. Untouched."

The lack of physical disturbances bothered her. Sullivan was not a weak demon, nor would he be easily taken by surprise. If he was attacked in his own home, there should be signs of a fight or a visitor. "And the neighbors?"

Finally looking at her, Fahd shook his head. "I didn't ask, but since the place isn't crawling with police, I think we're good."

"Natasha?" Raine's summons drew Natasha down the narrow hall to a wide entryway.

Darius dogged her steps, so close it raised her hackles. She fought the urge to turn and hiss at him like a pissed off cobra. Instead, she struggled to ignore his disturbing presence and concentrate on the scene greeting her.

The room was painted in carnage chic. The bed was a combination of wood and scrolled iron, but what lay in the midst of it was all gore. Nothing human could have accomplished this, which meant if the humans had gotten here first, the Kyn would be under a very ugly, very bright spotlight. The only way to tell it had once been Sullivan was his intact head on the pillow. The rest of him...well, she could understand why Fahd believed this was her handiwork.

Sullivan's body resembled a disjointed puzzle. Limbs had been savagely torn off at major joints, leaving them as individual pieces. His pale, gray and pink organs lay on his eviscerated torso, exposed in a way they never should be. Some even seemed to be missing but, from her position at the door, she couldn't be sure.

What looked like cables remained wrapped around what was left of his ankles and wrists, securing them to the bed frame. There was even a snaking crack along the footboard, a lone sign that Sullivan's initial struggles had proven too much for the bed.

Blood had soaked into the bedding, leaving a deep, reddish-brown stain to spread like a disease across the gray sheets. Cast-off blood spattered the walls. Yet there were no voids in the mess to indicate where the attacker had stood.

While the scene resembled a cross between mad doctor's dissection and an S&M scene gone horribly wrong, what concerned her most was the magical energy licking at her skin. This was why she wanted Raine and Gavin here. Together, they could retrace the magical signature, perhaps not enough to positively identify the one behind this, but enough to get a solid lead.

"What is it?" The question came from Darius, proving she wasn't the only one picking up on the lingering magic.

"Layered spells." Gavin moved carefully around the bed, his concentration focused on something unseen. "There's a containment spell holding everything in."

"What exactly is 'everything'?" Natasha asked.

"Not sure yet," he murmured.

Although she held no Magi blood, she understood enough of spell work to understand that each spell took on traits of its castor. Their will, their desires, helped to shape the magic to garner the hoped-for results. "What's the spell for?"

Gavin didn't look up from the bed, but answered absently, "Think of it like a catch-all. This spell is meant to keep things like noise, warring energies, and physical evidence of the struggle, within the four walls of this room. Similar to a Russian nesting doll set."

That did not sound good. And from the frown on Raine's face, there were good reasons to worry. "What happens when you break it?"

Strangely, it was Darius who answered. "Depending on what it's hiding, nothing we want to happen."

He went to step inside the room, but Raine jammed her hand against the opposite side of the doorframe, using her arm to bar his entrance. "Don't think so, not until Gavin clears the room."

Irritation flashed across Darius's face, but Gavin's murmured, "Give me a minute," held everyone in place.

Silence stretched, and the room's energy fluctuated as Gavin did whatever it was he did on the unseen plane. When he finally turned to them, he swayed, and Raine rushed to his side.

She slid an arm around his waist while he visibly resettled. "Hey, give it a second. You were under pretty deep."

Neither Natasha nor Darius moved from their silent sentry posts at the doorway.

"There are two, maybe three more spells still active." Gavin's voice was rough. Straightening, he gave Raine a nudge toward the door then followed her until they stood next to Darius and Natasha. "I recognize four of the six spells. Besides the containment spell, there's one for silence, probably so the neighbors won't come running. A third bears some resemblance to a blocking spell, one used by wizards generally to keep witches and Fey from reaching out to the natural magics, and the fourth is an immobility spell, which is what kept Sullivan in place while he was ripped apart."

"Wizarding magic?" Darius asked when Gavin paused.

Before Gavin could answer, Natasha interrupted, more concerned with the first part of his explanation. "You said there were two more active spells?"

Gavin studied them both. "The last spell is tangled with another. It could be a wizard's creation, but I'm not sure."

Tangled? Interesting choice of words. Next to him Raine's mouth tightened, so there was something Gavin wasn't sharing. Fine, Natasha would find out what it was later.

"Whatever Sullivan's own defenses were, they weren't enough," Gavin continued. "After he was immobilized, the next layer would have kept his magic out of reach. It's a nasty piece of work, which makes me lean toward a wizard. However, it's these last two spells that concern me the most. I don't recognize them."

Which meant it was some other kind of magic besides Magi. The shifters were out, because, while they could be brutal, even this kind of damage was beyond them. Fey could manipulate natural magics, but Gavin would recognize that. So that left...

"A demon." Natasha turned her head to Darius with reptilian slowness. Suspicions crept in. Her voice dropped into the deeper registers as her nature rose and stretched, her vision taking on a crimson hue. "Sullivan was of Blood of War. It would take a demon with tremendous power to hold him away from his abilities." Or two demons, like the ones currently invading her territory.

Unfazed by her show of temper or the unspoken accusation, he folded his arms across his chest and stared back, his own Amanusa nature setting a ruby flame in his glacial eyes. "There are some very old ones who could do it for giggles," he agreed, his smile far from pleasant. "Or give a younger one the necessary spell."

She felt a grudging spark of appreciation at his adept turning of the tables. "Ah, but Jamie and I both have witnesses to our whereabouts tonight. Can you say the same?"

"Could it have been mimicked by a wizard?" Raine cut through their stalemate. "If the other spells are tainted, why can't this be one we just haven't run across?"

"There's no sense of the castor on the last two." Cold calculation iced Gavin's voice, causing Natasha to look away from Darius. Gavin's focus was completely centered on Darius. "Just out of curiosity, Darius, what other blood runs in your veins?"

At Gavin's question, a small smile of cruel anticipation creased Darius's face. When Raine shifted aside, enough to give her and Gavin room to reach whatever weapons they had tucked away, Darius's smile widened. Gavin's low warning growl drew Darius's attention back to him, and the two males engaged in a stare down. Silence and tension pulsed through the room, waiting for the smallest spark to ignite.

While it amused Natasha to no end, nothing would get accomplished if the two men couldn't stop pulling their "who's the biggest bad-ass" routine.

"Or for gods' sake," Raine snapped, obviously just as disgusted with the two men. "We don't have time for this shit, you two."

"They're males, dear," Natasha chided. "They can't move on until they establish territory."

Raine stepped in between Gavin and Darius. "Yeah, well, they can piss circles around each other later."

Without dropping his gaze, Gavin's hands went to her waist to drag her out of the way. Her very feline hiss had him reconsidering his next move.

"Perhaps we should let them fight it out." Natasha's voice dropped to a husky purr. "It could be entertaining."

"For once, you might actually be right," the younger woman said.

Gavin finally looked away from Darius to stare at them in stunned amazement. "Did you two actually agree on something?"

Raine snorted, shrugged his hands away from her waist, and then pushed past Darius. "Come on, Natasha. We'll leave them to figure out who has the bigger dick in private." She threw a smirk over her shoulder. "Besides, I think you're being framed for this, so let's talk about who, besides me, wants you dead."

Darius watched the two women disappear down the hall, before turning back to the man standing next to him. "You deal with this all the time? Voluntarily?"

Gavin shrugged. "Normally they're at each other's throat." He smirked. "They must really not like you."

"Not my concern." Darius shrugged then stepped inside the room, moving over to the end of the carnage-strewn bed. However, whether the luscious little blonde liked him or not didn't change the fascinated pull she seemed to have on him. "So Natasha is being framed?"

Gavin walked to the far side of the bed. "Caught that, huh?"

Darius moved to the opposite side, careful not to breach the spell's magical boundaries. The concealment spell pulsed like sandpaper against his skin. Ignoring the discomfort, he tried to see through the mass of carnage that used to be an Amanusa. Something about the remains pulled at him. Unfortunately, he didn't have the luxury of unraveling the cause. "How exactly did Raine come to that conclusion?"

"She sees more than others," Gavin's comment chased his barely formed curiosity away.

Interesting non-answer. Time to see exactly what kind of Kyn this man was. "Shall we?"

Both men prepared to breach the spell surrounding Sullivan and the bed. The air in the room gathered, much like an electric charge before a lightning strike. Simultaneously, they stepped inside the edge of the concealment spell to better view the remaining energies.

Familiar power brushed against Darius. Like a lethal pet. it curled close, finding a sympathetic power. Like called to like, and he recognized the distinct traces of Amanusa coating the energies. But the knot in the middle, the one causing Gavin such concern, held the lightest taint of wizard. "These were set by a demon." He confirmed the origin of the interconnected spells, glancing at Gavin. "Yet, there's a bit of wizarding magic in this as well."

The other man nodded. "What I can't unravel is where these last two spells connect."

Studying the undulating power that lay before them, Darius realized why Gavin couldn't see the connections. "Give me a moment." Without waiting for an answer, he straddled the line between the Side and the mortal realm.

To Gavin, it would appear as if he phased out of the world for a moment, his form taking on a translucent appearance. Holding the in-between state was difficult, but necessary, as he found confirmation of his suspicions and returned to tell Gavin. "The spell is using Sullivan's blood to maintain a magical anchor in the Side. You'll need to stand guard while I unhook it."

"What should I expect?"

At the simple question, Darius's estimate of Gavin rose. The Side, or the Amanusa realm, was rarely talked about it. The fact that Gavin focused on the immediately important aspect of disarming what they faced spoke volumes. "The magic may try to reattach itself in the mortal realm, so you'd best keep your shields strong."

With that, Darius began to deftly maneuver the magical bindings holding the spell in the Side. He uncovered what appeared to be a deep crimson stone. With each line he unraveled, the small bloodstone shrank. There was considerable resistance from the magic, another indicator of a strong castor. Still, it wasn't long before he was done, the last of the blood falling to ash at his feet. He shifted fully back to the mortal world.

Gavin was holding his own rather admirably. Taking in the combative magics of the younger man and the lingering spell, Darius realized Gavin was an extremely strong Fey witch. But there was more there. Something he couldn't quite catch, an ability he didn't recognize. At least, not yet.

However, there would be time later to pursue his curiosity. For now, he added his own ability as a demon wizard, knowing it would answer Gavin's earlier question of what ran in Darius's veins. Together they managed to unsnarl the remnants of the complex spells.

"Wait." Darius reached an impressive magical knot. "Give me a minute."

It took a few breath-stealing moments to untangle the mess. Only then could he and Gavin continue to work on dismantling the two spells. Unfortunately, when they uncovered the last piece of the spell, it revealed an unexpected treasure.

"Ahhh," Darius murmured. "Aren't you a pretty one?"

"What the hell is that?" Gavin's voice was strained as Darius began to pluck at the dark magic lying like a thin blanket over Sullivan's severed remains.

"Just keep the containment spell in place, otherwise there will be more than these bloody pieces to pick up," Darius warned.

To disable this little gem, he'd have to trust in Gavin's strength to contain the disrupted magic. This was a complex melding of some very old, rarely used magic, the kind tied to blood and spirit. Most Kyn would never touch such power since it could so easily backfire on the user. *Could Natasha have crafted this?* As she was a scion of the House of Secrets, the probability was very high. Hidden knowledge was their bread and butter. This could be her.

Darius managed to unravel a piece, only to realize he tripped a trigger. "Son of bitch!" he hissed, abandoning his work as he threw up the strongest protective shield he could. "Shield!" he yelled at Gavin, hoping his warning gave the other man enough time.

The nasty spell detonated, like a mini bomb. It slammed against his mental barrier, clawing for a handhold but found nothing to grasp. Across from him, Gavin winced, his own shield holding steady under the barrage. The energy from the lethal blast washed over both of them, only to come up against the containment spell.

"Gavin!" Raine's voice sounded muffled even though she stood just inside the doorway.

The magic around Gavin flared, the dueling energies fluctuating before resettling into familiar patterns. Yet Darius noted Gavin's magic appeared stronger, deeper now. Busy keeping his own shield in place, Darius couldn't afford to look closer, but he filed away the anomaly. Too many damn questions kept popping up about these Kyn. It was frustrating.

"Darius, can you help me constrict the containment spell?" Gavin gritted out, his eyes glowing a deep, emerald green, while his jaw flexed under taunt skin.

Unwilling to waste energy on words, Darius simply added his strength to Gavin's and began to restrict the magic into tighter and tighter confines. Finally, the containment spell hovered over the middle of the bed, the magic roiling inside the globe like some dark disease.

"Any ideas on how to get rid of that?" Gavin asked.

"Yes." Gathering the spell, Darius pulled it with him into the Side and let his demon slip free. Almost as if it knew what was coming, the energy within the globe became agitated, pulsing against its confines. A black flame engulfed the globe and, within seconds, nothing remained but ash.

Sometimes, wielding the touch of death wasn't such a bad thing.

CHAPTER 11

"Wanna share why tall, dark and sinister has it in for you?" Raine asked Natasha as they stepped into the living room, ignoring Fahd who still stood at the foot of the stairs.

"I'd rather discuss why you think I'm being framed." Natasha fought her urge to pace by settling into a rather comfortable chair. Catching Fahd's dark look, she held it with her own and kept her condescending smile in place just to irk him. When red rode under his skin, she dismissed him and turned to Raine. "Do you think what lays in that room is beyond me?"

Raine snorted. "Please. I have no doubt you could do much worse." She leaned against the wall, arms crossed, her gaze intense. "The thing is, you'd never leave anything behind to find. This—" She waved one arm in the direction of the hall. "—is a great big fuck you. What I can't figure out is, is it to you or to us?"

"Us?"

"The Wraiths," Raine clarified, then her gaze darkened. "My money's on you."

With utmost care, Natasha crossed her legs, brushing her hands over her pants. Losing her patience right now would accomplish nothing, except cost her the tenuous alliance she and Raine currently shared. Unfortunately, Darius managed to push one too many of her buttons, leaving her a tad off-balance. However, with Fahd playing audience, it paid to remain careful in her conversation. "It would be more beneficial to identify who would set such a clumsy scene."

"I'm thinking the list of who has something to settle with you is damn long," Raine drawled, dark humor dancing in her eyes.

"Longer than you know," Fahd muttered, then he shut his mouth when both women looked at him.

"Want to share?" Raine invited.

He flicked a veiled look toward Natasha.

Oh yes, Fahd had ideas, but so did Natasha. Of course, one of her top names lay in pieces in the bedroom and the other was currently working with Gavin to uncover the one behind the mess. "Please share," she murmured, curious to see if any new names came up.

"I'd rather not say unless there's actual proof." He straightened, one hand passing over his chest, as if her marks still stung. "I'd hate to be the one behind an unjust punishment."

Really? Did he think she'd let him off that easy? Especially after his earlier behavior? "Perhaps, in an effort to preserve impartially, you could give the names to Raine. Let her question them." There was no mistaking her thinly veiled command or the prowling essence of her demon as it surged forward.

He stiffened, his jaw showing white through his skin as

he clenched his teeth in frustration. "Matt and Isolde have not been shy in their opinions on your recent policies."

"If we were to list those who disagreed with my policies, there would be many names beyond those," Natasha said. "Neither one has the patience to create such a subtle spell. Nor would the rest of the Amanusa feel confident in following either of them. The house would descend into chaos and turmoil under their continual bickering. Besides, this does not fit with their—" she paused, "—behavior. Neither would be quite so obvious."

"The foundational spell was very complex," Raine said. "That doesn't jive with leaving such a transparent scene behind. Hence the reason I think you're being framed."

"Unless that's exactly what she wants you to think," Fahd offered.

Raine scoffed. "Sorry, that's just too easy." She turned back to Natasha, her eerie silver eyes disconcerting. "Something bigger is at play here."

For a moment Natasha could see Ryan in his niece. The glimpse of a shrewd, quicksilver mind, maneuvering through the twists and turns of any given situation, tweaked against a tucked away portion of Natasha's heart. She had no doubt someone was setting her up. For once, she was glad to have Raine here, since she seemed to see the same thing.

Ryan's death, the isolation of her new position rested heavily on Natasha's shoulders. It was startling to realize how truly alone she was for the first time in hundreds of years. She forced an unconcerned curve to her lips. "Do share."

"How much do you know of this Sarielian Order?" Raine kept her voice low, her question darting off the expected course.

"Nothing concrete," Natasha answered, wanting to see where this would lead. "Throughout the years, there have been bits and pieces attributed to them, but nothing that would help here." The information Ryan shared came from an alliance he had forged before her time. But Fahd's presence hindered her from sharing. Perhaps she'd wait until she could confirm the nebulous inklings gaining form in her mind.

"So, for all we know, Darius could be involved." Raine looked down the hall, a worried frown creasing her forehead. "Maybe working with that Aimeric guy." Color leached from her face. "Gavin!" She ran toward the back bedroom just as a wave of concussive magic hit.

The force of it whipped across Natasha's skin like fine razors. She was up and moving before Fahd, coming up behind Raine to peer into the room.

The two men faced each other over Sullivan's remains while some sort of glowing orb hovered between them. As she watched, the orb expanded and contracted, as if fighting to free itself from some invisible binding.

Gavin visibly strained against the reverberating energy, the cords standing out along his neck. His lips were pulled back in a grimace, his eyes glowing a deep, jeweled jade. Next to Natasha, Raine's face tightened, her fists curled, her attention focused solidly on Gavin. The air shifted, and suddenly Gavin's tension dropped, his formidable shield strengthening, causing the trapped magic to shy back.

Fascinated, Natasha studied the couple, realizing they were combining their magic somehow.

A low grunt from Darius yanked her attention to him. The air around him shimmered, then an inky stain began to spread from him and surround the turbulent globe hovering over the middle of the bed.

"Any ideas on how to get rid of that?" Gavin's question came out tight.

"Yes." Darius's answer was curt, but the strange energy ball began moving toward him, completely engulfed by the tendrils of ebony.

Her only warning of what Darius was preparing to do was the unique tug under her skin, like a summons to her demonic side. It took a bare second for her to understand, then she made sure to stay with him.

Sure enough, he moved into the Side and his demon form snapped into focus.

Unwilling to miss his next move, she refused to allow the captivating combination of man and beast to divert her attention and maintained her observatory position in the Side.

He held the swirling magic between his lethally tipped hands, then a silent, black flame erupted. When it blinked out, his bone white claws were dusted in black.

Stunned, she slipped back into the mortal world, her mind whirling. Darius was a scion of the Blood of Death. Of the six demon bloodlines, Death was right up there with Secrets, their ability to change even the best laid plans legendary.

Darius could prove to be much more dangerous to her plans than anyone.

Darius sat next to Natasha in the back seat of Raine's SUV while Sullivan's neighborhood faded in the rear window. They left Fahd behind to work with Jamie's cleanup crew. Conversation was scarce, creating an edgy silence. An alluring scent, reminiscent of spice and smoke, drifted from the woman next to him. With nothing else to do, he studied her.

The delicate lines of her face were haunting, a sharp contrast to the core of strength he knew existed within. Her platinum hair was piled into some complicated knot, the kind that tempted a man to unravel it. Long, dark lashes veiled a startling combination of blue and violet, the thin red rings, inherent to their kind, an added jeweled layer. There was no mistaking her for anything other than female. Her tailored outfit emphasized her curves. Her entire demeanor screamed elegance.

Yet the blood red color on her nails gave a hint to what truly lay underneath. A ruthless, calculating mind hid behind her composed, professional mask. A uniquely contradictory package, she drew his curiosity like few others throughout his long years.

Watching her interact with the others had been educational. Confident and self-assured, she possessed the ego and arrogance inherent to her position. No weak individual could hold together the challenging collection of Amanusa she called her own. Yet, no matter how intriguing she was, he couldn't dismiss the possibility she had a hand in Sullivan's murder.

Yes, it was sloppy, but if he disappeared without a sign, suspicions would have fallen directly on her. This way, there was a sliver of doubt she could work with—who would believe someone as powerful as her would be so careless as to leave such a mess behind? Doubts, suspicions, questions, uncertainty—all part and parcel for her bloodline. The Blood of Secrets were the epitome of treachery. Why should she be any different?

"Is there something on my face?" she drawled, bring him out of his thoughts.

He let his lips curl up. "Just enjoying the view."

"Mmmm." She turned her attention back to the passing scenery.

He shifted until he could face her better. Leg room was a bit tight in the backseat. "You realize I'll be staying with you until we clear things up." A statement, not a question.

She whipped her head around, the red rings around her irises sparking. "Excuse me?"

He folded his arms and held her glare, unfazed by her icy tone. "Consider it a two-fold approach."

Her plump lips thinned, but even anger looked good on her. "Approach to what?"

"Finding out if you're the target or the killer."

Before she could respond, Raine cut in, "Natasha's the target."

He flicked his gaze to the rearview mirror, meeting those cool silver eyes in the reflective surface. "You have proof?"

Raine's attention went back to the road, but not before he caught the subtle, non-verbal exchange between her and Gavin. "Not that you could use."

When she didn't elaborate, he pushed, "Care to explain?"

"Not really," she muttered.

Gavin turned in his seat and spoke over her. "Every magic has a unique..." He visibly searched for a word before settling on, "...taste."

"You're telling me you can identify the individual behind the spell?" If that was true, Gavin and Raine could be problematic.

"No," Raine grumbled. "But we can tell you who it isn't. Natasha."

Darius was intrigued. "You have no doubts?"

Raine and Gavin shared another one of those unreadable looks, before she turned her attention back to the road.

Gavin picked up the conversation. "Which ever demon set this in play, it wasn't Natasha."

"A wizard helped set those spells." A taint Darius identified only because of his own heritage. "The physical damage indicates a demon was involved. That doesn't eliminate Natasha." He ignored the delicate snort next to him.

"It doesn't eliminate you or Aimeric either," Gavin pointed out in a bland tone. "Besides, you had no trouble weaving your own counter spells in there."

"Touché, but—"

"You mentioned the spell was old," Natasha interrupted.

Gavin nodded. "There was something strange about it, besides the age. Unfortunately, there wasn't enough time to figure it out."

Darius silently agreed.

"Anyone else notice a pattern here?" Raine asked as she navigated the streets.

"Like the age of the spell?" Natasha offered.

"Yeah, exactly that." Raine checked the side mirror and Darius caught her scowl. "Could the same person behind this spell, be behind the one that killed Mulcahy? Both spells were aimed at heads of houses."

"Then they're getting better with their aim," Natasha said. "The spell used on Ryan was probably intended for Vidis. This, as you pointed out in the kitchen, is very much pointed at me."

"If I didn't think it would be like looking for a needle in

a haystack, I'd make you hand over that list of those who might have something against you," the younger woman groused.

Natasha smirked. "That list is actually quite a bit smaller than you think, dear."

"And why's that?"

Darius caught the glint of wicked humor in her face before Natasha answered. "Those who have an issue with me, tend to change their minds."

"I'll just bet," Raine murmured. A bit louder she said, "Are we taking you two to Taliesin or your place?"

"Trying to keep tabs on me?"

"Nope, I'm going to let Darius have those honors."

"Then mine, please." Natasha rattled off an address ending in someplace called King's Heights. "At least I can be comfortable while playing prisoner." She pulled out her phone, her nails clicking against the screen.

"You calling in Ryder?" Gavin might be looking straight at Darius, but his question was aimed at Natasha.

"Hmm? No, just asking him to move my meeting with Carys to my house in the morning." She then ignored both men.

Darius met Gavin's silent challenge. "Do you think that young peacock could stop me?" Did Gavin really think him so easily thwarted? If he wanted to take Natasha out of the picture, he highly doubted any of the Wraiths could stop him. Of course, should they all hit at once, he might come out a little worse for wear. Somehow, considering the current level of discord in the group, he didn't think that would be an imminent problem. Once they uncovered who killed Sullivan, well, it might be time to reconsider.

Gavin gave him an evil smile, even as his eyes remained

flat. "Nope, but taking him out would give Natasha enough time to roast your ass."

Natasha's laughter rang through the interior, and even he had to chuckle at this unexpected ruthless streak. Perhaps Gavin might yet prove to be a worthy captain.

Natasha leaned forward and patted Gavin on the arm. "Don't worry, I don't need a bodyguard. Darius is going to be a good boy." Resting her shoulder against the back of the passenger seat, she turned to him with an arched expression. "Me dead doesn't fit into his plans."

"So sure of that, love?" Darius drawled, wondering exactly what she thought he wanted out of this mess.

Her periwinkle gaze traveled over him with a lazy sensuality. "Oh, no, not sure at all. However, I think you have something tucked up your sleeve. Something far more intriguing than our esteemed Council member Aimeric realizes." Her gaze landed on his mouth and that tempting chest rose and fell with a quick breath.

Amused by her innuendos, and curious to see how far she'd go, he reached out and traced her plump lower lip. He ran his thumb over the light sheen, satisfied when he felt the slight hitch in her breathing. "As I said before, I don't answer to the Council. I'm here to find out who killed Mulcahy and ensure the Wraiths have a qualified leader."

"And once you have that information, Darius, what then?" The husky tone of her voice caused an immediate, physical response.

He tried not be distracted by his reaction to her. Her constant challenge turned him on in a big way. So few females had the courage to take him on. But this one— inside his demon purred. Oh, this one was going to be so much fun. "Then, Natasha, I do what I do best."

"And that is?"

"Exact justice." He dropped his hand and resettled against the door, conscious of Gavin watching the two of them. He met the other man's stare head on. "One bloody piece at a time."

"Sounds damn good to me," Raine agreed as they turned into a long curving drive.

CHAPTER 12

THE CLASSICALLY BEAUTIFUL LINES OF HER MEDITERRANEAN-STYLE home fit Natasha to a T. Lush landscaping, sculpted into meticulous lines surrounded the white stone structure while strategically placed lights lent a sense of privacy to the property. Raine pulled to a stop under the covered porte-cochere. Stone stairs led to a deep burnished-mahogany door, inset with stained glass. The interior lights played through the colorful panes, lending a mystical, romantic hint to the entryway.

In the backseat, Natasha waited for Gavin to open her door. In the driver's seat, Raine leaned down and peered at the impressive entrance. "Who'd you kill to get this place, Natasha? An Italian Count?"

The door opened. Natasha took Gavin's offered hand then stepped out of the SUV before answering. "No, a lovely young architect out of Chicago owed me a favor."

Darius's door gave a muted thump, then he joined her on the tiled stone drive. The sharp click of her heels snapped through the night as she went up the short stairs to the expansive entryway, Darius keeping a silent presence behind her.

She stopped at the top of the stairs and turned, pulling Darius up short and catching Gavin in mid-turn. "Do let me know if any new developments surface."

Gavin gave her a short nod before settling into his seat and pulling the door closed behind him.

She watched the SUV's taillights glide down the driveway. Only when the night fell quiet once more, did she turn to the perplexing man next to her. "Are you seriously planning on staying here all night?"

He leaned against the stone balustrade. "Is that a problem?" He gave a significant look to her grand home. "I'm sure you can squeeze me in somewhere."

No, finding him a room wasn't the problem. Having him anywhere near her, was. Tonight, of all nights, she wanted to indulge in a luscious Merlot. Perhaps enjoy a little peace and quiet while she did some digging of her own on Sullivan, Zayn, and Darius. Something she'd be hard pressed to find time to do with him looming over her shoulder.

Pointedly glancing at his empty arms, she said, "Well, I'm sure by the time you get back with your bag, I'll have your room ready."

Giving him a patently false smile, she turned away, intent on putting the thick door between them. She just started to push the door open, when the hair at the nape of her neck rose as he came up behind her.

He crowded against her, deliberately invading her personal space. "I don't need a bag tonight." Low, intensely male, his voice curled around her, his exotic hint of an accent adding to his seductive purr.

That sound seeped into her pores, past skin and bones, a tangible lure to her curiosity. Her body woke up with a delicious shiver. Erotic images of how she could recreate that low rumble danced in her head. *Oh, the things she could do to this man.*

Slanting a sultry look over her shoulder, she smiled slowly as she let her gaze drift over him. "Sadly, I'm not sure I have anything..." she licked her lips, "...suitable for you to retire in."

An answering heat burned in his eyes, hard to miss when he was mere inches away. "That won't be a problem."

"It won't?"

Against her back, tension sang through his muscles. He lifted his hand from the doorframe and drew the tip of his finger along the side of her jaw, bringing chills in its wake. He leaned in until his mouth brushed her ear. "Skin is all I require for sleeping."

Her lids fluttered close for a moment. She took his spicy scent into her lungs, tempting her demon, who was suddenly way too pleased with this male. The woman, however, knew tangling with him now could hold long-term consequences, ones she wasn't yet ready to address. As enticing as he was, it was the wrong place and definitely the wrong time to follow him down this particular rabbit hole. Regretfully, she drew back, away from the temptation he offered, and led him into the vestibule without a word.

After he shut the door behind him, he reached around her to pull open the glass door leading into the house proper.

Before he could touch the wrought iron knob, she laid a hand on his arm. "Wait. I need to release the wards."

He studied the small room. Probably trying to pinpoint

her wards. However, since they were an intrinsic part of her home's defense system, they wouldn't be easily discernible. Otherwise, why bother?

Red mahogany and clear glass made up the alcove, offering a cozy area to remove coats and boots. A small statue of some ancient goddess merrily tipped a bowl, allowing water to dance into the well below, filling the space with a natural music. Ornate carvings twined over the wooden doorframe.

She reached out and covered one of the delicate oleander blooms etched into the warm wood. This particular carving contained sharp edges, and as she pressed her palm down, they sliced hair thin cuts, drawing minuscule beads of blood. Enough to unlock the ward. With the way now safe, she drew her hand back and waived Darius forward. "Welcome to my home."

Before she could drop it, he wrapped his fingers around her wrist and turned her palm up. "A blood ward?" His thumb wiped away the last remnants and then smoothed over her now, unmarked skin. "Seems a bit much for a home ward."

Gently tugging her hand free, she preceded him inside. "One can never be too cautious. I so dislike unwanted visitors." Let him read what he wanted into that. She turned to her left and went into her living room, kicking off her heels by one of the couches arranged around the stone fireplace. She made a beeline for the cabinet nestled in the corner. The Redigaff was calling her name. "Would you care for a drink?" she threw over her shoulder.

"Dare I ask for beer?"

"Plebeian," she mocked. Raising one of her most treasured bottles, she showed him the label. "Tua Rita,

2008, from Bolgheri, Italy, one of their finest Merlots." She poured, letting the wine warm in the glass. "However, if you insist, there should be something in the fridge."

"What? No butler?"

Holding her glass, she came back to the couch, taking the time to inhale the aromas of violets and licorice with subtle hints of brown sugar. "In case you missed it, I like my privacy. Having some droll individual hover around would get tiresome." She sank into the cushions, tucking her feet under her. Motioning with her glass, she said, "Kitchen's across the hall and to your right. There may even be food, if you're hungry. Help yourself."

He wandered away, disappearing on the other side of the stairs.

She didn't worry. Her secrets were safely tucked away from prying eyes. She sent a flick of magic to the fireplace, lighting the wood.

In a matter of moments, the quiet snap and hiss of a well-tended fire filled the room. The heat edged out the chill still very much a part of the spring nights. Taking a sip, she wallowed in the complex taste of light berries, chocolate, and the zing of orange. Even after swallowing, the notes lingered.

She enjoyed the moment, because tonight, or more accurately, this morning, would be long. Once she got Darius all squared away, she needed to reach out to a few key individuals. While Gavin and Raine would be most thorough in their investigations, Natasha could tap sources they couldn't. Sources who would be more likely to share with her. Not because she was the Head of House, but because if these individuals wanted to remain uncontested in their own positions, it was in their best interests to help her. No one did "keep your friends close, your enemies closer" better than demons.

She swirled her wine thoughtfully. Speaking of enemies, she needed to check on Tomás Chavez's whereabouts. Ensuring he was still grieving his psychotic wife, and not out hunting Brant Sutler, would enable her to explore other avenues. No disrespect to Jamie, but money, like that behind the dead human assassin, should leave a trail. And if that trail led to the Council, so much the better.

Old memories stirred, reminders of what happened the last time she stood against the Council. She shoved them away. That naive child no longer existed and, this time, there was no one left to betray her. Besides, she spent the decades since gathering the necessary weapons to hold her own against their esteemed leaders. Weapons honed with Ryan's help and encouragement. It had never been a question of if the Council would come back for them, but when.

Her instincts told her that when was now.

Which meant her first concern should be the two very old, very powerful, demons currently in her territory. Better than most, she understood the nature of her kind. Tricky didn't even scratch the surface. Diabolical, convoluted were more accurate. Why stay with simple, when you could maximize your path of destruction and chaos with multiple strikes? Why not send a team in? With Ryan dead, and things in disarray, they could cripple Taliesin and the Northwest Kyn with a few well-aimed pokes and prods.

Her stomach clenched in protest as vague strategies swirled, the possible outcomes playing out in her mind. She would definitely be making some calls tonight. Going up against Zayn and Darius would require every ounce of skill gained throughout the years. Even as her tension grew, so did the titillating excitement of pitting herself against the two formidable men.

Darius sauntered back in, a glass bottle in one hand and a plate filled with various foods balanced in the other. He bypassed the two empty couches to sit next to her and silently offered her the plate piled with fruit, cheese, crackers, and some thinly sliced lunchmeat.

Setting down her wine on the table tucked to the side, she took the plate from him and rested it on her lap. Picking up a grape, she dropped it into her mouth.

Next to her, Darius took a long drink from his sweating beer bottle. The firelight played over the light ale, turning it a mellow gold. For a few minutes, they existed in companionable silence, sharing bits and pieces from the plate. It was strangely restful.

When most of the food was gone, Darius finally spoke. "Why such a big house?"

His unexpected question caught her off guard. "It's not that big."

He tilted the bottled toward the door. "Darling, there has to be at least six rooms upstairs, and from what I could see from the kitchen, you're sitting on a pretty piece of land up here."

"Five," she murmured. He raised an eyebrow. "Five bedrooms, actually, and just over three acres." She continued to nibble on one of the last strawberries. There was a time, back when the house only existed on paper, she thought the rooms would be filled with others, but things change. "I'm not always alone, Darius." She licked the last of the fruit juices from her fingers. "Sometimes, my position requires I offer refuge to others or accommodations for visiting dignitaries."

He gave her a lazy smile. "So why isn't Zayn staying here?"

Because she didn't want the Council under her roof. "He choose to stay at the hotel, something about not wanting to impose." She left her *like you*, unspoken.

"Perhaps he doesn't trust you," he murmured.

She let a satisfied smile curve her lips. "Wise of him." Catching his expression, she laughed. "Did you expect to me to be offended? Zayn may be a pompous ass, but to sit on the Council requires a certain level of calculated intelligence." Her humor faded. It was time to show Darius who he really faced. "The Council sent you both in. There are numerous ways your presence can be interpreted, yet I think I'll go with the most obvious."

"And what would those be?" His blue eyes glittered, reflecting the firelight, but he watched her with an unsettling intensity.

"Ryan's death created an unexpected opportunity for the Council to slip into the Northwest." She picked up her glass and took a sip. "You and Zayn are looking for cracks, weaknesses you can exploit. The real question is—which faction are you aligned with?" She refused to look away.

"What makes you think the Council is fracturing?"

She refrained from rolling her eyes and arched an eyebrow instead. She so loved that gesture. It got her point across without words.

He made a noncommittal hum then reached out and tugged on a loose strand of hair, curling it around his finger. "Does the side matter?"

She tried to ignore his delicate touch. "Oh, yes."

Did he think she was so easily influenced? He might make her body sing, but her mind and heart remained crystal clear. Perhaps it was time to turn the tables. It shouldn't be hard. Distracting a male like him wouldn't take much.

She lifted her hand and cupped his jaw, enjoying the rasp of his five o'clock shadow against her palm. "Because knowing that will tell me if you're the one setting me up, or he is."

His smile was full of wicked promises. Promises she would love to explore. Just because he might want her dead, didn't mean he didn't want her. Or vice versa. There was no arguing the physical pull between them.

He angled his head into her touch, even as the hand in her hair slipped to curl around the back of her neck. "You love to play dangerous games, don't you?"

A warning flashed in her mind that this could be a very bad idea, but she refused to back away from the line they were about to cross. Some risks were worth taking. Focused on his lips, she murmured, "Are there any other kinds?"

He dipped his head, his mouth covering hers in a heated rush.

Kissing Natasha was not smart, but Darius really didn't give a damn. He explored those lush lips that tempted and teased all night. He kept his hand on her neck, knowing it provided some control should her claws come out, in one form or another. This had nothing to do with politics and everything to do with curiosity. His and the demon's that lived under his skin. Why this particular female managed to go where so many others failed, he didn't know.

He nipped her lower lip, insisting on entry. She opened and berry, tinted with the sweet spice of licorice, met his tongue. He delved deep, taking advantage of the breech.

Lust curled through him, his body hardening in anticipation. When her hand dropped to his shoulder and her nails bit deep as her mouth softened under his onslaught, he fought not to drag her under him and plunder what she was offering. Even as desire raged through him, he recognized this challenge for what it was, and he wasn't one to back down.

Determined to maintain control, he softened the kiss, pulling back to nibble her lips and drop teasing kisses over her jaw and down the delicate line of her neck. Needing to leave a lasting impression, he took the soft skin where her neck and shoulder met into a sucking kiss. When he lifted his head, satisfaction at the very distinctive mark swelled through him, allowing him to draw back.

Her chest rose and fell, her eyes a slumberous indigo while an alluring color fanned her cheekbones. Her lips were swollen and her hair fell in wild abandon around her shoulders. Instead of the elegantly composed woman, a sloe-eyed temptress curled before him.

Even as he watched, her small, pink tongue swept so slowly over her lower lip as it curled in feminine satisfaction. "Mmmm," she purred. "If this is a new interrogation technique, I quite approve."

Her damn purr made him want to pull her under him and—he slammed his prurient imagination to halt. To combat the urge to yank her back into his arms and make her purr again and again, he lifted his half-forgotten beer bottle to his lips and swallowed the lukewarm liquid, before answering. "I was just curious."

She lifted her eyebrows as she brought her wine glass up to her lips.

"Would you really fuck someone who was coming after you?" he drawled.

Instead of the expected fireworks, she lowered her glass, threw her head back, and laughed. Not the mocking kind he'd become use to hearing from her, but a true laugh. When she finished, she set her glass on the side table and uncurled her legs, dropping a hand on his knee. "Thank you, Darius."

She pushed to her feet and then raised her hands in a sensuous stretch.

He dragged his fascinated gaze away from the enticement of her breasts pressing against the material of her shirt. He couldn't let her get to him, even if on some level he knew it was already too late. "For what?"

He wanted to growl when she dropped her arms.

"The compliment."

"It wasn't meant to be one." He sounded disgusted even to himself.

Another one of those real laughs emerged. "I know." Then she did the damnedest thing. She patted him on the head.

This time he did growl at her.

Those periwinkle eyes brightened, but at least she didn't laugh. "Let me show you to your room."

He didn't move. "You think one kiss scrambled my brain?"

Her hands went to her hips and she cocked her head to the side. "Feel free to stay here then," she said. "When you're ready, take any of the rooms upstairs. Except mine. That one's by invitation only."

Cheeky wench, but he liked the snark and vinegar. "No invite?"

"You think one kiss scrambled my brain?" Throwing his words back at him, she made them sound suspiciously close to a challenge. She spun on her heel and headed out.

"Natasha." He kept his voice soft, but she still stopped. Her head turned, just enough to show him her profile as she waited. "I didn't set you up."

Why he felt the need to tell her that, he didn't know.

A shadow of sadness flitted across her face, before the familiar, haughty smile returned. "Good night, Darius."

It was a long while before he followed her upstairs.

CHAPTER 13

Natasha took her time preparing for bed, trying not to dwell on what had happened with Darius downstairs. Considering her body's reaction, perhaps she should make some time to curb her more physical appetites. When was the last time she found something worth exploring? A year? Maybe longer? Longer, probably. Things had been a bit hectic, leaving very little time to indulge in such dalliances. The realization left her feeling...tired.

Shaking her head, she tied the belt on her chenille robe and made her way to the small desk tucked into the corner of her bedroom. This room was her haven. She wasn't kidding when she told Darius no one entered unless by invitation. The only other person to see this room had been Ryan, and never in the capacity of a lover. Sitting behind her small desk, she let her gaze fall on the two chairs positioned in front of the fireplace...

"They will come for her," Ryan said, unusual lines of stress bracketing his mouth. He leaned forward, his arms on his knees, his hands curled into fists as he stared into the fire.

"You knew she would wake up one day. You've prepared her for this." Small comfort, but it was all she could offer him.

He sighed and sat back, his fingers drumming on the armrest. "She hates me, thinks I hate her. She doesn't know…" He trailed off, but he didn't need to finish, she understood.

"But she's right in one aspect."

He turned to her.

"She's your creation, your weapon."

He winced but didn't deny her words.

She leaned forward and covered one of those hands with her own, waiting until he met her gaze. "Catriona would have approved, Ryan."

A deep, hidden pain rose, drawing his skin tight over the bones of his face. "Would she, Natasha?" He turned back to the fire. "I'm not so sure anymore."

In all their years, she never witnessed him questioning himself as much as he did tonight. Tonight, when old decisions collided with new consequences, and secrets tore open hidden wounds, his niece's accusations cutting too close to home.

He gently tugged free of Natasha's touch and rubbed a hand over his face. It did nothing to erase his exhaustion and haunted expression. "Things aren't as clear as they once were."

Things never were. An unexpected lump made swallowing difficult. As much as she wanted to help him shoulder this, she couldn't. All she could offer was the same harsh slap he once dealt her. "You would abandon those who are counting on you now?"

Instead of the offended anger, his lips curved. He caught her hand and brushed a light kiss across the back of it. "Touché. No, I won't leave," he murmured, then sat there holding her hand. "So long as I have a choice."

The sharp snap of popping wood brought her back to the present. She wiped away an errant tear. Blowing out a hard breath, she gently pushed the memories away.

There were no answers to her current dilemmas in the past.

In minutes, her sleek laptop was up and running as she wound her way through the hidden paths of the Internet, into files she shouldn't have access to. Her first stop was one of the humans' many alphabet groups and Division's Sector Chief, Victor Osborn's reports.

She was keeping a close eye on these reports. So far, nothing serious had come up, despite Osborn's dire warnings, but it never hurt to double check. Following her normal routine, she did a search for that damn, sneaky geneticist, Brant Sutler. A brief mention of the murder Jamie mentioned was noted, but nothing else. Every damn lead on the human link behind Ryan's murder came up empty.

Undaunted, she switched angles. Maybe coming at the problem from a different direction would give her something. Whether Darius wanted to admit it or not, she knew the division in the Council was coming to a head. Those ripples would spread in to the human world. As she told Raine, some on the Council had no qualms about using the humans to do their dirty work. Even going so far as to use one to hide behind as they plotted the death of one of the Northwest Kyn was not out of the question. Deviousness was not limited to demons.

Moving into the memos and minutes of various committees, she checked a few other files. In the last one, she found a suggestion for a panel to discuss "developing concerns regarding existing partnerships." The panel included some names familiar to the Kyn community—a local general, a senator and his lobbyist lackey, and two politically active business leaders she'd dealt with in the past.

She tapped a nail against the desk as she considered what this would entail. The incident at the nightclub had rattled more cages than expected. The humans were piecing together their defense against the Kyn and their dealings. It would not be beyond the Council to use this to their advantage. Checking the time, she mentally adjusted for the difference. One a.m. There was a chance the person she needed would be coming in from an early night. Or preparing for a late one. Regardless.

She picked up the phone and dialed a number by heart, then listened to the other end ring.

"Natasha, I wondered when I'd have the pleasure of your call." The smooth, cultured voice drifted across the line.

"Thaddeus, did I catch you coming or going?" Leaning back in her chair, she closed her eyes, a trick she found better enabled her to focus on subtle vocal fluctuations.

"Coming home, for once." The faint sound of ice bouncing off glass filled his pause. "I'm sorry I wasn't able to make it to Mulcahy's wake." Genuine sympathy tightened his words.

importance has been decided. They are still in the idea phase."

"How long before they move forward?"

"If your people can keep it down, months."

His continued digs rubbed her the wrong way on every level and, this time, she let him hear it. Her voice deepened to warning levels. "My people are not the ones creating issues. They are the ones cleaning up the messes of those who want to see us trapped in the shadows. Remember, if the humans turn on us, you and yours are in the direct line of fire." She didn't wait for his answer, but gently disconnected.

A shiver of awareness crept over her, but she refused to look at the corner it emanated from. It took her a few seconds to loosen her grip on the phone. One by one, she relaxed her fingers until they were no longer bone white. Too many challenges left her temper, and demon, riding close to the surface. To combat the need to vent some of her frustration, she closed out the browsing windows and shut down her laptop, taking her time to focus on the minute things.

A few months, at best, to get ahead of what was coming. Not a lot of time. She rose to her feet and began to pace, clasping her hands behind her back. There were too many loose ends. For now she would let Thaddeus run interference with the humans. In the meantime, she needed to narrow her attention to the individuals causing her the most trouble: Brant Sutler, Zane Aimeric, and Darius Abazi.

As she hit the edge of the carpet, that tingle of awareness swept over her again. Again, she refused to acknowledge it.

Things were progressing, just not as fast as they needed to. It helped that Gavin was now the Wraith's Captain.

Initially she'd thrown her hat into the captaincy ring as a test of sorts, a subtle push to see who would step forward. Sullivan's bid was no surprise. The surprise was discovering Raine had enough self-awareness to realize Gavin, not her, would be the stronger leader for the group. Although Natasha was certain Raine wouldn't remain a silent partner. No doubt the two would become a very pivotal couple, and in turn, a source of strength for the Northwest Kyn.

Granted, claiming that position as her own would have been quite delightful, but Natasha had enough on her plate. Especially since she was now dealing with someone's attempt to frame her for Sullivan's death. She needed Gavin to step up the pressure on running Sutler down. Stopping the geneticist and his drug cocktail before someone else got to him was crucial. What he created took money, time, and power—three things the human did not have. It shouldn't take much to get the sneaky human to give up his backer. Chances were good the name would match the same person currently behind her problems.

Of course, the out-of-touch Council would be more than happy to jump at a chance to get rid of her and, by extension, the Northwest Kyn.

While Darius's presence was understandable from a political standpoint, was it a more personal threat? A way to remind her that the Council had not forgotten what sent her and Ryan to the new world? Either way, having both a member of the Order and the Council in her territory needed to be addressed. Most leaders wouldn't hesitate in their retribution, but she didn't have that luxury. The sticking point remained, who sent them?

Retracing her steps across the thick rug, she continued her musings, ignoring the shadows hanging in the far corner. Ryan, once part of the Order, held close ties to some of the Council, strong enough to call them allies. However, it didn't mean that those alliances would transfer to her, not until they could be reassured as to what her goals were, regardless of the fact that the Northwest Kyn were the only ones strong enough to stand against a fracturing Council.

So the true question became—which man truly answered to the Council, Darius or Zayn?

Darius intrigued her, which could be dangerous if she wasn't careful. He wasn't a simple man. She didn't need her trips to the Side to confirm that. She could taste the depth of secrets inside him, and exploring those secrets could be addicting. He was a distraction she could ill afford. Was that distraction a deliberate ploy on someone's part?

As for Zayn. In previous Council meetings he appeared to be neutral, more concerned with playing his private games. What did he expect to gain with his visit? How deep did the division in the Council actually go? She needed to know who sat on each side and where the Order fell. There was one person who could set her on the right path. He could help. It was just a question of would he?

Quickly running through the pros and cons of her next move, she decided the risks were well worth it. Striding to the desk, she picked up the phone and dialed.

"What kind of trouble are you bringing me now, Natasha?"

The disgruntled, grumble brought a smile to her face. "You love trouble, Rio."

Rio Castle, the Southwest Kyn's Amanusa leader, gave a laughing bark. "Are you sending your little instigators down my way?"

Walking over to the bay windows with the cordless phone, she curled up on the window seat. "Are you bored?"

"Humph, not yet," he groused. "But they certainly shook things up."

"For better or worse?"

"Tala's facing some heat from her motley crew of witches and wizards for bringing in Cheveyo."

Natasha gave a delicate snort. "Let me guess. They think it makes her look weak."

"The actual word was 'ineffective.' Of course, once she got done with the first one stupid enough to say it to her face, it hasn't been mentioned aloud again."

Rio's voice held a grudging note of respect. Of course, gaining the respect of a demon as old as he was took a certain amount of cold-blooded ruthlessness, a trait the Southwest Magi Head, Tala Whiteriver, carried well.

"And Tomás?"

"He's a mess."

"Are you certain, Rio?"

"What do you really want to know, Natasha?" His question was sharp.

Rio was not a demon she would trifle with, not if given a choice. "I fear he may be hunting on his own."

"I doubt it," he grumbled. "Damn wolf has lost what little was left of his mind. He can barely function. His Second has been covering for him." Rio paused, a sly note sneaking in his voice. "You might want to warn Vidis to watch his ass because Tomás isn't going to let go of this once he gets done tearing out his fur over his dead wife."

"He knows," she said. "If Tomás is stupid enough to come at him, you'll be looking for a new alpha."

"Would be a definite improvement," Rio muttered softly, then cleared his throat. "Now that we've caught up on all the little things, why the phone call, girl?"

She didn't take offense. Rio could call her a girl all he

wanted. Compared to him, she was. She was damn grateful to have him generally on her side, because going against him would be fatal. "Heard anything new about the Council lately?"

He chuckled. "Who'd you get?"

"Zayn Aimeric."

He clicked his tongue. "If he was all they sent, you wouldn't be calling, so there's something to the rumors you have another, much more troubling visitor."

She frowned. "Considering the amount of gossips we have, I'm surprised our presence hasn't been posted all over the human news."

Rio's voice sharpened. "Why are you stalling?"

Thank the hells he couldn't see her wince. "The Order sent in a proxy." Darius would not be pleased if his identity was shared far and wide. Although Rio was more than likely to hoard the information for later use.

"Ahh, interesting," he said, then went quiet.

"Why?" she pushed.

"What do you know of the relationship between the Order and the Council?"

Was this a test? "Not much. The Order is to the Council what the Wraiths are to us. They're supposed to protect us as a whole, not serve as personal enforcers for the Council. However, some Order members have close ties to specific Council members."

"And you think that has changed?"

She nibbled on her lower lip. "No, but could the current division seep into the Order?"

Would it sink deep enough to encourage a partnership between the Order and the Council? Together the two groups could arrange things to weaken the Northwest. Like set her up against her own house, the Wraiths, Cheveyo, and Vidis. Those were not comforting odds.

"So long as revealing the Kyn doesn't include revealing the Order, they may choose to remain observers," Rio said.

She found no comfort in his answer. "Yet, the Order has long held ties to the Council." She tapped her finger on her knee, dragged in a deep breath, and dove in. "Rio, would the Council use the Order to hunt us?" *Hunt me?*

A heavy silence spun across the line, until only her pulse sounded. Finally he said, "I don't know, Natasha, but if they did, you best watch your back, because you and yours won't stand a chance against that kind of combined power."

In the darkest shadows of Natasha's room, Darius stayed hidden, watching, thinking. The little demon queen looked a bit pale as she set down the phone. Interesting that Natasha would actually reach out to the other Amanusa leaders. It spoke to an unusual relationship, one that did not exist within the European houses. Perhaps there was something to the Council's concerns about the Northwest Kyn. Still, observing her had proven quite enlightening.

He came in halfway through her first conversation with Thaddeus. Even smiled a little when she rolled her eyes with exasperation as she soothed the other demon's prickly ego. Her ability to manipulate was admirable. Few others wielded that indefinable...tact.

Perhaps the Council was underestimating her. Ryan Mulcahy earned his lethal reputation one sharp edge at a time. Natasha? Well, too many on the Council viewed women as malleable. Strange, considering the most vicious predators he ran across tended to be female.

In fact, if Thaddeus wasn't careful, he would step that one inch too far, and Natasha would leave him in pieces. But Rio, now there was an interesting relationship. Darius swore he detected some true depth of feeling in that conversation. It was telling that her first move was to check on the human situation before the one sitting in her front yard. However, maybe not so unexpected after all, considering her years-long position as the chief marketing officer for Taliesin. Would she now find Mulcahy's CEO shoes a tight fit?

She stopped in front of the fire and the minor question disappeared like smoke. Those slim shoulders hunched, and she dragged a hand through her white-blonde curtain of hair, leaving it a tumbled mess—one his fingers itched to dive into. She turned her head, the firelight lining her profile with dancing shadows. Unexpected lust spiraled through him, his body hardening.

Her lips held a soft curl. "Are you going to watch me all night?"

He blinked as her question sank in. Releasing his hold on the concealing shadows, he faced her. "How long?"

Those violet blue eyes deepened into an inky mystery as they traveled over his loose, low-slung pants and bare chest. He reacted to the caress of her gaze as if it was a physical touch. His blood ran hot and thick, need coming up on point. When their stares finally locked, he found an answering desire flickering in her depths. Her pink tongue swept out over her bottom lip. A nervous tic or deliberate provocation? Did it really matter?

"Before I dialed Rio." Her voice was a husky rasp.

It took his brain a second to catch up. He gave himself a metaphoric head slap. *Get your head in the game, ass!* He prowled closer until he stood inches away.

She held her position, her face in profile above her shoulders, watching him from under those thick, dark lashes. Her unique fragrance of night-blooming jasmine, laced with feminine heat, drifted to him.

Keeping his hands at his side, he dipped his head and drew the scent deep into his lungs. His mark lay like a faint bruise against her alabaster skin, a temptation he choose not to ignore. He pressed the lightest of kisses to it, inordinately pleased with the rapid rise and fall of her chest. Lifting his head, he held her bemused gaze. "You didn't give him my name."

Her throat worked as she swallowed. "Rumors fly faster than light. He'll find you out soon enough."

"Perhaps." He searched her face, taking in the light rose under her cheeks, the widening of her eyes, and the small pants as she fought for air. He wanted to capture those lips and plunder until she could only breathe what he shared. The overly possessive urge made him straighten with a jerk and step back. The attraction between them was... uncomfortable.

Under his skin, his demon hissed and clawed, furious at what the man was denying them both. Darius shook his head sharply. No, fucking this woman would only complicate an already difficult situation. Needing to regain control, he struck out, using the tools at his disposal. "Do you think seducing me will keep you safe?"

She stiffened then deliberately turned fully toward him with haughty grace. Her rising signs of desire disappeared under a cold, mocking mask, her eyes flashing as her lips curled in contempt. "May I remind you that you invaded my bedroom, Mr. Abazi." Ice dripped from her words. "Is that normal for one of the Order? Do you normally whore yourself out for the Council?"

Her vicious implication shredded his tenuous control. Before he could rethink the wisdom of his actions, plastered her curvy body against his front. Those red tipped nails bit against the skin of his chest, his erection cradled against her stomach, while his hand tangled in the platinum mass as he held her captive. "No more than you whoring yourself for your precious houses," he growled, before taking her mouth with a barely leashed savagery.

No gentleness, only pure lust and need swirling in a savage storm. He ravaged with punishing intent, small bites and rapacious tongue, unwilling to give her room to escape. She met him with equal heat and passion. Hunger began to edge out his fury, allowing him to feel the sting of her nails as they raked against his chest. He loosened his grip, letting her yank out of his hold.

He looked down, unsurprised to find bloody gouges scoring his skin. His animalistic side took satisfaction in the sight. He lifted his head in time to catch the tail end of her wiping the back of her hand over her swollen mouth.

The wavering image of her demon hovered around her like a barely remembered dream. She faced him, her hands fisted at her side, chest heaving. "Touch me again, Abazi, and I'll shred your balls into confetti."

He smiled and crossed his arms over his chest, ignoring his still-seeping wounds. "Challenging me isn't in your best interests, darling, but you're welcome to try."

Those lips thinned and a feral hiss was all that escaped.

His smile widened. Rendering her speechless was quite rewarding, but it didn't last long.

Regrettably, she pulled herself together much faster than he liked, the revealing mirage of her demon whisking away, leaving the controlled corporate maven behind. "I have no intention of challenging you."

He raised an unbelieving eyebrow. "What intentions do you harbor?"

She studied him, her thoughts well shielded. "I intend to uncover who's setting me up, regardless of who's pulling the strings."

"And then?"

Her smile was all predator. "Then I'll remind them of what happens to those who go against me."

"Even if it brings you and yours unwanted attention?"

Her chin lifted. "It's never smart to rattle the cage of a beast you can't handle. Something someone's forgotten."

He titled his head in wry acknowledgement.

She strolled to the door and pulled it open. "Get out." A tremor ran through the low words. Fury or fear, he wasn't sure.

Knowing if he pushed her any further, one or both of them would pay for it—perhaps in flesh and blood—he strolled to the door, only to stop in front of her. He raised a finger and drew it down her pale jaw, impressed when she didn't visibly react. "You asked Rio a question. Would you like an answer?"

She remained stubbornly mute.

"You are being hunted, Natasha." He caught the flicker of unease she tried to hide. "But the Order doesn't have your scent."

CHAPTER 14

A COUPLE OF HOURS LATER, NATASHA FINISHED THE LAST DETAILS on a report for Taliesin. After kicking Darius's arrogant ass out of her room, sleep was impossible. However, it did allow her to catch up on business and tug on a few more investigative lines. It was surprising how a call from her in the wee hours of morning could garner such interesting information. Unfortunately, she couldn't act on it until a more reasonable time.

A blinding shaft of agony seared across her consciousness, causing her to hiss in pain, even as she jerked to her feet. Before the warnings of her breached wards could fade, a horrendous crash sounded from downstairs. She was moving before her vision cleared of the annoying little white spots. Yanking open her door, she darted into the hall, only to come to an abrupt halt as she slammed into something solid and warm wrapped in temptation and spice.

Darius.

Hands gripped her arms to steady her. "What the hell is going on?"

Ripping free of his hold, she spun toward the stairs. "Someone has decided to pay me a visit."

Staying on her heels, Darius followed her down the stairs. "Haven't they heard of knocking?"

"Obviously not," she snapped, rushing over the hardwood floor, her attention riveted on her living room.

The huge paned window now resembled a gaping maw with jagged teeth. Misty rain and cool winds whipped the heavy curtains back. Moonlight glinted off the glass shards now decorating her floor. Shadows, opaque and menacing, blanketed the room. Something waited in the inky darkness. Waited and watched, even as her wards continued to shriek their warnings inside her skull.

Curling her hand into a fist, she cut her palm with one sharp nail, allowing a single drop of blood to fall to the floor. The minute it touched the ground, silence rushed in and her magic swept out, slicing through the shadows. When it touched what waited, the magical reverberation raised more than the hair on her arms. Behind her, Darius's low, muttered curse confirmed her fears. Very old, very scary demon magic.

A pained bellow shook the room, even as the darkness peeled back revealing what waited. And it was not anything she had expected.

Demon.

Not just any demon, either. This one was different. His heavy chest was bare, tattered jeans covered muscled legs, and from his temples, two solid, twisted horns rose. No exotic meld of human and demon, instead this was the monster of human nightmares.

A demon's nature never translated well in the mortal realm. This one proved to be no exception. His features were an unholy mix of human and demon, something that should never exist on this plane. Claws existed where hands should be, and they were curling and uncurling at his side.

"A Bound?" Danger and pity swam under Darius's question.

Maybe, but such a thing was rarely done. "Only one way to find out." She didn't dare take her attention away from the one looming in front of her. Eyes of solid black, set against crimson where white should be, fixed on her. Something flickered deep inside the ebony wells, even as lips pulled back from serrated teeth and a hair-raising snarl rebounded through the room.

Undaunted, she moved forward until she stood just inside the room. "You shouldn't be here, pet."

"Brought you a gift." The voice was surprisingly normal, considering its source.

"Is that so?" This close she could feel the magic swimming around her late-night visitor like an electrical storm, preparing to strike. A faint nudge at her back made her step to the side, allowing Darius to move up beside her and snag the demon's attention.

"Considering your rude entrance, it better be a damn good gift." The fact that Darius could stand there in nothing more than drawstring pants and still look formidable was quite impressive.

She used his distraction to move a little more to the left, putting space between her and Darius while maneuvering the demon between them. "What gift?" she asked, allowing Darius to gain a few more feet.

Instead of answering, the demon took a step backward.

At his feet, a crumpled form lay like a broken doll. A woman. A dead woman. Her head turned toward Natasha and Darius, her eyes wide and glassy under the tangle of dark hair. More disturbing was the bloody furrows carved into the pale skin of her arms and torso, as if she tried to ward off the claws that ripped her apart. A torn hole remained where her heart once sat. The carnage covered remains of an oversized T-shirt and boxer shorts indicated the poor child must have been caught in bed.

As she studied the girl and recognition crowded in, Natasha's breath escaped in a furious hiss. Dull, almost invisible in death, pale red rings encircled her irises. They marked her as one of Natasha's. The delicate features triggered a name. Cleo James, Kevin Sullivan's lover.

Fury surged, bringing a vindictive urge to hurt the one who would brutalize someone under her protection. Red hazed her vision, her nails lengthened, and her nature rose in a shockingly feral wave, wiping out the woman and leaving only the beast behind.

Ignoring Darius's warning shout, she lunged.

While watching Natasha tear a demon to shreds was on his to-do list, Darius didn't expect it to happen like this. The little queen's fury roused her demon, which now surrounded her like a half-developed image. Her unexpected lunge caught their late-night visitor off balance, but that advantage wouldn't last long.

Even now, the creature swung out with a fist almost the size of Natasha's head. She ducked, raking her claws across his stomach. She continued to carve her way around to his spine as he spun to escape her reach. He kicked out, forcing Natasha to step back or take the hit in her stomach. Finally free from her claws, he picked up a couch as if it was a baseball bat and, with a roar, brought it around in a vicious swing.

Darius surged forward, his own beast straining against his leash in anticipation. He wrapped an arm around Natasha's waist, tucked her against his front, and turned so the couch slammed into his back. The force of the blow knocked him forward and shattered the couch. He landed on all fours, careful to keep his body between Natasha and the demon. Pain sang through his spine and shoulders, but it wasn't enough to quench the savage satisfaction of his beast as it broke through the last of his restraints, eager for the impending fight.

Under him, Natasha blinked and narrowed her eyes, now an entrancing combination of ruby and indigo. "Get off of me, Darius."

"What? No thank you for saving your ass?"

"I'd rather you kiss it." Then her gaze slid behind him and widened.

Heeding her silent warning, he rolled to the left, while she rolled right. The heavy wood that once graced the back of a couch sank into the wooden floor, right where they'd been lying. The following bellow of fury almost drowned out the shrill summons of a phone somewhere in the house.

"Who the hell is calling now?" Natasha rose to her feet and circled behind the maddened creature swinging its head between the two of them.

Darius straightened, cracking his neck and rolling his shoulders to shrug off the lingering tingles of pain. "Would you like me to see our guest out, while you answer it, darling?"

"Generous of you, pet, but I have a better idea." Under the edge of her rumpled nightgown, her bare feet slid a little more to the left. She gave him a veiled look. "Why don't we take our visitor someplace a little more private?"

Understanding clicked. "A grand idea, love." Beautiful and brilliant, the woman was such a delight. He reached for his magic just as the creature between them lunged for Natasha.

She didn't even flinch, simply stood still, haughty and assured. The only one surprised when her magic snapped into place was the creature caught inside. Darius let his own power slide over hers until the two energies met and connected, sending out a vibration like that of a tuning fork, resonating on both the mortal plane and the Side.

Natasha was beyond furious. Not only was another of her people murdered, but they dared to attack her in her own home. Her living room was reduced to a pile of kindling, and her exquisite wines pooled on the wooden floors. And, to top it off, Darius witnessed her small lapse of control. Someone needed to pay.

To find out who the grand-prize winner would be, she needed to question their captive. Since he insisted on visiting her at an ungodly hour, she would ensure he stayed until her questions were answered. Which meant she and Darius needed to keep the demon trapped on all three planes—the human plane, where he physically manifested; the Between, where the magic trapping him existed; and the Side, the Amanusas' playground.

To do that she needed to start in the Side. *But first...* "Who sent you?" Her question snapped like a whip, jerking the horned head back as if slapped.

Darius remained quiet, his arms folded over his bare

chest as he watched. Somewhere in the house, the thrice-damned phone began to ring again.

The demon's mouth opened, revealing sharp, serrated teeth, but no words emerged. This time, she didn't miss the ugly wave of fear swimming in the obsidian depths. The demon's muscles visibly locked and his body began to shake. All signs that things were about to go south.

She tightened her magical hold even as Darius snapped, "Natasha, take him now!"

There was no time to snarl at his bossiness. Instead, she sank her magic into the demon, using it to yank him into the Side. Between one breath and the next, her living room disappeared, only to be replaced by a circular room. Ever-shifting ambient light drifted from above, sliding down smooth, stone walls. Her demon surged forward, sublimating her human form, her magical cage strengthening as her focus sharpened. Across from her, Darius's towering demonic form rose, his magic reinforcing hers.

Symbols burst into eye searing life as they came fully into the Side, dragging their captive with them. Those symbols were a personal affront, an indicator of a binding. An ear-torturing shriek ripped from the demon caught inside their combined cage. Natasha's fury hardened into something cold and lethal.

Darius flicked out a hand, his claws nicking the edge of the binding, sending a cascade of black sparks tumbling down the magic's surface. The horrendous noise cut off, even though the monster's mouth remained open, stretched into a jaw-breaking scream. Darius stopped next to her and folding his arms across his chest. "He's Bound."

"Half-Bound," she corrected, eyes narrowed against the glare as she studied the symbols on the floor. The magical chains weren't as tight as they should be for a full binding. "Regardless, if we undo his ties to the Side, we'll sunder his spirit from this form, trapping the man here, while leaving the beast free to roam in the mortal realm. Plus, it won't leave much of his mind behind." And since her answers resided inside that mind, they needed another option. One that wouldn't leave the demon searching for a new host in the mortal realm.

She glided around the edge of the binding circle, taking note of each symbol. One of the Amanusas' greatest weakness was bindings, a process the race as a whole made damn sure to hide as many details about as possible.

A couple of reasons made the binding process problematic. One was the amount of magical strength necessary to hold both the human and demon forms on three different planes: the mortal, the Side, and the Between.

If you could harness that much power, then was the vital key of Naming, using the correct names—all of them, in the right order—of the demon you were trying to bind. If you failed to do so, you ended up with a Half-Bound. A hellish proposition, as undoing a half-assed binding never ended well for anyone. Those names were never shared, but she wasn't stupid. The demand for that kind of power created a bustling black market in the Amanusa world. Of course, she collected her fair share of names, most belonging to those in her house who might forget their place. Names she discovered purely by skill alone. Another perk of her bloodline—secrets rarely remained secret.

"He's young." Darius's comment brought her back to the immediate situation.

"Quite, and not very strong." She completed her circle. The demon trapped within kept circling to keep her in sight. "Which means he left enough of his name unguarded for someone to use." She shook her head. "Stupid."

"Or he shared it with someone he trusted." Darius watched their captive. "Who is he?"

"Not sure yet," she murmured, still working through the symbols. Something about them bothered her. Problem was she didn't have the luxury of time to figure it out. *Oh well, no time for delicacy.* "Let him speak," she told Darius.

The ear-piercing wail resumed.

She straightened, pulled on her power, and clamped it around the demon's will like a vise. "Who Bound you?" Her voice emerged deep, sinking past skin and bone, pounding into the spirit of the demon trembling before her.

The wails dampened to whimpers. He opened his mouth, the muscles in his neck straining but remained mute.

Something cold and cutting pushed back against her hold. It didn't belong to the one caught inside the circle. It was older, darker, and much more dangerous. She flexed her magical muscle. "Tell me."

Caught between the two warring magics, hers and his summoner's, the demon's body snapped into a painful arch. The strain moved from visible to audible as bone after bone began to snap. The whimpers turned to screams.

Stunned by the ferociousness of the reaction, Natasha withdrew her magic. "What in the hell?"

The demon collapsed, eyes open, blood seeping from his ears, eyes, nose, and mouth, his claws scraping against the floor.

Darius crouched, a low growl emanating from him. He lifted his head, his eyes frigid with fury. "Part of the binding. It won't let him answer."

"Maybe not that question. Perhaps another one?"

He turned back to study their captive, considering. "Possibly, but you'll have to work fast. Once he starts talking, the binding will take over. We'll be racing against the clock."

Someone out there considered one of hers disposable. She refused to let Darius see how much that angered her. "Can you run interference while I readjust the runes?"

She couldn't alter the symbols on the floor and hold the binding back at the same time. Besides, her request would keep Darius out of her hair while she worked. Taking his nod, she shifted her attention to the runes.

As Darius took over the binding, wisps of black spread like ink in water around the demon still writhing on the floor.

"Don't kill him." The last thing she needed was another dead demon.

She caught Darius's disgruntled look. The symbols on the floor faded in intensity, but remained visible. Identifying the three she needed, she began.

Reworking the runes took skill, strength, and patience. She had the first two, but not much time for the third. When it came to bindings, the summoner created the symbols specific to the demon they called. Those symbols represented the various objectives the summoner wanted accomplished. Adding in the true name of an Amanusa tied the demon's wellbeing into the summoner's goals. If the demon failed to complete their task, they lost everything. If they succeeded, they kept their life and soul, but were forever leashed to their summoner, unable to disobey given commands. Summoners tended to be a greedy bunch of idiots. Each success bred a thirst for more—more violence, more power, just more. Until the only possible outcome for the Bound was failure.

Breaking through the unholy compulsion depended on the age and strength of the one Bound. In this case, because he couldn't be past half a century old, she should be able to get at least a confirmation of what he was sent to accomplish. Retrieving the name of his summoner might be a possibility, since his binding wasn't complete. The outcome would remain elusive until she began to unravel it.

Darius growled. "What are you waiting for, woman?"

She curled her lip then got to work, slipping through the demon's fractured mental shields. Readjusting the symbols was like working with molten metal. Their power seared across her psyche. Tied as symbols were to the demon's spirit, they fought against her attempts as if sentient, when in actuality they were part of the summoner's inherent defenses.

Relying on the additional strength of her own demon, she forced the runes to bend to her will. Overriding a summoner was never easy, and this time proved no different. In fact, there was a unique depth of age to the magic holding the binding together. Each change she wrought caused the demon to react and she swore the binding shifted as well.

Once the first symbol was in place, she tried again. "Why?"

The thrashing demon lurched on to all fours, ignoring the obviously shattered bones in his arms and legs. It threw back its head and howled.

She drew her magic tighter. "Why did you attack?"

"Divide—conquer—" Spittle flew as the words hissed out. "Musssttt—removvvee—" the rest trailed off into incomprehensible squeals.

Firmly inside the demon's mind, she caught glimpses of the summoner's. To share with Darius, she repeated what she saw out loud. "First order, cause dissension among my house, second, remove key leaders." No surprise there, considering who he attacked, but it made her curious. "Who's next?"

The demon didn't answer, but turned its head with reptilian slowness toward Darius.

The damn man laughed. "Your master's not very bright."

The black mist solidified into ebony ribbons. As they wrapped around the demon's limbs, he began to scream. Blood began to seep along the ribbons' edges. Just as the demon began to babble, the ribbons reverted back to their previous, smoky state. The demon collapsed into a sobbing heap.

"Stop playing with him," she bit out.

The demon's mental acuity began to crumble and the binding fluctuated against Darius's hold.

"You better figure out who he is or who called him because he's not going to make it," Darius warned.

"Can't you hold him?"

Her frustration rose as she realized the binding was leaving her no choice but to utilize brute force to get the information she wanted. There was no saving this demon. Hardening her heart against the tortured sounds, she forced the last two symbols into shape, then played observer to his broken memories.

A smoke filled room.

How cliché.

Cards on a green felt table. Male laughter and half-hearted curses. Switch to cool night air. Stone against his back, smoking a cigarette. A shadow coming up next to him.

No surprise there, so probably someone he knew.

The beginnings of his name, his true name, in a resonant voice. Fear sliding through him, his body refusing to respond as the names curled tighter and tighter, like barbed chains around his mind and will. As despair threatened to suck him into oblivion, the voice stopped. A bright, fleeting spark of relief. The summoner forgot to name his maternal line.

"Jared Pick," she murmured, sharing the demon's name with Darius.

The memories continued. Now warped and broken pieces, nothing made much sense. No clear image of the summoner, just a driving need to complete the instructions given. Flashes of blood, Sullivan's rough shout, more blood, hunger, feminine screams and pleas, shattered glass, and rain.

Natasha kept scrolling forward and caught images of her home. Hope pierced the mindless compulsion, pulling her up short. Something about seeing her home? No, seeing her, had given Jared hope. *Hope for what?*

If she dug deeper, she'd chance losing more answers as his human intellect crumpled under the pressure. His death was a foregone conclusion, but she wanted to ensure she tried everything before it finished.

"Natasha, hurry the hell up." For the first time, strain colored Darius's voice. "Whatever you've hit, it's triggering the Binding."

Sure enough the links began tightening, tearing through the fragile spirit twisting in torment. Jared fought back, struggling to override the compulsion curling around him. His determination to reach her was painful to watch. "He wants what you have—careful—"

She tried one more time. "Who?"

But it was too late.

The binding flared and Jared's scream choked into a gurgle. His inner demon clawed forth, his intellect swallowed by primal instinct. The binding stretched and the magical links warped.

When the first link snapped, what was Jared snuffed out under the Binding, leaving only a demonic beast behind.

CHAPTER 15

Darius muttered a quick oath. When the first link broke, he slammed a protective shield around Natasha. He didn't stop to question why protecting her was his first instinct. He felt her powers slide into place under his, adding another layer of protection. Still, some long-forgotten instinct hadn't wanted to take any chances with her safety.

The skin of the trapped demon began to split, spilling a reddish orange light from fast widening cracks. His wails turned into demonic growls and his body morphed into the horrific forms of human nightmares.

Broken bones disappeared under a patchwork of leathery skin and scales. As the body twisted and turned, Jared's demonic nature took over, coming out to play in the Side. It wasn't even close to pretty—tortured thoughts and twisted desires given horrific form. Fueled by mindless hunger for chaos and destruction, it would tear through the boundaries between realms searching for a new host. Which meant they needed to stand guard on the mortal plane and take it out.

It slammed against the magic holding it captive. Each

hit reverberated through Darius like a physical impact. He could withstand those, but it was the rampaging emotions trying to chip away his remaining control offering the biggest peril.

The Bound's animalistic nature began to bleed through the barriers, threatening to infect Darius. The air was heavy with hungering rage, and it called to him like a forgotten lover. The hot rich taste of blood. The intoxicating high as all hell broke loose. The primal satisfaction of rendering his enemies limb from limb, while the world broke under the terror. The visceral need to replace control and logic with the seductive lure of chaos.

When a particularly vicious hit to the magic's confines left him leaning over to gasp in much needed air, that rage coated his mouth like the spicy aftertaste of mulled wine. It urged him to indulge in another sip, another thirst-quenching drink. A ravenous need to destroy darkened his vision, narrowing it to a laser fine focus.

He and the Bound locked gazes.

Darius's own demon howled for blood. Through sheer will, he held himself in check. Knowing he would pay for it later, he shoved his primal nature back, shackling it with chains forged of ruthless control and rigid discipline. Snapping and snarling, his primal aspect retreated, leaving behind the warrior.

"Darius, dammit, are you listening to me?" That was Natasha, and from the sounds of it, she'd been trying to get his attention for a while.

"Am now," he growled back, unwilling to take his gaze off their captive.

"We won't stop him until I get back and sever Jared's ties to the mortal realm." Nice to know the little queen understood what needed to happen next. "Can you hold him?"

Was that doubt in her voice? What the hell gave her the impression he couldn't hold his own against a Half-Bound demon fledging? He cocked his head and met her frown. At the same time he adjusted his magic.

Lethal, black ribbons whipped around the demon's wrists and ankles. As if yanked by invisible hands, the demon's limbs snapped into an X shape, even as it continued to struggle. Darius arched his eyebrows in a silent, mocking question.

Even in full demon form, her eyes were expressive. Right now, they said as much as the narrow lines of her lips and her crossed arms. Funny, but he found her annoyance as intriguing as her passion from earlier. What would it be like to get her truly riled up? What lay under all that cool restraint? The challenge she presented enticed both natures residing under his skin—man and demon.

An enraged yowl snagged his attention, reminding him to keep his focus on the problem at hand. He blinked, pleased to see Natasha mimic the action. She gave a small shake of her head. He followed her gaze back to the restrained beast floating above the floor. The summoner's bindings wreathed over the struggling figure, competing with his own implacable restraints. A tiny flicker of pity flared to life. "He's beyond saving now."

Something darkened in her expression. "I know," she agreed softly. Her familiar arrogant mask fell into place. "If we don't time this right, there's a very good chance he'll be set free among the humans."

She was preaching to the choir. Since a Bound was tethered to all three dimensions, breaking those ties needed to be nearly simultaneous. If any link remained behind in any realm, the mindless animal would be freed. While their combined efforts managed to currently hold him in the Side and in the human world, it still left the Between unguarded.

With just the two of them, covering all three realms simultaneously would prove difficult. "We can't sever the ties individually. We'll need to time our hits. You'll need to break the ties in the Between and mortal realms when I break these."

"And how, pray tell, do you expect to do that?" She shot him a look. "It's not like cell phones work here."

"Give me your hand." He didn't bother hiding his grin when she tucked her delicate claws behind her back instead. "Scared?"

"Cautious," she corrected. "Only a fool would blindly trust the one sent to hunt her."

His demon purred at the backhanded compliment. "No harm. My word, Natasha," he rumbled. He held out his hand and waited.

After a moment she placed hers carefully in his.

He turned it palm up, tracing a delicate line across the surface. She blinked rapidly. "You are Blood of Secrets. I'm Blood of Death." He lifted his gaze to hers. "What do the two share?"

He watched her devious little mind rapidly work through the connections. "Whispers." Whispers of intrigue, of secrets and half-truths. The initial seed of all discord. However, this time, it wouldn't be lies, but a way to synchronize their actions.

The next pass over her palm laid open a thin line, leaving a crimson streak behind. As her blood seeped from the cut, he repeated the movement on his palm. This time she didn't hesitate as she pressed her hand into his. "The blood connection won't last long," he warned, "but it'll allow us to work across realms."

Their blood mingled, their magic twining together, forging a delicate link between them.

Her fingers tightened against his then slowly pulled away. Her voice was husky. "Be ready."

She stepped back and opened the door between the Side and human worlds. Before she stepped through, she lifted her palm to her mouth. Her tongue flicked out with a leisurely sweep, licking her palm clean. A low hum of hunger escaped as her gaze darkened.

The sound and sight sent heat and lust curling through him. "Tease."

Her lips curled in satisfaction. "Don't disappoint me, Darius."

Then she was gone.

The exotic flavor of Darius's blood still lingered on Natasha's tongue as she reentered the mortal realm. The intriguing taste brought a slew of questions as the whispers his blood offered began to murmur. Did he realize what he so casually offered her? Sharing of blood, even such a light sip, could be dangerous, even fatal, in their world. It was so tempting to delve deeper into the secrets held in that small taste before the potency faded, perhaps finding something she could use later. Unfortunately, the snarls and growls coloring the air took precedence. So did the small problem of how to sever the magic in both the mortal and Kyn realms.

"What the hell is going on, Natasha?"

The harsh unexpected demand snapped her attention beyond the struggling creature before her. *Ah, a solution.*

Gavin stood inside her demolished living room, crimson staining the side of his T-shirt and aggression surrounding him like an invisible cape.

What had the boy been doing? "You seem to be leaking, dear."

"Appreciate the concern, but still doesn't explain what you're doing."

With her more volatile nature so close to the surface, there was no stopping the warning growl vibrating from her. She was getting damn tired of pushy males. She turned her head and let Gavin see what he was poking. He stood a few feet away, a lethal blade held at his side, his face grim.

She opened her mouth to answer, only to shut it with a distinctive snap as Darius's voice swept through their blood connection, his voice curling around her mind. *"Stopping checking out the witch and get to work, woman."*

Considering how clear his exasperation was their newly formed connection was far from weak. Resentment at his unfair admonishment heated her face. She redirected her and her demon's earlier irritation at him. *"Jealous, pet?"*

She deliberately added a mocking edge to her question, needing to knock the arrogant ass down a peg or two. Or three.

Still, they didn't have time to engage in petty emotional games. Ignoring the mutters from the disgruntled male demon in her head, she turned to Gavin. "Can you reinforce the containment spell?"

"What is that?" Gavin's attention didn't waver from the Half-Bound demon caught in her living room.

"Durand, focus!" Beyond frustrated and highly aware of the clock ticking down, she snapped, "Can you hold him?"

Gavin moved farther into the room. "Not unless I know what I'm dealing with."

"This is a Bound demon, which means it's anchored in all three realms. We need to time our attacks or we will have more than this to worry about." Like possessed humans running around. Or, if luck was having one of those days, a lethally talented possessed Kyn armed with a sword. "Can you hold it?"

"Here and Between, yes." Those jade eyes turned to her. "Wherever you and yours go to play, not so much."

Sounded like he finally figured out where she held her little discussion with Fahd earlier. Good, perhaps it would save them time now. "Our 'playground' is called the Side, and Darius is there, so no need to visit. Besides, it doesn't play well with other Kyn."

Gavin arched an eyebrow even as the light touch of blue-tinged energy slipped around her hold on the struggling captive. His magic didn't touch hers, but it came uncomfortably close. Such disparate energies never mixed well and the two powerful magics filled the room with skin-tingling electricity.

"What are you going to be doing?" Gavin asked.

"Amanusa are dual natured, physical, and incorporeal. You and Darius must simultaneously destroy the human and demon's physical form to break the ties here and in the Side. What's left behind will do whatever it has to in order to survive." One of those survival techniques would include the demon's essence looking for a new mortal body to occupy, or escaping into the Between. Neither was a viable option. "You best ensure your personal shields are impenetrable, Gavin." Gods above and below knew she didn't need an infuriated Raine on her ass if something should happen to him.

Gavin tilted his head to one side then the other, the simmering energy taking on a new depth, the jade glow in his eyes gaining intensity. He lifted his blade, rotating his wrist until it was held at the ready. "Head or heart?"

"Heart."

The head would be Darius's responsibility. Holding the essence of the demon away from the three realms, that was on her.

Trapped under the combined magics, the demon began to struggle in earnest. All signs of Jared were erased, replaced by the mindless, destructive monster.

Knowing how fast things could change Natasha freed her demon. Hardening her heart as Darius's countdown sounded in her head, she tightened her grip on the magic slowly closing in on the maddened demon. Coiling her power like a whip, she wound the loops of a destructive counter spell around the snarling, unaware monster.

Next to her, Gavin stepped between her and the now vibrating magic. He raised his blade, anticipatory tension singing through his body.

Snapping the magical loops into a strangle hold, she echoed Darius's signal. "Now!"

As if dozen of chains moved in tandem, the captured demon rose from the floor, his body jerking into a painful, suspended arc. His scream of combined rage and pain hit mind-numbing decibels.

Gavin's blade moved in a blur of light, finding its target with efficient accuracy. The metal severed tendon and bone. Natasha gritted her teeth and cinched her power tighter. The demon screamed, unable to deflect the deadly combination of Gavin's blow and Natasha's steel will.

Jared's body burst apart in a silent explosion. The pieces evaporated and, for just a moment, both containment spells collapsed inward. Natasha braced as the released essence of the Half-Bound demon refilled the gap left by his body and surged against the spells' barrier.

The magical discharge splattered like a mad artist's temper tantrum, turning the containment spell into a whirling vortex of colorful magic. The light show became a pretty display, hiding the energy's destructive nature. In the center of the mystical snow globe, a figure came into focus.

"Durand, look away!" Natasha's command demanded Gavin's instant obedience as it echoed in a deep and sonorous tone as she and her beast straddled the mortal world and the Side.

She gave a brief thought to the hope Gavin would listen before turning her attention to their captive. Having Gavin look away was for his own sanity, not hers, because what stood trapped between worlds and magic was nothing remotely human, but a mishmash of mind-bending nightmares. Nothing made sense—the features morphing from one horrific visage to the next. Demons drove humans insane for a reason. Their impact on Kyn, well, it differed. Still, she was unwilling to take chances. Drawing on the power flowing through her, she began to turn the magic opaque, hoping to shield Gavin from what lay within.

Inside the spell, the demon's essence glided to face her. Magic didn't take up much room, and the demon stood mere inches from her. Refusing to look away, she met the soulless pits where a blood red flames flickered in inky orbs. A feral intelligence stared back. The murky curtain of magic between them, blurred the monstrous image.

Using the connection they had forged, she checked in. *"Darius?"*

The demon's misshapen maw twisted into a smirk. A long, forked tongue swept obscenely over his rough lips.

"Almost."

"Hurry up," she hissed, the hair on the back of her neck rising as the demon prepared to strike. All it needed was one small chink in her spell, the smallest tear, to escape and hide in any living form. Or, if she was extremely unlucky, in Gavin.

"Don't rush me, woman," Darius snarled.

There was a reason women were so damn good at multi-tasking, they had to compensate for their male counterparts. "Whatever you do, don't let it escape," she told Gavin without looking away. "Otherwise things will get messy."

"And this isn't?"

She ignored Gavin's mutter and reinforced her magic lying under his, just as the demon threw its entire metaphysical weight against the spell. Her magic shuddered. Blood thundered through her head and she shoved back, knowing this much strength meant the demon was drawing on its summoner's will. She was so focused on holding it, she almost missed Darius's mental shout.

With a ruthless twist, she triggered the power hidden within her containment spell. It joined with Darius's to create a lethal wave that echoed through the mortal realm and the Side. Unified, they tore through the Half-Bound demon, demolishing the summoner's chains.

In front of her, the demon's image began to shred as if a gale force wind whipped through the spell, ripping the figure apart, piece by piece. The screams and growls reverberated, vibrating in her bones like a tuning fork.

The move didn't come without a price.

Agony burst into violent life, setting its hooks deep. She gritted her teeth and rode it out, unsure what this unexpected reaction heralded. However, as the Summoner tried to latch on to her in a desperate attempt to replace what he was losing, other more immediate concerns rose. His desperation meant if she didn't move quickly she would lose her current hold in this battle of wills. She and her demon joined their wills, unwilling to bend. For anyone.

A heartbeat, then two and the summoner's greedy grasp, unable to find a purchase, slipped away. She gave Gavin an abrupt, "Hold it until I get back."

Stepping fully into the Side she found the demon cowering at Darius's feet. Magic swarmed the creature in ribbons of ebony, burrowing deep, capturing him in a tight fist. There was a lessening in the magical pressure, allowing her to add her strength to Darius's. The lethal ribbons tightened and the stone room filled with a massive surge of power.

Their captive threw back his head, his throat exposed, an earthly howl escaping. Between one breath and the next, black lightening sliced over his exposed throat. Even as the head began to fall, their combined abilities snuffed the remaining pieces of the demon out, leaving only the echoes of his agonized scream to fade with the dull ache in her head.

The sudden drop of energy in the room intensified the harsh rasps of their breathing as they stood there. Two massive demons, one white, one black, and a pale layer of ash on the floor. Silence filled in the now empty space.

"Well," Darius drawled. "That was fun."

Fun? No, it hadn't been fun, but it had been interesting, in a very unsettling way. Consciously relaxing her jaw, she considered the strength behind the Jared's last escape attempt. There was an unprecedented amount of vehemence behind that effort. A surprising depth that spoke to the summoner's inherent will. Because the summoner made a rookie mistake in failing to garner Jared's entire name, she had underestimated him. It wouldn't happen again.

"Just because he made an error in the initial stages doesn't mean he doesn't know what he's doing."

Stiffening as Darius's voice cut into her thoughts, she glared at him. "Excuse me?"

He tilted his head, those horns catching the shifting light, a small, irritating smile playing at his lips. "You're thinking too loud."

Damn blood bond. How long would it last? She carefully cloaked her thoughts, but shared some of her speculation. "Making such a critical error in the naming would generally indicate a lack of knowledge or experience. Naming is a key component to binding. Why make such a novice mistake?"

Those powerful shoulders shrugged. "Because they are a novice?"

"Or perhaps there are more players than what we are being led to believe?" Especially if this was a Council ploy. They abhorred the simplistic, and leaned toward manipulative and layered. Using someone as a patsy, yes, that wouldn't raise an eyebrow. This could have served as a test, a way to see how strong her hold was on herself and her territory. What better way to monitor it than to set things in motion when one of theirs was already here to lend a helping hand? Her lip curled at the last thought and, without sparing Darius a glance, she stepped back into the mortal realm before her budding anger could erupt.

Unfortunately, Darius was right on her heels. As they materialized in her living room, his hand wrapped around her arm, spinning her around to face him. "I may not have caught all of that," he snarled. "But rest assured, Ms. Bertoi—" He fairly hissed her name. "—I am not some Council toady."

She held his flinty gaze with her own. "That remains to be seen, doesn't it, Mr. Abazi?"

His fingers tightened almost painfully on her arm. "You want proof? Taste the blood, Natasha. It doesn't lie."

And that was exactly what bothered her. Did she dare believe what his unexpected offering could show her? Blood may not lie, but it could hide things. Dangerous things. Once before she trusted a blooded connection. It hadn't ended so well. She lifted her chin, allowing condescension to tilt her lips. "Perhaps." She pulled free of his grip, knowing she escaped only because he let her, and turned to Gavin.

He watched the two of them, his face impassive. "Are you two done?"

Blighted hells, save her from the male species. Holding on to her composure by sheer stubbornness, she gave a brief thought to ripping both of them verbally and physically to shreds just for relief. She refrained. Barely. "You're missing a shadow."

He arched a maddening eyebrow. "She's not too far behind. I'm more interested in what the hell just happened here." He motioned to the shattered remains of her living room and the crumpled body feet away. "And who and why she's here."

"Cleo James." Pity and anger settled heavy in Natasha's stomach. "Sullivan's lover."

Gavin gave a slow blink, weaving a little on his feet. "She seems to be missing some pieces."

"The demon consumed it," Darius answered from behind her.

When Gavin's mouth opened, probably determined to ask more questions, she stopped him with a raised hand. "This is not the time for a lesson on getting to know your Amanusa better."

Cool night air swept through the room, causing the curtains to billow. As the chill seeped over her skin, she gathered the edges of her robe together and tightened the belt. "This demon answered to someone else, a powerful someone else. To ensure Cleo's silence, he consumed the heart. I'm sure when I receive Jamie's report on Sullivan, he'll be missing one as well."

"They were dead," Gavin gritted out. "What does eating their hearts accomplish?"

"It's ensures a demon stays out of a necromancer's reach." It was difficult to keep her voice brisk and unaffected, especially when her own nasty tempered demon prowled under her skin, hungry for retribution. Needing to get away from the room filled with needless death and infuriating testosterone, she went to step around Gavin, drawing both men behind her into the entryway by the front door. "Let me grab you something for that scratch of yours before you stain my floors."

"And it took two to take Cleo out?"

Gavin's question made her pause and turn. "Two what?"

"Half-Bounds or whatever you called that."

"There were no other demons, Gavin." She narrowed her eyes. "Are you sure you haven't loss more blood than you think? And why, exactly, are you bleeding?"

He grimaced. "Little stone freak out front didn't want to

let me in." Before she could probe further, he asked, "Why kill the girl? What purpose does her death serve?"

The urge to leave and investigate his story clawed at her, but she remained still. One crisis at a time. "Other than angering me, nothing."

"Except to serve as an indication that your House may not be happy with your current leadership," Darius drawled.

Spinning on her heel, she took in his calculating consideration and clenched her fists. Lifting her chin, she made sure that her answering smile held nothing remotely friendly. "I don't think it's my House we have to worry about, pet."

CHAPTER 16

G{\small AVIN} {\small SPLIT A LOOK BETWEEN} D{\small ARIUS AND} N{\small ATASHA}, {\small BEFORE} settling on her. "Is that true?"

Natasha gave a negligent shrug. "To those stupid enough to grasp at straws, yes, it could be seen as such."

Gavin's face darkened. Not that it took much considering his initial pale tone. "Dammit—"

Whatever he was going to say was cut off by the front door bursting open in a rush of cold night air and one very irate feminine growl.

"What the hell, Gavin?" Raine's mercurial glance swept over the entryway and landed on him. More specifically, on the red staining his T-shirt. She barely acknowledged Natasha and Darius as she went to stand in front of him, her hands pulling the saturated material away to see the damage. "Couldn't you duck?"

"Got stuck between a rock and a hard place." Curling his arm around her neck, he dropped a brief kiss on top of her head. "You got here fast."

Raine shifted to the side, peering over her shoulder,

silver gaze zeroing in on Natasha. "Got any towels around here?"

Realizing none of her questions would be answered until Raine saw to Gavin, Natasha marched out of the room, throwing over her shoulder, "Let's move to the kitchen."

Maybe she could get a glass of wine while Raine played doctor. In the kitchen, she opened a drawer and removed a small stack of dishtowels. She handed them over to Raine, getting a tiny nod of thanks in return.

"Would've been here faster, but Carys showed up." Raine pressed the wadded towels against Gavin's side as he leaned against a counter, earning his sharp hiss.

A headache picked up behind Natasha's eyes, joining the many questions waiting to be asked. *Where to start?* "Dare I ask where you were?"

"Mulcahy's place."

While Raine had any number of reasons to be at her uncle's, what would be Carys's? "Was she looking for you or something else?"

"I didn't ask." Raine kept her attention on tending to Gavin's injury, but it wasn't enough to hide the slow rising tide of color along her cheekbones.

The need to find that elusive wine pressed closer. Folding her arms over her chest, Natasha leaned against the counter's edge, pointedly ignoring Darius as he settled on a stool at the island with undisguised interest. "What did you do, Raine?"

Raine's lips tightened but she didn't look up. "I didn't do anything. I just didn't have time to be polite while Gavin was busy holding his own against a demented demon."

If Natasha closed her eyes and counted to ten, would it be enough to stop the urge to shake the maddening girl until her teeth rattled? Taking in the press of bone against skin as Raine gritted her teeth, probably not. *Maybe a hundred would help?* "What did you do, McCord?"

"She shoved me into a car created by midgets." The hint of Ireland didn't soften the cutting edge of irritation. Carys Iver stood in the doorway, hands on jean-covered hips, the soft Angora sweater doing nothing to hide the curves underneath. Her red hair was pulled back into a restrained tail, a few curls making mad escape attempts. "No explanation, just growls. Hello, Natasha." Her eyes flashed as they landed on Darius then cooled as she took in the rest of the room's occupants. "Gavin, you're looking a little battered. Explains Raine's lack of effective communication."

Not missing the newest head of house's reaction to the other man in her kitchen, Natasha decided to stir the pot a bit. "Carys, have you met Darius Abazi?"

Carys made her way to Raine and Gavin, giving Darius a quick, dismissive once over. "Mr. Abazi, dare I assume you're a friend of our visiting Councilman?"

And with that one haughty question, Natasha knew that, at some point, Zayn had said or done something to push the normally cordial woman into a temper. Discovering what that something was could work to Natasha's advantage in setting up the Northwest's unified front against the Council—a move seeming more necessary as each minute ticked by.

Unintimidated by her reception, Darius watched them with an amused detachment. "Assumptions can be dangerous."

"Pity the Council doesn't seem to remember that." Nudging Raine out of the way with a small hip bump, Carys removed the now stained towel from Gavin's side. She made a clicking noise, passed the towel to Raine, then met Gavin's gaze. "Brace yourself."

She pressed her hands against the wound. Gavin hissed in a sharp breath. A soft, warm light emerged from Carys's hands. A teasing scent of sun-warmed wood wafted through the room. As the scent and light faded, then disappeared, the tall Fey female stepped back, dusting her hands off. Straightening, she faced Natasha, her green eyes turning into sharp shards of sea glass, the feral beauty of the Fey seeping around the human lines of her face. "Now that we've taken care of that, perhaps someone here would like to explain why there's a dusted gargoyle in your front yard, a dead girl in your living room, and the stench of a Bound demon wafting through your home."

"Gargoyle?" When the regal redhead leveled a cold glare in his direction, Darius stifled his sigh. Whatever Zayn had said or done to Carys, it looked as if Darius would be paying for it now.

Raine bent closer to Gavin, ostensibly checking out Carys's handiwork, while Natasha turned and rummaged in a cabinet. Since the others were busy actively ignoring the exchange, he straightened in his seat, prepared to go out and see the gargoyle in question for himself.

"Sit," Carys snapped. "It's dust. You won't get anything from it." She gathered the bloodied cloths and tossed them in the sink.

Since dust couldn't answer questions, no use wasting his time. He slowly resettled in his chair. Gargoyles were puppets, stone statues given limited will.

Any of the Kyn could tie such a creature to their will, if they knew how. They were useful because, once destroyed, they crumbled into dust, leaving nothing behind to trail back to their handler.

"The girl is Cleo James." Natasha didn't turn around as she answered the second half of Carys's question.

"The name means nothing to me."

"It wouldn't." The slight clink of glass meeting glass preceded the soft shush of liquid being poured as Natasha kept her back to the room. "She was Kevin Sullivan's lover."

"And one of Natasha's people." Gavin's bland tone belied his watchful gaze.

Standing between Gavin and Natasha, Carys rested a hand on the thin lip of counter in front of the sink and studied Natasha's stiff back with a little more care. "You're in the midst of someone's crosshairs, dearest."

The dull thunk of the wine bottle hitting the counter coincided with Natasha's harsh laugh. "Oh, Carys, haven't you learned? If someone's not pissed at you, you aren't doing your job correctly."

"Your job is turning into a godsdamned mess," the redhead grumbled.

Natasha turned around, smile sharp, wine glass in hand, and tipped it to Carys in acknowledgement. "That it is." She leaned against the counter, one arm wrapped around her waist, the other holding her wine. "I'd offer, but this seems to be my last bottle, and I'm a bit selfish."

"How about some answers instead?" Next to Raine, Gavin gingerly straightened, rolling his shoulders. A small wince came and went with the movement.

"Yes, answers would be nice," Natasha murmured, then took a delicate sip of her wine. Lowering the glass, she stared into it as if it held something of great importance.

"Sullivan's death is a direct strike to my position as the Head of the Amanusa. His desire for my seat was common knowledge. Easy enough to arrange his rather messy removal while the esteem Council was in town. What better way to demonstrate the slipping holds of a head of house on her rather volatile people?"

"And Cleo's death?" Raine chimed in.

"Now that one puzzles me." Natasha lifted her head, her indigo gaze resting on Darius, before moving on to the others. "What could she know to be considered worthy of such overkill? She's a bit of a flirt, but not the brightest bulb in the bunch."

Natasha's casual tone didn't fool Darius. Their fading blood tie only allowed the faintest traces of her emotions to seep through in bits and pieces. Vicious bites of fury tainted with a wild hunger for retribution and grief.

To catch even that much indicated a savage emotional storm hiding behind her calm countenance. A storm he understood all too well, because he'd been there a time or two. Leadership and responsibility were harsh mistresses. And when someone under your protection was harmed? Well, that mistress turned into an exacting bitch.

"Whatever she knew," Carys said, "sending a Bound demon after her ensures her silence."

"The demon was Half-Bound."

Darius narrowed his eyes at Natasha's correction. *What was she up to?* The Amanusa rarely spoke about the Bound, zealously guarding the information for obvious reasons, much less discuss Half-Bounds. No one wanted to hand their enemies an open book on how to take your ass out. Not that some of it hadn't leaked. Tonight was proof of that. Still, what game was she playing? Unfortunately, her thoughts remained shrouded from him.

"Shall we test your collective knowledge?" Natasha didn't wait for an answer. "How much do you know of Bindings?"

Gavin folded his arms across his chest. "To bind the demonic nature of an Amanusa, you need a summoner, a cast circle, and their name."

"But if you manage to bind a demon, you best make sure you hold on tight." Raine put her hands against the counter behind her and hitched herself up to take a seat on the hard surface. "There are warning tales of how a Bound can take the tiniest loophole and rip your throat out."

Or other, much worse things, Darius silently added.

"Good start." Natasha carefully set down her wine glass. "Let me increase your education. Binding the essence of an Amanusa is contingent on naming them. If you don't have intimate knowledge of their ancestral names, you will never achieve a fully Bound demon."

Impressed by her artfully crafted explanation, Darius listened to Natasha dance along the razor thin paths of half-truths. Granted, you needed a demon's ancestral name, but it meant nothing if you didn't know their actual bloodline, or have the power to override an individual's will. The small tightening of Carys's mouth indicated she caught Natasha's elegant dodge, but she, too, remained silent. Instead, the Fey turned and began to rinse out the soiled cloths in the sink.

Natasha continued, "A demon's name will anchor their essence to the Side, which allows the summoner full control of the demon. If you miss one piece of their true name, you end up with a Half-Bound demon—"

"This Side," Raine cut in. "Is that where you and Abazi held your little conference with Fahd?"

Natasha gave the woman a nod. "Every demon is dual

natured, much like the shifters, however, our other form only comes out to play in the Side."

"Why?" True curiosity vibrated in Raine's question.

A flash of discomfort tweaked through the fading bond Darius held with Natasha. The unusual sensation triggered that damned latent protective streak from earlier. He stepped in before she could answer. "Have you ever seen a demon's true form?"

As the attention shifted to him, he caught the slight lessening of tension in Natasha's stiff shoulders as she picked up her wine glass.

"You're talking about that weird image they get when you piss them off," Raine said.

Piss them off, challenge them, or anything else that would push an Amanusa to the edge of their control. Something he was sure Raine had plenty of experience with. "That's the one. The Side is the Amanusa's playground," he deliberately used Gavin's earlier analogy, "one most other Kyn avoid as it's easier on their brain and eyes. There, our true forms don't need to be cloaked in understandable illusions."

Raine opened her mouth, but before her question could escape, Gavin cut her off. "That's why you told me to look away."

Natasha raised her glass to Gavin. "I have enough to deal with, adding a temper tantrum from Raine should your brain become a bit scrambled, just isn't worth it."

Raine snarled. Natasha simply smiled and took another sip of wine. It was like watching cats fight—all hisses and claws.

Gavin attempted to get the discussion back on track. "Half-Bound means, what, exactly?"

Surprisingly, the answer came from Carys. "Exactly what it sounds like." She wrung out the wet cloths and turned around. "The demon's essence is partially Bound. If the summoner isn't paying close attention, at some point the demon will strike out, looking to get free. To break the bindings, whether Bound or Half-Bound, the anchors in all three realms must be broken at the same time. And to break the one in the Side, you not only need to be Amanusa, but you need to have enough magical strength to crush the summoner's psychic hold."

Darius watched the Fey woman with a great deal more consideration. She deftly skipped the lethal repercussions if a Half-Bound's Bindings were incorrectly handled. "And how do you have so much information?"

"I've been the chief legal counsel for Taliesin for years." Carys's voice was coolly composed, even as she dried her hands. "Not to mention working by Ryan's side for far longer than that. When you have to deal with four different houses filled with highly dangerous beings, each with their own quirks, such information is a good thing to have."

"I couldn't agree more," Gavin murmured, his attention arrowing on Natasha. "So want to share what about this Half-Bound demon was different, then?"

"Let me guess," Raine hopped down from the counter to stand next to Gavin. "If it took you and Abazi to break through the Binding, we're dealing with a damn powerful summoner, aren't we?"

Natasha's jaw tightened, but she dipped her chin in a sharp nod. The tension in the kitchen began to climb. Enough so that Darius pushed to his feet, unwilling to sit and watch the impending storm—amusing though it would be.

"How powerful?" Raine went to take a step forward, but Gavin's grip on her wrist brought her to a halt.

Natasha's spine straightened. Carefully setting the wine glass on the counter, the arrogant demon queen made a comeback. "Not powerful enough, considering I'm still here and Jared isn't."

"Jared?" Gavin asked.

"Jared Pick," Darius supplied coming up beside Natasha. "Ring any bells?"

Gavin frowned. "No, why?"

Darius shrugged. "Just curious if you had run across the name during your investigation into Mulcahy's death."

"Why? Worried the name might lead back to your partner on the Council?" Finished drying her hands, Carys tossed the towel aside and confronted Darius, resentment and suspicion clear in the feral delicacy of her face.

And there it was—the first true glimpse of the Northwest's leanings. Anticipation hummed. "Zayn had no part in Mulcahy's death. However, the same can't be said of you and yours, now can it?" His gaze swept over those gathered, finally landing on Natasha. "Rumors abound, darling, and your name keeps popping up."

Those intriguing eyes narrowed, a flame of pure fury igniting deep within. "Yes, rumors abound, Mr. Abazi. Rumors and coincidences. Take for instance the sudden appearance of two very old, very strong demons in my territory just as the most vocal opponent to my seat is found torn apart in a very blatant way. Then one of my younger demons is trapped in a clumsily executed, but cleverly planned Binding, one that requires a great deal of power, power none in my house could wield unless they worked together. Something they've yet to accomplish on mere agenda items, much less the complexity involved in a Binding."

Hiding his amusement at her attack, Darius held the fuming queen's gaze with complete unconcern, curious where her deft mind would take her. "You think Zayn or myself did that to Jared?"

"What I think," she all but purred, "is that to sit upon the Council demands not only a certain arrogance, but an unprecedented strength. A strength you or Zayn could easily disguise. The same strength behind the summoner's hold on Jared."

"Am I missing something? Because I'm damn sure I was right next to you, trying to take his ass out."

"Yet, here you stand, no worse for wear, while the bodies of my people begin to pile up."

Seen from that angle, yes, he could understand her suspicions. But he knew damn good and well that Half-Bound demon had no intention of sparing him or the infuriating woman glaring at him. "And what do I gain by creating such an abomination?"

"Leverage, pet. What better way to undermine my leadership than to force me into unfriendly scrutiny, by humans and Kyn alike." While she didn't move from her relaxed pose, her voice took on a dangerous depth. "Of the three American Kyn regions, the Northwest holds the most lethal of our people and the closest working relationship with the Division and the U.S. Government. I'm not unaware of our perceived influence with the humans or the threat the Council imagines we pose. It would not be beyond them to send in one, if not two, agents to wreak havoc under my roof."

Her persistence in insinuating he was nothing more

than a Council tool was beginning to piss him off. "I do not work for the Council."

"But Zayn does," she snapped.

"That means nothing."

Those periwinkle eyes locked on him, an incandescent fury burning within. "According to your blood still whispering in my ear, it means everything, Mr. Abazi."

CHAPTER 17

"Enough!" Gavin's rough command cut through the rising tension, but not before Natasha caught the flash of awareness in Darius's eyes. Her lips curled. Poor pet. *Did he really think his secrets were safe with me?*

Oblivious to their silent exchange, Gavin continued, impatience lending a sharp edge to his words. "There are plenty of individuals trying to rip us apart. Let's not give them hand. Considering what I walked into tonight, I'm thinking whoever has it in for you, Natasha, has no qualms about taking out Darius as well."

The air behind her shifted as Gavin moved to her side. Only then did she release Darius's gaze and turn to the younger man. "Appearances can be deceiving, Gavin."

He didn't back off. "Think about it, Natasha. If I hadn't shown up, there's no way the two of you alone could have stopped Jared."

Fury and frustration did not make for a happy demon, and hers was more than willing to come out and play. The air around her began to waver as her more volatile nature pushed against her frayed control, but the brave boy kept going.

"You said it yourself. The spell's anchor had to be cut in all three realms. Logic dictates that whoever sent this Jared after you, really didn't give a damn who else he took out."

Behind Gavin, Carys spoke up. "The spell that killed Ryan was meant for Vidis."

"That spell and tonight's little get together have one thing in common," Raine said. "Each one would eliminate a Northwest leader."

Natasha leaned around Gavin to pin the girl with a narrow-eyed glare. "Then they should have sent more than one Half-Bound demon to do the job."

"But they did." Darius's comment brought everyone's attention back to him. Those startling ice-blue eyes were fixed on Natasha with unnerving intensity. "The summoner tried to trap you."

She stiffened. How in the blighted hells did he know that?

Wicked intent curved his lips under the dark goatee. "The blood tie is a two way street, darling."

Forcing her spine to relax and her mind away from his implications, she said, "Tried being the operative word here."

Raine came up beside Gavin. "What the hell is this blood thing you two keep referring to?"

Unwilling to stay trapped between the three, Natasha placed her palm against Darius's bare chest, trying to ignore his body heat seeping through her skin, or the reaction it invoked. She dug her nails in, just enough to bite, and pushed.

Humor softened the challenging edge of his mouth, but he stepped back, allowing her an escape route.

"It's a blood-tie, dear." She edged around Darius then made her way to the bay window where a small table nestled, keeping her back to the others. "It's a temporary psychic connection two demons can utilize to communicate."

"How temporary?" Raine pushed.

"The duration depends on the amount of blood taken. As does the depth of the connection." It served no purpose to go into details she preferred not to share. Besides, the faint connection she could sense between Darius and Zayn was something she wanted to explore privately, without an audience.

"Should we be worried about this link?" Carys's cool query wove through the kitchen.

Darius's dark chuckle answered. "Never fear, our connection fades by the minute. Your demon queen is safe from me and my supposed nefarious intentions."

And wasn't that a shame? Some secret part of her whispered, even as she kept her attention focused on the inky dance of the dead of morning outside the glass. Tonight's events were piling up fast and furious. Her demon surged against her self-imposed chains, until it threatened to swamp the calculating logic of the woman she needed to be. Taliesin could not afford its leader to react instinctively, not now when so many vultures were circling.

"Natasha can take care of herself. We just don't want the Council whining if one of theirs comes back with a boo-boo." Gavin's dry response made her lips tilt just a bit.

"I'm sure Zayn is perfectly fine," Darius drawled, unruffled by Gavin's not so subtle dig.

"Considering the nature of the attacks we've been under, it might be best to double check on Zayn's wellbeing." Natasha had no qualms using Darius's suspicious nature against him if it got him out of her house. The silence behind her rippled out to lap against her spine. Slowly turning, she met Darius's unsettling gaze, refusing to give under his cool appraisal.

"Threats?" Soft menace lingered under his question. Around him, barely visible, the air wavered. He set a hand against the counter, the silver ring on his finger catching the light.

Seemed she wasn't the only one riding a thin line tonight. As fun as it would be to continue poking, a cautionary voice held her back. No matter what Darius proclaimed, he and Zayn had a connection. One that would be unwise to ignore. And, yet...

Maybe she was banking too much on Darius's possible relationship with Ryan, the one hinted at by his ring. Ryan never named his link to the Council, but if it was Darius, could she reestablish his alliance? It would benefit not just her, but the Northwest. His anger and need for retribution at Ryan's death seemed real. Predatory, lethal, and shrouded in secrets was nothing new in their world, but her instincts hummed he would make a vital ally.

And if you're wrong? that insidious voice whispered. Hells knew, she made the mistake of trusting her instincts before. Now, with the weight of Taliesin on her shoulders, screwing up was not an option. Exhaustion and worry tugged at her. She held so little information on him. If she made the wrong choice the fallout would be nothing short of disastrous. Still...

"No, pet, no threats." For once, her endearment held no mocking bite. "Go, check on Zayn."

The air around Darius calmed as he studied her. Thoughts raced over his face, too fast to be recognized, leaving behind his familiar, arrogant mask. "We're not finished."

Now, who was issuing threats? His overbearing tone scraped along her waning patience but she refused to give in to the need to snarl back. "There's nothing to finish."

His only answer was a slow, decadent grin.

She fought back the rise of color as heat that had nothing to do with anger, simmered in her veins.

He turned away, gave the others a slight nod, and strode out of the kitchen.

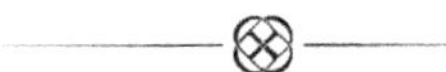

After Darius headed upstairs, Natasha turned to Gavin. "Before we get into what brought you to my door at such an hour, I need to take care of a few things."

He looked beyond her to the devastated remains of her living room. "A cleanup crew?"

"Top of my list," she murmured. "I'll make a call upstairs."

"At least we don't have to worry about nosy neighbors." Raine crossed the kitchen and headed toward what remained of the living room window.

"No, the wards would've dampened the sound." Which reminded her, she'd have to reestablish the damaged house wards. She shifted the items on her mental to-do list as she started for the stairs.

"Natasha, we'll need someplace private to talk."

The heavy weight of seriousness in Gavin's comment stopped her. Turning, she considered his somber expression. "There's a library on the other side of the house. It's far enough away from here to ensure privacy."

And her wards would still be intact to let her know if her current houseguest wandered too close.

He nodded and trailed after Raine.

Natasha turned back to the stairs. Her hand reached for the railing and she was surprised to see a small tremor.

"I'm sorry about your home."

Carys's soft sympathy created an unwanted pressure behind Natasha's eyes. Damn, she must be more tired than she thought. Delicately clearing her throat, she said, "It's merely a structure, it can be rebuilt."

A truth, though the ache in her heart seemed as raw as the splintered wood and shattered glass marring the room behind her. Needing distance and solitude, if only for the few moments necessary to get dressed, she continued up the stairs, spine straight.

Once in her room, she collapsed into a chair and pulled her feet up under her. For a moment, she soaked in the silence. When her wards vibrated against her skin, indicating Darius's departure, she blew out a soft breath, some of her tension bleeding from her shoulders.

The fading whispers of Darius's blood gathered on the edge of her thoughts. Not strong enough to be heard clearly, but enough to tease. She let them linger, knowing that, given enough time, the pieces would fall into place. He unsettled her on more than one level, and right now she couldn't afford the distraction. His leaving gave her a chance to find her footing in the deceptive landscape taking shape.

She needed to call Jamie in for cleanup, but did she really want another person to invade her home? Not that she believed Jamie had anything to do with what happened tonight, but someone did. Between Sullivan's and Cleo's death, the discontented whispers in her house would grow into rumblings. If Cleo's death got out, too many of the Kyn would see only what they were meant to see—Natasha's slipping grip on her people.

Perhaps, it would be best if she took Cleo's body to the Side, just until she could get a lead on who was behind the deaths.

What could that child possibly have known to be considered such a threat? To send a Half-Bound demon was overkill. If they sent it solely after Natasha, that she could understand. But, Cleo? It made no sense.

She gave a soft, inelegant snort. As if attributing common sense to whoever was behind this was an option. Look at who they choose to Bind. Jared was such a young demon, not known for traveling with the older crowd. The mistake of not fully naming him showed a lack of age. Combined with the fact, that Jared knew the individual who set the Binding in place, pointed to someone he knew. But it contradicted the amount of strength behind the Binding.

Could someone be using a younger demon as a patsy? Maybe. While it didn't ring true with what little she knew of Darius or Zayn, it didn't mean it wouldn't hold true for someone else. The power behind the summoner had been strong, stronger than she had expected. And that amount of power could only come with age. A great deal of age. Maybe paranoia or past experiences, or both, were raising their pesky heads, but she was more inclined to think whoever the puppet master was, he—or she—was not one of the Northwest Kyn.

The dull sounds of a hammer echoed from downstairs, dragging her out of her uselessly spinning thoughts. Gavin and Raine must have found the toolshed in the back. She rubbed a hand over her face, the grit of dust scraping over her skin. Shower first, then she'd take Cleo's body to the Side. Afterward, she'd deal with whatever Gavin brought to her door.

Upstairs in the room he claimed as his own, Darius crossed into the Side, both man and demon happy to leave his human form behind. The urges the Half-Bound raised still churned under his skin, leaving a dangerous craving behind. Here, where the Amanusa could straddle the human and Kyn worlds, he could travel between Natasha's home and Zayn's hotel unseen, while allowing his more primal nature a brief respite from civility's demands.

Besides, the early morning darkness still chased the dawn, its win a few hours away. Time enough to touch base with Zayn, especially since he owed the Councilman a report on the Wraith's meeting.

Had that only been a few hours ago?

Between the meeting, Sullivan's murder, and the Half-Bound demon, time had warped. Too much, too soon, and no time to process the ramifications. However, one thing was crystal clear. The one hunting the Northwest had their next target. Natasha.

Normally he wouldn't have budged at Natasha's demand to leave, but considering the three individuals staying with her, his concern at a second strike was diminished. Rising in its place was another worry. Had whoever targeted the Northwest decided to turn their attention to the Council's representative?

Unlike Natasha, he knew exactly where Zayn's loyalties

lay. Yet those loyalties wouldn't matter if the one behind the current string of bodies managed to add Zayn's to the pile of corpses littering the Northwest. If a Council member was murdered, there would be no more need for games. The Northwest Kyn would be eliminated. Possible problems solved.

Using the strange pathways between realms shortened his trip considerably. He put his thoughts on pause as he approached the street where Zayn's hotel stood. He took his time to scan the surrounding area from his hidden position. Quiet reigned.

Satisfied that he was alone, Darius donned his human skin and stepped out into the heavy shadows under a burnt-out streetlight. Within minutes, he was through the deserted lobby and in the elevator. It took him to the top floor, where he made a beeline to one of the two doors lining the expansive hall.

Zayn opened the door before Darius could knock. He stood aside, allowing Darius entry. Darius strode down the elegantly appointed hall and into a warmly lit living room. Behind him the door closed with the sound of the security bolt latching into place.

Leave it to Zayn to get the best suite at a hotel. The fire in the far corner snapped and curled over the logs in a quiet frenzy, flanked by comfortably elegant chairs book-ending a small table.

"You've been busy." The dry observation came from behind him, even as Zayn slipped past and headed to the built-in bar, a cup in hand.

Darius settled into one of the two chairs facing the fireplace. "A bit early, isn't it?"

A cup, heat wafting from it, appeared over his shoulder as Zayn handed it to him. "It's tea, you idiot." The

Councilman took the other chair, casually propping his foot on his knee as he took a sip of his own. "Although I wouldn't mind something stronger, the personalities here are..." he hesitated, obviously searching for the right description, "...challenging."

"You expected open arms?" Darius took a sip, letting Zayn's unruffled presence chase the lingering worry from his bones. The taste and scent of the strong, black tea was comforting in its familiarity.

A wry twist of lips echoed the spark in Zayn's gold eyes. "Not quite."

"Good." Darius stretched out his legs and balanced his cup on his stomach. "When did you talk to Carys Iver?"

A low hum escaped Zayn and his long fingers rose to rub the bridge of his nose. "About the time you were meeting the Wraiths. Why?"

Darius studied him. "Whatever you said sent her to Mulcahy's place tonight. She ran into Raine." If he didn't know the other man so well, Darius might have missed his tiny wince.

"Perhaps I mishandled things," Zayn muttered.

Wasn't this interesting? Mister Suave and Sophisticated managed to strike out with the Amazonian redhead. "You losing your touch?"

Zayn grunted. "After dealing with those close mouthed bastards, Vidis and Cheveyo, my approach was harsher than planned."

Raising his cup, Darius hid his grin at Zayn's grumpy response.

Not one to wallow in frustration, Zayn lightened his tone. "You'd think these chiefs would have more respect for their Council members. Instead, they're almost as arrogant as we are."

"And you like that?"

"Admire it, actually." Zayn set his cup on the small table perched between them. "They're going to need every iota of arrogance and confidence in the face of what's coming. Unlike the Council, the Northwest seems prepared to do what they must to protect their people. Some of my associates could learn a thing or two from them."

There was no missing the disgust and contempt underlying the words. "You could always step down, Zayn," Darius said. Only their centuries-long friendship allowed him the ability to state such a treasonous suggestion. One did not step down from the Council.

"No, I made a promise. I'll see it through." The weight of the promise was reflected in his serious tone and implacable expression.

"Still determined to convince the Northwest Kyn you're just another Council blowhard?" Darius's lack of patience with the devious subterfuge was evident in his harsh question.

Unperturbed, Zayn answered, "It's a necessary evil. For now."

Silently, Darius disagreed, but maybe after he explained what happened tonight, he could change Zayn's mind. Studying the set lines on his companion's face, he revised that opinion. Zayn was nothing if not stubborn. "Your presence seems to have prompted someone into action."

Zayn arched an eyebrow. "Mine? Are you certain it's not yours?"

"Not this time. Kevin Sullivan was killed tonight."

Zayn frowned in thought. The expression was familiar and an indication that he was sifting through his mental files. "One of the Wraiths and a vocal upstart in Natasha's court." He tilted his head. "Did she finally get tired of his mouth?"

This time it was Darius's turn to frown. "That's what someone wants everyone to think."

"You don't believe it." A statement, not a question.

Darius shook his head. "No." Killing one of her own for disobedience was not out of the realm of possibility, but that spell wrapped like ivy around Sullivan? No, that belonged to something older, darker. Besides, Natasha had a point. After seeing what was left of the girl and dealing with the Half-Bound demon, Darius felt chances were damn good that Sullivan's heart would be missing as well. A very brutal, heavy-handed way to cover one's tracks.

Besides, Natasha would never stoop to a Binding. Such soulless slavery revealed a narcissistic need for power. She might be many things, but narcissistic was not one of them. Plus, there was a wisp of familiarity in that spell. The problem was, he couldn't quite catch it. And that was worrisome.

"Why not?" Zayn steepled his fingers under his chin, his gaze direct, calculating. When Darius remained silent, he pushed. "According to all accounts, Sullivan was a pompous pain in the ass. Natasha is the epitome of ruthless practicality and well versed in the art of manipulation. Convincing you of her innocence?" He answered his own question with a Gallic shrug. "Much like Sullivan's death, it would be far from problematic."

"Exactly." Ignoring his companion's not-so-subtle dig at his fascination with the woman, Darius set his almost empty cup aside and pushed to his feet, the need to prowl propelling him forward. "Sullivan was nothing more than a pesky nuisance. Natasha doesn't believe in short term solutions. His death might shut him up, but it would only serve to strengthen his complaints. Natasha isn't stupid. She wouldn't give him that much influence."

"Or you're giving her too much credit."

Darius stilled and glared at his oldest friend. "If Sullivan was the only new development, I might consider it, but he's not." Unlike the Northwest leaders, he and Zayn had access to some very disturbing information, information but no proof. "We have another problem."

Zayn straightened and leaned forward, his attention caught by Darius's seriousness. "We have many problems. Which one are you worried about?"

"The one behind Sullivan's death? He killed again. This time, Sullivan's lover."

"How do you know they're one and the same?"

"Because the Half-Bound demon ate both their hearts."

"Half-Bound?" Zayn's olive-tone complexion paled, his lips thinned, but a baleful spark blurred the red rings in his gold irises. "Start talking." The command came out in a near hiss.

"We were attacked." Keeping the details short and sweet, Darius related all that occurred at Natasha's home. "It took both Natasha and I to banish it. At one point, the summoner tried to take Natasha."

Shock widened Zayn's eyes then they narrowed with speculation. "How do you know?"

And here was where Darius put his trust in a centuries-old friendship and something much older, because his answer could cause all sorts of backlash. Backlash not even their well-hidden family tie could block, because Zayn wasn't just his friend, he was also Darius's brother. Which meant tonight's actions could ripple farther than intended. "We shared blood."

With a muttered curse, Zayn surged to his feet. "What

the hell are you thinking, Darius?" He dragged his hands through his hair, the gold strands glinting under the flickering firelight. "Such a tie could destroy all our carefully laid plans."

"What would you have me do?" Darius snarled, going toe to toe with the last of his family. "Let a Half-Bound demon escape? Once we destroyed his bindings, there was no choice but to combine our abilities to ensure he couldn't escape. If we didn't, and he got loose, we would have more than the humans on our asses. A possessed mortal or Kyn would bring attention even the Council wouldn't want."

Zayn spun away, his shoulders a solid line. "And blithely handing the reigning power of the Northwest Kyn an inside track into my plans is what we need?"

"The blood tie is already fading, Zayn. If she didn't make the connection by now, she won't." He didn't blink at the small lie. Natasha had picked up something, but how much remained a mystery. However, as he watched his brother fight for composure, Darius knew it could work in their favor. "You wanted an ally."

Zayn spun around. "An ally, not a damn psychic Peeping Tom, Darius." He blew out a hard breath and dragged a hand over his face, wiping away his expression. "And the summoner?"

"Far from a novice. But something bothers me."

"What?"

"They didn't name Jared's maternal line. It gave us a loophole." Darius paused, letting Zayn process. "It's a mistake someone with that much power shouldn't have made."

They both fell quiet, each lost in their own thoughts. Finally Zayn broke the silence. "What are you thinking?"

Darius's stomach tightened. He didn't want to put his

suspicions into words. It was too much like tempting fate. Yet, no matter how he twisted and turned the facts, he couldn't escape it. "I think we're dealing with more than one person."

Zayn grimaced, blowing out a hard breath. "Yeah, me, too." He dropped his head. "Fuck me."

CHAPTER 18

NATASHA RETURNED FROM HER TRIP TO THE SIDE WITH CLEO'S body to find a sheet of plywood covering the hole in her living room. She spoke briefly to Jamie and Fahd who were working on cleaning up the remaining debris. "Sullivan's house?"

"Clean," Fahd answered, his dark eyes steady, his anger from hours earlier tucked neatly away. "He's on a prolonged business trip, should his neighbors ask."

She nodded. "Jamie, reschedule my morning meetings, please. I won't be in until the afternoon."

"Will do." Jamie's gaze slid behind her and narrowed. "Natasha?"

She turned her head at Gavin's voice.

He stood near the back hall leading to the library. "When you're ready."

"I'll be there in a minute."

He gave her a short nod, turned, and walked away.

"What the hell is going on, Natasha?"

Jamie's question brought Natasha's head back around.

He and Fahd stood in front of her, Fahd's attention on Gavin's retreating back, Jamie's focus solely on her.

"That, my dear, is what I'm about to find out."

Jamie frowned. "Do you want me to come with you?"

She gave him a small smile. "I'll be fine, Jamie. Once you and Fahd are done, go home. We can talk more tomorrow."

Jamie's mouth pressed into a tight line and his hands curled into fists. "I don't like this. Where's Darius?"

Her patience rapidly fading under his continued questions, she snapped, "Gone."

He blinked. "Excuse me?"

Exasperated, she threw up her hands. "I didn't kill him. He left."

"Before or after whatever redecorated your living room?" Fahd asked softly.

Interesting. She didn't mistake Fahd's shifting suspicions for caring. Demons never took kindly to outsiders. "After."

"Was this attack aimed at you or at him?"

Curious to unravel Fahd's thinking, she asked, "Why couldn't it be both?"

"Both?" He frowned. "No, that doesn't make sense. You alone would be difficult to defeat. The two of you, together?" He shook his head. "What did they send? A Bound?"

"Please," Jamie scoffed. "If that was the case, there wouldn't be a room left to clean up." He and Fahd shared a look. "When are you expecting him back?"

"If I'm truly blessed, when Hell freezes over." She cocked her head, studying the two demons before her. Niggling whispers circled her thoughts. How close was the one behind her headaches? Could they be standing in front of her? "Why the sudden interest in his social calendar?"

This time it was Fahd who answered. "With an individual such as him in our territory, we would rather be overly cautious than caught unawares."

As much as she wanted to pursue this conversation, another waited for her. "He's busy checking on the well-being of our visiting Councilman."

Jamie smirked. "Must suck to be a babysitter. Wonder what his hourly rate is?"

The snide twist in Jamie's tone rubbed her the wrong way. "I dare you to ask."

Jamie's smirk died a quick death, but the red rings around his eyes began to glitter. "Might be fun."

She smiled. "Let me know. I'd love to watch."

Resentment chased arrogance and left behind a frustrated male ego. "Maybe I'd surprise you."

Teasing really wasn't nice, but what crawled under her skin wasn't feeling nice toward anyone tonight. "Maybe, maybe not." Unwilling to indulge her nature, she turned and left Fahd and Jamie without another word. It was safer that way.

Natasha stepped into her library to find Raine and Carys already seated. Raine was on the small reading sofa, while Carys laid claim to the nearest of two plush reading chairs standing on either side. Gavin perused the bookcases stretched along the walls, where shelf after shelf held multi-hued bindings.

Natasha headed for the chair framed by the moonlit window, leaving Gavin to close the door behind her. "Jamie and Fahd should be finished shortly," she said.

Gavin crossed the room. "Something's happened with the investigation of Mulcahy's death."

Tension tightened her stomach, but Natasha forced her

body to relax into the overstuffed chair. "Something you don't want to share with Darius."

"Unless you're entirely certain he's not behind our latest string of disasters."

"No," she murmured, allowing her doubts voice. "Not entirely. What happened?"

"Axel Kayzer is missing."

The unexpected name startled her, but she put two and two together. "The Wraith you assigned to track down Dmitri's movements?"

Gavin settled next to Raine on the small reading sofa and gave a short nod. "He was following up on a few names linked to Vidis's brother. He's gone dark."

Natasha tucked her feet under her. "Who was Axel tracking?"

"We don't know exactly," Raine hedged.

Gavin stretched out his legs, crossing them at the ankle. "Last time he checked in he mentioned he had a couple of possibilities, but was having a hard time finding them credible. He planned on digging a little more before he shared the names. He indicated that if he shared them and they turned out to be false leads, the fallout could be catastrophic."

"He must have given you some indication of who they were." Carys reclined deeper into the chair opposite Natasha. "I find it hard to believe that if there was even the smallest chance the leads could pan out, he wouldn't have given them to you."

Natasha agreed. "He may not have given you specific names, but I have no doubt the two of you have ideas of who he was following."

Gavin and Raine shared a long look, then Gavin took a deep breath. "We have it narrowed down to three:

Leopold DiMarcco, Corwin Westbrooke, and Zayn Aimeric."

Each name was a power in their own right and each brought serious complications. Those complications made Natasha's demonic nature sit up in eager anticipation. "You do realize that, with those three, calling the fallout catastrophic is putting it mildly." She drummed her nails against the fabric covered armrest, arranging and rearranging the newest pieces of the puzzle.

"Information on DiMarcco and Westbrooke has been hard to come by," Raine said.

"Understandable," Carys murmured, sharing a knowing glance with Natasha. "But Natasha is right. If any of those names is behind this mess, we better have solid proof of their involvement or there will be no more Northwest Kyn."

"It won't matter if we have proof or not." Natasha forced her voice around the ball of sick certainty growing in her gut as the pieces began to click. "If they are behind this, we have only one chance at survival." One very slim, very dangerous chance, especially if she put the pieces together wrong.

Carys's face remained grimly composed even as her skin paled. She flicked her fingers.

Magic singed Natasha's skin causing her to hiss. "What are you doing, Carys?"

"Silencing spell," the woman answered, her gaze fierce. "You want to speak about taking out the members of the Council, you best ensure there are no ears nearby. Especially considering who is sleeping under your roof."

"Or those currently on cleanup duty in your living room," Raine said.

Reaching for her dwindling patience, Natasha refrained from splintering the uncomfortable magic. Instead, she reinforced it with a barrier of her own. Carys was correct to be cautious, because their upcoming discussion could not be overheard. "Why those three?" Natasha directed her question to Gavin.

"All three are European based Kyn, yet in the last year, they've made several trips to the States."

"That's not unusual, Gavin." Time to play devil's advocate. "As the oldest member and reigning leader of the Council, Leopold DiMarcco may reside in Europe, but his business interests stretch over various countries, including America. Corwin Westbrooke isn't Council, but he is the key liaison between the European Kyn and their human governments. Politics or business could draw him our way. As for Zayn, between the Southwest Alpha's disagreement with Vidis and Ryan's death, the Council has every right to send in a representative to evaluate us. That they chose him is not surprising. That he brought Darius with him, also understandable as he serves as a bodyguard and evaluator. You'll need more than a series of easily explained trips to lay at their door."

"It's not the trips, so much as who they met on those trips and the timing." Raine leaned forward. "Did you know that Westbrooke met with head of Talbot Foundation, Jonah Talbot, in late August, a month before Talbot approached Mulcahy to find out who was behind the deaths of his employees? Why? What interest would the European Kyn liaison have with the son of the man rumored to have experimented on Kyn?" Those eerie silver eyes focused on her with unblinking intensity. "Then in January, DiMarcco met with a hush-hush sub-committee in Washington, DC. According to the information we found, that committee was attended by key military figures, including one General Matthew Cawley. The same man who was working with Dr. Lawson under Talbot's nose to create a super soldier based upon Kyn genetics."

"And who did Zayn meet?" Natasha asked.

Raine hadn't lumped him in with DiMarcco and Westbrooke. *Why?* Natasha had her own suspicions, but best to wait and see what they found first.

Gavin shared a look with Raine then answered. "He covers his tracks better than others. We found signs of a trip to Vancouver, British Columbia, around early June of last year, and another to Denver a couple weeks into December. No indication of who he was meeting or why he picked those places."

"Aimeric wasn't alone. He had a shadow, the same one who followed him here," Raine took over. "We have no idea how long they've been in town, but they only made themselves known after Mulcahy's death. Who's to say our problems didn't start because of their presence." Her lips lifted into a feral grin. "I don't believe in coincidences."

Neither did Natasha. But, there were things these two didn't know. "We need proof."

Raine stiffened, but Gavin's touch on her arm kept in her place. He looked at Natasha. "What kind of proof?"

"The infallible kind," Carys answered, drawing everyone's attention. "The kind that when presented to the other Council members can't be argued with or twisted." Although she remained coolly composed, the green of her eyes had deepened, something old and calculating swirling in their depths. "Identifying the one behind Ryan's death would be a grand start. Looking to the Council for our prey is tricky. They don't like to see too much power in one individual's hands, especially since they spend so much time trying to snatch it out of each other's grasp."

Raine's smile was sharp and nasty. "They must have

hated it when Mulcahy created the Wraiths and Northwest Kyn, then."

Natasha found Raine's vindictive pride amusing. "The Council's relief when Ryan left to head west was short lived. They were not pleased when they realized what he was building here. But Ryan is the only one I've ever known who's held multiple positions of power at one time."

"The Wraith's captaincy and Head of Fey House," Gavin said.

"And Taliesin," Carys added. "You hold those three positions, and you hold the majority of political power of the Kyn in America."

"And the Council would definitely not like that," Gavin mused. He turned to Natasha. "Is that why you set your sights on the captaincy?"

She gave him a serene smile. "I never said I wanted it. I only provided alternate options for consideration."

Raine muttered something that sounded very close to "Manipulative bitch," but Natasha chose to ignore it.

"Yet you still managed to gain one out of the three," came Gavin's dry rejoinder.

"True, but I have my hands full with my own house and Taliesin's CEO position." She slid a mocking glance at Carys. "I've never envied Carys her position."

Cary's quiet laugh would have had sent chills skittering over a lesser woman's skin. "Had you asked earlier, I may have given it to you. There were those under my roof who felt older, more experienced individuals should be sitting in my place." Anger glittered in the sea-glass green of her eyes, and her smile held a cutting edge. "However, Ryan was no one's fool. He made it quite clear who he expected to follow in his footsteps. Something I took great pains to remind them of earlier tonight." She met Natasha's gaze and a dark satisfaction crawled behind the beauty. "He wasn't one to leave things to chance."

"A leader never does," Natasha murmured, recalling all the late night discussions with Ryan. The hundreds of "what-if" conversations and solutions they'd shared, the goals and dreams they'd held of what the Northwest Kyn would be. All of it coalesced into a quiet clarity. If she was to lead the Northwest Kyn, it was time to ensure Ryan's legacy wasn't torn apart by petty aspirants and jealous, power-hungry ghouls.

Carys inclined her head, losing some of that feral rage.

"We're getting off track," Raine growled. "Let's get back to these trips of Aimeric's. Just because his trips aligned with Mulcahy's doesn't mean they met."

Carys clear her throat. "As much as I'd love to pin this on Councilman Aimeric or Mr. Abazi, I think we can remove them from our list." She looked to Natasha, a shared knowledge flaring to life.

"Agreed." Natasha knew where Carys was headed. Her fingers slowed their dance against the chair's armrest.

"Why?" Gavin spoke over Raine's growl, going so far as to put a restraining arm around her shoulders.

Natasha let Carys take over the conversation. Better Gavin and Raine hear it from Ryan's successor, than from her. They wouldn't trust her. Wisely so.

"Ryan has been grooming me as his replacement for a while now," Carys explained. "The last few years, he turned more and more of the House matters over to me. It left him able to concentrate on Taliesin and his other interests. However, there was one aspect he refused to hand over, Council meetings." A small tightening around her mouth indicated Ryan's decision had not set well with her. Still, heir apparent or not, you did not argue with your head of house. "The Council meets twice a year, Midsummer in June and Winter Solstice in December. Ryan took numerous trips within the last year, some documented, some not."

Raine straightened in her seat. "Are you telling us those two were meeting with Mulcahy? Before the Council meetings?"

Carys's smile was serene and full of secrets. "As I said before, when it came to Council matters, Ryan was completely hands on. While I can't confirm who he met, what I can attest to is that two of those undocumented trips coincide with the dates in question."

"Son of a bitch." Raine ran a hand through her hair, loosening black strands from the long braid. Veiled thoughts swam behind her composed expression, changing the gray of her eyes to mercury silver. As her hand dropped to rest on Gavin's thigh, she turned to Natasha. "Before Abazi showed up, we thought Aimeric was the one in the Order. However, Abazi is the one wearing an Order ring, not Aimeric. How do we know which one to trust?"

"Order?" Trepidation turned Carys's question sharp. "For goddess's sake, Natasha, is Darius with the Order?"

Natasha raised her hand to halt Carys's outrage. "Yes." She lowered her hand and turned her attention to Raine. "Darius."

Raine's lip curled at her answer. "I told you before, Natasha, you put too much stock in a supposed friendship."

"And I told you, his connection to the Order could supersede even the Council. I still believe that."

"Why?" Raine pushed. "What do you know that we don't?"

How to explain the secrets gathering strength in her mind, even now after the blood-tie she shared with Darius remained nothing more than a remembered taste. "Nothing worth sharing just yet, but it shouldn't take me much to get the information we need. Darius and Zayn are connected. It's just a matter of figuring out how. Until then, we are best served approaching Darius first."

Amusement lightened Gavin's eyes, edging the darkness back a bit. "You think you can get Darius to spill his guts?"

She arched an eyebrow.

He snorted. "Natasha, I realize you believe most men are more malleable than clay, but Darius isn't one of them. You're treading dangerous ground going up against him."

A little miffed at Gavin's statement, Natasha sharpened her voice. "Are you insinuating I'm just another beautiful face?"

This time, a true laugh escaped the man watching her. "I would never dare say that, but you may have met your match with him."

"I don't know," Raine said. "My money's on Natasha."

"I'm with Raine," Carys chimed in. "Males too often underestimate the predatory nature of females."

Darius didn't strike Natasha as one of those males. "Darius is no one's fool. His reaction to Ryan's death is not faked. Something tells me he allows the Council to believe they have sway over his actions, so long as it benefits him."

Carys frowned. "Ryan's death, planned or not, brought Darius and Zayn to our door, and that benefits the Council. If our leaders are proven unable to control the escalating situation the Council can justify sweeping in and taking over. They would claim it's in everyone's best interest."

Natasha considered her words. "It would make perfect sense if you're a politician, not a warrior."

"Which rules out Abazi." Raine's hand flexed against Gavin's thigh. "But not Aimeric."

He looked down at her, a subtle intensity in their exchange. Silence trickled in, and Natasha let Gavin think. She could practically hear his brain speed through the information at his disposal. Finally, he lifted his head, and brought his attention back to Natasha. "Darius says he's here to evaluate the Wraiths and find out who killed Mulcahy. So why not use that to our advantage?"

"By what? Giving him Zayn's name as our prime suspect? It's obvious the two must work together. What would that accomplish?"

"Nothing, which is why we don't give him any names. It's too dangerous. We know the Council is splitting. We have no idea if the Order is following suit. Until we can be sure who falls on which side, we need to pick our way carefully. If Darius wants the truth, it wouldn't take much for him to uncover the same three names we have. Especially if we tell him Axel went missing because he was sniffing around something big."

"You think he'll believe you have no idea of who Axel was following?"

"Doesn't matter if he does or doesn't, he can't prove it. Regardless, it'll be enough to rattle some cages and maybe uncover both his and Zayn's agenda."

And this was why Ryan had chosen Gavin as his successor for the Wraiths. The warrior came with razor-sharp intelligence and well-honed instincts. Instincts Natasha now counted on. "That's a hell of a balancing act, Gavin."

"My footing's good." He sat up and leaned forward, studying her. "It'll confirm if you're right about those two being connected. If neither Darius nor Zayn have anything to do with Mulcahy's death, it will take us down to two, very tricky names."

"Leopold DiMarcco and Corwin Westbrooke," Raine murmured. "Would they work together?"

"I highly doubt it," Carys said. "DiMarcco is a traditionalist in every sense of the word. He's held his position on the Council the longest."

Carys's answer left Natasha perched on the edge of some pivotal realization. One she probably wouldn't be able to identify until much later, but the impression lingered. Instead of dwelling on it, she said, "Which means, if the Kyn decide to change directions and reveal themselves to the humans, his proclivities will come under scrutiny. That is not a light he will want to be under."

"Let me guess," Raine cut in. "He believes in keeping the Kyn bloodlines as pure as possible?"

Natasha gave her a small smile. "He'd never be so crass as to state it quite so bluntly, but yes. Under his very tactful rhetoric beats the heart and soul of a bigot, one who fanatically believes the Kyn should be the dominant race. To him, humans are disposable, easily controlled. Yet, he's not above using whatever tools he can to accomplish his end goals." She had been up close and personal with DiMarcco's viciousness before, and the end results were disastrous.

"Even humans?" Gavin asked.

"Even humans."

"Sounds like a prime candidate for our troublemaker," he drawled.

Even though part of her agreed with Gavin, she shook her head. "It's almost too neat." Plus she needed to ensure her own history didn't interfere with their current evaluations of the players.

"And Westbrooke?" Raine asked.

Carys tucked her legs under her, adjusting her position

until she fully faced Raine and Gavin. "Best guess, he's vying for a position on the Council."

A brief quiet filled the library as the impact of Carys's observation filtered through those gathered.

Raine finally broke it. "And since there aren't any current openings, he's going to create one?"

It reassured Natasha to see the girl held a firm grasp on just how brutal Kyn politics could be. "Exactly. Not only does he have the ear of many Kyn leaders through Europe and America, but he works regularly with the human governments. These relationships could prove very vital to the future of the Kyn. All he would need to complete his control is to have sway over the Council. Since he's popular with leaders on both sides, it wouldn't take much to accomplish that."

Gavin laced his hands behind his head and slouched a little farther into the sofa, studying the ceiling. "And how does having a modern thinking Kyn on the Council, who the mortal leaders already look to, become a bad thing?"

And this appeal was why Westbrooke could be so dangerous. "A wolf in sheep's clothing," Natasha murmured.

Her comment brought the room's attention back to her.

"Westbrooke is very good at appearing to be the charming mediator." She leaned forward. "He can walk the political lines with unerring balance and grace, but what you'll never see is the shift of his foot as he trips those beside him, or the not so helpful nudge off the edge. He may claim to want what's best for the Kyn, but in actuality he has only one concern—himself. When the dust settles, he wants to be the one manipulating the puppet strings, no matter if those strings control the humans or the Kyn. If he achieves his goal of a Council seat, mark my words, within ten years there won't be one familiar face sitting at that table."

Gavin dropped his dismissive pose and sat up, listening. "If that's true, why hasn't he been caught?"

"Hard to catch someone if all the witnesses and victims are dead or missing."

"But you know about him."

She nodded. "True, but I have nothing but hearsay and assumptions. Nothing concrete to bring to the Council. Plus, while it may answer who's behind the concentrated efforts to weaken the Northwest Kyn, it still doesn't solve who's sowing seeds of discontent in my house. The chances are good we could be facing more than one opponent."

"From what you've indicated, either DiMarcco or Westbrooke have enough sway to hit us from multiple fronts," Raine piped up. "Hell, they could use our own people against us."

Her comment reminded Natasha of Jared's fractured memories, and a piece of the puzzle slid into place with a soft, but resonating click. "They probably are."

That comment brought every individual in the room on point. Only Gavin asked the question they all wondered about. "Who?"

And therein lay the problem. "I don't know. Yet." One thing at time. "To pinpoint the Council's mole, we need to unravel the web surrounding us."

"If we can uncover who's betraying us, we could use them to lead us to which of the three is really behind this mess."

Too much anticipation hovered in Raine's observation. Perhaps Natasha should make sure Gavin kept watch over the wildcat once their rat was caught.

"We need to be sure. Some of these trails could be

false." Personal experience taught her a valuable lesson on that nasty tactic. One favored by some Council members. "We may find that things aren't what they seem, and we may not be the only ones being fooled."

"Careful, Natasha," Carys warned. "Just because Darius serves the Order, doesn't mean he can't work alongside a Council member. If any of the three are behind this, they'd have no problems setting each other up."

Gavin looked between both women. "Or setting up Darius."

It wasn't a question, but still, Natasha answered, "Or setting up Darius. Perhaps when he realizes that, we may find ourselves with a rather weighty ally."

"If we're on the same side." An appreciative calculation glittered in Gavin's gaze. "And if he's against us?"

She let her lips stretch, revealing a sharp, predatory grin. "Then it's time to even our odds."

"We'll need to update Cheveyo and Vidis," Carys said. "We have too many wolves circling to waste time. We'll have to plan our approach to Darius."

Natasha gave her a nod then switched her attention to Raine and Gavin. "The Wraiths must hunt. We need solid connections. Find out what Sullivan and Cleo knew that necessitated their deaths. Comb through Jared Pick's associates and link them to whoever was whispering in Sullivan's ear. Figure out how Brant Sutler ties in, before his body shows up. We need all the information on what Axel found out before he disappeared, because I'd bet if we put all the pieces together, we're going to come up with a name."

"And Abazi?" Raine asked.

Natasha shared a look with Carys, getting a subtle nod in return. "Leave him to us." Unfolding from the couch, she got to her feet, indicating that the impromptu meeting was over. The other three rose as well. "Gavin, would you be so kind as to let me know the minute you find anything new?"

"I'll keep you updated." As the silencing spell rippled away, he turned to Carys. "Are you staying here?"

She waved him off. "Don't worry about me, Natasha and I are big girls."

"Besides, Darius will be returning shortly," Natasha added. "I'm sure he wouldn't do anything overtly threatening to the two of us."

Gavin looked between the two of them. "Should I be concerned?"

Natasha only smiled.

CHAPTER 19

Darius stepped into his room at Natasha's as dawn finally breached the horizon. The early morning light joined forces with a soft rain to create a watercolor painting of pastel colors against his window. He and Zayn spent over an hour debating the wisdom of revealing their suspicions to the Northwest Kyn. While Darius was convinced it was the right move, Zayn stubbornly insisted neither of them could afford the Council catching wind of their shifting allegiance, especially when they weren't sure how many moles the Council had within the Northwest's ranks.

His brother's pigheadedness left Darius gritting his teeth. His finely honed survival instincts whispered they were running out of time and if they didn't get their pieces in line, they would lose before the battle truly began. Yet, no matter how much Darius pushed, he couldn't get Zayn to budge.

Darius had finally given up and returned, hoping some breathing room would allow him to find a way around Zayn. Under his skin, his demon snarled and clawed, frustration and exhaustion never a good influence on a demon's temper. The smell of bacon drew him to the door. Opening it, he wandered to the head of the stairs, the murmur of feminine voices reeled him down to the kitchen.

He passed the darken living room, absently noting the plywood covering the hole left by the Half-Bound. He stepped into the kitchen and, in sync, the blonde and redhead turned to face him from the counter.

He leaned against the entryway and folded his arms across his chest. "Natasha, Carys, good morning."

"Mr. Abazi," Carys acknowledged, her voice as cool as her gaze. "I assume your councilman is all safe and sound."

"His night was much quieter than ours."

"Help yourself to breakfast." Natasha waved a hand toward the stove while Carys raised a delicate teacup to her lips. "Carys and I were just discussing some pressing business matters."

Considering the sharp speculation of both females, he found himself very curious as to what transpired in his absence. And something had definitely happened. As he made his way to the stove, he took a surreptitious glance around. Nothing seemed out of place. No new damage.

He opened a cupboard, found glasses, closed it, moved to the next, and found plates. Taking one down, he loaded it with scrambled eggs, decorated with chopped peppers, then added a few slices of bacon to the side. As he dished up the food, he could feel the combined weight of the women's gazes on his back and barely managed to keep from hunching his shoulders. It wasn't until he was he fixing a cup of coffee that they resumed their conversation.

"How long before the contracts are ready for approval?" Natasha's voice remained low, but clear.

Cup in hand, he reclaimed his plate and took the seat on Natasha's other side.

"With the negotiated terms, we should have the final copies by late Monday. I have my team working on the materials Division sent over as well." Carys made a notation on the tablet in front of her with a small stylus.

Natasha's nails tapped lightly against the rim of her coffee cup. "Are you having issues with Osborn?"

Carys shook her head. "No, but I have concerns with some of the details Division is considering sharing with the public on what happened at the nightclub. I spoke to Xander to clarify some points, but the way Division's report reads could open up us to unnecessary litigation."

Natasha frowned. "What do you need me to do?"

"Nothing yet, but I'll let you know if that changes." Carys tapped a few more times on the screen then closed the cover of her tablet. "We'll need to set aside some more time to go over the recent set of contracts from Sterling as well. They're requesting a long term security detail, but their non-disclosure agreement is questionable."

"Ask Rachel to schedule a time for us to meet, possibly Tuesday." A discrete chime sounded. Next to him, Natasha shifted, pulled out a slim phone, and checked the screen. "It seems your ride has arrived."

"Lovely." Carys took one last sip of her coffee and pushed her cup away. "You'll be in later?"

"This afternoon. Hopefully, I'll have more to share."

Carys rose, tugging her sweater into place. "I wish you luck then."

The peculiar note in Carys's voice drew Darius's attention. He lifted his head, fork half way to his mouth, to find a complacent smile on Natasha's face, while Carys sported a pleasantly neutral expression.

"Something I should know about, darling?" he drawled, torn between amusement and irritation. The two were up to something, but they weren't letting him in to play just yet. After dealing with Zayn, Darius's normal patience for games was quite exhausted.

"Don't worry, nothing nefarious here, we're simply dealing with challenging business decisions. Are you always so grumpy in the morning?" Natasha asked, a provocative light in her eyes.

Whatever she had planned must be big, because the minx was proud of herself. "Mornings seem to be a busy time around here."

"Much easier to accomplish things with a fresh mind," Natasha murmured, pushing to her feet.

"I'll keep that in mind for future reference." He remained seated, finishing his breakfast and sipping his coffee

"I'll walk you out," Natasha said to Carys. Together the two headed to the front door. Her voice drifted back to Darius. "I'm interested to see what you find out."

The heavy door closed behind them, cutting off their voices and his chances of catching anything more. He sat, enjoying his coffee and the momentary quiet as Natasha saw Carys off. He finished his breakfast, took the plate to the sink, and rinsed it. Knowing Natasha would take her time, if for no other reason than to keep him waiting, he gathered his coffee and roamed to the other side of the house. It didn't take him long to find the library he discovered on his first go through.

He sank onto the small sofa situated between two comfortable chairs. He rested his coffee on his knee and let his head fall back, closing his eyes. Under the soothing silence, some of the night's tensions began to bleed away. For such a volatile woman, Natasha's home was quite serene and he found it comforting. This unusual peace offered an escape from the demands of reality. Perhaps that was the reason she guarded it so zealously.

Minutes ticked by before the muted sound of the front door opening and closing reached him. It wasn't long after that he felt her standing in the doorway, watching him. He slit his eyes open. "You've been a busy girl."

"Business stops for no one." Instead of taking a seat, she remained in the doorway. She leaned her shoulder against the doorjamb and folded her arms across her chest, settling in to watch him.

He let the quiet stretch between them, recognizing the waiting game for what it was. He studied her fine boned face, noting the brush of lavender shadows under her eyes and the slight slump to her shoulders, visible tolls from the long night. Considering the same weight perched on his own shoulders, he decided to forego the games and finally get some answers. "What are you up to, darling?"

"What makes you think I'm up to something, pet?"

"Instinct."

"Perhaps your instincts are off."

He sighed. "I wouldn't be who I am if they were." He narrowed his eyes as she hummed a questioning note under her breath. Yes, something was definitely up. "What did Gavin bring you?"

"Why the sudden interest?"

"Do you realize in the handful of hours since I've made my presence known, I've stood over two eviscerated bodies and crushed a Half-Bound demon?"

She shrugged those delicate shoulders. "We wouldn't want you to get bored."

"Oh, I'm very far from bored. I'm curious."

"About?"

"What you plan to do to stop those who are hunting you."

"Who's asking, Darius? You or Zayn?"

"Does it matter?" Seemed his little queen was beginning to put the pieces together. If so, Zayn would need to tread very carefully. And, perhaps, so would he.

"Very much so." Voiced low and soft, there was no hiding the lethal edge under her answer. "I'm very particular about who I choose to work with these days. I've found some relationships are not worth the headaches they bring."

Something had changed in his absence. Something serious enough for her to move beyond the verbal parrying they indulged in for the last day or so.

He leaned forward and set his now-forgotten cup on the low-slung table. "Yet some bring unexpected benefits." He took advantage of the opening she gave him. "Like your relationship with Mulcahy."

Grief and anger lit those indigo eyes and brought much needed color to her cheekbones. Instead of snapping, she dipped her head in a silent nod. "Or yours with Zayn."

How much had she gleaned from his blood? Would it be enough to work around Zayn's stubborn refusal to come forward? "Friendships are very rare in our world."

Her lips twisted slightly. "So is loyalty."

He refused to give her any more, not until he could figure out where she was headed with this.

The silence grew. Her attention drifted to the window on the far end of the library. "Do you think he knew?" Echoes of loss whispered through her question.

Strangely, he had no problem following her jump in conversation. "About his death?" He kept his voice soft.

She turned back to him, allowing him a glimpse of the

upheaval Mulcahy's death left behind. "He had a way of seeing things before they happened. Do you think he knew?"

He didn't answer right away, but gave it thought. "He once told me that being able to see the future was a tricky business, so he never fully believed in what he saw. He never took it at face value, said the future was fluid, changing from moment to moment. I don't know if he did, but I know he wouldn't have shared if he had. He wouldn't put that on those he left behind."

In the quiet room her small sigh sounded overly loud. She straightened and glided over to claim one of the chairs. "Why did you let Ryan leave the Order?"

Her unexpected question left him choosing his words carefully. "Once he made up his mind, it was smart not to stand in his way." Anyone who dealt with Mulcahy knew that.

She shook her head. "I don't want platitudes. Every leader understands the importance of their people. None want to lose them. Ryan was a key component to numerous missions for the Order. You're the Order's leader. Why would you let him walk away?"

Sitting back, he stretched one arm along the back of the couch and considered her. "You give me too much credit. Mulcahy recruited me. Why would you think I could have stopped him?"

She held his gaze, studying him. "Because, he trusted you."

He let his lips curl up. "So certain of that?"

Her gaze slipped to his hand, and the silver ring resting there, then rose back to his face. A silent but pointed statement. She remained quiet, waiting. A tactic she probably learned from Mulcahy.

A burst of memories of other times, other places, other situations where one of the few men he ever considered a friend had challenged him in the same silent way. The eroding combination of anger and grief scored a new gash across his heart before he managed to stuff it back into its box. "When he decided he wanted to move on, I tried to convince him to stay. No matter how hard or long I argued, I couldn't get him to change his mind. He made it clear that as soon as he finished his current assignment, he was gone."

"Did you ask him why?"

"Repeatedly."

When he didn't elaborate, she pushed, "Did he ever answer you?"

"One night, in a Turkish Bath." He leaned back and rubbed a hand over his face, stifling a yawn. "It was pure coincidence. I had tracked my quarry to this particular establishment. When I went in to ask around, I found Mulcahy." He smiled in memory of Mulcahy's disgruntled expression when Darius had stepped into the steam room. "He wasn't in the best of moods. He'd been tasked with his current assignment by one of the Council, but it was turning out to be stickier than anticipated. He thought I was sent in by another interested party. When he finally accepted I wasn't there to play shadow, we got to talking. This time when I asked, he answered."

He fell silent, memories coming back as if had been days instead of years—the remembered feel of humid heat curling over him, offering a false sense of privacy. The lingering scents of soaps, melted candle wax, and lotions added a tantalizing layer to the air. And Mulcahy, towel wrapped around his lean waist, sprawled on the bench, considering him through half-closed eyes...

"If you're not here to check up on me, Darius," his friend drawled, "what brings you here?"

Darius's skin itched with the thin layer of dust that somehow settled between every piece of clothing and his flesh. Gods, how he wished he had time to join Mulcahy and wash this crap off.

"Callipso's favorite servant disappeared about the same time as some very sensitive letters," Darius said. "So far, I've tracked them here."

The twist of Ryan's lips couldn't be called a smile, more a disillusioned grimace. "Let me guess, Callie's worried her letters will find their way to her husband."

Darius snorted. "If only it was that simple. She's worried they'll end up in the hands of her lover's husband."

Ryan shook his head. "Someday, that woman will end up dancing with the wrong partner at the wrong time and her father won't be able to help."

"For now, being a Councilman's daughter is keeping her safe."

The harsh bark of laughter cut through the quiet bath. "How much longer do you think it will be before the Order will be nothing more than the Council's cleanup crew?"

Darius leaned against one of the tiled walls and studied his friend. "Is this why you want to leave?"

A flash of teeth flicked through the curls of steamed air. "Partially. The Order was founded to serve as a check to the Council and a way to ensure the Kyn's survival. Hard to do if we're running around wiping childish asses and cleaning up their messes."

Darius tucked his hands behind his back as frustration

curled his hands into useless fists. "You leaving the Order won't help."

A glint of sympathy sparked then disappeared behind Mulcahy's composed mask. "The world is changing, my friend, and leaving the Council behind. If our people are to survive, they need options, something besides hiding. We have to find a balance with the humans, or we'll die under the hands of both humans and our own misguided leaders. The first step is to carve out our own place in the New World and, right now, I'm one of the few who can do it without pissing off the Council. My leaving the Order gives our people a fighting chance."

"So you'll abandon the Order?"

Genuine humor lightened the shadows on Mulcahy's face. "No, I'm giving it to the one person I know who'll ensure its mission won't be corrupted."

Tired, frustrated, and tangled up with resentment, Darius didn't bother hiding his sneer of contempt. "Who's the lucky bastard?"

He should've been warned by the beatific smile, but still the answer shocked him. "You."

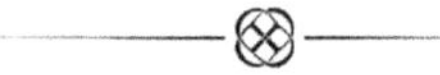

"Darius?" His name in feminine tones dragged him away from the past. "Darius?"

He captured the small hand waving in front of his face and blinked.

Natasha knelt in front of him, her other hand a warm weight on his knee for balance. Periwinkle eyes met his, setting him solidly in the present. "You back with me?" He dropped his chin in a short nod and slowly released her.

"Why did Ryan leave the Order?" she asked. More than curiosity lurked in her alluring face.

"To save the Kyn." His answer was rough. Hindsight was always twenty-twenty. He could see the value of Mulcahy's decisions now, but then—then it had been difficult to accept.

A frown creased Natasha's brow. "He had to know the Council wouldn't just let him walk away."

"Not without a price." The woman was damn beautiful, even tired and exhausted. Unable to resist the temptation to touch, he traced a finger along the side of her jaw, feeling the slide of silky warmth against his finger. "The Council doesn't let anyone walk away," he murmured, letting his hand fall. If the arrogant bastards did, his brother wouldn't be walking such a tight line.

She tilted her head to the side in silent question.

"I don't know what price they asked of Mulcahy," he answered. "Whatever it was, he paid it in full, but they never took their eyes off of him."

"So which ones weren't happy with his decision?" A new inflection appeared under her question, adding an unexpected weight to his answer.

He began to get a glimmer of where she was headed. "The Council was divided in their responses. There were some who found him amusing and waited to see what would become of his experiment in the New World."

"Hoping he'd fail?"

Darius nodded. "But when the American Kyn Houses began to grow in power and influence, their amusement turned into contemplation."

Pressing both hands on his knees, Natasha pushed to her feet and looked down her elegant nose. "Oh, let's not sugar coat it, Darius. They began to worry about losing their power. You forget, Ryan wasn't the only one who came over to the New World. I remember how 'polite' the first few Council emissaries were. How their suggestions were thinly veiled orders from the Council."

"Orders he chose to ignore," Darius reminded her. "He could be as arrogant as any Council member, and forcing them to treat him on equal footing didn't endear him."

Her hands went to her hips. "Maybe one of them decided they'd had enough, then."

As her implication sank in, he straightened, his instincts clamoring for attention. "You think Mulcahy was targeted by someone on the Council."

Her lips thinned and, as he rose to his feet crowding her personal space, her eyes narrowed, but she didn't step back. "I think it's an option I'd be foolish not to consider."

Her mulish expression didn't falter. The thrill of an impending hunt twined with an unusual spark of fear. She really believed someone on the Council was behind Mulcahy's death. His little demon queen was about to step on a very treacherous trail. "What did you find out, Natasha?"

This time, she did step back, evading his hand as he failed to grab her, drawing him up and away from the couch. "Don't worry, Darius." She flashed a patently false smile. "If something concrete comes to light, we'll let you know. For now, I'm just exploring various options."

He stalked her out of the library, stopping at the foot of the stairs to watch her ascend. When she reached the first landing, he called out, "Natasha."

She stopped and half turned, her hand tightening on the mahogany railing.

"Don't go hunting your options on your own." It was a futile request, but he had to try. The stubborn woman was about to start poking a very lethal wasp's nest in her quest for answers. "It may not be safe."

Her lips took a disdainful curl. "Threats, darling?"

Ignoring the sharp edge of her tone, he answered, "Consider it more of a warning."

Feminine pride and arrogance stiffened her spine and added color to her cheeks. "I'll take it under advisement." She turned away.

"You do that," he murmured, knowing he just doomed himself to becoming the demon queen's unwanted shadow.

CHAPTER 20

After a brief, but intense meeting with Cheveyo, Vidis, and Carys, Natasha finally made it to her office in the early afternoon. It took the combined efforts of her and Carys to convince Cheveyo and Vidis of the wisdom of approaching Darius about Axel's disappearance, while not revealing the names at their disposal. Walking through the front doors of Taliesin, Natasha was greeted by a waiting Rachel and a long list of needed decisions. The afternoon flew by as Natasha went from one minor fire to the next, hammering out contract negotiations, juggling public relations requests, and fielding the morbid curiosity of various business contacts and reporters. It gave her very little time to dwell on her earlier conversations or the memories they evoked.

She was wrapping up an appointment with her executive marketing staff, when Rachel's discreet chime sounded. Knowing the receptionist wouldn't interrupt unless it was important, Natasha held up her hand to halt the ongoing conversation. "Yes?"

"My apologies, Ms. Bertoi, but Mr. Durand is asking to meet with you."

Natasha's pulse picked up, anticipation thrumming through her. "Give me five minutes to finish up."

It took her four minutes to ensure everyone had their assignments and usher them on their way. She watched her team leave as Gavin stood off to the side, his face impassive. She turned, heading back to her desk, knowing he would follow. The door closing sounded overly loud as she took her seat. Then she waited until Gavin dropped into one of the chairs in front of her desk.

"You found something?" And judging by his grim expression, the news wasn't good.

"Our missing Wraith." His flat declaration had her suspicions taking front and center. "But Axel's not talking. He's in a coma. The only thing keeping him alive right now is his link to Vidis and his pack."

Reigning in her urge to spew a stinging mass of curses, she fought to keep her emotions and the more volatile aspects of her personality in check. Her lack of sleep and the mounting stresses of the last few days were starting to pile up. It took a great deal of damage to render a shifter comatose. Perhaps she should be grateful for small blessings like pack ties, but right now she rather have Axel articulate. "What happened?"

"He ran into someone bigger and badder than him."

Gavin's sarcastic rejoinder scraped against her already stretched temper. Her fingers tightened on the pen in her hand. Instead of snapping his head off, literally, she took breath, carefully set the pen aside, and reminded herself why ripping into him would not be productive.

However, some sign of her waning patience must have made an appearance since Gavin's slumped posture slowly straightened. His voice was carefully neutral as he continued, "I sent Chayton to join up with Axel when he called with his trio of names."

She held his gaze, managing to hide her impatience with a soft observation. "Yes, considering who those names are, sending another Wraith was wisely done."

"I'm captain." Gavin's reminder emerged equally soft. "I wanted someone covering Axel's back."

Understanding that her stare was being taken as a challenge, she blinked. The small movement allowed Gavin to continue, "When Chayton got into town and reached out, Axel wasn't answering. After Chayton informed me Axel was missing, he started hunting. When he finally found him, he was unconscious and barely breathing. He was dumped in a junk yard on the Anacostia Waterfront neighborhood in Washington, DC."

Gavin's word choice caught her attention. "Dumped?"

"I'm assuming, since Axel can't confirm. Chayton thinks the place was picked deliberately."

Unfamiliar with the area, she arched a brow at Gavin for more details. "He thinks this, why?"

"It's near Bolling Air Force Base." He watched her closely. When she didn't visibly react, he continued, "I sent Chayton in on Taliesin's jet since commercial flights are hard to come by in the dead of morning. He managed to pick up Axel's trail fairly quickly. If Chayton hadn't found him when he did, Axel would've been discovered by the military police."

Leaning forward, she rested her elbows on her desk and steepled her fingers. Pieces of what he was leading to began to fall into place. "Which you believe is what someone wanted."

Gavin nodded. "Not sure exactly what they hoped to accomplished since Axel can't talk, but still..."

"A Kyn showing up on a military base never goes over well," she murmured, her mind clicking through one possible scenario after another, testing each piece with the scattered information at her disposal. "Axel's injuries, what are they?"

An ominous cloud descended over Gavin's face. "Physically he's been beaten to hell and back." He pulled out his phone, thumbed through some screens, and then passed it over to her.

If Gavin hadn't told her who was in the brutal photo, she wouldn't have recognized the mangled form. Her memory of Axel filled in the blood-stained hair as brown, the swollen and bruised face as a craggy combination of calm capability and stubborn resourcefulness, one that allowed him to blend into seedy bars and executive lunches with equal ease.

What stared back from Gavin's phone, made her wonder if his physical appearance would ever again approach anything close to normal. The violence wasn't limited to his face. His body was ripped and torn. As she brought up the remaining pictures, she noted the wounds varied, some with the smoother edge of a blade, while others bore the ragged edges of claws, possibly teeth. "At least he still has his heart."

"A small blessing."

As much as she could admire the fact the wounds were meant to hurt, not kill, the damage told her one thing. "Someone had him awhile to achieve this much damage." And they weren't looking for information, just punishment. Otherwise they wouldn't have spent so much time erasing his face.

"It took Chayton five and half hours to get there."

"That would do it."

"That's not all. They set a spell," Gavin added.

She looked up from the gruesome gallery. "Spell?" Why did that little tidbit manage to surprise her? Whoever they hunted liked to play with magic.

"According to Vidis, if it was a simple beating, he would have known Axel was in trouble and been able to assist his healing through the pack bonds. The fact Vidis had no inkling of what was happening with Axel means someone was deliberately blocking his tie to his alpha. And whatever is blocking that tie is making it so Vidis can't prod him out of his coma to find out what happened."

"Is it the same magic used against Vidis last time?" Vidis recently lost one of his wolves when his traitorous brother used their shared blood to block the pack ties. She handed Gavin his phone back. "Or similar to the one used to kill Ryan?"

"We won't know until we get Axel back here and check it out." He took the slim device from her and tucked it away. "Right now, Cheveyo's acting as a mediator between Vidis and Chayton. They're trying to work around the spell and keep Axel breathing while they're flying home."

"Why not let him heal under the eastern alpha's care?" Even with a shaman babysitting, bringing a critically injured shifter home in a plane did not inspire confidence.

Gavin grimaced. "From what I can gather, the eastern alpha doesn't want to be involved in any way with Vidis, says whatever trouble is stalking the Northwest Pack doesn't need new prey."

"Is that so?" Perhaps the eastern alpha was simply being cautious, but she would make a point to carve out some time to do a little digging, just to be certain.

Information was always helpful when you needed to ensure proper responses to future conversations. Regardless, the Northwest Houses would not forget the eastern alpha's lack of assistance. For now, she needed to concentrate on more immediate issues. "When do you expect their flight?"

He checked his watch. "In about two and half hours."

Doing some quick mental calculations, she sighed. "Darius will be here soon, but I'll have Jamie and Rachel reschedule my other meetings."

"You are not meeting him alone, Natasha."

The male arrogance in his statement made her back teeth grind. "Aren't you a dear boy for trying to protect me?"

"It has nothing to do with your protection."

"No?"

"No, it has to do with what keeps peeking out when you're not paying attention." He shook his head. "If you decide to stop playing civilized, I'm not sure Taliesin could handle the increase in remodeling costs."

His rather astute observation drew her attention to the unsettled nature stirring under her skin, a sure sign she was much more off balance than she thought. Perhaps coming in this afternoon was the wrong decision. "It has been a damn long day," she admitted. One that showed no sign of ending anytime soon.

"Tell me about it." His momentary commiseration wiped some of the exhaustion off his face. "Move the meeting to Vidis's house. Let's set the board in our favor."

She leaned back in her chair, thinking. "No, not Vidis's." With one of his own coming in injured there was no way Vidis would be able to maintain the calm needed to deal with Darius. Considering the topic under discussion, Gavin had a point though. They needed someplace private, where curious ears couldn't listen and, if things went badly, eyes couldn't witness. Her house was currently overrun with construction crews. She smiled as the perfect solution rose. "I'll have him meet me at Ryan's."

"Meet us," Gavin corrected.

"Chayton's flight," she reminded him. "You won't have time."

He eyed her for a moment then came to some internal decision. "I'll text Raine and have her meet the plane." He suited action to words. "Depending on how this plays out, we can join them at Vidis's afterward."

"If Cheveyo hasn't already, we should bring in Cassandra." If anyone could break through a spell strong enough to block a pack's bond, it would be Cassandra Miwa. The powerful witch was second to Cheveyo and saved both Gavin and Raine at various times, not to mention numerous other Kyn. Remembering the older woman lived an hour and a half outside of Portland, she added, "Have Raine send someone to pick her up, if need be."

Gavin gave a quick nod and continued texting.

She waited until he finished before she spoke. "I'll relay the change of venue to Carys and Darius."

Gavin got to his feet. "Do you need a ride?"

She waved off his offer. "No, I need to gather a few things before heading over. I'll have Jamie drive me over if he's available."

Gavin frowned.

Reading the unspoken concern in his expression, she blew out a short breath. "He's one of ours. I sincerely doubt he's working for the Council. What he wants, he can't get without me."

"You sure about that?"

She opened her mouth to respond, but the automatic reassurance never emerged. *Was she?* Someone close to Taliesin had to be working with the Council. Otherwise these strikes wouldn't be made with such accuracy. When faced with Fahd and Jamie earlier, suspicions began to form, but there was nothing concrete to give it substance.

The last few days—hell, the last few weeks—proved fertile ground for growing paranoia, but heeding them could be even more dangerous. The Northwest couldn't afford to fracture, especially as the Council seemed to be crumbling from within. Still, she couldn't ignore her instincts, no matter how much they seemed to confuse things. "If someone near and dear is playing with the Council, it would be best to keep them close."

"I know you've all but crossed Darius off your list, but are you sure he's not behind Axel's beating?" Gavin rolled his shoulders. "If more than one person is involved, we could be looking at a team. What if Zayn sent him out to dead end our investigation?"

He had a valid point, but—

"The timing is wrong. The only time Darius wasn't with us, was this morning. Even traveling between realms, he wouldn't have enough time to pay Axel a visit or spend the time needed to accomplish that beating."

Plus the same voice whispering to keep an eye on those closest to her, also nudged her attention elsewhere for the one behind the current string of problems facing the Northwest. That bond Darius and Zayn shared, the depth of it, had her looking to DiMarcco or Westbrooke. If either of those two knew just how close Zayn and Darius really were, they would not be above exploiting it and getting rid of two very powerful males in one fell swoop.

Calculation entered Gavin's gaze. "Let's hope you're

right, Natasha. If we slip now, we'll be torn apart before we can regain our feet."

"I've always been light on my feet, dear."

Natasha looked up from her paperwork as Jamie slowed the car for the turn to Ryan's house. "You made good time." She began to tuck the papers away in her slim briefcase.

"For once, traffic wasn't bad." Jamie continued to guide the car down the long drive.

She made some non-committal noise and set the trappings of business aside. Carys asked her to arrive a few minutes early, an indicator she had more information to share. Which reminded her. "Have you made any further progress on running down Sutler's whereabouts?"

"There were a few flare ups with the Kensington campaign today, so I haven't had a chance to check." He flicked his gaze to the rearview mirror. "Durand getting anywhere on who's behind Sullivan's recent misfortunes?"

"Some, but nothing solid." She caught his frown before he turned his head. "What?"

"Why aren't you sharing with me?" There was a definite edge of a growl to his voice.

His temper sparked her amusement. "You don't get to play in my sandbox all the time, Jamie."

He blew out a hard breath. "Look, I'm just worried. Between Sullivan's death and whatever happened at your place last night, you and I both know someone's gunning for you." The car rolled to a stop next to another sedan and a low-slung sports car. He shut off the engine then turned in his seat to face her. "What's going on?"

The worry in his face tugged at her. No denying she had

a soft spot for this boy, but it wasn't enough to blind her to the possibilities. Her sister's betrayal drove home how even those closest to you had weak spots, and weak spots could always be exploited. The Council was very, very talented at exploitation. "We're being tested."

"By?"

She gave him a small smile and opened the door to get out. "Someone who wants what isn't theirs. Unfortunately, I don't feel like sharing."

Jamie reached over the back of the seat, his hand wrapping around her wrist, holding her in place. "If I don't know which direction trouble's coming from, I can't help."

She stared at him until he let her go. "The only help you can provide me is a connection between Sullivan, Sutler, and Dmitri." More than blood would chill from her tone. Red washed under his skin, but Jamie just gave her a curt nod. Satisfied her message was received, she slipped out of the car and gently closed the door behind her.

If her knee jerk reaction to Jamie was any indication, her upcoming meeting with Darius did not bode well. Her temper prowled too close to her skin, making it difficult to remember to keep a gentle touch on her words. Stress, exhaustion, and frustration did not make for a happy demon queen.

As she drew closer, Niall's tall form emerged from the shadows gathered around the front door.

The echo of Jamie's door closing sounded behind her. "Jamie, keep Niall company." She forced herself not to stalk across the drive.

"I enjoy my solitude, Ms. Bertoi," Niall said, as he held open the door for her.

She paused in front of him, tilting her head back to address him. "So do I, Niall." Perhaps if she shed her human skin, she could wipe away the traces of amusement lingering behind the Fey's bland expression. If nothing else it would allow her to loom over him. The temptation almost proved too much.

Niall's eyebrows rose as the air visibly wavered around her, but wisely said nothing.

She continued into the house, feeling the weight of Jamie's glare until the door closed behind her. Standing alone in the entryway, she took a deep breath, then another. Only when she was satisfied her first response wouldn't be to literally rip someone apart, did she move farther into Ryan's home.

Light spilled from the living room, and the low murmur of voices drifted to her, a combination of light and depth. Carys and Gavin. Their conversation came to a stop when she stepped into the room. "Don't let me interrupt."

Ryan's living room combined natural elements of wood and stone into an elegant, casual blend. The floor-to-ceiling windows provided the only barrier to the lake and forest existing outside the structure. Carys's stood near one of those windows, her green silk blouse and black pencil skirt a perfect foil for her porcelain skin and red hair, currently tamed in a neat chignon.

Gavin sprawled in the smaller sofa, his face grim. "You're not going to like this."

Just once Natasha would rather be greeted with a more positive note. Sighing she made her way around the matching set of chairs to the larger of two sofas congregated around the fireplace. A unique wooden table cut from some ancient tree sat in the middle. The flickering flames and warm light from the lamps played across the table's polished surface, light and shadow dancing among the tree rings preserved under a high gloss.

She sank down on the edge of the sofa. "Carys, do you mind?"

The redhead dipped her chin, and the skin-prickling magic ran over Natasha's skin as the silencing spell fell into place. Considering Darius's predilection for hiding in the shadows, it would be best if this part of the conversation remained private. "What happened now?"

Strangely it was Carys who answered. "We finally found a connection."

Cautious excitement bloomed. "And why wouldn't I like that?"

Carys and Gavin shared a look then Gavin said, "Ever heard of Cinar International?"

"Sounds vaguely familiar."

"It's a European-based corporation housing several different companies. One of which supplied a rather large anonymous donation to Biovita—one with a string of zeros behind it."

"The biotech company in Hillsboro, the one Brant Sutler was working for?"

Gavin nodded. Instead of the expected relief for finally having a solid lead, he looked more grim than ever.

A European corporation funding research in an American lab, one situated in their backyard? It didn't take a rocket scientist to put it together. Dread curled in her stomach. "This Cinar, who's behind it?"

Carys clasped her hands behind her back, her shoulders straightening. "I pulled some strings and uncovered their board of directors, both silent and public."

Natasha rubbed a hand over her face, a sudden ache taking residence in her temples. "Let me guess, Zayn Aimeric, Leopold DiMarcco, and Corwin Westbrooke all have seats?"

"Got it in one." Gavin sat up and leaned forward. "What if we're not dealing with one or two, but all three?"

She looked between the other two, not missing the worry under the anger. "Then having Darius on our side just graduated from a want to a necessity."

"And if he's involved?" Gavin pushed.

She carefully locked away the small voice whispering about Darius's innocence. Ryan built the Northwest Kyn so their people could survive the upcoming changes. She wouldn't let one intriguing male stand in the way. "Then we remove him and Zayn, before sending our own message to our esteemed Council—one they can't misinterpret."

CHAPTER 21

Darius stepped out of the taxi in front of the unlocked gate standing guard at Ryan's home and began walking down the drive. Evening was just settling in, and the still cool air carried a hint of rain. After finally getting some much-needed sleep, he woke to find Natasha's home empty. However, she left behind a written summons, requiring his presence this evening.

He tucked the note away and spent the main part of the afternoon with Zayn. It took a few hours, but he finally got his brother to grudgingly agree to approach the Northwest leaders. Zayn's one caveat—unearth the Council's mole first before dragging his name into it. Considering Darius was already determined to do so, that wasn't much of hardship. Unfortunately, his brother's stubbornness cost Darius time, time he could have used to dig deeper into the players of this interesting group.

His first stop, Natasha's court. Knowing his presence would taint what he heard, he kept to the shadows and listened. His patience eventually paid off as the discontented whispers rose and revealed themselves.

Unfortunately, they were thin on strength but fat on petty jealousy. The more he listened and watched, the more convinced he became that support of Sullivan's bid for Natasha's seat had more to do with envy than an actual grab for power. The death of Sullivan's lover hadn't filtered through her court as yet, which meant Natasha was keeping that piece of the night's adventure hidden. A decision he highly approved of, not that she'd care.

However, Sullivan's death dominated conversations. While the majority agreed Sullivan's attitude and mouth had pissed off the wrong demon, it wasn't Natasha's name being bandied about. Not because she couldn't do it, but because popular opinion believed if she wanted to kill him, she would have done so in full view of her people, leaving no question as to the who in the equation.

She was a formidable leader, one both feared and loved. Feared because she enforced the rules of her house without fail, and loved for the same reason. The Amanusa were, by their very nature, volatile. It was why self-control was so highly prized among the demons. Without that, the havoc they could wreck would wipe out not just them, but all they touched. Amanusa leaders established strict rules, and the punishments could be harsh. To be the one enforcing those rules required an intimidating amount of strength, balanced by compassion. His little queen would never admit to compassion, but it was there.

For every sly insinuation from petulant wanna-be power players, there were others willing to defend their leader and her actions. Other names were tossed out. Strangely enough, one of them belonged to Natasha's little toy, Ryder. As much as Darius would love a reason to tear the prick limb from limb, there was nothing behind the speculation, just simply passing commentary on the possibility of Ryder ending Sullivan's petty aspirations before they got in his way.

The end of the drive came into sight, cutting Darius's musings short. Two men stood in place before the entryway —just beyond two parked sedans and a deep blue, almost black, sports car—the prick in question and a tall Fey, one of the Wraiths from the previous night's meeting. It took a moment to pull up the name. Niall. The glint of the porch light flickered off of Niall's glasses as he dipped his head in acknowledgement. Next to him, Ryder straightened.

It took a few minutes to cross the remaining distance. He stopped in front of both men. "I'm assuming Natasha's inside?" Darius kept his attention on Niall, effectively dismissing Ryder.

Niall stepped to the side. "They're waiting for you."

They? Considering who stood watch, he bet Carys was in there, maybe even Gavin and Raine. He should have never left Natasha's the night before, because something was definitely going on.

Before he could move up the steps, Ryder stepped in front of him, the red rings in his eyes blazing in a tight mask of anger. "I don't know what's going on, but you better not have anything to do with the mess of shit sitting at Natasha's door."

"I don't create messes, I clean them up." Darius let his demon rise and stretch, a reminder of who and what Ryder confronted. Ryder's barely disguised flinch pleased both halves of his nature. "Better hope I don't find your stench lingering around."

His taunt found its mark as Ryder's hold slipped, his eyes bleeding crimson while the air around him shimmered with his other form. Before the little shit could sign his own death warrant, the door opened.

"Do I have to separate the two of you?" Smoke and spice, laced with feminine exasperation, cut through the mounting tension.

With his back to Natasha, Ryder flashed his canines at Darius as he issued a silent snarl. Darius returned it.

"Jamie, move." The curt order revealed Natasha wasn't unaware of their exchange.

The younger demon reluctantly moved aside, only looking away when Natasha gave a quiet huff of impatience.

Darius's snarl turned into a lazy grin as he faced her, he and his demon appreciating the picture she presented.

Cunning intelligence and wells of secrets swam in those periwinkle eyes, offering an unwanted challenge to the man and beast. Her white-blonde hair was caught in a deceptive tangle, a few lone strands brushing her shoulders. The soft, seductive material of her deeply hued sapphire dress clung to her curves with tantalizing precision. Danger and beauty in one small, alluring package.

Perhaps Zayn had reason to be worried about Darius's fascination with this woman. Either that, or Darius needed to get laid. "And here I thought you finally decided to trade up."

"Trade up?"

"For a more mature challenge." He moved up the steps, deliberately crowding Ryder aside. "I wouldn't want you to become bored, darling."

Devilish amusement glinted in her gaze. "No, I believe boredom is the least of my worries." She stepped back and let him enter the house.

He offered her his arm. "Shall we?"

She placed her palm against his arm, the heat of her

touch bleeding through his shirtsleeve. Without turning, he pushed the door closed in Ryder's face.

Opening the door to find Darius and Jamie engaged in some sort of testosterone-driven showdown piqued Natasha's interest. When she realized the tension screaming between the two males had to do with her, she found a perverse pleasure in the situation. Jamie's possessiveness was new, but amusing. Unfortunately, he would never find himself in the running for her attentions. She wasn't blind to who came first in his heart—him. Besides, not only was he young, he wasn't strong enough to capture both halves of her nature. Both woman and beast would eat him alive. Literally.

As for the male walking silently beside her, that was another story. Memories of the kiss they shared brought a surprisingly intense need to life. Before it could burn too bright, she shut it down. Tall, dark, and deadly could elevate any female libido, but it was what existed behind the face that fueled her fascination.

Most males proved predictable, and nothing Darius did came close to that. Perhaps it was because she was uncertain of what his goals were, but Darius drew her beyond the physical. There were depths there, secrets calling to her blood like a drug, tempting her to delve deep. It didn't matter that, as a scion of Blood of Death, death could ride his touch as easily as passion. In fact, it added to his allure.

If it wasn't for the web of conspiracy surrounding the Northwest, she might have considered sating her curiosity. Instead, she would have to be satisfied with small indulgences until she was certain of the part he played. Her hand flexed against his arm, her nails pressing a quick bite before she let him go as they stepped into to the living room where Gavin and Carys waited.

"Our guest has arrived," she announced unnecessarily as she swept into the room, leaving Darius to follow.

Gavin still lounged on the small sofa, but Carys had picked one of the two chairs on the opposite side.

Natasha waved a hand toward the empty chair next to Carys and made her way across lush carpet to resume her seat on the sofa. "Darius, have a seat."

Ignoring her silent direction, Darius took the seat next to Natasha. He leaned back and propped an ankle on his knee, before stretching his arm along the back of the sofa, the picture of unconcerned interest. Natasha caught his raised eyebrow, but refused to frown, knowing he would view it as a challenge.

It didn't stop his lips from curving into a small smile. He turned to Gavin. "Finally decided to share the reason behind your unexpected visit last night?"

"I'm more than happy to share," Gavin drawled, sarcasm coating every syllable. "But let's make sure we're the only ones taking part in the conversation." He looked at Carys, who dipped her chin just before the skin-ruffling magic of a silencing spell settled into place.

Sitting so close, Natasha caught the razor-sharp curiosity lurking under Darius's arrogant amusement. Still his voice remained relaxed. "You've found something."

Gavin's smile didn't reach his eyes. "Does Cinar International ring any bells?"

Although his position didn't change, the air around Darius did. Natasha felt his tension crest even as the red brightened around the arctic blue of his pupils. Oh yes, Darius recognized the name.

"A large European umbrella corporation, it houses numerous companies around the world." His words were clipped.

"It also makes some rather sizable donations to various ventures as well." Carys pulled Darius's attention away from Gavin. "Large anonymous donations, such as the one to a local business known as Biovita."

There was no discernible reaction from Darius as Carys dangled the name in front of him. Buried deep within Natasha something loosened a fraction, but it didn't stop her from continuing with their combined attack. "Biovita employed a human geneticist, Brant Sutler."

Still no visible reaction from Darius.

"When Dmitri went after Vidis, he used a drug to turn our wolves feral," Gavin added. "Sutler is the scientist who created that drug."

Now that did get a reaction. When feral werewolves began attacking humans, Division demanded a name. Natasha gave them one, Sebastian Reiner, Vidis's Third, and Dmitri's puppet. The same man who just happened to die in the explosion that killed Mulcahy.

The Council, however, was given what truth the Northwest could prove, Vidis's brother, Dmitri had manipulated the pack's Third into playing Trojan Horse for a spell that killed the Northwest's leader. Only she and the other Northwest heads knew there was someone much more powerful and well hidden behind Dmitri. The same individual they now hunted.

Darius scowled, and his hand near her shoulder curled into a fist. "Sutler was working with Dmitri." A statement not a question. "The amount of money necessary to fund drug development is not something Dmitri Vidis would have access to."

Gavin didn't move. "No, it's not."

Darius's gaze narrowed, and his jaw flexed while the air around him shimmered, a sure sign of volatile emotions.

Natasha refused to allow her demon to rise in answer. Best they sit and watch, because the next few minutes would determine who would leave this room alive.

"You think Cinar was backing Dmitri," Darius gritted out between clenched teeth.

"Cinar is a very interesting corporation." Carys's cool voice wove through the rising tension. "The companies gathered beneath it are both human and Kyn. We find it strange that the only board member names we could uncover were human."

Natasha noted, for future reference, the ease with which the Fey leader lied.

Gavin leaned forward, his elbows resting on his knees. "Even more interesting, the individual who gave me their names is currently in a coma, fighting for his life against a spell." His attention focused on Darius with cold calculation. "Since I'm not the most trusting person, I'm wondering what names Cinar buried. You say you're here to get justice for Mulcahy's death, so I'm going to ask you one more time, does Cinar International ring any bells?"

Under his skin, Darius's beast clawed and gouged for freedom. Gritting his teeth, he fought through the blind fury burning like a phosphorous candle, dripping corrosive rage against the chains holding his beast in check. *Had he heard of the godsdamned company?* Blighted hells, his brother sat on the board as a silent partner, along with two other very dangerous Kyn.

A fact he would be willing to bet the three facing him already knew. But that wasn't what was pissing him off. No, his murderous fury could be laid directly at the feet of Leopold DiMarcco and Corwin Westbrooke, because those two bastards were setting not only Zayn up, but by extension, Darius. Not something he'd soon forget. Or forgive.

Under his rage, an unfamiliar emotion awoke, apprehension. Had DiMarcco or Westbrooke discovered the carefully laid plans he and Zayn had in place, or were they simply taking advantage of an available out? Were they working together or was it just one of them? Questions screamed through Darius, almost drowning out the rising silence of the three watching him. Knowing if he didn't answer, blood, probably his, would spill, he finally managed to growl, "Yeah, it rings a damn big bell."

The tension dropped fractionally and he could have sworn Natasha let out a breath of relief. Under Gavin's unforgiving countenance, a flicker of satisfaction was there and gone, a moment so brief, Darius would've missed it if he'd blinked.

Yet Gavin's voice remained even, "Your turn to share."

Yes, it was, because with this connection the game entered a whole new level. He'd bring Zayn up to speed later. For now, he would do what he always did, cover their asses and ensure their survival. "Three Kyn sit on the board—Leopold DiMarcco, Corwin Westbrooke, and Zayn Aimeric. I can vouch for Zayn, but not the other two."

Gavin looked at Carys. Next to Darius, Natasha tapped her fingers on the edge of the couch.

When Gavin turned back to him, Darius wasn't surprised. "I thought the Order didn't serve the Council."

"The Order was founded to serve as a check to the Council, and a way to ensure the Kyn's survival." Words uttered decades ago, their weight unchanged. "It doesn't."

"Do you?"

"No." The denial snapped out. He curled his hand tight, feeling the metal of his ring cut into his skin. The need to hunt and stalk those who would willingly sacrifice him and his brother stripped away the civilized version of his voice, leaving a sonorous growl in its wake. "I serve the Kyn."

Natasha sat inches from him. "That may be, pet, but there is one other you serve."

He turned to her, knowing his beast ranged around him, moving like a mirage over his human skin.

Yet, she faced him with a regal serenity. "There is something between you and Zayn, something you don't want others to know. If you want us to trust you, we'll need more than your say-so. Those under my protection have learned too well how little weight words hold."

No, his word alone wouldn't be enough. Not for these Kyn. The cost of trusting those around them had already proven too high. However, his cost for trusting them could be more than he was willing to pay. "What do you want, Natasha?"

Those fingers stilled their dance against the armrest. She held his gaze with an unsettling intensity. "The truth behind the game you and Zayn are playing. Give us a reason to follow Ryan's lead and trust you."

"This isn't a game." He abruptly stood up from the couch.

Gavin mirrored him, coming to his feet with a predatory grace, revealing the warrior.

Darius sighed. "You're being hunted by powers you can't comprehend, and those stalking you won't stop until nothing is left of what Mulcahy created." Darius deliberately stared at Gavin. "Not the Wraiths, not his niece, not one vestige of the Northwest Kyn. You want to survive, you're going to need not just me, but Zayn as well."

A low growl escaped Gavin, but before he could step into Darius's space, Natasha was there. "Enough!"

It would have been laughable to expect such a small female to hold apart two formidable men, but what lived inside Natasha had obviously reached its limits. The form wavering over her body held no vestige of humanity. The temperature in the room dropped noticeably. Power so cold it burned, whipped around both men.

She faced Darius, crimson snaking through indigo. "The Council has no idea what exists in my territory, nor do they fully understand what it means that the Northwest is now mine and not Ryan's. If they think we are less because of Ryan's death, they will soon learn very differently."

"Will they?" Frustration rode Darius hard. "You have more rats than a sinking ship. You think what's happened here in the last year is coincidence? Everyone has a weakness. You know that better than most. The Northwest is no exception. Ryan's was his niece, Vidis's is his pack, Cheveyo's is his past, and yours is your arrogance. The Council may be fracturing, but those on it are there for a reason."

Fury thinned down Natasha's face, creating something inhumanly beautiful and terrifying.

He leaned closer, determined to drive home the danger circling her and her people. "It may have taken years to set the board, but I am here to let you know, you are behind in this game." He spat the last word out. "And if you don't readjust your strategies, you'll be wiped off the board."

"What, exactly, makes you and Zayn valuable to us?" Directly behind him, Carys's frigid question was accompanied by the kiss of metal against his neck.

Still staring into Natasha's eyes, he smiled then abruptly straightened. His hand snapped out, trapping Carys's wrist in his unforgiving grip. Her reflexes were quick enough, but not enough to avoid him slicing his neck along her blade. He pulled Carys's hand and the bloodstained blade forward, dragging Carys against his spine, his own blade lying in silent warning against her kidney.

"He and I are all that stands between you and the Council." Without looking away from Natasha, Darius exerted pressure against the bones of Carys's wrist, drawing a sharp hiss of pain as he shoved the Fey's blade closer to Natasha. "Taste the blood, Natasha. Tell me if what I've said is a lie."

CHAPTER 22

Natasha felt the moment Gavin decided to act and stepped back, blocking his movement. "No, Gavin, stand down." She eyed Darius who still held Carys's wrist with casual ease, his blood smeared across the blade held between them. His other hand was hidden behind him, but since Carys remained still and the only blood scenting the air was his, Natasha was sure he held an equally sharp threat against Carys.

She studied the demon in front of her, recognizing his challenge for what it was. Blood could lie, if the one offering was stronger than the one taking. "Let her go, Darius. If you want me to take the secrets from your blood, that paltry offering won't work."

"Paltry?"

"Truth exists in gifts given, not taken." She flicked her fingers at the bloodied blade. "That's not a gift."

The arctic blue darkened with a disconcerting mix of hunger and heat, but he lifted his fingers, one by one, from Carys's wrist.

The redhead yanked her hand and blade free, then

stepped back. "I could always carve a bigger hole for you, Natasha."

"You could try," Darius murmured, amusement lacing each word, even as he continued to hold Natasha's gaze.

"Thank you for the offer, Carys, but let's hold off just yet." Natasha closed the distance between her and Darius, until only inches separated them. She placed her palm against his chest, feeling the heavy beat of his heart. Her gaze drifted over him. Vicious want and calculated control warred in the stark lines of his face and vibrating muscles. This close, she couldn't miss the bloody line along his neck or escape his savory scent. The temptation to delve into his secrets was almost stronger than common sense. "So, pet, willing to let me play with your secrets?"

Darius captured her hand, lifting it from his chest, and brought it to his mouth. He nipped her palm, the tiny pain triggering a deeper hunger. "If I'm to bare my neck to your tender teeth, Natasha, I expect the same consideration."

His words had her fingers involuntarily curling around his. "Why?"

Unlike her, he wouldn't gain access to her innermost thoughts and needs through her blood.

"Consider it a formal acknowledgement of alliance."

His answer reminded her of an ancient custom, one not much practiced in the last few centuries. At one time, the six demon bloodlines, or Bloods, warred amongst themselves on a continual basis. Only when the humans had turned their attention to decimating the Kyn populations, did they stop and refocus their combined attention to outside threats. During those wars, ruling members of each Blood would forge necessary alliances with blood exchanges, combining the gifts of two bloodlines together to defeat a shared enemy.

To combine Darius's line of Death with her own Secrets could create an unprecedented advantage. Darius's strength rivaled hers. If she was honest, perhaps even surpassed hers. Together they could not only stand, but possibly triumph over the Council. Especially if Darius brought in the Sarielian Order.

The temptation was vast. Such an alliance would be a game changer. Only a fool would dismiss such a powerful tool. And she was far from a fool. "If the Blood of Death proves true, and our enemy is the same, the Blood of Secrets shall stand beside them."

"Then shall we?" Dark satisfaction hummed through his voice.

Behind her, Gavin protested, "Natasha, I don't like this."

Delicately pulling her hand free, she stepped back from Darius and turned to face Gavin. "I don't expect you to, however, if you and Carys would please make sure we aren't interrupted before we finish, I'd appreciate it."

Gavin shot a dark look over her head at Darius then glanced back at her. "You're going to the Side."

Not a real question, but she answered. "Yes. This is best done in our true forms." Besides, she and her demon were too intrigued by Darius. Sharing and tasting his blood, even for something as practical as an alliance, could turn so very intimate. The Side would offer the buffer of privacy. Whatever existed between her and the male behind her was not something she wanted up for consideration by others.

"Take Jamie with you, then."

She was already shaking her head. "No. This will remain between the four of us and no one else." She held Gavin's jade gaze, letting her skin slip enough to impress her determination. "Until we know who is ours and who isn't, it's best to keep this quiet."

He ran a hand through his hair, turned away, paced a few steps, then came back. "And if he decides to kill you over there? Then what?"

Amused by his concern, she smiled. "Take his heart."

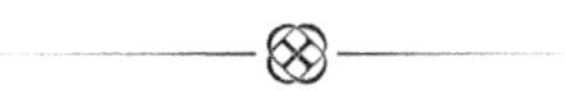

Natasha shed her human skin as she made her way through the barrier between the mortal realm and the Side. The magical barrier between the worlds resembled a mist-shrouded cloud bank. Darius moved silently alongside her, his form towering above hers, a study of inky shadows and mysteries.

The barrier thinned, bits and pieces of a room coming into focus. A few more steps and the barrier disappeared, leaving behind a room draped in exotic colors and lush furnishings. Hedonistic comfort oozed from the low-slung couches covered in plush piles of pillows clustered around an enormous fireplace. Large windows covered one side of the room, letting in red-tinted light. Trees, not seen in the mortal realm, reached for the sky. Their green, so deep as to be mistaken for black, draped the branches, while thick trunks sank into a carpet of vegetation. The landscape of the Side was a far cry from the human's version of Hell.

"Your private rooms?" Darius deep voice stroked along her spine.

"If I find out you're lying, it's best no one sees us together, pet." As she walked across the room, she waved a hand at the windows. Curtains fell with a quiet whisper. Stopping near the fireplace, she turned to face Darius. "Shall we?"

He stalked toward her, muscles flowing with mesmerizing strength under obsidian skin, the disconcerting blue eyes focused on her, his bone white horns rising from silky strands of black. He stopped in front of her and traced a delicate line from temple to chin with one white claw. "So eager to start?"

She titled her head back, careful not to scrape her horns against his. Such intimacy was generally reserved for lovers, unless contact was made in the heat of battle. She set both hands against his chest, her black tip claws curling in just enough to prick skin. "On your knees, Darius." The husky edge to her voice wasn't deliberate, just a byproduct of the image her words provoked.

His smile held the temptation of every fantasy she entertained. He sank to his knees with masculine grace, never taking his gaze from hers.

She stole a moment to bask in the feminine thrill it gave her to have this very lethal, very powerful male in such a position. She stepped in, using her hands on his shoulders for balance. His heat seeped through skin and bone, sinking to touch parts of her long ignored. Desire rose, churning brighter with each breath. This strange, intense intimacy was why she hadn't wanted to do this in front of Gavin and Carys.

His hands circled her waist, providing another anchor, another point of heat. His breath blew softly across her chest, causing her body to waken and yearn. Her claws tightened and released, testing the muscles under her touch.

He watched her with the predatory focus of a hunter. Heat, hunger, need, all swirled together. Her breath sped up as he leaned in and pressed a kiss against her thundering heart. Pulling back, he held her gaze then tilted his head to the side, offering his neck.

The bloody line left by Carys offered a temptation Natasha refused to ignore. A purr escaped as she leaned in and dragged her tongue in a delicate rasp along the wound. His deep, vibrating groan made her claws tighten, even as she licked her lips and lifted her head. The spice of his blood tingled, awakening a need for more.

She curled her left hand along his jaw, the brush of his goatee against her skin sending a delicate shiver through her. "*Qan üz illüziya yandirmaq edilir.*" Blood shall burn the illusions away. The words fell, weighted with promise and magic, triggering the ancient ritual. Energy sang between them, finding a home in both of them. Focusing on her most pressing questions, she sank her teeth deep.

An emotional storm rose and enveloped her, dragging her under. Black, bestial fury rose and crashed into white-hot lust, while male arrogance rode the waves, whipped along by the ravaging winds of duty and discipline. Unfazed, she sank beneath the battering waves, following his blood's siren song. The farther she dropped from the rampaging storm above, the quieter her surroundings became, allowing the whispers to share their voices. Memories surrounded her, each one an unprecedented insight into the warrior kneeling at her feet.

Long ago battles rose and fell. Pieces of conversations cut in and out. Friendships gained and lost left distinctive marks in their passing. Yet each spun by her as she wound her way closer to the answer she sought. The temptation to peer closer beckoned, but she ignored it. A deeply ingrained honor refused to allow her to look beyond her needs.

What connection does Darius hold to Zayn?

The whispers fell quiet with a startling suddenness. In

front of her two men stepped out of the shadows. So close in height, it was difficult to determine which was taller, but there was no mistaking who they were—Darius and Zayn.

Standing side by side, their coloring captured her attention. Both bore the distinctive olive tone reminiscent of desert vistas, but where Darius was the inky color of whispers, shadows, and mysteries, Zayn was the distracting play of light on sand, variations of gold and whites. Different, but somehow very much the same.

"Two sides of the same coin." With the sound of her own voice the connection clicked into place. "Brothers," she breathed. In front of her both men offered her identical bows. The eerie movement triggered another realization. "Twins."

But siblings weren't immune to betrayal. Her own twin left her to die in a bleak room in Turkey hundreds of years ago, simply to please a power-hungry male. How had she missed this relationship?

Darius's voice echoed through her. *"Our tie was buried in the dust of history per Mulcahy's advice. We felt no need to give the Council or anyone else such information."*

Her second question drifted forward. *"Where do your loyalties lie?"*

The image of Darius frowned at her, while Zayn simply watched. The scene wavered, shifted until it reformed...

Low slung couches with jewel-toned pillows took shape. Zayn sprawled along one, Darius on the other. "The Council will see us hunted by not just the humans, but our own." Gone was the condescending Councilman. In his place was a hard, unflinching male. "I have no intention of dying to appease the Council's ego."

"Then play your part well."

The familiar voice, one she thought never to hear again, spun her around. Ryan Mulcahy stood in front of her, cup in hand as he leaned against a wooden table, his attention solely on the two men behind her. For a moment she forgot where she was and reached out. Her fingers passed through air and Ryan didn't react.

She dropped her hand, letting it curl into a fist. Determined to catch every piece of this memory, she stepped back to watch all three males.

Zayn frowned. "Have I ever not?"

"Well, there was that one time, with the artist in Paris," Darius drawled.

Zayn cursed and threw a pillow at him. "Don't be a dick." He turned back to Ryan. "Do we have any idea who's on which side of the line yet?"

Ryan shook his head. "Other than Malachi, and possibly Antonia, I'm uncertain of the others. Chances are they are waiting to see what happens."

"They'll be coming for you." Concern hovered behind Darius's statement. "A few others in the Order have heard rumors, but can't pin anything down."

Ryan's smile was all teeth. "They've come for me before and been sent home with their tails between their legs."

"Which only makes them that much more dangerous," Zayn said. "They're going to be looking for cracks among your people, Mulcahy."

Ryan set his cup aside, hiding his face. "And they'll find them, but it won't give our enemies the openings they expect."

Darius dropped his feet to the floor, sitting forward on the edge of the couch. "What have you seen?"

Ryan lifted his head, facing the two before him. "Nothing concrete. Things are changing too fast to follow." He ran a hand through his collar length hair, the shifting strands of sable catching the light. "Regardless, I know my people. The Council will find a much more difficult prey than they anticipated."

Darius frowned. "Only if they stand together. Yet we all know if the Council can set them against each other, they will. Not just to create an opening, but to enjoy the show."

"My people will stand." Conviction rang through Ryan's voice.

Zayn tapped his knuckles against the back of the couch. "I'm not worried about Cheveyo and Vidis, or even your Wraiths. The one that worries me the most is Bertoi. She's more dangerous that the others combined."

Some of the tension dropped from Ryan's face and a small, private smile rose. "Something I'm counting on."

Darius raised his eyebrows. "What do you know that we don't?"

Ryan studied the two men for a moment, his thoughts well hidden. Finally he shook his head. "Not my place to share, but rest assured, Natasha will never side with the Council. She'll do whatever it takes to keep the Northwest Kyn safe, even from their own."

Zayn and Darius shared a look filled with unspoken words. Zayn turned back to Ryan. "Her mother sits at the table."

"And she is one treacherous bitch," Darius murmured.

Ryan propped his hands on the table behind him. "It's a trait both share."

"Yet, you still persist in trusting the daughter?" Zayn pushed.

Ryan nodded.

"Why?"

"Because the daughter has something her mother lacks. Loyalty."

"To who?" Zayn snapped. "Herself?"

"No." The rejection came from Darius who was studying Ryan closely. "To her own."

Ryan acknowledged Darius's answer. "She will protect those she considers hers, use whatever tool she can, regardless of the cost, so long as she can keep them safe. Even when they're blind to her reasoning."

Zayn narrowed his eyes. "Have you told her about us?"

Ryan shook his head. "There's no reason to reveal our position yet. It wouldn't do any good. For now, it's best to let the Council believe its actions are going unnoticed. In the meantime, I'll make sure to prepare me and mine for what's coming."

Letting out a hefty sigh, Zayn pushed up to his feet. "We'll meet again before the next meeting. I'll do my best to gather what information I can."

Darius rose as well. "I'll have the Order keep an ear to the ground."

Ryan straightened. "Be careful. If things progress how I fear, I may need you sooner rather than later."

The memory fractured, dissolving as Natasha processed the truths hidden in Darius's blood. Forgotten brothers, secret alliances, and oaths bound by more than honor. She turned each over as she drew back from the blood's whispers.

Blinking, she cleared her vision until Darius's face loomed before her. Still spinning from what she discovered, the fact she was cradled in his arms didn't even register.

"My turn," his deep voice rumbled, dragging her stunned attention to him. His head lowered, and his teeth locked on to her neck, piercing deep.

"*Qan qan, iki bir olmalidir.*" Blood to blood, two shall be one.

Natasha's blood hit Darius's senses with the battering force of tsunami—smoke, spice and sex, rolled into one overwhelming wave. It threatened to drown both man and demon. Her taste and the magic held within triggered his most basic instincts—to take, to dominate, to claim. His hold tightened and a hungry growl escaped.

The animalistic sound snapped him out of the red haze of need and want. He battled against his primal nature, forcibly relaxing his clawing grip as he struggled against the rising, mindless need.

It was like slogging through thick syrup. Finally, he managed to reestablish control. His jaw relaxed, easing his bite on the delicate neck under his teeth. Even as a husky moan filtered from the female demon in his arms, he ran his tongue over the mark. Once. Twice.

Then he lifted his head. Natasha was cradled in his arms. A position he would bet she rarely, if ever, found herself in. Considering the softened lines of her face as she blinked at him, he gave her about thirty seconds before she pulled herself together and jerked away.

He licked his lips and her gaze focused on his actions, darkening to a deep indigo. A deep breath, then another one. She reached up and traced one ebony nail over his mouth, the move strangely intimate. While her thoughts remained masked, he could see her reclaim her normal composure, one sure piece at a time. Her hand fell, and she pushed upright. Within moments, she put distance between them.

He let her go. Only because he didn't want to. And that was not something he could afford. Unlike Natasha, he couldn't read the secrets hidden in blood, but this exchange would cement their alliance.

However, blood, like magic, held its own power.

With the gifts at his disposal, having Natasha's blood leveled their playing field. As one of the Blood of Secrets, she could uncover and use the secrets she found against him. But as one of the Blood of Death, he would now be able to use his tie to manipulate her as well.

Death and torment against illusions and nightmares. It could prove an entertaining battle. If they could work together, they would become a formable force. If not, well, then neither he nor Zayn would have to worry about their secrets, because nothing escaped Death.

CHAPTER 23

"You're telling us we're down to DiMarcco and Westbrooke?"

Gavin wasn't happy, but then Natasha really didn't give a damn. Unsettled by her encounter with Darius, her patience and concentration were shot to hell.

Gavin gave Darius a narrow-eyed glare. "And if this is just another trap?"

"It's not," she snapped, curling her fists until her nails bit into her palm.

"Because blood doesn't lie?" The sneer in Gavin's question shredded her strained control.

She stalked across the room, ignoring Carys's gasp, as her demon surged against her skin, making its presence known. The surrounding air took on a chilling bite. Her nails thickened, the tips streaking black as she grabbed Gavin's T-shirt and yanked hard enough to bring his face down to hers.

Her voice deepened with promised pain. "Blood can't lie. Not to me." She cocked her head to the side and smiled, baring sharpened teeth. When Gavin paled, her smile stretched wider. "Shall I take yours and prove it?"

Wary but undaunted, Gavin didn't resist her hold. "It's my job to question, Natasha. The situation is too treacherous not to."

The young fool was right. Zayn and Darius were not the only ones with secrets to protect.

Carys kept her distance, but sidled closer to Gavin, deliberately moving into a defensive position. "Fighting among ourselves will do nothing but help those coming against us."

Natasha snarled then let Gavin go with a small push.

Darius watched in silence.

She spun on her heel to pace away, her fingers curling and uncurling. There was one way she could convince him, but—

"You can't tell them." Darius's drawl slipped in her head, pulling her up short. *"Not until you unearth the one carrying stories back to the Council. I will not risk him."*

With her back to Gavin and Carys, she slowly turned her head to look at the demon plaguing her and let out a slow hiss. Between the blood connection and her unsettled temper, keeping her thoughts masked from Darius was proving difficult.

Unwilling to indulge in their private connection, she answered him aloud. "We uncover the rat in our midst, and he holds any connection to Zayn, I'll kill you both myself." With their chance at linking their traitor to Zayn scuttling away, she still might hurt Darius anyway. Purely on principle.

Darius had the audacity to laugh. "Promises, promises."

From behind her, Carys said, "I'm not comfortable

bringing Zayn in, Natasha. Not when we have no idea which of ours is working against us."

Standing before the fireplace, Natasha stared at the fire merrily gorging itself on wood. Considering how much damage the Northwest leaders had suffered, Carys's concern was well founded. Whoever it was had to be close. While that narrowed their pool of suspects, it didn't make it any easier to accept. "We're not bringing Zayn into anything. What is discussed here remains between the four of us alone."

Realization hit even as Darius's mental agreement left her gritting her teeth. Locking her thoughts down against his voyeuristic tendencies as she, too, had people to protect from the Council, she considered who else would know about tonight's meeting. Raine. No doubt, Gavin had already clued his lover into this mess.

Natasha's agreement did little to appease Gavin. He demanded, "If you believe he isn't behind this mess, why not?"

She turned to face him. "Because if the traitor tells the Council he's siding with us, Zayn's life expectancy will dramatically decrease, and we will lose a necessary ally."

Darius finally spoke up. "So long as DiMarcco and Westbrooke believe Zayn is under suspicion, they'll simply view him as a possible scapegoat, not a threat. It'll give us time to uncover who's working against you."

Gavin glared at Darius, opened his mouth, only to snap it shut when his phone rang. He fished it out of his pocket and answered. "Durand."

The voice on the other end was too quiet to pick up, but Gavin's gaze settled on Darius with calculating intent. Gavin turned and gave his back to the room, walking over to the windows.

No one spoke as he took his call. Natasha watched the shift of muscles along his back as tension tightened his shoulders. She checked her watch. Ah, it must be Raine on the other end with a progress report on Axel.

A few minutes later, Gavin pocketed his phone and came back to stand in front of the other three. "Axel's at Vidis's, along with Cheveyo and Cassandra. It's not looking good."

Of course it wasn't, because their luck couldn't possibly shift for the better.

"Who's Axel?" Darius asked, coming to stand next to Natasha.

"Axel Kayser." Gavin folded his arms over his chest. "One of mine."

"Axel Kayser." Darius tested the name. When it clicked, his gaze sharpened. "One of the Wraiths, a shifter?"

Suspicion honed an edge to Gavin's voice. "How do you know who he is?"

"I told you, I'm your evaluator. Can't do that if I don't know who I'm evaluating." As bland as Darius tried to make his voice, he didn't really succeed.

Gavin's face darkened.

Natasha raised a hand before the two bull-headed males started butting horns. "Axel was attacked after tracking down leads on Mulcahy's death."

Darius looked between her and Gavin. "These leads, they were the three names?"

She nodded.

"And he's still alive?" A hefty amount of disbelief weighted Darius's question.

The muscles in Gavin's folded arms flexed with tension. "You sound surprised."

"Considering what he found, yes." Darius turned away to pace. For a moment, they all watched him. "To get that much and escape with his life is actually quite impressive."

Natasha didn't think Axel would consider it impressive. Lucky? Maybe. If he ever woke.

On Darius's third pass, he stopped. "Did he give you anything besides the names?"

She considered him. Was Darius looking for something specific? "Such as?"

Darius shrugged. "What led him to find the names in the first place? Was it a person? A place?" He faced all three of them. "I need to talk to him."

"He's not talking." Carys came up Gavin and rejoined the conversation. "If he was, we wouldn't be here." Somehow her unspoken *wasting time with* you came through loud and clear.

"Enough!" *Gods above and below, how had Ryan managed these personalities without hurting someone?* Egos and arrogance would be the downfall of this fledging alliance, leaving easy pickings behind for the Council. "Did we not agree to work on the same side?" Natasha waited for the round of grudging nods. "Then start acting like the adults you are, instead of squabbling children. If we continue questioning every choice and every move, we'll do the Council's job for them." Facing Darius, she said, "The reason the Northwest is the force it is, can be found in the leaders Ryan choose. Don't lessen the validity of his judgment with your insinuations." Turning to Gavin and Carys, she continued. "As for you two, do you think Ryan would align with a fool? There is a reason he picked this man to work with against the Council. It's in our best interests to maintain that partnership."

She wanted to tear her hair out in frustration. When the queen of demons became the voice of reason, it was time to worry.

Carys was the first to back down, stepping back to give Darius some breathing room, although Natasha didn't miss the spark of amusement in Carys's gaze before she turned away. Gavin soon followed suit, dropping his arms as the tension in his spine dialed back. He moved to one of the chairs and leaned against it, waiting.

Darius smiled.

That smile tripped her temper, but she refused to let it go. Wouldn't do a bit of good to have her slap him after her little speech to the other two.

His eyes lightened and she knew he caught that thought. His voice, however, remained serious. "You said he was alive. Why can't Vidis help him heal?"

"He's in a coma," Carys answered.

His forehead furrowed in confusion. "A coma?"

"A spell induced coma," she clarified.

His confusion cleared, leaving behind intent focus. "What kind of spell?"

"Considering how old the magic our enemies tend to play with is, perhaps you should go with Gavin to answer that question." Natasha gave the order wrapped in silky suggestion.

Darius dipped head. "At your service."

His courtesy extended only as long as it served his purposes. She forced her smile into less revealing, more natural lines.

"Natasha—"

She cut off Gavin's protest with a raised hand. "Go, both of you. We need whatever we can get from Axel before he dies. A link we can use. Otherwise we're back to fishing in an endless hole."

Gavin shut his mouth, but his jaw continued to flex. Finally, he said, "Are you coming?"

"Jamie's here, waiting. Besides, you'll only fit Darius into your toy." Gavin's sleek little two-seater didn't leave much room for passengers. "It's probably best you two leave now. You'll make better time."

Carys dropped the silencing spell, and the disconcerting feeling accompanying her magic drifted away. The two men took their leave, and the tension lingering in their wake dissipated.

Only after the sound of the front door closing, did Carys turn to Natasha. "Are you sure about this? Allowing Darius to work with us, tying him so close to you, it's dangerous."

Natasha moved about the room, turning off the lights. "More dangerous for him than us." Stopping next the fireplace, she studied Carys. "Worried about me?"

Carys gave a delicate snort and clicked off the lamp next to her, leaving the two women bathed in firelight. "Worried about the blood connection you two share." She moved to the edge of the sofa and leaned against the arm. "How much does he see, Natasha?"

Sincere, but cautious concern underlay her question, and it snuck past most of Natasha's guards to brush up against the aching spot of Ryan's loss. Strangely touched, Natasha turned away, her answer equally serious. "Only what I want him to."

For a moment or two silence waited between them, then Carys asked the unexpected, "What's his bloodline?"

Once again Carys proved Ryan had chosen his replacement well. Eventually Natasha would get use to

Carys's insightful questions. For now, it wouldn't hurt to share. Just in case things went horribly wrong. "Death."

Carys closed the distance between them, her hand curling around Natasha's arm. "What have you done, Natasha?"

The fear and worry warring over the other woman's face made Natasha wonder just how much information Carys held on the Amanusa.

"What was needed, Carys." Natasha gently pulled free of Carys's hold. "Death may be final, but Secrets—those can reap long lasting and far reaching damage."

"Only if you're alive to use them."

"He's had more than enough chances to kill me." Natasha waved a hand along her body. "I'm still here, alive and well."

"Only because you fascinate him." Carys's teeth worried her bottom lip. "You and I both know a man's need to shag a woman only goes so far."

The blunt remark surprised a laugh from Natasha. "I don't think seducing him is necessary, though I appreciate the backhanded compliment."

Carys rolled her eyes. "Are you planning on blackmailing him to keep him in line? Because, if so, I've got some serious concerns with that approach."

"No, I don't think I'll have to resort to that either." Well, at least not yet. Down the road? Hard to say. She had no doubts if it came down to the Northwest or his brother, the Northwest would lose. Unless she managed to change his priorities. Hmmm, something to consider.

"Why?" Carys's blunt question snapped Natasha out of her musings. "Because he was Ryan's inside man on the Council?"

Partially, but—"Because without us he can't get what he wants."

"Which is?"

Natasha smiled at Carys. "Revenge."

Carys considered her closely. "And what do you get?"

Ah, such a pleasure to work with another intelligent female. "Power, darling."

CHAPTER 24

With Carys at her side, Natasha stepped outside, locking Ryan's door behind her. Niall emerged from the shadowed recesses of the porch and stopped at Carys's side.

In the drive, Jamie stood in the faintly lit opening between the driver's door and the car, waiting.

"I'll see you at Vidis's?" Carys murmured.

Natasha nodded and navigated her way down the steps.

As she closed the distance between her and Jamie, he leaned his arms on the roof of the car. "Osborn called while you were in your meeting. He wants you to call him back as soon as you can."

Her pulse spiked. Maybe they finally caught a break. She stopped, turned, and called out, "Carys."

The redhead had reached the end of the steps. She and Niall both stopped at her voice. "Yes?"

"I may be a few minutes late."

"Everything all right?"

"A call from Division, one I can't ignore. You'll inform the others?"

Carys nodded.

Satisfied, Natasha turned back and walked around to the door Jamie held open for her. She slipped into the interior, the door closing behind her with a soft thump. Within moments, Jamie got into the driver's seat and retrieved her cell phone.

He handed it back to her. "Do you want me to wait until you finish your conversation before we head out?"

She took the phone. "Please." Reception was sometimes spotty and this was not a phone call she wanted to miss. She pulled up the last incoming call and hit the screen to call it back.

Jamie watched her.

She raised a questioning eyebrow, the sound of the phone ringing through a mild distraction.

"Am I allowed to stay for this?"

Considering the not so hidden whine of petulance sneaking out of his question, she guessed someone wasn't finished pouting about their earlier conversation. However, it wasn't worth the impending argument just to prove a point. "Are you sure you can handle it?"

He opened his mouth to answer, but Osborn's greeting had her raising a hand to cut Jaime short. "Chief Osborn, you rang?"

Sandpaper rough, Osborn's voice came over the line. "Good evening, Ms. Bertoi, I wanted to call you with an update regarding our conversation on Wednesday."

Had that only been two days ago? Time flies when you're being hunted. "You've found something in regards to Sutler?"

"Actually we've found him."

She straightened, her gaze flying to Jamie's.

Considering his avid attention, he was hearing every word. "Any possibility of letting one of our investigators interview him?" Or at least get close enough to eliminate him.

"Only if they can talk to the dead."

Her fingers tightened on the phone. "Where did you find him?"

"Some kayakers found a piece of him at a marine park south of Columbia City."

"Piece?"

"Partial torso."

"Not to impugn your investigation, but are you certain it's Brant Sutler?" A partial torso wouldn't give anyone much to go on.

"We're still waiting on the DNA test to confirm, but he had a distinctive birthmark just below his shoulder blade. It's a match."

"That's...unfortunate. Any ideas on how he came to be in such a state?"

"The coroner is still trying to determine what weapon was used." The careful blankness in Osborn's voice made her suspect the damage to the torso could probably be attributed to teeth and claws versus the smoother edge of a blade. That did not bode well for the Kyn or their carefully constructed veil of secrecy.

"How bad is it?"

"Bad." He paused. "Even worse if any other parts turn up with the same marks. Right now, it's a tossup between teeth or claws."

"Could be a killer salmon," Jamie muttered too low for Osborn to hear.

She frowned, but made a mental note to warn Gavin. Perhaps together they could ensure a different story emerged. "Wolves, bears, even cougars have been spotted in some areas, Mr. Osborn."

A harsh grunt that could only be mistaken for a laugh with a great deal of imagination sounded in her ear. "Wolves? Like the one that tore through the 88 Ivories a few weeks back?" He let out a hard breath. "Dammit, Natasha."

The level of exhaustion and stress in those two words tugged at her. She could empathize. "Could you keep me posted on what is determined to be the cause of death? I'd be happy to offer Taliesin's services if needed."

"We'll see."

His tone indicated she would wait quite a while for that particular call. "Were you able to find any other connections to Sutler?"

"Maybe, hang on." The sound of movement came over the line, objects or papers being rifled through. "Does the name Cleo James mean anything to you?"

For a moment, her mind blanked in shock. Not the name she expected to hear, not even close. "Cleo James?"

Jamie straightened to attention, red flashing in his eyes before they narrowed.

"Yeah, seems Sutler deleted some online conversations with her just before he disappeared. We've been trying to locate her, but she seems to be out of town."

"It sounds familiar." Excitement and rage mixed into a pulse pounding high. It took a great deal of control to keep her voice casual. "Could I do some research and let you know in the morning?"

"Sure. If I'm not in, just leave me a message, I'll call you back."

"Will do. Thank you."

They rang off. Cradling the phone in her lap she raised her head, her gaze colliding with Jamie's.

"Why do you look so happy?" he asked.

"Cleo James is our key to unraveling this mess."

He raised his eyebrows. "Cleo James? Seriously?"

"You know her?"

He snorted. "If you're male and making your way up the corporate ladder, she'd come sniffing around. Fun to flirt with, but not my first choice for stimulating conversation."

Interesting. "She was Sullivan's girlfriend."

"Sullivan's girlfriend was messaging Sutler? Why?" He paused, his eyes widened. "Wait, you don't think Sullivan was behind the whole mess with the werewolves?"

"No." Although she suspected that was exactly what someone wanted her to think. "Sullivan's death was a rather useless attempt to discredit my authority. No, someone is tying up loose ends."

"And if we don't find Cleo, she'll be next." He looked away, thinking. "According to Osborn, she's in the wind. It's going to be hard to find her."

"Not as hard as you think," she murmured.

Jamie turned back to her, watching closely. "You know where she is, don't you?"

Natasha sighed. "She's dead."

Shock and something else ran over his face, too quick to read. "What? When?"

"This morning."

His mouth tightened. "Are you trying to tell me Cleo attacked you? Are you shitting me? There's no way she could have done the damage Fahd and I cleaned up."

Stuck in the car with Jamie, there's no way he'd drop it until she gave him the whole story. She kept it as short as possible. "That wasn't Cleo. That was Jared Pick."

Jamie rubbed the back of his neck. "Who's Jared Pick?"

"The Half-Bound demon who tore apart not only my living room, but Cleo and Sullivan."

He dropped his hand and blew out a hard breath. "What the hell is going on?"

She leaned forward and patted his shoulder. "I told you, we're being hunted."

"By?"

"The Council, dear." She sat back, crossed her legs and smoothed her skirt. "Unfortunately, they've decided to use someone close to us to assist them."

Jamie blinked at her, his face a tad pale. Not an unusual reaction considering her answer. "Who?"

She gave him a small smile. "The answer to that is at Vidis's, so we should be on our way."

He shook his head and turned in his seat. He pulled his seatbelt into place then started the car. "Who, or what, is at Vidis's?" He turned the car and around and headed down the drive.

She looked out into the darkness pressing against the windows. "Axel Kayser."

As Gavin drove toward Warrick Vidis's home, night settled over the landscape, replacing the multitude of lights with a thick curtain of trees.

Neither man spoke during the ride, leaving a rather strained silence behind.

Gavin slowed then turned onto a winding, gravel road, snaking deeper into the surrounding forest.

Darius winced at the sounds of rocks pinging against the low-slung car's undercarriage. He turned from his contemplation of the passing scenery just in time to catch a similar expression crossing Gavin's face.

"This road isn't doing your ride any favors," Darius drawled.

Gavin glanced at him before returning to the road in front of him. "Yeah, but trying to get Vidis to live closer to town is pointless. Besides it'd be like setting the big, bad wolf on a town full of little pigs."

Darius chuckled. Lights broke through the night, first one, then another, until Gavin pulled to a stop in front of a breath-taking home.

Too big to be labeled a cabin, the two-story, wood-and-glass structure blended in with its surroundings. The expansive front porch wrapped all the way across. As Gavin shut off the engine, a small figure stepped out to lean over the railing. Light bounced off short, spiky blonde hair, even as an arm rose in a casual wave.

Darius exited the car and followed Gavin around and up the stairs.

"Hey, Gavin." Xander Cade, Vidis's mate, waited for them. Behind her, the heavy wooden door stood partially open, allowing a bit of light to spill across the porch.

"Hey, Xander. Everyone make it back okay?"

"For now. Cheveyo sent Chayton to one of the bedrooms upstairs to crash. Holding on to Axel during the flight, just about did him in." She slid a glance at the open door then back at them. "Thanks for sending Raine and Cassandra."

Gavin gave a small nod. "Things okay?"

The little blonde wolf grimaced. "It doesn't look good. Every time Cheveyo or Cassandra make some progress, Axel slips further away." She was tense and pale. Even the delicate tattoo on her face couldn't hide the strain of the night's activities. She turned her attention to Darius, her eyes taking on a lupine glow. "Why is he here?"

Darius hid his amusement when Gavin shifted a bit, as if to protect him. "Natasha wants him here."

Xander continued to stare. "This isn't his territory."

"No, but it is mine." Warrick Vidis stepped out onto the porch then continued until he could wrap his arms around his mate. "If Natasha wants him here, he may stay."

Darius didn't mistake Vidis's unassuming appearance as an indicator of his strength. Standing close to six foot, with shaggy brown hair and brown eyes, the Northwest alpha hid his power well.

Darius dipped his head in acknowledgement. "Natasha felt I might be of help with what ails your wolf."

"Did she?" Vidis murmured.

"Natasha and Carys are on their way in, they should be here soon," Gavin said.

Xander shook her head. "Carys will, but Natasha's running late. She took a call from Division."

"About?" Gavin asked.

Xander shrugged. "No idea."

Warrick's shoulders hunched, his eyes closed, and Xander let out a low hiss. In front of him, Gavin stiffened.

Before Darius could ask any questions, all three turned and rushed inside. He followed in their wake, closing the door behind him. He made his way into a rather impressive living room, complete with an enormous fireplace framed in river stone. A large, three-piece leather sectional was shoved back, creating an empty space on the hardwood floor in front of fireplace. Cheveyo sat cross-legged on one side of a still form Darius assumed was Axel. Raine mimicked him on the other.

Axel's head rested in the lap of an older woman, whose

white hair hung in two incongruous braids. Such a style belonged to someone much younger, but it somehow worked.

Even as Gavin crouched behind Raine, careful not to touch her, Vidis and Xander settled in between Cheveyo and the older woman. Drawing closer, Darius crouched at Axel's feet. That close, he couldn't miss the ebb and flow of magic surging between Vidis, Cheveyo, Raine, and the other woman.

"Cassandra, I can't hold it back much longer." Cheveyo's voice was tight with strain.

"Just a little more." The older woman's soft response seemed to ease his tension. "Raine, dear, can you reinforce this?"

Raine swayed, but nodded. Her actual answer didn't sound anywhere Darius could hear. Not surprising, since all three were working on the metaphysical plane in an attempt to heal the badly injured Wraith. If the damage on the outside was any indicator of what they faced on their end, Darius held little hope for Axel's continual survival.

What was left of the man's face was a horrific mask of wounds. Not to mention the rends and tears decorating his torso. Those injuries slipped below the towel lying across waist and groin, offering a modicum of privacy. Darius set one hand on the ground beside Axel's thigh and leaned in to examine the wounds strafing the shifter's legs. "Claws," he murmured.

Cheveyo turned to him, power swirling in the inky depths of his obsidian gaze, making it hard to hold. "Claws, teeth, and magic. Old magic."

"Will you allow me to help?" Darius held that uncomfortable gaze, refusing to relent, even as the subtle challenge riled his own demon.

For a moment, the witch didn't answer, then slowly he nodded his head. "Sit. Join, but be careful. Things are not what they seem."

Taking the warning under advisement, Darius settled on the floor at Axel's feet. Wrapping his hand loosely around Axel's bare ankle, he concentrated on the magic, bringing it into focus, feeling the flux of energy against his skin.

Much like Sullivan, Axel was encased in a multilayered spell. It took a few moments to identify what kind of magic was at play as he carefully examined each layer. Cassandra and Cheveyo managed to unravel the first few layers, and that magic seemed to be contained in some kind of energy trap. Unusual and very intriguing. He'd have to remember to follow up on that nifty trick later.

Turning his attention to what he could identify, Darius tested each bit of magic. Definitely wizard. The oily stain darkened all it touched, seeping through each layer. Deep inside its mental cage, his demon growled as he brushed up against the faint vibration of fur and moonlight. Pack magic, probably. The energy in the final layer kept slipping away, only detectable on the edges of his awareness. The minute he tried to pull it closer, it drifted away like smoke.

"There's something there, I can't catch it," he murmured.

Cheveyo pointed to Axel's barely moving chest. "Look, here."

Puzzled, Darius asked, "The bruise?"

"That's not a bruise, young man," Cassandra chided him, reducing his decades to single digits. "That is the spell keeping Axel from us and his alpha."

"And it's damn touchy," Raine gritted out.

He looked over and saw that the girl's eyes fairly

glowed and something clicked into place. The energy trap holding the other spells at bay, it belonged to Raine. "Touchy?"

"Every time we go to unravel it, it slithers out of sight, like it's hiding in an invisible hole."

Raine's explanation sent shockwaves reverberating through Darius. She could actually see magic, not just sense it. Bits and pieces of the couple's previous behavior—the way they seemed to read each other's mind or the way Gavin's magic seemed to deepen—fell into place. Half-formed stories tugged at his mind, but now was not the time to listen. He narrowed his eyes, his attention sliding to Gavin, sitting behind her.

A dangerous emotion flared in Gavin's eyes, turning the green into depthless dark jade. His hands curled over Raine's shoulders. Recognizing the protective threat, since all too often his own reflection held the same cold image of death, he simply asked, "Like it did with Sullivan?"

Gavin nodded.

Darius stifled his curse. If Raine could see magic, and this particular spell kept disappearing from her sight, it could mean it belonged to someone with demon blood. "You realize what this means?" he directed his question to Gavin.

"Yeah," Gavin growled. "We're dealing with the same shit who spelled Sullivan."

Turning back to the other two who watching their byplay, Darius said, "I need to check on something."

Cheveyo stopped him. "Check on what?"

"Since this is acting like the spells Gavin and I encountered with Sullivan, chances are we're looking at the same castor. If that's the case, there's a damn good chance the reason you can't counter it yet, is because that nasty bastard on his chest is tied to the Side." And if he didn't work fast, they'd lose the man lying before them.

"Hold up," Raine snapped. "How is the spell anchored in the Side if Axel is a shifter? I thought you needed demon blood to hold it in place?"

He didn't want to answer her, especially since a horrible suspicion was swirling through him. Yet if he didn't, they'd continue to argue with him and Axel would die. Natasha would not be happy with that outcome. "There's another option, part of Axel's spirit could be trapped in the Side."

Xander's small gasp didn't hide Vidis's low growl.

"Will you be able to free him?"

Much like the power she wielded, Cassandra was a center of calm control. He'd met a few witches like her, powerful, but unable to violate the witches' three-fold law —unable to cause harm to any, in fear it would revisit them threefold.

He gave a short nod. "But you'll have to work fast. I'm betting the spell is set to take out its anchor if anyone tampers with it."

"You mean it will kill Axel," Xander snarled.

"Yes, so as soon as I break the link, use the pack ties and drag his ass back over." Darius aimed his next command at Cheveyo. "You need to hold a protective shield in place." He canted his head slightly at Cassandra, an unspoken warning to protect her as well. Unlike his companion, Cheveyo didn't strike him as one to hold too tight to the three-fold law.

Cheveyo gave a barely perceptible nod, and the brush of magic rushed against Darius as the protective energy settled into place.

Darius turned to Raine and Gavin. "However you're holding the other spells back, keep it steady. Don't let them trigger or we're screwed." Not waiting for assurance, he looked up to meet Vidis's amber gaze. "I'll do what I can to bring your wolf back, Alpha, but if this is Amanusa magic, it won't let go of him easily."

"Neither will I," the man growled.

Knowing he'd done all he could to protect Natasha's people, Darius followed the magic into the Side.

CHAPTER 25

STANDING IN BETWEEN REALMS, DARIUS STUDIED THE DISTURBING scene before him, holding his human form intact. Without Natasha here to act as his go-between, he had to be able to communication with the others, even as he worked in the Side. Very few Kyn did well in the Side. Unlike the Between, where most Kyn pulled their magic from, the Side played hell, literally, with any magic not tied to an Amanusa.

Axel wasn't doing well at all. Rage and pity swam through Darius in a stomach-churning storm. Even his demon hissed in displeasure. His suspicions proved correct. The castor managed to anchor the spell in the Side, but he also tied the spell to Axel's spirit.

Unfortunately, shifters, much like Amanusa, were dual in nature—two spirits sharing one body, a fact this nasty-ass concoction used with twisted deviousness. While Axel the man lay in a coma in the mortal world, Axel's wolf was trapped in a realm he was never meant to see. No wonder Vidis wasn't able to use pack ties to help his wolf. Those ties couldn't reach into the Side, not unless they had help. Help,

Darius planned to provide, just as soon as he figured out how.

The wolf snarled and snapped, nothing sane lingering behind the amber gaze. The edges of the spell encircled the wolf, the disturbing energy fluctuating in a mind-bending ribbon, keeping Axel inside its boundaries. Darius didn't dare break the visible edges of magic until he knew what he was dealing with. The more he studied it, the more he began to recognize what was at work. Someone took one of the Amanusa's most hated spells and turned it into something much, much more disturbing—a weapon to be used against other Kyn.

It was a warped version of a constraining magic Amanusa used on their adolescents, when hormones and rising demonic natures did not mix well. If an Amanusa's offspring wasn't strong enough to control their chaotic nature, it would drive their more human half insane. When that happened, a spell was used to lock the teenager's demonic nature in the Side, limiting the amount of damage they could inflict on themselves and those around them. However, in the mortal realm the human form would be in a coma. Then it became a waiting game, as the Amanusan nature and intellect battled and fought for dominance. Either the child found the mental fortitude to accept themselves, or they died.

In Axel's case, they trapped his wolf in a realm guaranteed to drive him insane. Plus, the more Darius studied the spell, the worse it got. The energy appeared to weave in and out of the wolf. Whatever it was doing, had to hurt, because the animal would break off from his snarling to snap at his own skin, leaving bloody wounds in its wake. Somehow the spell severed Axel's connection to the

Between, cutting man and wolf apart, while weakening the bond to his alpha.

Since blood was the basic key of most Kyn magic, Darius took a chance. Elongating one nail, he sliced a narrow line across his palm, waiting until his blood welled. If blood was the basis of the spell, then he needed to destroy that base before it snapped the last line between Vidis and Axel.

"Vidis, can you reach Axel's wolf at all?" Darius needed to get in close and would much rather not get bitten if given a damn choice.

Instead of a verbal answer, small fireflies of light began to flicker to life all along Axel's fur, the heaviest concentration centered on his chest. When the spell reacted, stunned fury raced through Darius. The bastard who cast the spell set the anchors inside the wolf's spirit.

Darius leapt forward, powering through the edges of the spell, feeling it rip along his skin with serrated teeth. As the pain rose, so did his demon. His hold on his human skin wavered. He tackled Axel's wolf, managing to hit the beast from the side and take him to the ground.

The sickening magic whipped around him. His demon's howls joined Axel's. Ignoring both beasts, Darius used his body to pin the wolf, using his forearm just behind the creature's ear, to keep his jaws from Darius's skin. He struggled to not just hold the head in place, but keep his eyes covered. If the maddened werewolf caught sight of a real live demon, Darius might as well kill him now because there'd be nothing left to save.

Axel was a stubborn bastard. Even weak and in tremendous pain, he kept trying. Executing a particular vicious twist, he managed to sink his teeth into the underside of Darius's upper arm.

Darius bellowed at the hot, bright pain. All pretense at humanity dropped away. Now in full demon form, his hands were bigger, able to cover more of Axel's vision, and still hold him in place. He almost missed the click when his blood connected to something inside the wolf and claimed it as its own. Acting on instinct alone, Darius slammed his magic out in a protective rush.

Death rode along the energy, attacking anything not connected to Darius or Axel. When it collided with the still dancing light of Vidis's connection, it paused in recognition then shifted to encompass that link as well. It slammed into the sickening magic snaking in and out of Axel. The resulting, silent explosion shattered the remaining spell into hundreds of ashy shards, leaving behind three distinct anchors.

Axel writhed, his howls agonized.

Together Darius and Vidis continued to pour their power into Axel, rebuilding his connection to his pack. On some level Darius worried what damage they were doing to the wolf, but he still refused to stop. Vidis's magic gained strength, the fireflies growing into embers, then into eye-searing flames as Darius turned his attention to the last remaining anchors.

"On my count," he gritted out. "One…" He smashed the first anchor then sent his magic along the next one. "Two…" He ripped it free even as Axel's wolf convulsed. Surrounding the last one, he hammered it to pieces. "Three!"

The light surrounding the wolf flashed white hot then disappeared, leaving Darius blinking in the aftermath. He barely noted the smeared remains of the shattered spell littering the ground at his feet, before he dropped back into the mortal realm. His head spun at the abrupt reentry.

Panicked shouts and rough curses swirled around him, even as his hands reflexively clamped down on Axel's drumming heels.

"He's seizing!"

"Put this between his teeth!"

"Hold his head still!"

"Godsdammit, we're going to lose him!"

Darius blinked, clearing his vision, even as the movement under his hands slowed. He looked along Axel's twitching body and ran straight into the amber gaze of a wolf trapped in a battered human face. "Betrayed…" Axel's hiss was caught between pain and fury. "Betrayed us…" His words choked off as his body arced into a cruel bow and an inhuman howl escaped.

Darius winced as Axel's body slammed back into the ground.

Then Vidis was there, kneeling next to the raving wolf, his hands catching Axel's wildly thrashing head, framing his face. "Calm." One word, but even Darius could feel the weight of power behind it.

Blocked by Vidis's back, Darius couldn't see what happened next, but the soft reassurances continued, urging Axel to relax and breathe. There were no false reassurances that he'd be okay, only that he "was safe for now." After a handful of moments, Axel's guttural growls slowed and his abused body stilled.

Then a small whine escaped. Unsure how long the calm would last, Darius lightened his grip on the wolf's ankles, but didn't release him. Not until Vidis indicated it was safe.

"Tell me." Vidis's soft, inescapable command cut through the combined noise of heavy breathing and pants.

"Called in…" Axel's voice held broken edges. "Heard

something, needed to share with Gavin." His heavy breathing picked up.

"You gave me three names," Gavin reassured him.

Even with Vidis's back in the way, Darius saw Axel shake his head. "No, something more. Another connection. Little prick, hiding right in front of us—have to warn you —" His body began to shake, cutting off his words.

"Get what you need quickly, Alpha." Cassandra laid her hands over Vidis's, and Axel's tremors slowed.

The alpha gave a short nod. "Breathe, Axel. No, don't look away." Pause. "That's it." The alpha and his wolf took another breath. "Give me the connection."

"Connected Brant Sutler to Cl...cleo James, Sullivan's woman."

Darius and Gavin shared a look. Cleo James. The girl the Half-Bound dragged into Natasha's home.

But Axel wasn't done. "She's also con—connected to another Wraith—has been for years. They just hid their relationship." Another violent tremor wracked his body.

Cassandra hissed in warning.

"Give me a name," Vidis demanded.

"Jamie fucking Ryder," Axel snarled.

Disgust and fury hazed Darius's mind as he paced from one end of the expansive back deck to the other. He refused to allow his underlying panic for Natasha to gain a foothold.

Axel's announcement sent shockwaves through Vidis's living room. Exclamations of disbelief and vile curses abounded. Hostility and anger erupted from Gavin, Raine, and Xander—the three Wraiths woefully unprepared for betrayal from within. As for Vidis and Cheveyo, they held their cards closer to their chests, but Darius knew they would soon be chiming in on the massive clusterfuck they now faced. Only Carys's arrival stopped things from spinning farther out of control and gave Cassandra a chance to reclaim the room. The older witch directed Vidis to take Axel upstairs, then she all but ordered Carys to follow. Unable to stay in the living room, where rioting emotions only urged his own beast closer to the surface, Darius retreated to the back deck.

Nothing eased the gouging urge to hunt down the duplicitous shit. *Why had he listened to Natasha?* Damn fool woman and her arrogance. How had she missed this? Hell, how had the little fuck managed to fool so many for so long?

Gavin stepped out of the house, stopping to watch him pace. Darius ignored him. He didn't trust himself to open his mouth. Instead, he continued to wear a private path along the wooden planks.

"I can't reach Natasha."

Gavin's quiet words brought Darius to an abrupt halt at the far end of the deck. He deliberately reached out and curled his hands over the wooden rail. The wood squeaked under the pressure. Gods above and below, what he wouldn't give for the wood to be Ryder's fucking neck right about now.

"Can you?"

Darius jerked his head around at the question. "Can I, what?" he growled, his demon so close the words were almost unintelligible.

Gavin walked over and stood just out of arm's reach, the night shadow's masking his expression. "Can you reach her?"

Darius gritted his teeth and shook his head. Not that he

hadn't tried. The minute Ryder's name fell from Axel's mouth, Darius reached out, trying to use the blood tie. No smart ass remark, no sense of the complex woman he was beginning to discover. Not one damn spark. Instead, all he found was a disturbing blankness. "She could be out of range."

"Out of range?"

"The farther apart we are, the harder it is to communicate. All I can tell you is, she's still alive." He hoped.

"I'd rather you tell me where she is," Gavin bit out.

Darius flexed his hands against the wood, allowing blood to return to his fingers. "It's a blood tie, not some damn mate bond."

"Blood tie?"

The growled question came from behind him. Darius spun around to face Vidis as he stepped away from Cheveyo, who closed the door behind the two of them. Since they had the name of their traitor, keeping this information from the other two leaders now became pointless. Still the alpha's question scraped against him, and Darius snapped back. "Alliances based on words alone mean less than nothing."

Undeterred, Vidis stepped in until he violated any personal space Darius could claim. "What alliance?"

His demon surged, and the night took on a reddish tint. "The one I forged with Natasha to keep you and yours safe from the Council."

Vidis's lips curled back from his teeth and he rolled up on his toes.

Darius held the amber gaze with ease. His demon was so riled, he bled through—his nails sharpening into thick claws, his teeth elongating until he was snarling back.

"Cease." A solid gust of wind slipped between Darius and Vidis. Strong, invisible hands shoved against Darius's chest. The unexpected move sent him stumbling back a step. In front of him, Vidis mimicked him.

Both turned to the tall witch standing next to Gavin, arms folded across his chest as Cheveyo glared at both of them. "We have enough predators willing to tear us apart. We don't need to do the job for them." He eyed both of them. "Agreed?"

Darius inclined his head and deliberately leaned back against the railing. He folded his arms across his chest, tucking his claws out of sight, and dragged in a deep breath, striving for a calm that seemed absurdly out of reach. Right now, rage would gain him nothing but unnecessary delays in locating Natasha.

Cheveyo let both men draw back then broke the quiet. "I was unaware of any alliance being made tonight." And whatever his reaction was to that, was well concealed.

"It's a rather recent development," Darius was careful to keep his voice level.

"Does it have anything to do with the three names Gavin mentioned tonight?" Vidis turned away to gaze over the forest sprawled below.

"Yeah," Gavin answered. "Axel was attacked shortly after he shared three names as possible leads in Mulcahy's death." He paused. "Zayn Aimeric, Leopold DiMarcco, and Corwin Westbrooke."

Darius gave Cheveyo and Vidis credit, as Gavin dropped the three bombshells, both of the Northwest leaders barely blinked.

"And Natasha was able to rule out Mr. Aimeric." Carys's voice carried over the deck. All four males turned to face the redhead coming through one of the French doors. Light and shadow played over her face as she came closer to their impromptu huddle. "Thanks to the blood tie she forged with Darius, here."

Cheveyo and Vidis turned their attention to Darius. He refused to react. If they had questions, they could damn well voice them. Then he'd consider answering them.

Cheveyo didn't look away from Darius. "That's not a strong enough reason to forge an alliance, Carys."

"Not for you, perhaps," Carys said. "However, maybe this will help sway your opinion. Not only is Darius a member of the Sarielian Order, but he was Ryan's inside source to the Council. Natasha felt it was in the Northwest's best interest to maintain that partnership." Her voice hardened. "I tend to agree with her."

"Why?" Vidis snapped.

Her smile wasn't nice. "Ryan knew the Council would eventually hunt us, so he created relationships that would give the Northwest an added element against them. If we try to face down the Council alone, we'll fail to protect our people. We're not strong enough to convince those wavering on the Council to side with us. We need something more to offer by way of protection. Darius can do that for us, can't you?"

He smiled and inclined his head. "As I've said before, the Order serves the Kyn, not the Council."

"Can you guarantee every member of the Order feels the same?"

Darius understood the bitterness running along Gavin's question. For the new captain, discovering a snake curled around your ankle with fangs sunk in deep could make one wonder about the wisdom of trusting anyone. "For one of the few times in my life, yes, I can."

"How?" Vidis asked.

Surprisingly, it was Carys who answered, "Because aligning with us gives Darius something he wants very badly."

Curious to her answer, Darius asked, "And what is that?"

Danger and something much more primitive glittered in her green eyes. "Revenge for one of your own."

Cheveyo frowned. "One of your own?"

Next to him, Gavin shifted his weight. "She means Mulcahy."

Vidis studied Darius. "Mulcahy was with the Order?"

Darius shrugged. "Before he came here and created the Northwest houses, yes."

Vidis tilted his head to the side, the patchy moonlight reflecting off his eyes. "You came thinking one of us was behind his death."

A statement, not a question, so Darius remained silent.

"Where does Zayn fit in?" Cheveyo asked.

"He doesn't," Carys said, her voice flat and cold. "And he won't."

"Not until we have Natasha back and absolute proof the Councilman isn't working with Jamie," Gavin added, his gaze never leaving Darius. A not so subtle threat.

"Do you expect me to argue?" Darius asked.

"You vouched for him," Gavin said. "Even as Carys held a knife to your throat. You changing your tune now?"

"Let me repeat what I said earlier, he and I are all that stands between you and the Council." Darius turned and dragged his gaze over the four Kyn standing around him. "Until your rat problem is exterminated, Zayn remains free of this mess. However, if you continue to grill me, you will lose another leader. Your choice on which one, because I have no intention of leaving Natasha alone with Jamie."

Carys blinked. "You think Jamie could kill her?" She shook her head. "You have met our Amanusa queen, correct? She's not going to need you to ride to her rescue."

"I'm not the one with blinders on when it comes to Natasha." Darius battled back his frustration. "You think Ryan's death shook your world? What do you think it did to one of his oldest friends?"

Uncomfortable looks flashed across the gathered faces. Natasha would carve his eyes out for this, but he needed these leaders to fucking think. Grief played vicious games with even the most intelligent leaders. "Ryan and Natasha go back hundreds of years. Farther than any relationship you all can claim. If you think his death didn't leave its mark on her, then you are the ones who don't know your Amanusa queen. If it wasn't for Ryan's death, she would've seen Ryder coming from miles away. Treachery isn't a new thing for her. She learned its lesson at the hand of her twin sister, so don't stand here and snidely insinuate that I don't know who I'm dealing with, because I have a hell of a better idea than any of you. You see exactly who and what she wants you to see. You don't see the bigger picture."

He looked right at Gavin. "Ryan's gone. He can't protect his niece any longer. The abilities you and Raine share, who do you think keeps it from the Council?"

Gavin's lips tightened.

Darius wasn't done. "Tell me something. If she hadn't thrown her name into the ring for the captaincy, would you have stepped up?"

Understanding finally sparked in Gavin's jade gaze.

Darius turned back to Carys. "No, I'm not trying to ride to Natasha's rescue. I'm more concerned with what twisted spell Ryder's going to use on her. Look at the magic thrown at the Northwest. The common denominator—it's ancient, powerful and twisted. It's enough to make even me pause."

Carys held up her hands. "Enough. You've made your point."

Darius damned well hoped so.

She dropped her hands and rubbed them along her thighs. "If the blood you two shared doesn't allow you to track her, then how do you plan on finding her?"

"Xander, Niall, Raine, and I will start scouring any location associated with Ryder," Gavin said.

"Vidis and I can start combing through his computer records," Cheveyo offered. "See if we can't narrow the list of places down."

"And you?" Carys directed her question to Darius.

Relieved they were finally doing something, he said, "I'll take the one road none of you can."

She canted her head. "Can you track her through the Side?"

"Not her." He began to loosen the chains holding his demon in place, letting the need for the hunt rise. "Ryder."

"How?" Gavin asked.

"I'm going to use the blood traces he left in Axel to run his ass to the ground." The words were low and difficult to get out.

"Blood traces?" Tension made Cheveyo's question sharp.

"The spell he used with Axel," Darius forced the explanation out. "He used his blood to set it in motion and interfere with the pack ties. All I need is enough to taste." He moved toward the back door, only to have Cheveyo's hand on his arm stop him.

"We need to know who Ryder is working for." An

unnecessary reminder that the Northwest wanted their traitor alive.

Darius held that obsidian gaze, the red from his eyes reflecting back to him. "If I can get to him before Natasha does, I'll try to make sure he can talk. I won't promise you more."

Cheveyo dipped his chin and let him go. Wasting no more time, he headed indoors to pick up Ryder's trail.

CHAPTER 26

Natasha swam her way out of a smothering blackness and straight into a wave of throbbing pain. When she tried to move her hands to hold her skull together, the harsh rasp of chains on metal tore along her awareness while needles stabbed down her arms, adding to the excruciating overload. Those thrice-cursed needles followed the path of her spine, hit her hips, and shot fire down her legs. Instinctively she tried to curl them tighter under her, only to have the harsh surface she sat on scrape over her exposed skin and bare feet.

Her soft groan escaped before she could capture it. The weak sound filtered through the haze of pain, shocking her into an acute awareness. Smells hit her first—salt tinged metal, nose-curling rot and mildew, air tainted with diesel—which meant she was down by the river. Probably one of the many cargo docks. Unfortunately, she couldn't tell which river, the Columbia or the Willamette. Her ears strained beyond the echoing hollow pants of her breaths and found the slap of water against a solid surface, matched by the low drones of machinery.

The pins and needles crawling over her legs and spine started to fade. Carefully, she tried to adjust her legs, cursing the fact she chose to wear a damn dress on today of all days. Pants would've given her skin added protection.

A cold sweat popped out on her brow, the first few drops stinging her eyes. Turning her head she managed to rub her face over one restrained arm to wipe the dampness away. The chain locking her hands shifted, the heavy metal links scraping against the wall. Echoes chased the sound.

Under the pounding pulse in her head, something nagged at her. More concerned with trying to figure out where she was and why she was chained, she ignored it. Blinking, she lifted her head, slowly so not to increase the pounding ache, and tried to see beyond the pressing darkness. It took longer than it should have for the shadows to give up their secrets.

No windows. The only light seeped around the blurred edges of what she supposed was a large door at the far end of her cell. Slowly, she tilted her head back, trying not to grit her teeth since she wasn't sure her head could take it. Solid darkness stared back. The chains holding her seemed to glow softly, or maybe that was just her, since her vision didn't seem to be working right yet. She blinked again, hoping it would help. It didn't.

Around her wrists, inch-wide bands circled, no visible locks or hinges. She frowned. That wasn't right. You couldn't lock or unlock someone if the bands didn't open, so how in the hell did they end up around her wrists? Twisting her arms, she realized the actual chain links and cuffs seemed to be formed of the same piece of metal, with no obvious seams or soldering. Her gaze traveled further up the chains, trying to see how they connected to the wall above her head. Her stomach sank when the same phenomena appeared there as well.

Considering what it took to mold and mutate metal to such an extent, a sickening knowledge slowly unfurled. Only one person close to her could manipulate metals to such an extent. Jamie Ryder. A scion of Blood of Earth, and a Fundo demon, he held complete control over the alloys of the Earth.

Memories pushed their way forward, each one piling on the next until the weight was almost crushing. The car sputtering to a rattling stop. The side of a road, devoid of lights or homes. The headlights flickering then blinking out completely. Jamie's soft curse, followed by his apology. His door opening, then closing as he got out to check the car. The hood raising, minutes passing, until she came around to see what the issue was. Cool night wind playing over her, a teasing edge of moisture promising rain later. The sound of her heels against gravel. Using one hand on the car for balance. Rounding the hood, asking what was wrong. Jamie frowning at the engine and motioning toward it. Coming to stand beside him for a closer look. His arm snapping around her with a startlingly suddenness, yanking her off balance. A cruel, unexpected blow against her jaw. A tumbling well of blackness swallowing her whole.

Rumbling, vicious growls echoed around her metal box, chasing her back into the present. Fury, dark and deep, pushed away the accumulated body aches, leaving her shaky and weak.

Weak?

Her growls abruptly cut off. Staring unseeingly into the darkness, she focused on what should exist under her skin, only to come up empty. Her other half, her demon half, was...gone?

Her mind spun, her chest ached. Beyond rattled, she continued her internal evaluation even as the pressure on her chest grew. Little black dots fuzzed out the edges of her vision, vision that couldn't pierce the shadows because she couldn't reach that half of her who lived in darkness.

A harsh sob broke the silence, and only then did Natasha realize she was holding her breath. Her pulse spiked, heat rushed over her skin, only to be replaced by a cold sheen of sweat. *Dammit, Nat, pull your shit together!* Panic wasn't new, but it hadn't stopped in for a visit in quite some time either. First, she got her body back under control, concentrating on evening out her breathing, until her muscles finally unlocked. Satisfied her body wouldn't melt down, she began to think.

Very few things could keep an Amanusa's demonic nature out of touch. Bindings subsumed the human intellect, and since she was terrifyingly trapped in a human body with her mind intact, she could cross that one off the list. A spell infused poison might work, if a wizard knew what the hell they were doing.

She swallowed carefully, searching for any strange, lingering tastes. Nothing, so no for the poisoned spell idea.

Panic nibbled at the edges of her mind, but she ignored it.

There was one, very dire period in an Amanusa's life when shutting off the link between intellect and instinct was necessary. Adolescence. When hormones created more havoc than even demons enjoyed, then a constraining spell was put into place. Could this be a variant of that spell? Considering that Jamie seemed to prefer utilizing old magic and spells, it was quite possible. How difficult would it be to stretch a constraint spell to accomplish the one thing guaranteed to even his odds?

Time to find out. Since getting physically loose wasn't happening any time soon, she took her time to do a mental check. Without pain clouding her thoughts, she managed to uncover Jamie's nasty little gift. It was as if she was trapped in a small box with impenetrable, misty walls. She threw her magical weight against them to no avail.

It was useless to wear herself out, smarter to find a weak point. Of course, easier said than done. If she didn't manage to break through Jamie's spell, the link between her two halves could be damaged beyond repair.

The longer her more bestial half remained free from her intellect, the stronger the urges, that made the Amanusa who they were, grew. If she strained, she could make out a dense shadowy form on the other side. Her other half she was sure, but the damn walls kept them apart.

To reestablish the balance between her two sides, she needed to figure out a way through the barriers. Whatever Jamie did to alter the spell, caused it to act like a steroid infused constraint spell, but different. The different worried her. Based on the spells used on Ryan, Sullivan, and Jared, the chances were damned good that a lethal trigger existed. Unfortunately, she couldn't find it. Yet.

Part of her gave Jamie credit. He might be a treacherous little shit, but he was far from stupid.

Considering where she was and why, perhaps she should be more concerned with her own powers of observation. *How in the thrice curse hells had she missed the signs with him?*

Yes, Ryan's death had thrown her, but was it something more than that? Had losing her friend blinded her to what stood beside her? Or had grief colored her perceptions? She honestly didn't know.

Unfortunately, the reasons behind Jamie's actions were

much easier to understand. The promise of power was a seductive lure, especially when the one dangling it was so very, very good at making it appear so. She watched it happen before, with her sister, Irina. If her sister, who had been much older and wiser than Jamie, could be fooled, the boy never stood a chance.

Anger, disappointment, pain, and pity all swam together, making her heart ache. It no longer mattered to Natasha which man, Westbrooke or DiMarcco, had turned Jamie against her. Regardless, she would ensure they suffered for it.

Only if you can get yourself out of this mess. Her lips curled in disgust. Gods above and below, she hated that snide little voice. Until recently, she managed to beat it into submission. After Ryan died and left her, it made a comeback, popping up when least wanted. Like right now.

Something rattled and scraped against the door at the far end, then the small sliver of lighter darkness began to widen. Voices drifted in, two separate pitches, both male. Time to play possum. She let her eyes close, forcibly relaxing each muscle until she hung lax in the chains, the picture of unconsciousness.

Then she listened.

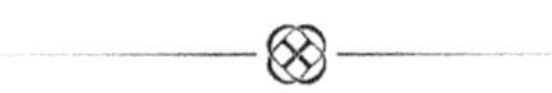

Metal grated over loose gravel. As the door opened, she watched from under the veil of her lashes. With her demon locked away, she didn't have to worry about the telltale red glow in her eyes. Still, she let them shut completely as the voices drew near.

Footsteps drifted closer, words becoming clearer. "You pulled me out of a key meeting." The older voice held traces of Europe that not even the bright burn of anger could wipe away. "Why?"

"Would you rather I approached your fellow Councilman, Zayn Aimeric?"

Even expecting it, the sound of Jamie's cocky voice, hurt. Yet, anger at proof of his betrayal quickly swallowed it.

The footsteps stopped. "Aimeric is nothing but a posturing idiot." Derision coated every word and cut through memories, bringing her a name. *Leopold DiMarcco.*

Natasha fought not to react, her blood chilling in her veins. A deadly force, DiMarcco's presence skewed the odds decidedly out of her favor. She couldn't afford to sit and wait.

Hiding behind her unconscious charade, she tested the limits of the spell Jamie wrapped around her. Unfortunately, she couldn't completely tune out the conversation, but working on two separate mental levels required a delicate balance. Lucky for her, that balance was second nature.

The urge to check where the two men stood tempted her to lift her lids, but she fought it back. Considering the echo of their voices, they were still by the door.

"And yet, he holds the favor of other Council members."

No missing the jealousy in Ryder's voice with that one. The mist in the barrier around her picked up speed.

"And?" DiMarcco's one word question snapped with a frigid bite.

Jamie, either too stupid or too arrogant, missed the warning. "And that concerns you."

"It won't be a concern for long."

Natasha filed away the implied threat under DiMarcco's words. She'd have to make sure to warn Darius to watch his brother's back. If nothing else, this disastrous night managed to clear all her doubts about Zayn.

"Is that so? What do you have planned for him?" Jamie didn't even bother hiding his dark glee. A thin streak of black zagged across the barrier holding her from her demon.

"Nothing you need to worry about." Decidedly unamused, DiMarcco dodged the question. "Perhaps you should explain why I shouldn't walk away right now?" Metal gave a soft creak as someone shifted their weight. "Being seen with you is not in my best interests."

And considering the cold heat weaving through DiMarcco's voice, Natasha bet Jamie was teetering on a very shaky ledge with the Councilman.

"Trust me, no one of importance will know you're here," Jamie answered, blithely unaware of the danger he courted.

"When someone tells me to trust them, I've found it's better to sever any and all ties with them from that point on." Silky menace softened DiMarcco's voice.

Chills raced over Natasha's skin. In front of her mind's eye, the dizzying mists slowed, catching her attention. As she watched, the mists seemed to thin. Taking advantage of the apparent flaw, she prodded the magic. For the first time, it seemed to give.

Realization flooded her. The spell's weakness was Jamie's emotional state.

"Why should you be any different?" DiMarcco's quiet question left her holding her breath.

If the Councilman killed Jamie, she would stay trussed up like some stupid, virgin sacrifice. Some weird bit of mental hysteria escaped. Perhaps not virgin, but a sacrifice all the same.

Instead of Jamie's answer, footsteps crossed the floor. A soft, rasping click preceded a flood of light against her closed lids as the mists around her pick up speed.

A sharp inhale followed.

"You wanted to break the back of the Northwest. I'm giving you the last straw." Arrogant satisfaction dripped from Jamie, even as footsteps drifted closer. The magical barrier began to solidify, gaining strength with his confidence.

The air around her shifted, indicating someone was close. When a hand tangled in her hair, yanking her head back against the metal wall, she almost opened her eyes. Every bit of will went into not wincing.

"You like?" Jamie's voice sounded right next to her.

Every part of her ached to attack. Only DiMarcco's presence held her in check. And the chains still holding her to the damn wall. And the thrice damned spell.

More footsteps. DiMarcco had come a bit closer. "Is she alive?"

"For now." Jamie ripped his hand from her hair, and she let her head fall forward, hoping her hair would be an added protection from DiMarcco's scrutiny. The spell turned opaque.

"Do you understand what you've done?" This time there was no way for Jamie to mistake the cold fury in DiMarcco's voice.

The spell fluctuated violently and Natasha used Jamie's distraction to slip a thin line of her magic through, like a wire thin needle. When it connected with her demon, the resulting power shock almost had her missing the rest of the conversation. Like a flood being forced through a straw, the ache of its return almost ripped her magical hold free.

"What is it you think I've done?" Jamie's caution finally emerged.

He stood, the leg of his pants brushing against her shoulder. Light and shadow danced across her closed lids with his movements. She struggled to thin out her tenuous connection. If she could keep the energy signature low enough, Jamie would never notice.

DiMarcco took a step closer. "Set a pretty target on your back." Then another one. "And by extension mine." The last was a hissed accusation.

Natasha managed to get control of her link, just as the spell's wall began to solidify around her. Foolish child was preparing to face down DiMarcco. "There will be no target."

A wave of breath stealing power slammed into Jamie and, by extension, her. She choked back a groan at the oppressive weight. DiMarcco wasn't done. "Then why her? Why now?"

Above her, Jamie snarled as he struggled under DiMarcco's magic. "She was getting too close. There's no way either of us could afford for her to put the pieces together."

"You left loose ends?" The Councilman's voice became softer, almost kind, in direct contrast the increasing magical pressure.

"No." Jamie's denial emerged in a harsh gasp.

"Then how is she getting too close?"

Natasha held on to the thin connection through sheer strength of will, hiding her fierce joy at reestablishing her link to her demon. In front of her, Jamie's battle played out, the spell's haze dissipating as he struggled to hold his own against DiMarcco.

"Division." Jamie's one word answer emerged through gritted teeth.

"Humans," DiMarcco spat, "are easily dealt with. This mistake you've created. Rectify it. Now."

"This is not a mistake."

Stunned, Natasha could barely believe Jamie was still arguing. For once, she agreed with DiMarcco. Jamie made a critical error in taking her. How could the boy not see that?

A short bark of laughter followed. "Do you really believe the other Northwest leaders won't put two and two together and come up with your name?" DiMarcco's power receded. "And if they manage to add mine to it, you better pray someone else finds you first, because it won't come close to what I'll do to you, boy."

"You need me."

Tiny fissures ran through the spell surrounding her, Jamie's doubt weakening his hold.

"No, you need me." Utter ruthlessness laced DiMarcco's response. "Shall I remind you? I did not come to you, you came to me."

The scramble of feet over the ground preceded Jamie's accusation. "Without me, the humans would've never come to the table and your grand plans would be nowhere."

The sound of flesh impacting flesh filled the air, followed by a choking sound. "Did you think you were my only agent in this?"

"Nnn—no."

A body hit the ground and someone, probably Jamie, dragged in air with greedy gulps. The idiot still managed to get out, "But I am the most valuable."

If his betrayal hadn't made her reconsider his intelligence, that last comment certainly did.

"Valuable? More like liable." Footsteps moved away, and the door opened with a groan. "Clean up your mess,

Ryder. All of it." DiMarcco's words drifted back crystal clear even as his footsteps faded into the night.

CHAPTER 27

Silence crawled back in and settled around Natasha. A half a minute passed, then, "I know you're awake, Natasha."

Her bluff called, she lifted her lids slowly, giving her eyes time to adjust. Harsh light from the bare bulb above fell around her. She blinked a few times, hoping to clear the shadows veiling Jamie's face as he stood in front of her. "Was that little display for my benefit?"

Jamie dropped into a crouch until their faces were level, his arms balanced on his knees, hands dangling from his wrists. The distinctive red rings of the Amanusa flared around his brown eyes, yet the rot within didn't show on the boyish face. "It shouldn't have come to this."

Ignoring the now dull ache from her jaw, Natasha forced her lips into a mocking smile. "This? Where your greed and ambition have made you the perfect tool for the Council and their agenda?" She leaned forward, pulling against the chains. Their rattle followed her movement, even as Jamie instinctively leaned back. "Your choice to take us here, pet."

He shook his head. A small, sad smile accompanied the glimpse of pity in his gaze. "Not my choice, yours. The Council is the only one who will keep us safe."

"Safe?" There was so much was wrong with his statement. She didn't bother hiding her scorn. Not that he'd recognize it. He was too far gone in DiMarcco's game. "From who?"

"The humans."

The depth of conviction behind his answer stunned her. Slowly she sat back, thinking. "There are worse things than the humans, Jamie."

Anger darkened his face. His hands curled into fists. "Like you?"

Had he expected her to agree with him? If so, he'd be waiting a damn long time. "No." Would he admit the truth, even if she gave it to him? "Why don't we start with the master you serve?" Catching his flicker of unease, she pushed. "You do realize he'll kill you as soon as he gets all he wants." And knowing DiMarcco's conniving ruthlessness as well as she did, if she didn't kill Jamie, it would be a matter of hours before death came for him.

He jerked upright, his lips curling in a sneer as he glared down at her. "You're not the biggest or baddest power out there."

If he really believed that, she hadn't been doing her job. An oversight she'd be sure to correct. As much as she wanted to leap to her feet and get in his face, the chains made the move impossible. Not to mention the fact she wasn't exactly at her best.

Instead, she forced her muscles to relax and leaned back, as if seated in her office chair, and not sprawled on the unforgiving metal floor. "You aren't paying attention then."

Jamie's eyes narrowed, even as the red brightened and bled over the brown color. "But I'm not the one chained to a wall, missing a rather vital piece of myself, though, am I?"

Choking out a carefree laugh, she hoped it distracted him enough to not notice her testing the damn spell again. Or the slowly strengthening link between her and her demon. *Just a little bit longer.* "If you think that what makes me dangerous is my demon, darling, you are not as smart as I thought."

The magic holding her fluctuated as her taunts found their marks and his emotional status began to crumble. His gaze shifted just that tiny bit, revealing his worry, even as he tried to mask it. "This spell, Natasha, it's not some simple thing."

No, far from it, but the strength of the one holding it in place was no match for her—with or without her demon's presence. However, if he would give her another minute, she'd be happy to prove it to him. "I never mistook the spell that killed Ryan or Sullivan as simple."

He lifted his chin at her comment, his smile full of vicious satisfaction, creating a chilling contrast to his boy-next-door look. "No, those were pieces of fucking brilliance."

Needing to crack his composure and weaken his hold, she held his gaze, letting every ounce of contempt and disgust she felt for this twisted child shine through. "Which is how I know you had nothing to do with creating either of them."

Her dig did its work, a little too well.

Jamie's face went startling blank. He moved, too quick for her to react, and backhanded her.

The dull thud of her head crashing into the metal wall behind her was lost under the explosive echo of his hand meeting her face. Copper burst on her tongue as her teeth cut the inside of her mouth, almost enough to mask the wrenching in her shoulders as her body jerked against the chains.

Jamie's harsh breaths fell over her.

She smiled despite her cut lip and burning cheek. Slowly, deliberately, she turned her head toward him, full-fledged fury burning bright under her cruel amusement. "Temper, temper, Jamie."

The cracks in the surrounding magic widened, bringing her two halves a little closer.

"Shut the fuck up, Natasha!" he spat. "Those spells were mine." He leaned closer. "All mine!"

Undaunted, she called his bluff. "No they weren't." She curled her lips, ignoring the sting of the cut and the slow slide of blood. "The magic that killed Ryan had nothing whatsoever to do with you. That was all DiMarcco."

Jamie dropped in front of her, slamming his hands into the wall beside her head.

She didn't flinch.

He leaned in, crowding her and dominating her field of vision. "DiMarcco didn't have the balls to go after Mulcahy."

Undaunted, she strained forward until mere centimeters separated them. "And you did?" Did he really think she believed Ryan was his intended target? Perhaps she over estimated his intelligence. "Tell me another lie, Jamie. Ancient and powerful are not two words I'd associate with you. Now, DiMarcco, on the other hand…"

The sound of metal shredding under nails screeched across her eardrums. Fury brought Jamie's demon to the surface, further signaling his loss of control.

"Ryan was never the target. Not for DiMarcco, and not

for you." She continued to bait him, hiding her relief as the first stirrings of her demon's answering rage found its way through the spell.

"He's still dead," he snarled.

"Not because of you." *You demented bastard.* The pure wave of malice swept away any lingering traces of pain. Oh yes, her demon was making a comeback. Fury, rage, and a need to destroy the one in front of her clawed against her relentless control. She couldn't afford for Jamie to know just how close she was to breaking through.

She relaxed. leaning back to put a bit of breathing room between the two of them. "Whether it was luck or planning, it doesn't make a difference."

Her ability to read what lay in his blood rode the magic holding her and found its way to Jamie. Idiot had used his own blood to set the spell.

"Difference in what?"

"The depth of your betrayal." She tilted her head and dropped her lids partway, hoping her thick lashes would veil any revealing red tint in her eyes. "Or did you think it was just me you had to deal with? Did you happen to forget the other Wraiths? You killed their captain. They're not ones to take betrayal lightly. Maybe Gavin will make an example out of you. Oh, what I wouldn't give to be a fly on the wall when Raine gets her hands on you." Keeping her mental touch delicate, like the whisper of spider's silk, she wove her way deeper into Jamie's mind, ferreting out his secrets.

"Gavin and Raine? Please." The low rumble of Jamie's snarl vibrated between them. Then he rocked back on his heels. "Those two think they're hot shit. They have no idea what's coming for them."

"And you do?" She kept the question soft as she worked.

Her first goal, patiently unbinding the metal on one of the chain links even as she kept Jamie talking. Unfortunately, her demon was done waiting around. She let her eyes close briefly as she shoved her more primal wants and needs back. Intellect, not instinct, was needed now.

Jamie grabbed her chin. "Look at me!"

She slitted her eyes and yanked her chin free, keeping her face turned away.

Undeterred, he duck walked until he was at her side. "Do you understand what's coming?" He spat each word. "The Kyn won't survive if they don't stay true to their natures."

Fairly confident she'd beaten back her demon, for now, she finally raised her gaze.

Satisfied he had her attention, he continued. "Messing around with magic and genetics doesn't make them better, it makes them less."

She arched an eyebrow. "I'd have to disagree."

"You would."

"What's that supposed to mean?"

"You want these 'new' powers because it gives you something no one else has." He stopped and waited, his expression expectant.

She didn't bow to his ploy and kept her mouth shut.

He gave her a small smile. "Weapons to use against the Council."

It was too hard to navigate Jamie's twists and turns of deluded logic while picking apart his touch with metal. She let him ramble on as she unraveled the magic holding the chain together, grateful when the metal showed signs of weakening.

"You think DiMarcco is blind to how much you hate

him?" Jamie tapped her nose, his unusual move startling her.

Her gaze jumped to his.

"Ah, don't worry, Natasha, you hid it well," he crooned in a voice full of false sympathy. "It took me years to figure it out. But once I realized you'd never turn against Mulcahy and take what was yours, I went around you to the next best thing."

"Next best thing being DiMarcco?"

"He has no problem rewarding those who serve him."

"You think DiMarcco's going to share with you?" She laughed. "He doesn't share. Ever. He didn't get to be the head of the Council because he shares, you idiot." She shook her head. "Did you miss the whole liability thing, Jamie?"

"He's not the only one with sharing problems." He shoved to his feet and spun away, running his hands through his hair in a visible struggle to regain his slipping temper.

Taking advantage of his turned back, she got to her knees, using the movement to pull, with slow and steady pressure, against the chains. The weakened link gave, just enough to spike her pulse and ignite a predatory anticipation. She stilled when he stopped.

"Why couldn't you just give a little?" he asked his back still to her.

She gave an inelegant snort at the plaintive note in his question "Oh, please, you're not going to start whining how it was all my fault now, are you?"

He spun around on his heel, the skin of his face pulled tight over his skull, the wavering apparition of his demon rising like mirage at high noon. "Don't." He stalked closer.

There was no more brown left in his eyes, just pure crimson fire. Jamie's demon teetered on the crumbling edge, right where she wanted it.

The spell holding her shifted. The fractures she manipulated widening. Jamie's darkest desires bubbled to the surface. Endless craving for power. A driving need to dominate. An addiction to violence writhing underneath it all. She needed just a little more. "Don't, what?"

"Don't twist this back around."

"Oh, I'm not the one twisting things around, pet." Her muscles coiled. The roiling energy of her enraged beast flooding her, filling all those empty spots with a pure, incandescent rage. That rage grew as it consumed more and more of Jamie's hidden desires. "That's something you're doing just fine on your own."

He closed the distance between them in two long steps then snarled in her face, "You're a bitch, Natasha."

Her lips curled back in a teeth-filled parody of a smile. "You have no idea, Jamie."

Her demon slammed home. With a blood-chilling snarl, she yanked her hands down and out, shattering the weakened link. Then, before Jamie could jerk out of reach, she struck. Black tipped claws ripped across his face, and blood scented the air.

Jamie howled then fell back on his ass as he tried to scramble out of reach.

Undaunted, she whipped the dangling end of the metal chain still attached to her wrist across his jaw and temple, opening a bloody gash in its wake.

He covered his face with both hands and rolled to his side on the ground, his legs curling up.

Even as her muscles screamed, she shoved to her feet and took a step toward him.

He lashed out with both legs, slamming the hard sole of his dress shoes into the muscles of her upper thigh.

She stumbled, her leg going numb from the hit. She fell to the ground, her palms and knees slapping the rough metal floor.

Crouched on all floors was not where she wanted to be. Especially when next to her, Jamie kicked out again. This time hooking his heel for her unprotected jaw.

With the barrier between her and her demon shattered, her muscles coiled and reacted with inhuman agility. Even as his heel barreled toward her, she shoved against the ground then pushed off. The force of her move allowed her body to spin over his kick. She landed in a crouch.

Even as Jamie rolled to his feet, she attacked. Using the thick black nails tipping her fingers as weapons, she raked out. He stumbled back, even as material and skin shredded and four bloody furrows bloomed across his chest.

He swung at her.

She turned, taking the bruising blow along her ribs. Her claws flashed and ripped another vicious trail from ribs to spine.

Jamie bellowed, spinning to keep her in sight.

They circled each other, animalistic growls emanating from both. No more taunts. It was down to brutal savagery. No finesse, no grace. Pain and punishment were the only players. They exchanged blows and kicks, neither gaining nor losing ground.

Claws and teeth tore skin, and still it wasn't enough. It didn't sate her need for pain and blood. Under her demon's feral haze, Natasha struggled to think instead of react with mindless rage. A physical beating wouldn't stop Jamie. Not now. The spell he used to trap her—it was starting to warp into something much more dangerous.

The magic twisted, gaining strength, from both of them. *How?*

Whispers circled in her head, sharing bits and pieces of the magic used and how Jamie had set it. The spell was based on the dual nature of the Amanusa and blood. The more they lost, the closer their destructive natures rose, the stronger their rage grew, the stronger the magic raged. But there was more.

Jamie closed in, viciously swiping his claws across her stomach, leaving deep gouges behind.

Her blood fell. The magic spiked.

Instead of backing off, she slammed both hands against his arm, curled her claws deep, and pushed, spinning out of reach.

Off balance, he stumbled, his skin tearing under her nails.

More blood. Another magical spike, the spell between them tightening.

Jamie straightened slowly as he faced her.

Both of them were breathing hard, their bodies savaged by teeth and claws.

She watched as Jamie lifted his hand, coated in her blood, and deliberately ran his tongue over one finger, all the way to his nail. "Mmmm...tasty." The word was barely discernible.

The crushing urge to spill more blood rose in a fiery wave. Realization clicked into place. The damn magic fed on their combined blood, just like their rage. To hold her from her demon meant Jamie linked the spell's magic to his blood and hers.

It was a link she needed to break before they became even further tangled. But she couldn't do it here, not when her demon battled for dominance. Messing with the spell had only fouled the magic, not broken it.

Knowing she'd pay for it later, if later came, she barreled into Jamie and dragged him into the Side.

CHAPTER 28

Darius left Natasha's home in the Side, frustration and worry tangling his patience and fraying his temper. An hour and half had come and gone since Natasha disappeared and he was out of places to check.

Tracing Ryder's blood was proving problematic. It seemed the duplicitous shit didn't spend much time in the Side. So far, he tracked Ryder to a condo near downtown, an office at Taliesin, Mulcahy's home, an abandoned bar in downtown Portland, and Natasha's house. All of which were dead ends.

Time to touch base with the others. Leaving the Side, he stepped into the mortal realm under one of the tall trees guarding Natasha's manicured backyard. Digging his phone out of a pocket, he dialed Gavin. "Anything?"

"Just found the company car over by the Ross Island Bridge, tucked in a parking lot."

"I thought the GPS wasn't working?"

"It wasn't. Cheveyo found the last known location and we've been moving out from there."

"What's down there?"

"Warehouses, a couple of shipping yards, and quite a few businesses." Gavin's voice was grim. "You got anything?"

"Not a damn thing. He's been careful to stick to familiar places. Nothing sticks out." Darius blew out a frustrated breath. Time to combine efforts. "I'm at Natasha's. How far away are you?"

"We're roughly four miles south."

"Send me your location." Darius crossed the gardens to the house. "I'll be there in ten minutes."

"You going to fly?"

"Going to borrow Natasha's car." He hung up.

Two minutes later he started up the Aston Martin and followed his phone's directions down to the Willamette riverfront. Just under the ten-minute mark, he pulled in next to the dark SUV in a parking lot nestled by freeway overpasses and the river.

Leaning against the SUV, Raine waited for him, her arms folded across her chest.

He opened his door and got out.

"You better take care of Natasha's ride, Abazi." Raine said in lieu of a greeting, before she straightened and waited for him to approach. "Xander's checking out the top floor of the warehouse." She hitched a thumb over her shoulder, indicating the large, looming building behind her. "The river's messing with her nose, but she managed to pick up traces of Ryder's stench from the car."

"Where is it?"

"Inside."

She turned on her heel, leading him across the parking lot toward the two-story structure. Metal containers clustered on the end near the river, four or five deep, two to three high.

He gave the containers a nod. "Anyone check those?"

"Gavin's on the far end, he's clearing them as fast as he can."

Which would take hours. Hours he was damn sure Natasha didn't have. His stomach clenched. "Not fast enough," he muttered.

Raine came to an abrupt halt and turned around to him, her hands curling into fists at her sides. "I'm all ear—"

His demon roared inside his skull, cutting Raine off. The blood-tie he shared with Natasha seared into brilliant life.

"Darius." Just his name, but what filled her voice enraged both man and beast. Anger, panic, and fear. Something was very wrong.

"Natasha!" he hissed. Refusing to waste time explaining, he heeded his instincts and rushed into the Side. Between one blink and the next, all traces of the human world disappeared.

What took its place was a haunting landscape of abandonment. Buildings, tall and strong on the human realm, resembled bombed out structures in the Side. Their skeletal, twisted fingers reached to a pitiless sky for help. The metal containers were no longer neatly stacked, instead they tumbled in haphazard fashion across the rock-strewn ground as if thrown by some giant hand.

He forced himself to stop and look around. Natasha and Jamie were here. He just had to find them. Lifting his head, he drew in the scents of rot and decay, rust and salt. And copper. Spilt blood.

A rumble of satisfaction vibrated in his chest. He followed the trail at a run, weaving his way through the scattered containers. Rounding the far corner, he pulled up short.

There, under the cold light of the moon, he found them.

The alabaster white of Natasha's demon was spattered with dark abstract patterns. She was crouched over another demon, this one dull copper with yellowed horns. She lifted her head, moonlight glinting off her obsidian horns.

He rushed forward. "Natasha!" He skidded to his knees, facing her over Ryder's jerking body and reached out to touch her.

"Don't!"

The unexpected vehemence in the word halted his hand in midair.

She grimaced. "Don't touch me, Darius. You can't."

"Why not?" he growled, tearing his gaze away from her. What the hell was going on? Natasha's hands were buried in Ryder's chest. Or what was left of it. "He's dying."

"He's not the only one."

Her calm statement sent shock ricocheting through him, giving dread a foothold. "Start talking."

"When I broke through Jamie's constraining spell, it triggered a gift from DiMarcco."

"DiMarcco?" *Son of a bitch!*

"He used Jamie to fracture the Northwest. They're working with some humans. Ryan's death—" She took a shuddering breath, a soft groan escaping even as Jamie's body jerked under her hands. She lifted her head and held his gaze. "Ryan's death wasn't intentional, but he's not crying any tears over it either. He has plans for Zayn, for my people." Rage burned bright in her red-tinged purple gaze, yet it wasn't enough to mask the regret underneath. "You're going to have to stop him."

"We're going to stop him," he corrected, furious at her casual acceptance of her death.

She shook her head. "No, you, and you alone." Fury sparked in those unusual eyes. "There is no physical evidence of DiMarcco's involvement. My word against his gains us nothing."

He growled at the grain of truth in her statement, but nothing said he couldn't share her information.

"Don't you even dare," she hissed, narrowing her eyes.

Damn blood-tie. He carefully shielded his emotions. "Dare what?"

"You can't tell Gavin, much less Raine. If she has a name, no one will be able to stop her from killing herself to get to him."

Anger and worry almost blinded him to the slide of panic under her voice. He cocked his head. "You're protecting her? Why?"

For one quick moment that beautiful head bowed, her shoulders slumping. She took a deep breath and the arrogant Amanusa queen made a comeback. "She's mine." She held his gaze and, beneath the arrogance, he saw why Ryan chose her to stand beside him, an unending streak of protectiveness for those she considered hers. "They're all mine."

Intrigued, he studied her, deciding to chance a question. "And me?" His question was soft, like a dangerous secret being shared.

Her lips twitched even as a light red ran under her cheeks. "So long as you remain useful, you may stay."

Her rare flash of feminine interest pleased him, more than it probably should. "You and I are far from done, darling. Are you really going to let a piece of shit like this—" he motioned to Jamie, "—cheat us of our vengeance?" He forced a teasing note into his voice, determined not to lose her. "Cheat us of finding just how much fun you and I could have hunting down our enemies?"

She choked on a weak laugh, even as her eyes darkened

with anger and grief. "Darius, you idiot, I can't escape this. DiMarcco's tying up loose ends. When Jamie dies, so do I."

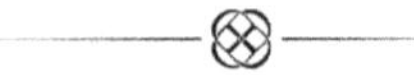

Natasha's legs gave out and she sat down suddenly, almost losing her grip on Jamie's artery. Fiery pain crawled through her, leaving icy numbness behind. Gods above and below, she'd almost missed DiMarcco's trap. Caught up in her feral haze, she dismissed the whispered warnings hovering in her brain until it was too late. She brought Jamie into the Side so she could destroy the anchors he set between them and free herself from his thrice-damned spell. Instead, when she shattered the first one, she ended up on her ass, feeling as if pieces of herself were among the fragments left behind.

Jamie didn't have it much better. He, too, had been laid out flat. As she struggled to sit up, he laughed. A crazed, desperate sound, even as he rolled to his feet. It sent ants crawling over her skin.

They met again in a hail of claws and teeth. Determined to end it once and for all, she ripped into Jamie's chest, tearing through tissue as if opening a Christmas present. She found the second anchor and decimated it even as she killed the boy who once belonged to her. His howl of agony was drowned out by the blinding, white pain that wrapped her in a strange silence. Only then did the reality of her situation become frighteningly clear.

Jamie was not the only creator of the spell, there was one other. Leopold DiMarcco. The Councilman who wanted to bring both the humans and Kyn under his control. The Magi held hundreds of years' worth of knowledge, making it easy to ensure whoever took out his puppet, followed his fate.

"Natasha!"

The sharp sound of her name had her blinking back to the present. Her hands, still buried in Jamie's chest, twitched. Jamie's eyes fluttered open, hazy and unfocused, his moan of pain escaping.

Struggling past her body's protests, she focused on the warrior kneeling in front of her. She studied his face, the strong lines under ebony skin, the core of determination burning in those ice-blue eyes. A distant part of her wished there was more time to explore him. It would have been a very interesting adventure.

He reached out. "Natasha, are you listening to me?"

She jerked back, a slick slide of fear turning her voice cold. "I'm listening to you. Would you extend the courtesy of doing the same to me?"

His claw tipped hand curled into a fist, but he slowly drew it back. "Tell me something that isn't complete bullshit, and I will."

Arrogant ass. "Jamie used my blood and his to anchor a modified version of the containment spell. Unfortunately, by tying us together, he created a link DiMarcco's magic could use."

"Blood."

She nodded and drew in a shaky breath, the numbness now crawling over her hips and up her stomach. "Something I couldn't see until I broke the anchors of Jamie's spell."

Darius frowned. "How many anchors?"

Not the question she expected. "Two. There's one more left." She stared at him. "So no touching."

Although hell waged in his eyes, his voice remained

calm. "Darling, it's a little late to worry about that." His hand shot out and wrapped around her arm, just above where it disappeared into Jamie's chest. "You've forgotten. We already share blood."

Unable to jerk away for fear of losing her grip, stunned realization left her cursing. The blood tie from their oath. "Godsdammit, Darius, I need you alive." For more reasons than what hid deep in her mind.

He leaned in and stole a hard kiss. Then he pulled back just enough so she wouldn't go cross-eyed looking at him. "Ditto, darling. So let's fix this, shall we?"

Damn stubborn male. "I'm open to suggestions, pet." Sharp sarcasm covered her worry that even his strength wouldn't be enough to counter DiMarcco's treachery.

"First, we need to buy ourselves some time."

She raised an eyebrow. "And how do you plan on doing that?"

Black mist began to gather around him, curling close like an adoring pet. "We get Gavin and Raine to do their thing and keep Jamie around long enough for me to work around DiMarcco's spell."

His answer didn't make sense, but she was too tired to pursue it.

Those inky ribbons gathered above Jamie's chest, waiting. Darius watched her, giving nothing away. "You need to let me take him back."

Trust, he was asking for her trust. Strangely, it wasn't that hard to loosen her grip, allowing him to replace her hold with his magic. Her hands fell into her lap as Darius gathered Jamie's battered body in his arms. She stared at her gore covered hands, and considered how she was going to get up since she couldn't feel her legs. She could crawl, but crawling in front of Darius wasn't happening.

An ebony hand tipped in bone white appeared in front of her face. "If you wanted me to carry you, you should've asked."

Calling on drained reserves, she placed her hand in Darius's, allowing him to draw her upright. Her fingers curled tight as she fought to maintain her balance even as her body protested. "I'll walk, thanks."

His grip tightened on hers then let go. He adjusted his hold on Jamie and dipped his head in acknowledgement. "As you wish."

The first step was the hardest. The racing wave of pins and needles over her shaky legs had black eating at the edge of her vision. She dragged in air, concentrating on not releasing the moans caught in her aching chest. The second one hurt, enough she reached out and placed her hand on Darius's back, steadying herself. His heat seeped into her, giving her something beside the pain to focus on.

"Still with me?"

"You can't get rid of me that easily." Too bad her voice shook.

The next step brought them back into the cool Oregon night. Salt and rot perfumed the air. Rough asphalt appeared under her battered feet. Her next step brought her bare foot down on a sharp edged rock. It was enough to send her stumbling into Darius.

"Natasha!"

"Darius!"

Two different voices rang out. In front of her Darius stopped, so she took advantage of his stillness and rested her head against his back. Just for a moment.

"We need someplace out of sight," Darius said.

"This way," Raine answered. "Want me to take that?"

"No, but help her."

Strong arms wrapped around Natasha, pulling her away from Darius and out of her exhausted daze. She stiffened.

"Relax, Natasha, it's just me." Gavin's familiar voice had her muscles unknotting. "You're barefoot, let me help."

Any other time, she'd slap his offer away. Tonight...well, she was too damn tired to argue. She gave him a short nod, then curled her arm over his shoulders as he lifted her. The movement proved too much for her and the looming blackness swallowed her under.

CHAPTER 29

Raine led Darius inside the darkened building. A small ball of floating light hovered near her head, illuminating their way. "Hang on. I think there's something we can use as a table."

Darius stilled, looking over at Gavin who came to a stop beside him, Natasha cradled in his arms. The sight of her in another man's arms, battered and bruised, sent a cascade of conflicting urges through him. Darius wanted to toss Ryder's body aside and snatch Natasha out of Gavin's arms. As if that was all it would take to keep her safe. The urge to see Gavin loose a few strips of skin along the way seemed perfectly acceptable. The strange, animalistic possessiveness was a key indicator that his demon was riding close.

Darius laid Ryder's body down on a dusty metal table then turned to take Natasha from Gavin. "I'll take her."

Gavin arched a single eyebrow, but said nothing, simply handing her over gently.

As Darius settled her close to his chest, he felt, more

than heard, her soft groan. His chest vibrated with a near silent rumble.

Her heavy lashes fluttered then finally lifted, revealing a wary panic, which faded as she recognized who held her.

He brushed his lips over the top of her white-blonde hair, then he raised his head. Raine and Gavin both stared at him, their faces carefully blank. Time to test his deductive ability. "You two are going to help me save Natasha."

"You have a plan, I assume?" Raine asked from the other side of the table.

"Gavin, you need to keep Ryder alive until I say otherwise." Darius walked over to a fairly clear spot on the floor near the table. He sat down, careful not to jostle Natasha too much.

"Is he the one behind the spell that killed Mulcahy?" Raine's question was too even.

Darius looked up, Natasha's earlier warning echoing in his ears. "If Ryder dies, so does Natasha." That strange silver gaze didn't move from him, the unblinking intensity reminding him of a large, predatory cat. "You're going to make sure that doesn't happen."

Raine's lips curled in a silent snarl.

"Start explaining." Gavin's voice broke their staring contest, even as he moved up beside Raine. He gave her a gentle nudge, as he studied Ryder's injuries. "Because I'm not inclined to save his sorry ass unless I have no other choice."

"You're not saving him," Darius bit out. "You need to give your girlfriend and me enough time to unravel the spell holding him to Natasha."

Gavin lifted his head, the muscles in his forearms

tensing as he gripped the edge of the table. "What exactly do you think Raine can do?"

Darius's snarl filled the interior of the warehouse. "I don't have time to play games, so let's just lay it all out there, shall we?" He watched both Raine and Gavin. "Raine can see magic, and the two of you share some sort of psychic connection. If I had to hazard a guess, I'd say it was damned close to the mate bond shared by shifters." Although neither one physically reacted, the tension between the three of them mounted, his observations cutting too close for comfort. "We don't have time to discuss fairy tales and ponder the wonders of magic, but I'd be willing to bet Raine can not only see magic, but manipulate it, correct?"

Raine stiffened, and something very lethal moved behind Gavin's stony expression.

Although Darius understood their inclination to hide their abilities, abilities that would set them in the middle of DiMarcco's racial purity war, they were racing against the clock. He let his demon surge forward on a wave of frustration and fury. "I am not, however, willing to gamble with Natasha's life. So before you decide covering your own ass is more important than her, know this. She dies, you will follow." His threat wasn't an empty one. Death followed his will and if Natasha died because they refused to act, he wouldn't hesitate take this damned couple out.

Natasha stirred in his arms, and her hand rose to cup his jaw. "Darius."

Just his name, but it was enough for him to answer. "What?"

"Your word to protect what is mine."

He looked down at who he held. "No." Part of him

wanted to howl in denial at her request. The chances of this not working were astronomical.

Ruthless determination stared back. "Yes."

He clamped his mouth shut, but it didn't stop the rumbles trapped in his chest.

"Say it," she hissed, desperation beginning to crawl under her steely gaze.

"I vow it," he snarled the oath, the weight of his words falling into place, leaving him no choice but to see it through, regardless of the outcome.

She patted his jaw. "There now, that wasn't so difficult, was it, pet?"

Torn between exasperation at her manipulation and fury at their situation, he did the next best thing. He growled.

"Is he telling us the truth, Natasha?" Raine didn't take her attention off of him, but came around the table and closer to them.

He felt Natasha turn her head toward Raine. "About?"

Her question made Raine frown and look at her. "If Jamie dies, do you die?"

"Yes."

The blunt answer seemed to shock Raine. She blinked, a mixture of complicated emotions flying over her face. She finally settled on stubborn refusal. "Not happening."

Natasha's laugh was far from normal. "Already is, dear."

Raine looked over her shoulder at Gavin. He gave her a small nod.

She turned back and, with a big sigh, sank to sit on the ground in front of Darius and Natasha. "What do you need us to do?"

"Ryder used the same type of spell on Natasha as Axel. Difference is there was a failsafe embedded in the magic."

"Not Ryder's," Gavin said.

"Not Ryder's," Darius confirmed. "That failsafe binds Ryder's fate to hers."

Raine's lips tightened and her hands flexed against her thighs. "Sounds like someone wanted to make sure their part in this mess stayed hidden."

"More than you know."

"Who?" she snapped out.

Darius held her gaze even as Natasha stiffened in his arms. "We don't have proof."

Raine leaned forward. "I want a name."

"It's not his to give," Natasha said, garnering Raine's anger. "Nor can I share my suspicions with you until I have proof."

"Dammit, Natasha."

"Listen very carefully, McCord, because I will not repeat myself." Obviously even with death hovering nearby, Natasha had her limits. "The ones hunting us are not to be taken lightly. You do not have the luxury of rushing out and hunting them down without evidence of their betrayals. Your grievances do not outrank the safety of the Northwest Kyn. Your uncle taught you better than that. Think for gods' sake. Be the warrior he created, not the grieving child."

For a moment the air around him fairly vibrated with explosive tension. The two women stared at each other. Raine obviously fighting herself and the situation.

"You can't fucking die, Natasha. It's not fair." For the first time, Raine's voice cracked.

A fierce pride lit Natasha's drawn face. "Then work your magic, girl, and make sure we give our enemies a reason to fear us."

Darius wasn't sure what to expect, but it wasn't being shuffled to the sidelines. Gavin took over with Ryder, leaving Darius to focus on Natasha. In front of him, Raine slipped into the psychic plane only she and Gavin seemed to see.

"Do you want me to call Cheveyo?" Xander had rejoined them moments ago. A quick debrief brought her up to speed.

"He'd never make it in time." Darius carefully set Natasha on the ground in front of him. "Besides, the only ones capable of destroying this spell are in this room. No use in endangering any others." He lifted his head and considered her. "Perhaps you should wait outside?"

Affronted, she jerked back, amber lighting in her eyes. "Excuse me?"

Females were damn touchy. He shook his head. "I have enough on my plate without adding Vidis to it."

She smirked. "Then don't screw up." Then she deliberately sat at Natasha's feet and wiggled her fingers at him. "What are you waiting for, tick tock."

Oh, for the love of—

"Found it." Raine's voice snapped his head around. Worry clouded her face. Her eyes swirled like liquid mercury. "It a mess, Darius."

He wasn't surprised. A spell like this was complex. "Describe it."

Raine worried her bottom lip. "It's like a tangled web of knots. I'm not sure where to start."

"Can you tell who's tied to what?" There had to be a starting point.

"Okay," she muttered, a frown marring her forehead. "I've got Ryder's link. If I follow it this way…" Her voice trailed off and lines of concentration deepened on her face, her eyes studying something only she could see. "There she is." A pause. "I can't untangle the two. Part of it disappears every time I reach for it."

He hissed in a sharp breath, brushing a hand over his goatee. "Because it's attached to the last bloody anchor in the Side." He ran his hands through his hair, his mind spinning through options. "Okay, we can't touch that until we break through the failsafe. Can you find that?"

"Any idea what it would look like?"

"How the hell should I know? Magic is magic," he snapped, feeling the press of time slipping away.

"What kind of magic," she shot back. "Demon, Fey, Shifter, Magi?"

"Magi." His oath to Natasha tugged at him but since he hadn't specified a name, it let his response slide.

Raine didn't answer, instead another handful of minutes ticked by, then he felt something brush against his magic. Startled, he turned his attention inward, trying to determine what happened.

His demon paced under his skin, as he checked his link to Natasha. She was holding on, but she seemed to be fading. He did what he could, sending his strength along their tie. Death prowled closer, but he held it back. No way in hell was he ready to let it in.

Again something brushed against the blood-tie. This time even Natasha reacted, a violent refusal of whatever was happening. He reacted without thinking, protective magic flaring to life shoving the strange presence back.

Raine's reactive hiss barely registered. "I'm trying to help. That tie you two have won't last long."

He snarled. "Leave it alone. Find the damn failsafe and destroy it."

Whatever Raine was doing, Natasha didn't want any of it, and that was good enough for him. Playing with magic required a skill he was pretty damned certain Raine was still acquiring. Guess neither he nor Natasha wanted to be anyone's guinea pigs.

The unsettling sensation disappeared. Another minute ticked by.

"There you are," Raine's voice was soft. Her head tilted to the side as if she was looking at something. When she straightened and blinked, she licked her lips. "Want the bad news first or the really bad news?"

Nerves stretched tight, Darius was in no mood for games. "Talk."

"I can destroy the failsafe, but if I do, it'll take Ryder with it."

"And by extension, Natasha."

She nodded. "That anchor used the blood they exchanged during their fight to cement its hold. The way it's created, if you destroy it, there's a high chance you'll destroy Natasha's bitchier half."

Which would kill her any way. His stomach churned at her words. "But if we don't?"

"We'll lose her when I destroy the failsafe."

Dread roiled through him. Locked under the thin veil of skin, his demon threw back its head, roaring a denial of the choice being forced on him. Damned if he did, damned if he didn't. No matter how he looked at the situation, death was the only escape option for Natasha.

For the first time in his very long existence, he was paralyzed by indecision.

A hand brushed his. "Darius."

He blinked down at Natasha, unable to answer.

Her fingers curled around his, and he held tight. "Do it."

His grip tightened, but she didn't look away, resigned knowledge adding a grimness to her features. Unmitigated fury raged through him, his demon battering at his precarious control.

One man's arrogance and greed had brought him to this—to protect her he had to kill her.

Darius crouched over Natasha as sulphuric winds whipped through the Side, wailing through the skeletal remains of the warehouse—his grief and anger given physical form. He held her hand even as he gritted his teeth and sent the ebony ribbons of his magic to curl gently around her, careful not to let it touch her skin. Not yet.

She watched him, her gaze never wavering from his face.

"I'll kill him for this alone."

She gave him a small smile. "Make sure it hurts, pet."

He growled, his claws flexing, his free hand scraping deep furrows in the ground.

"Gods above and below, Darius, don't be so dramatic," she huffed out on a shaky breath. "You're a scion of the Blood of Death with centuries of experience. This is not beyond you."

Hiding his trepidation behind an arrogant mask, he said, "Normally I'm not under a damn shot clock. It's not a fucking light switch, Natasha."

Amusement glittered in her gaze, but her voice remained droll. "Oh, I don't know. On. Off. Dead. Alive. I'm sure you'll figure it out." *Please figure it out.*

Her unspoken plea sent a crack snaking across a hidden part of his heart. Another sin to lay at DiMarcco's feet. "I'm sure I will, darling."

He tugged his hand free and cradled her face, brushing his thumb over her chin. Strange to find such a women at this time. She fascinated him, touched places he though long buried. Such a protector who'd use anyone and anything to keep those that were hers safe, regardless of the cost.

What would it be like to have that aimed in his direction? She'd manipulate and scheme until she got what she wanted, what she thought was best. An intelligent, sneaky, beautiful, wicked woman full of contradictions. And he wanted time to discover all of her. Wanted her beside him as they pulled DiMarcco's world apart, piece by bloody piece.

Ruthless determination rose, shoving his unusual emotional turmoil to the side. Natasha was right, death was his territory. Quick or slow, it answered to him.

Quick or slow.

An idea bloomed, awful and tricky. Death could happen between one breath and the next, or it could stretch the span of minutes, hours, or days. It was flexible. The anchor existed in the Side, set deep within Natasha's demonic nature. Yet her human body remained unhindered in the mortal world.

The original spell was designed to cut off the link between an Amanusa's two halves—intellect and instinct. It trapped the demonic essence on the Side, leaving the remaining spirit locked inside the untouched, mortal form. For all intents and purposes, the Amanusa became two separate beings.

Of course the spirit would eventually fade away, while

the demon grew more and more lost in a feral rage. That's why the longer the containment spell stayed in place, the less chance there was of recovering an Amanusa.

But magic wasn't a thinking adversary, it followed rules.

If Ryder's original spell was the containment spell, then there was a very slight chance Darius could fool the magic into believing her death was very real. If it required death, then he could give it death, just not the one DiMarcco intended. There were so many ways to kill someone. Darius had played with them all through the years and he discovered some very interesting results. The transition between life and death was never instantaneous. There was a brief window in time where neither state existed. It wasn't long, a minute at most, but a lot could be accomplished in a minute.

Like destroying a spell's anchor.

Killing Ryder.

Setting Natasha free.

Dark anticipation curled through him, his demon purring with violent joy at the risky solution. He bent down and ravaged Natasha's mouth, her stunned gasp lost as a primal heat roared into place.

She wrapped her arms around his shoulders, her nails biting deep even as her tongue dueled with his. When she finally tore her mouth away to drag in air, he took advantage of her exposed neck, nipping his way down the slender column until he covered his initial mark.

His tongued stroked over it, once, twice, then he sank his teeth deep. Even as a moan that had nothing to do with pain escaped her, her body bowed under his, her hands clawing at his shoulders. He curled his arms and magic around her, wrapping her in death's embrace.

CHAPTER 30

The heat of Darius's kiss burned away the cold tendrils of apprehension curling around Natasha like clinging ivy. Even as the desire she kept locked away rose in a cresting wave, she knew what he was doing. She gave him credit. As distractions went, he hit the damn bull's eye.

Heat, hunger, need, all twisted together into one bright inferno. It burned away the ragged edges of betrayal and drowned out the distracting whispers of what might have been, leaving only crushing sensation and the incandescent moment in its wake.

Darkness began to creep along the edges of her awareness, edging out desire with a rising panic. Frigid ribbons glided over her, leaving a curious numbness in their wake. Fear had her eyes fluttering open even as her pulse began to slow.

Ice-cold blue lit with a savage determination dominated her vision. "Let go, Natasha. I've got you."

As if she had a choice. The blanketing darkness crawled closer, covering her in a smothering weight. With a quiet sigh, she let her eyes close for the last time.

She never imagined the kiss of death being quite like this.

CHAPTER 31

Watching Natasha's chest still and her arms fall limply to her side made Darius clench his teeth. Doubts and sick fear fought for purchase, but he couldn't acknowledge them.

The clock was ticking. He whipped the coil of his magic around the last anchor and, with a vicious jerk, shattered it into ash. Within seconds, he was back in the mortal realm. "Now!"

Across the warehouse, the floating light glinted off of the blood covering Gavin hands as he lifted them from Ryder's decimated chest. Ryder's body convulsed against the table. In Darius's arms, Natasha's body did the same. He turned his attention to Raine, her pale face set in grim lines. Seconds ticked by, each one more ominous than the next. Natasha's body stilled. So did Jamie's.

Then just as he was ready to launch himself at the girl, those eerily silver eyes opened. "Done."

Wasting no more time, he burst into the Side, and yanked on the magic tethered to Natasha's spirit, dragging her ruthlessly back from the crumbling edge between life and death. His heart raced, his other half snarling at her resistance to his demands to return as she slipped farther than he anticipated.

He tightened his hold, denying the greedy demands of death, the pull stronger than expected, but still no match for what fueled him. Once certain she wouldn't slip out of reach, he palmed the back of Natasha's head.

"Breath of my breath." He covered Natasha's slack mouth with his and sent air deep into her lungs. Raising his head, he slashed a line along his inner arm until blood ran warm against his skin. "Blood of my blood." He held his arm over her mouth, rubbing her throat, forcing her to swallow. "Spirit divided, sundered no more."

His magic, still twined about Natasha's spirit, swept into her still body anchoring her spirit to its mortal shell. Then he focused on the energy binding her two halves together, the one the spell left in tattered ribbons. They flailed in the magical wind sweeping around him, dancing out of reach, while every hair on his body rose. Gritting his teeth, he focused, determined not to lose her now.

Another energy joined his, adding to his strength. Female, fierce, and uncompromising. Raine. She brought Gavin's healing touch, adding it to Darius's energy until it became an unstoppable force. Together they gathered the magic and forced it to bend to their will, reestablishing the vital bonds between Natasha's dual natures.

The magic whipped around him and the precious body he held. He felt ribbons of energy sinking deep within the alabaster skin. He waited and, for the first time, prayed for a fucking miracle. Had he kept her hovering in that in-between state too long? Would this work? Had he misjudged his ability and killed her?

Suddenly, light burst from every inch of Natasha's body,

searing his retinas with such intensity he roared, giving voice to all the brutal emotions clamoring inside him.

The body in his arms convulsed. He drew her closer, trying to still the bone jarring movements. They faded, and his head bowed over hers.

"Open your damn eyes," he whispered.

Between one breath and the next, his wish was answered. Natasha's eyes flew open revealing a feral, crimson gaze. His heart stuttered, his relief replaced by grim realization.

Natasha's demon was in full control and she was beyond pissed. At him.

Her claws swept out. He barely managed to get his arms up in time to block the blow. Her nails tore strips from wrist to elbow. She twisted out of his lap, landing on her feet with cat-like grace. Crouched in front of him, her lips curled back from razor-sharp teeth, she hissed in fury. That crimson gaze fixed on him with lethal intent. Her head lowered, bringing those deadly horns into play. Her body began a slow, mesmerizing weave back and forth, her maddened gaze never moving.

He rolled to his feet. "You want to play, darling?" he drawled, curling his fingers in a come-hither motion. "Let's play."

Whether following his voice or the insolent curl of fingers, she snarled and rushed him, her instinct overriding any trace of intellect. He let her in close then stepped to the side, intent on immobilizing her, not hurting her. She, on the other hand, had no such intentions. Anticipating his move, she went in low, her claws flashing as she slashed toward his hamstrings. A twist and turn got him out of harm's way, but set him off balance and straight into the kick she aimed at him.

He took the blow meant for his ribs on his back. The force of it wrenched a grunt from him, but he managed to wrap his hands around her leg. He pulled and twisted, yanking her off balance and torquing her body face down on the ground. He didn't waste time, but followed her down. Dropping to his knees on either side of her hips, he locked one hand on her wrist, twisting it up and between her shoulder blades, forcing her thumb toward her spine.

She smashed her head back, the edge of one her wicked horns, slicing a line of fire along his cheekbone, perilously close to his eye.

He cursed and clamped his other hand on the base of her skull, holding her head in place, her cheek pressed to the ground. He leaned in and growled, "As much as I enjoy this rather testy side of you, could you save it for someone who actually deserves it, darling?"

The thrashing body under him stilled. Her spine rising and falling with her harsh breaths. Small tremors ran through her. Her muscles locked as if fighting something from within.

"That's it," he crooned, hoping to get through to her. "It's just me, Natasha. I need you to come back. We have a few things to finish."

A violent shudder wracked the demon under him, before she went limp. Silence hung for a breathless moment, then a hesitant, "Darius?"

She was back. Relief thundered through him. "Yes?"

"Get off me before I show you what testy really means."

He laughed as he rolled off of her, gathering her tight in his arms. "Welcome back, darling."

CHAPTER 32

Hours later, Natasha drifted through the quiet of Vidis's house, careful not to disturb Cheveyo, sprawled asleep on the massive sectional. Carys had gone home, leaving Cassandra to watch over a stabilized Axel upstairs, while Gavin and Raine had retreated into another room. Vidis had been gracious enough to offer Natasha one of the rooms upstairs to rest. She tried, gods above and below knew she tried, but sleep eluded her. And from the sound of running water, Darius was still in the shower, which meant she could slip away unnoticed.

Carefully, she opened the French doors and slipped into the quiet of the pre-dawn night, pulling the door closed behind her. Right now, the last thing she wanted to do was field the questions and concerns the night's events would bring. Time enough to shoulder it in the morning.

The moon chased the horizon, leaving Vidis's wild yard bathed in silver light. She took the steps down to the ground and made her way across the yard.

The night was far from quiet. The constant hum of insects followed her. The soft hoot of an owl drifted on the breeze as it danced through the leaves to add a soft shushing counterpoint. A fine mist drifted over her, making her glad she hadn't taken the time to dry her hair earlier. She stopped in the middle of the yard, steps from where the forest held watch, and lifted her face to the sky. Closing her eyes, she just breathed. In and out. In and out. Taking Nature's unruffled calm in deep.

The irony didn't escape her. A being of chaos looking for a moment of peace.

Finally she dropped her head, opened her eyes, and stared at the trees in front of her with unseeing eyes. As if a dam had broken, everything—Ryan's death, Jamie's betrayal, Taliesin's weight, the treacherous path looming ahead—crashed into her.

Without Ryan to talk to, who could she trust to understand her decisions? They could so easily be misconstrued. Who would keep her in check? With DiMarcco hunting the Northwest, one wrong move would cost more than she could bear. How could she keep her people safe when she couldn't even see the snake curled around her neck?

Jamie's betrayal cut deep, deeper than she thought. She spent years with him, but the minute something shinier came along, the minute she stumbled, he left. Who else stood by, waiting for her to make another mistake? Who would die this time? Silent and hot, tears fell unchecked. For one brief, dark moment, she wondered if her death wouldn't have been the better option.

"I didn't think you were that breakable, love." Ryan's achingly familiar voice haunted her from the past.

"Dammit Ryan, everyone breaks." She ran a shaky hand through her damp hair, a harsh sound—half sob, half laugh—escaping. "You left me. Left us."

"Not by choice." The dark, deep voice had her spinning around to find Darius behind her.

Her tears vanished as she choked back a snarl. "Why are you following me?"

"He'd have stayed if he could, Natasha." He ignored her question, instead cocking his head to the side, allowing the moonlight to chase away the shadows hiding his face. A kindred grief darkened his eyes even as he searched her face. "He trusted you, trusted those he left behind to see this through. He would not leave something so precious as his people to someone weak." He stepped closer and carefully cupped her face with both hands. "You are so far from weak, you wouldn't know how to break if you tried."

She studied him from inches away. "I made a mistake, and he paid for it with his life." She forced the painful confession from her aching throat.

"Everyone makes mistakes, Natasha." His thumb traced away one last damp trail before slowly letting her go. "Even Ryan." He captured her hand and tugged her into walking with him. He didn't look at her, but continually scanned their surroundings, alert even here. "Ryan's mistake cost him the life of his sister, Catriona."

Natasha held her tongue and listened.

"When Ryan left the Order, he knew there were those who wouldn't be satisfied with just letting him go. He held too much power, too much influence to be allowed to just walk away. Threats were made, some even acted out against him and his sister, until he was forced to leave Europe. No one could live under the constant strain of never knowing who or where the next knife would strike. Catriona was his weak spot, and his enemies knew it. The target on her back burned much brighter than his."

"Over the years he became very protective of her, too

much so, he later admitted. Catriona wouldn't push him on things, unless it was worth it to her. Twice she faced down her brother, refusing to bow to his version of protection."

"Raine's father," Natasha murmured, as memories of Ryan, furious and frustrated, when his sister refused to name the man she was involved with, despite his repeated pleas for a name.

Darius nodded. "And raising Raine on her own, away from Ryan's protective shadow. It was the center of their last argument. Ryan told me it got so bad, he said things he couldn't take back, and Catriona wouldn't talk to him for years. They'd barely starting talking again, when she and Raine disappeared. And when he found her…"

"It was too late," Natasha finished, remembering Ryan's devastation when he returned with Raine, leaving Catriona's body behind. Little things began to click into place. "He kept a distance between himself and Raine out of guilt, not grief."

Darius's jaw tightened. "He could never forgive himself for Catriona's death, but he also knew if he showed any tenderness to Raine, his enemies would once again switch their focus. He wasn't willing to take that chance. Especially when he found out Catriona had been worried she and Raine were being hunted, but hadn't gone to him. He always thought if he hadn't held on so tight, Catriona would've reached out sooner. He didn't want to make the same mistake with Raine."

Natasha stepped over a log, using Darius's arm for balance. "So he pushed her away?" She shook her head. "Damn idiot, did he learn nothing?"

Darius tightened his grip on her arm, bringing her to a halt. He waited until she looked up at him. "And will you learn from your mistakes?"

What had she learned? She looked away, thinking. She twisted her decisions around and around, running through her would've, could've, should've scenarios, while quiet minutes ticked by. Darius stood patiently waiting, giving her the time to face her own realizations. Finally, she answered, "How does that saying go? 'Those who don't learn from the past, are doomed to repeat it'?"

His lips twitched. "You really want a repeat of tonight?"

She gave him a small smile. "Not really, no."

She began to pick her way through the forest. With each step, her grief loosened its hold and she made her decisions. Ryan tried to protect his people by standing in front of them. Well, perhaps it was time for a change in strategy. DiMarcco held his position for centuries, using a politician's proven tools—lies, manipulation, and slight of hand. If she wanted her people to survive, they would need something DiMarcco would never consider—trusted allies and unexpected weapons.

Allies like the one behind her, who gained her trust by killing her. She smiled to herself. It made a twisted sort of sense, if you were into that kind of thing. And she definitely was. Time to play the game for keeps. "We'll have to give Gavin and the others DiMarcco's name." She shot Darius a look over her shoulder. "And we need to bring Zayn to the table." She turned forward, leading the way. "Your choice to share your relationship or not."

"Gracious of you, darling," he drawled with dry amusement.

"I thought so, pet."

His silence as they continued through the woods assured her he was considering the pros and cons of sharing. Finally, he said, "It may serve us better to keep that connection quiet for a bit longer."

"Why?"

Darius reached above her, tugging a drooping branch out of her way. "Until we have actual proof against DiMarcco, we'll need every advantage we can get. We have no idea how far or deep his reach goes."

He had a point. "One of the many things we'll need to uncover before the Council meeting in June."

"You think we can unravel which humans are working with him by then?"

"We? No." She stopped and half turned back to him. "We are going to leave that task to Gavin and Raine. They seem to have such fun interacting with the humans. Besides, it will give the two of them the chance to hone their new-found skills."

He arched an eyebrow, wicked amusement dancing in his eyes. "And give you a chance to evaluate their potential power."

She put on a pout. "You say it like it's a bad thing."

His lips twitched. "You sure that's wise?"

Dropping the pout, she shrugged. "Wise? Perhaps not, but it will definitely be effective and necessary. DiMarcco wants to eliminate what he doesn't understand, so why not use what he fears against him? We need every weapon we have. He won't go down without taking everyone and everything he can with him. I don't intend to let the Northwest be part of his collateral damage." She turned back to resume walking. "Besides, you, Zayn, and I have something more important to do."

"What's that?"

"We need to figure out who's standing on which side of the line before the Council meeting."

"Easier said than done, darling."

The serious undertone to his comment slowed her

steps. "I'm sure your brother is more than up to the challenge."

"Of that I have no doubt." Darius fell into step beside her. "But are you ready for what this alliance between you and us will trigger?"

"What exactly do you think will happen?"

"The Northwest is the only one capable of garnering the type of support needed to bring DiMarcco down. It's why he's targeted you to begin with. You know he'll make a move before the meeting, especially if you enter the game officially."

"Oh, I truly hope he does." Dark satisfaction purred under her words. The trees thinned and then disappeared, leaving behind a small clearing where a shack stood, semi-camouflaged by fallen branches and leaves. "In fact, I'm counting on it." She stopped and turned to face him, not bothering to hide her savage needs behind a civilized mask. "Do you happen to have your knife handy?"

Darius slipped out a sharp, lethal blade, and handed it to her hilt first. "Something I can help you with?"

"No." Her smile was all teeth as she took it from him. "I just don't want to chip a nail."

CHAPTER 33

Leopold DiMarcco took one last sip of coffee as he finished the morning paper. Setting it aside, he rose from the comfortable chair tucked on the small hotel balcony in downtown Portland. He'd be happy to leave this city of gray, weeping skies and enjoy the sunnier climes of his home. Unfortunately, he had to stop in Washington, DC first, to ensure the legitimacy of his business trip. This spontaneous trip to the Northwest had not turned out quite as he expected. While the arrogant little prick, Jamie Ryder, managed to pull together quite the impressive list of influential humans, he pushed his streak of initiative too far.

DiMarcco glared down at the crawling traffic below. Kidnapping Bertoi was a critical error, especially so soon after Mulcahy's death. His lips twisted in a smile. Now, that particular plan had ended brilliantly in his opinion, even if it did miss its originally intended target. Which was why he added a little something extra to the spell he gave Ryder. The same spell the idiot used on Bertoi. It wouldn't matter if the cocky shit did his job or not, because the spell would do it for him. All with the added benefit of keeping DiMarcco's name out of this mess. Just like he preferred.

He turned from the view, leaving the cup and paper outside. He stepped back inside the hotel room only to come to an abrupt stop. On the dresser sat an inconspicuous box. Narrowing his eyes, DiMarcco scanned the room. His bags were still stacked by the door, waiting to be picked up by the bellhop. His jacket lay on the bed, next to his phone and wallet. From where he stood, he could see that the lock was engaged on the door.

Trepidation crawled up his spine and he fought the urge to dash into the room. Using his magic, he swept the room for any hidden traps or cloaked presence and came up empty. Just like his room. All except for that mysterious package.

Cautiously he moved forward until he stood in front of the dresser, peering down at the box.

No label, no writing of any kind to indicate where it came from or who it was for. Though the fact it appeared out of thin air in his locked room seemed to make it pretty damned clear who it was intended for. Again, he tested it with his magic, searching for any sign of anything.

Again, nothing.

Gingerly he lifted the box. A weight inside shifted and he stilled, his heart picking up speed as cold sweat trickled down his temple. When nothing more happened, he set it back down on the dresser. He looked around for something to cut the packing tape with.

Spying his key card, he snatched it up and applied the sharp edge of plastic to tear through the tape. Using his fingers, he pulled back the box's edges. A dull roaring flooded his ears. Ice crept through his veins. His vision tunneled until all he saw was a bright, red ribbon wrapped around Jamie Ryder's severed head.

Rage, bright and brilliant, swept away the chilling tendrils of unease, until his hands shook against the cardboard. It took every bit of his control honed through hundreds of years not to smash the gory contents against the wall. Who had brought this here? How had they known he was even here? Was it that bitch, Bertoi or one Mulcahy's pet freaks? Questions swirled in a dizzying rush.

A buzzing sounded, cutting through his fury, giving him a chance to breathe. The reddish hue clouding his vision receded, leaving him staring into the ghastly gaze of dull, brown eyes.

The buzzing drew his attention away from the unexpected delivery and to the phone next to the bed. Uncurling his fingers one by one, he let go of the box and walked over to the persistent phone. He lifted the receiver to his ear. "Yes?"

"Sir, are you ready for your bags to be collected?" The young, professional voice belonged to the front desk manager.

"Yes, I'm ready to leave." DiMarcco's voice remained even and unfettered by his earlier rage. He barely acknowledged the manager's answer and hung up the phone.

Walking back to the dresser and the mocking box, he studied his gift. After a moment's pondering, he smiled. He carefully tucked the boxes edges down. Perhaps he'd keep this a memento, a reminder to expect the unexpected.

He turned and gathered his suit coat, pulling it on and pocketing his phone and wallet. Looking into the mirror, he straightened the edge of the jacket's cuffs. When he gazed at his reflection, he wasn't surprised by the glittering excitement staring back.

It didn't matter who sent the gift or why, it only mattered that the game had truly begun. Until now, he simply played with destroying the Northwest. Now, though, now he was going to have such fun bringing them to their knees.

Gathering the box under his arm, he tilted his head toward his reflection. "To the most powerful goes the win."

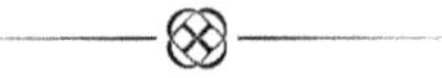

Discover Cheveyo's biggest regret when he returns to the woman that haunts him, only to stumble into a treacherous plot designed to fracture the Kyn in SHADOW'S DREAM .
Now available at your favorite bookseller!

KYN APPENDIX

GLOSSARY

Amanusas:
One of four Kyn races, delight in chaos, half-demon and
half-human or Kyn. Six bloodlines—War, Earth, Secrets,
Enticement, Death and Inequity—referred to as 'Blood of'.
For example: Natasha is Blood of Secrets.

Amá:
Navajo for "mother".

Ape':
Shoshonee for "father".

awéé':
Navajo for "baby".

ayóo-anííníshní:
Navajo for "I love you".

Baide':
Shoshonee for "daughter".

Between:

The second realm between the mortal and magical worlds, accessible by the Kyn.

Bitten:

Humans transformed to shifters through vicious attack. Magic needs human to be on brink of death to complete conversion. They are lower in the pack's structure as the control of wolf is tenuous at best. Tend not to live long.

Biovita:

A biotech lab in Hillsboro, OR where Brant Sutler, a human geneticist worked creating drug to turn Kyn wolves feral.

Blood ward:

A magical construct based on a castor's blood to defend or protect a place or person.

Bonded:

Rare metaphysical tie between Kyn, generally shifters, that connects two individuals at soul level. A step above mated. Partners generally don't survive the passing of the other.

Born:

Kyn Shifters who are born, some are Pure Bloods—rare few bloodlines.

Bound:

An Amanusa, caught in a casted circle by a summoner who uses all their names, to enslave—body and soul—to do the summoner's bidding. If a name is missed, they become half-Bound.

Chindis:
Vengeful spirits of the dead, raised by witches, however can be done by anyone with the ability, controlled by their summoner. Torment victims and rip them apart psychically. Generally are spirits of those who died violently or before their time. Once vengeance is taken, they'll rest.

Cinar International:
European based corporation.

The Council:
The ruling eleven members of the Kyn, chosen from around the world and headquartered in Turkey.

Division:
Preternatural Crimes Division, a group of talented and/or psychic humans who work for US Government and assist the Kyn on supernatural crimes.

Feral:
Wolves whose animal nature has taken control. Tend to attack humans and those closest to them. Nothing of the thinking man is left behind.

Fey:
One of four Kyn races, Sidhe descendants.

Kyn:
The entire preternatural community, composed of all four houses: Fey, Lycos, Amanusa, and Magi.

Lycos/Shifters:

One of four Kyn races, shape shifters, generally predator animals.

Magi:
One of four Kyn races, made of witches and wizards.

Mated:
Emotional bond created when two shifters commit.

Mavericks:
Lone wolves who have chosen to leave packs and roam on own. Can be Born or Bitten.

Mirroring:
Ability to send part of yourself into another by merging two magics, can add strength, but only as passenger. Empathic magic, deep level merger gives access to individual's mind/heart. Witches can mirror.

Pinnanku tease em puinnuhi:
Shoshonee for "See you again next time."

Sarielian Order:
The ultimate group of Wraiths, made of nine of the most dangerous Kyn of the world.

Shadowed Paths:
The walkways in Between, used when Shadow Walking.

Shadow Walking:
Ability to travel in the realm that exists between the waking world and the magical one.

Side:
A realm accessible to the Amanusa, not easily borne by other Kyn, completely unbearable by humans. A third plane of existence.

Sisna:
Sanskrit demon slur, lewd version of tailed demon or phallus-worshipper.

sitsi':
Navajo term for daughter.

Soul Stealer:
Nomâhtsé' héõo' Adanta - Eater of Souls, a psychic being created by black magic from the remains of a soul, tied to summoner. Gains strength eating the souls of others.

Taliesin Security:
The public security company housing the Northwest Kyn.

Tachair:
Gaelic word for "light", Raine uses it for light spell.

Three-fold Law:
Witches follow concept: What you do, will come back to you three-fold.

Tracker:
Shifters who are outside Pack hierarchy, their duty is to hunt/execute rogue shifters and threats (internal/external) to Pack.

Witches:

Practitioners of natural magic/white magic who follow the Three Fold law.

Wizards:
Practitioners of spells, potions, tend toward dark magic, use science and rituals.

Wraiths:
Twelve member highly skilled collection of North American Kyn who serve as the ultimate police for the Kyn and human monsters. They are not publicly acknowledged, basis of Boogieman stories for Kyn, even human not sure if they exist.

Yázhí:
Navajo equivalent of "little one".

88 Ivories:
Music/dance club in downtown Portland

CAST OF KYN

NORTHWEST KYN

Ryan Mulcahy (d.)
Former Head of Fey House,
Captain of the Wraiths,
Chief Executive Officer (CEO) of Taliesin

Natasha Bertoi
Head of Amanusa House,
Current Chief Executive Officer (CEO) of Taliesin

Warrick Vidis
Head of Lycos House,
Chief Financial Officer (CFO) of Taliesin

Cheveyo
Head of Magi House,
Chief Information Officer (CIO) of Taliesin

Carys Iver
Current Head of Fey House, Chief Legal Council for Taliesin

NORTHWEST WRAITHS

Raine McCord
Gavin Durand
Xander Cade
Jamie Ryder
Axel Kayser
Niall
Gideon
Dorian
Chayton
Fahd
Kevin Sullivan
Killian

SOUTHWEST KYN

Rio Castle
Head of Amanusa House

Tala Whiteriver
Head of Magi House

Tomás Chavez
Head of Lycos House

KYN COUNCIL SO FAR...

Leopold DiMarcco

Zayn Aimeric

Corwin Westbrooke

Malachi

Antonia

SARIELIAN ORDER SO FAR...

Darius Abazi

KYN KRONICLES

SHADOW'S EDGE

Raine's spent a lifetime hunting monsters, but can she stop her prey from exposing the supernatural community one bloody corpse at a time?

SHADOW'S SOUL

When a simple assignment turns into a nightmare, can Raine and Gavin unravel old vendettas before they both pay the ultimate price?

SHADOW'S MOON

Compromise isn't in Warrick's vocabulary and Xander won't abandon the hunt. As the line between instinct and intellect blurs, will they survive the fallout?

SHADOW'S CURSE

When the queen of chaos locks horns with death's justice, Natasha and Darius set a dangerous game in motion, leading two predators into a lethal dance of secrets.

SHADOW'S DREAM

Tala can't forget the past. Cheveyo can't change it. As the dreams they shared linger, can they escape the encroaching nightmare before it's too late?

SHADOW'S FALL

A trail of missing Kyn leads a powerful new threat into Raine's backyard. Will she and Gavin be able to hold their own or fall under the weight of secrets haunting the shadows?

About the Author

"This story is an emotional roller coaster, from betrayal, anger, fear, love..." —InD'tale Magazine

Jami Gray is the coffee addicted, music junkie, Queen Nerd of her personal Geek Squad, Alpha Mom of the Fur Minxes, who writes to soothe the voices crammed in her head. Her series combine high-stakes urban fantasy and edgy paranormal romantic suspense into books you don't want to put down. Buckle up and get ready for a wild ride through the fascinating worlds of the Arcane, the Kyn, the PSY-IV Teams, and the Collapse.

Come visit Jami's website at **https://www.jamigray.com** and stay up to date on what kind of trouble she's getting into and when you can expect to join in.

amazon.com/author/jamigray

instagram.com/jamigrayauthor

facebook.com/JamiGrayWriter

threads.com/@jamigrayauthor

goodreads.com/JamiGray

bookbub.com/authors/jami-gray

9 781948 884235